Bryan's mind began to fill with images of his family, of happy gatherings, of Hannah. He sensed an unbearable sadness, felt his throat closing, tears nearing his eyes.

He blinked rapidly and looked straight ahead into the face of a Tan, his rifle now aimed at his shoulder. A dozen rifles pointed over the wall. The Tan directly in front of him couldn't meet his eyes directly and shifted his aim slightly.

Bryan thought that the man was wanting someone else to fire first, that he didn't want to initiate the killings himself.

The seconds passed like minutes. There seemed silence all around. Bryan tried to think of a prayer. None came to mind. He wanted to say something but couldn't.

And then the rifles exploded . . .

Look for these Tor books by Robert Perrin

ALL THE RAGING SEASONS
NOONDAY

NOONDAY

ROBERT PERRIN

TOR

A TOM DOHERTY ASSOCIATES BOOK

NOONDAY

Copyright © 1984 by Robert Perrin

A Tor Book edition, published by special arrangement with Pan Books Ltd.

First Tor printing: April 1987

A TOR Book

Published by Tom Doherty Associates, Inc.
49 West 24 Street
New York, N.Y. 10010

ISBN: 0-812-58708-1

Printed in the United States of America

0 9 8 7 6 5 4 3 2 1

For my dear friend and second father,
Bob Wyatt, who might read this elsewhere.

"I have made their widows more in numbers
than the sands of the sea;
"I have brought against the mothers of
young men a destroyer at noonday;
"I have made anguish and terror fall upon
them suddenly."

Book of Jeremiah, Chapter 15, Verse 8.

BOOK
ONE

Chapter 1
December, 1913

The men crowded into the meeting room in Convent Street were of every age and size. Their faces shone with zeal, sweat, and enough porter to carry a man through such an important evening in Listowel's history as this.

Those near the front of the room pressed closer to the small, raised platform. The younger ones chattered away excitedly, speculating or boasting, while the older men tended to remain silent except for perfunctory greetings. The light from the new electric bulbs hanging from the ceiling left pools of dark shadow near the walls and corners.

Jack Aherne had carefully positioned himself in one of these darker places. In his sixtieth year, Jack found himself becoming more and more detached from the people closest to him. Perhaps, he reckoned, it was nature's preparation for the final, loneliest event in anyone's life. When he was more cheerful, he blamed it on a lifetime spent teaching history and geography to the children of Listowel. Jack gazed around with a rueful smile: he was surprised that the reaction to the protests in northeast Ireland against the Home Rule Bill had been so long coming.

Demonstrations had begun in Ulster even before the Bill had been introduced into Parliament more than two years earlier in 1911. The Unionists had gathered in their tens of thousands to march past their leader, Sir Edward Carson. A year later, nearly 450,000 Ulster people signed a covenant opposing any change in the links between Ireland and England. They were not in the least concerned that the majority of the Ulster members of Parliament were in favor of an Irish legislature for Irish affairs. When the bill passed the Commons in 1914, they formed the Ulster Volunteer Force.

Jack Aherne knew that the rest of Ireland would form a body equivalent to the UVF with its many dummy wooden guns for public drilling, its real weapons for private target practice, its implicit threat of military action if Home Rule became a reality. It was the oldest natural law: every action had a reaction.

He wondered how many of the men at the meeting had sized up what was happening in Ireland and how many were simply being borne along on the emotions raised by the police brutality in Dublin a month before, when one man had died and hundreds of others, including women and children, had been injured in baton charges during a transport strike. The call for the formation of the Irish National Volunteers had started in Athlone, spread to the Dublin strikers who called themselves the Irish Citizens Army, and now had reached even a remote market town like Listowel.

The schoolmaster had read the names of the Provisional Committee running the Volunteers in the nationalist *Freeman's Journal*. From his own guesswork and knowledge, almost half the committee were sworn members of the Fenians, the secret Irish Republican Brotherhood.

Jack had long ago declined to join the Fenians. He talked politics only with his family or closest friends. People usually attributed his reticence to the childhood trauma of his father's untimely death, which had occurred in 1867, during his father's attempt to free Richard O'Sullivan Burke from Clerkenwell prison. Jack liked to think and observe, not to participate. The town regarded his scholarly idiosyncrasies fondly. Those standing close to him at the meeting nodded their greetings and received a nod in return. That was all they normally got from "Old Jack," as he was nicknamed by hundreds of schoolchildren.

"To order, gentlemen!" a voice called from the platform. "To order, please!"

A man stood up behind the trestle table on the platform, removed a homburg hat and unbuttoned a thick overcoat.

It was Jack McKenna, the chairman of the county council. Aherne raised his bushy, grey eyebrows in some surprise. He hadn't expected the man to come out into the open. Surely everyone knew McKenna had been sworn into the IRB in 1910? He'd expected the Fenians to be a little more circumspect in their efforts to infiltrate this new organization.

McKenna waited for a hush to settle over the room.

"We're all aware of the object for which we're assembled here tonight. It's for the purpose of what I consider doing a good night's work for the good old land that bore us.

"We have before us at the present time what I regard as a very good example set by the North. And that is that the best way to insist on having our rights observed by an alien government is to take the rod into our own hands. Carson has been going round preaching what some call sedition, urging people of the North to defend their rights by might, in the way God intended.

"Now, we're going to take the names of every man and boy tonight who wants to join the Volunteers. We're not having any informers, no cadgers, no cads. We want true, manly men and we want nothing to do with any other kind."

The spindly schoolteacher at the back of the hall snorted contemptuously at the poor rhetoric, and headed for the door. He'd heard and seen enough. As he left, the rest of the crowd in the hall started to queue at the foot of the stairs leading to the platform. One by one they walked up to the trestle table, placed their right hand on an old Lee-Enfield rifle and signed their names on a large sheet of paper. McKenna's beam embraced each volunteer, including Jack Aherne's fourteen-year-old grandson, Bryan, who, unknown to his grandfather, signed his name along with four of his schoolfriends.

Jack Aherne walked home slowly, savoring the ceiling of stars in the sharp night air. To his right, the steeple of St. Mary's Church announced the presence of the Catholic faith to the dark mass of St. John's Anglican Church, set in the middle of the square not forty yards away.

It was a symbolic juxtaposition, Jack decided, that couldn't have been mere coincidence. First the centuries of Protestant ascendancy; now, the growing, perhaps overwhelming, demands of the native Catholic majority.

Catholic and Protestant, a singularly petty and stupid way of deciding Ireland's future. It gave the extremists of both persuasions the chance to obscure their true motives under the cloak of religion. Now, Jack was certain, the battle lines were being drawn up.

From this night, Catholic volunteers in Listowel were prepared to face Protestant volunteers. And few could see the wider storm signals in Europe. He felt resigned. His life's studies had taught him that men could shape history but never control it. History had a way of making up its own mind, of playing its own hand. So far, he thought, history had dealt Ireland's cards from the bottom of the pack. Why should it be different in the years to come?

Slowly Jack paced around the square, musing that events in Listowel during his lifetime had reflected fairly accurately those in Ireland as a whole. Here, he'd seen the glorious, heady years of Parnell, revered like no Irish politician since Daniel O'Connell, who had often visited Listowel during his times of influence. He'd also come there when he was ruined by his love for another man's wife.

Jack remembered when Parnell, a sick man, had spoken last from the front window of the Listowel Arms Hotel in the corner of the square. 1891, wasn't it? Well, if he wasn't sure of the date, his memory of that evening was crystal clear.

There'd been brass bands to welcome the great man. Dozens of policemen were drafted in, most taking notes in case Parnell uttered seditious words. And the crowd . . . the huge crowd . . . and the heckling led by Father O'Callaghan from Duagh, protesting at Parnell's adulterous relationship with Mrs. Kitty O'Shea, now the politician's wife but for too long his mistress during another marriage.

Parnell had refused to accept that his career had been destroyed by the Catholic Church's abhorrence of his private morals. Defiantly he had battled on, his voice with its clear English accent growing hoarser, weaker, against the continuous shouts of "How's Kitty?" and "Sinner" and "Adulterer" and "Whoremonger."

Parnell had died within weeks, and his party had begun to decline. When the second Home Rule Bill failed in 1893, the vacuum had been created for a new political party.

They called it, in Gaelic, Sinn Fein. "We Ourselves" Jack translated literally as he strolled out of the square and northwards up Church Street, but Sinn Fein accepted that foreign policy and defense should be left to the Imperial Parliament in London. Distasteful as some of its leaders found the concept, Sinn Fein said publicly that it didn't want to sever Ireland's links with the British Crown.

In that, Jack believed, they represented the views of most Irish people. But Jack also knew that within Sinn Fein there was the hidden enclave of Fenians, the Irish Republican Brotherhood, which wanted complete independence as a republic and believed that this would come about only through violence. The Fenians lived within Sinn Fein like a dormant, yet malignant, growth, retaining links with the American organization, Clan-na-Gael.

Jack realized that his hatred of Fenianism stemmed from the circumstances of his father's death and his mother's reaction to it.

The day after Matt Aherne's headstone had been blessed at Drombeg, his widow had called the children together. Her black mourning dress emphasized the paleness of her complexion. Her eyes were pools of grief.

"Children," she said quietly, "you know how and why Daddy died."

Bernadette snivelled into a handkerchief edged with black lace.

"No, dearest," her mother chided, "no more tears. There should be no more crying. Daddy wouldn't have that, I'm sure."

Mary looked down at her hands, pressed into her lap, knuckles whitened.

"It was a brave thing he was trying to do for a friend,

brave but very foolish. I shall say that once more but then never again. It was foolish. But that doesn't mean your daddy was foolish. He was misled by wicked men he thought were his friends. They used him for their evil work because they knew he loved Ireland, that he would die for his country. They weren't interested in him or our land: they only wanted power for themselves. They tricked Daddy like they tricked all the others who were killed or put in prison during the uprising. They're called Fenians and you must promise me that you'll never have anything to do with them. Do you promise?"

Mary asked the question of each of the children in turn. The girls nodded, both with tears glistening on their cheeks.

"I promise, Mama," Jack piped up, realizing that this was quite one of the most solemn moments of his young life. He ran to his mother and pressed himself against her bosom. Mary smoothed his hair gently while she went on talking.

"Now we've agreed, haven't we, that the town shouldn't know how Daddy died. So we've to be very careful in what we say. One day, perhaps, there'll come a time when we can tell the whole story but you must allow me to judge when and if that time arrives."

And so it had been. His two sisters had worked with their mother at "Aherne's" while Jack pursued his studies. He was reminded constantly that he was the hope of the family. Jack didn't mind studying. The men who drank in the tavern opposite the barracks were too like his father with their changeable moods, sometimes cheery, often morose. His memories were too precious, too few, to be risked. He preferred the unchanging world of his books and immersed himself between their covers.

His mother always wore black, a woollen shawl usually drawn tightly about her head; otherwise life seemed almost unchanged. There was still enough money to satisfy most childish whims and fancies. Jack realized from envious remarks that he was regarded as well-off although the Ahernes never employed servants nor owned a horse carriage like the wealthier farmers and shopkeepers in North

Kerry. In adulthood, he learned that his comfortable upbringing and university education in Dublin were not only due to the tavern's income, reasonable as that was, but also to money drafts which arrived every quarter with unfailing regularity from Alderman Finucane, his grandfather, in Boston. After the alderman died in 1870, a well-loved and respected man throughout New England, the drafts continued. Not long after, when Jack's grandmother was laid to rest, the responsibility was taken over by his mother's sister, Aunt Kathleen.

She inherited the Finucane cooperage factory and the taverns-cum-eating houses, but sold them in favor of railroad shares. Her husband, Edwin Aicheson, had become one of Boston's leading and most sought-after surgeons.

With the money draft invariably came a detailed, gossipy letter describing the increasing stature of Mary Aherne's relatives in America. She insisted on reading these to her children, sometimes more than once. There was never any trace of envy in her voice or comments.

Sometimes when she was alone, Mary thought wistfully of Boston and what might have been. She was never tempted though from the decision she reached after Matt's death. The children would make their lives in Ireland. He would have wanted that, she was sure. As the years went by and her children married and produced grandchildren, she began to treasure the cozy intimacies of life in the small Kerry town. She had to concede that she truly felt at home.

Mary took a delight in continuing the tavern's tradition of being the clearing-house for news of Kerry people who'd gone away. She became the acknowledged expert on Listowel's genealogy, often sorting out whose third cousin, once removed, had married into which family and what that relationship entailed. She never contemplated marrying again herself: the tavern and the closeness of her family ensured that she never felt really lonely. Even when Bernadette married a farmer and moved to just outside Ballylongford, visiting her mother once a week at best, Mary still had Brigid to confide in.

There had always been Brigid, Jack reflected, as he

strolled along Church Street. He looked across the road at the lights burning in the family home, and wondered whether to call on his elder sister. Brigid had never married, preferring to stay with her mother. She still worked a few hours a day at the tavern with Jack's son, Sean, now the licensee, and spent the rest of her time helping Sean's wife, Finoola, look after the children. Bryan was the eldest, followed by Sinead, May, Kevin and the late arrival baby Michael. Sean cheerily called him the froth on the porter.

It was a happy, close family. Sometimes Jack wished that he and his wife Maude had been able to have more than one child. After a day with his beloved grandchildren, however, he was all too glad to escape to the solitude of his books and his thoughts.

No, he decided, he'd go straight home tonight. He'd only wake the children if he dropped in at the house and he guessed it would be a late night if he stopped at the tavern further up Church Street. Everyone in the bar would be excited by the formation of the Volunteers, plenty enough excuse for a hooley.

The old schoolmaster turned off Church Street, a few yards past the police barracks, and into his neat, terraced house in Forge Lane. From its front window, he could look across to the town's imposing, square-built courthouse, set amid wide lawns. Some visitors dismissed the town's regular architecture as boring and uninteresting, but Jack found it reassuring. It was a town with a place for everything and everything in its place, he'd say.

Jack recounted the evening's events while he ate his supper.

"Is it serious, you're thinking?" his wife asked when he'd finished and placed the tray carefully on the floor beside him. He filled his pipe before replying. He and Maude had always been able to talk together, which was a great satisfaction and comfort to Jack.

"What are you meaning by serious?" Jack replied at last, for a moment forgetting that he was not addressing schoolchildren. "I'm sorry, dear," he continued, tapping the stem of his pipe against his nose. "Of course, it must be serious. It's the old, old story of the unstoppable preparing to meet the immovable." He ran a hand back through his wiry, grey hair, scratching his scalp. "Mother used to tell the tales she'd heard about the faction fighting round here, how the Cooleens used to go against the Mulvihills."

"Even in Listowel itself," Maude Aherne agreed, her fingers busy with her needle.

"And at the races," Jack went on. "Oh, yes, they used to beat each other to death for a name or a colored piece of ribbon. Remember Mother's tales about the last great faction fight at Ballyeagh. Half of them didn't know why they were fighting. Well, that's how I'm reckoning it is now. They're picking sides for another faction fight and, blow me, Maude, I'm thinking most are being led by the politicians like bulls with rings in their noses."

"Do even the politicians know?" she asked shrewdly.

"Know? Know?" Jack echoed, peering deep into the fire. "They are like steeplechase jockeys who can only see the next fence. When you get two sets of people in the same country arming themselves against each other, it doesn't take much to reckon that they want a fight and they're determined to have a fight."

Maude was silent. She knew better than to interrupt when Jack was in one of his pessimistic moods.

"You would think their love of Ireland would bind them together, wouldn't you? A love to win independence together and then build the country to our ways. Now they're squaring up like they've nothing in common except for a love of their own religions. I don't know, Maude, I really don't. Whom the gods wish to destroy . . ."

The next Sunday, Jack and Maude Aherne had a grandstand view of the first parade of the local Volunteers from their bedroom window. More than a hundred gathered on the lawns outside the courthouse to march off in columns of three behind the stirring music of the town's fife and drum band.

"Don't they look brave and smart in their Sunday best?" Maude commented, tapping her feet in time to the music.

"Daft more like," Jack replied grouchily. "On the march

with no guns and nowhere to go. The little people have stolen their brains."

"Oh, you!" Maude laughed, as they leaned out of the window. "I do declare you're becoming a crabby old man, Jack Aherne."

Her husband merely grunted. Inwardly, though, he had to admit to a slight stirring of pride.

"Oh, look, Jack!" his wife cried, pointing down at a youngster carrying a crudely made green flag with a golden harp at its center. "Isn't that our Bryan?"

All Jack could see was the top of the boy's large cap. "Nothing like him," he muttered. "Nothing like him at all. Anyway, Sean wouldn't let him join this rabble."

It was a good four months before they discovered that their grandson was indeed a Volunteer. By then, Bryan had persuaded his father, who'd also experienced a hot flush of nationalism, that there was no harm in being simply the flag-bearer and, anyway, weren't a lot of his schoolfriends in the Volunteers as well?

Jack Aherne, who knew that some of his pupils had even been sworn into the IRB, expressed his displeasure forcibly. He realized, however, that it would be wrong to interfere too much with his son Sean's family. He did toy with the idea of revealing to Bryan how Matt Aherne met his end, joining an organization he didn't understand. But then he remembered his pledge to his mother—a pledge from which he'd never been released—and stayed silent. Nevertheless, he remained deeply worried about his grandson because he recognized how ominously the events in Ireland were drifting.

In March of 1914, sixty British officers at the Curragh Camp signified that they would rather resign their commissions than put down any rebellion by Ulstermen. This further weakened the resolve of Asquith's Liberal Government to force through an unchanged Home Rule Bill. They no longer needed the assent of the House of Lords, but the thought of an uprising in Ulster horrified the Cabinet. Back and forth went the proposals for compromise, but it was

deadlock. And in the deadlock, those persuaded that
violence was the only solution took action.

A month after what was popularly termed "The Curragh
Mutiny," the Ulstermen managed to land nearly twenty-five
thousand rifles and three million rounds of ammunition at
Larne, north of Belfast. There was now hard muscle behind
the threats of those who totally opposed relinquishing any of
their ties with the British Crown. After all, they told
themselves, hadn't their Protestant ancestors been settled in
the North nearly four centuries ago precisely to provide a
bastion against the recalcitrance of the native Celts, the
Irish?

The Irish National Volunteers responded in late July by
bringing ashore two thousand rifles at Howth, just south of
Dublin. Later the same day, four people died and nearly
forty were wounded at Bachelor's Walk, by the River Liffey
in Dublin, when troops of the King's Own Scottish
Borderers, tired of hunting the gun-runners, fired on a
jeering, jubilant mob.

Jack Aherne studied these events in the quiet backwater
that was Listowel.

He thought it inevitable that the conference about Ireland,
held at Buckingham Palace, would fail. Neither side was
happy with the suggestion that any Home Rule Bill should
exclude the Ulster area. The proposal was that these
counties could, if they so wished, later vote themselves
under control of an Irish Parliament in Dublin. Such a
proposal would be an Amending Bill to the Home Rule Bill.
Since no one could even agree on what time scale should be
used such a move inevitably would have brought intersec-
tarian strife to Ireland.

Ironically, the certainty of war in Europe helped heal the
breach. The Conservative leader, Andrew Bonar Law, and
his staunch ally, Sir Edward Carson, suggested that a united
front had to be presented against the German threat; that, in
the best interest of all, the Home Rule Bill, which they both
opposed so vehemently, should become law but should be
suspended until a new Amending Bill could be introduced
when the greater European crisis was over.

The Nationalist leader, James Redmond, seized the moment. As the First World War formally began he declared that the British government could remove its troops from Ireland and that Ireland would be defended by the Irish National Volunteers combined with, he hoped, the Ulster Volunteer Force.

Support for Redmond's pledge flooded in from all over Ireland except, not surprisingly, from members of the Irish Republican Brotherhood hidden in the ranks of the Volunteers and the Sinn Fein Party.

The last hurdle had been cleared in a blaze of patriotism, not only for Ireland but for the British Empire.

On September 18th, 1914, the Royal Assent was given to the Home Rule Act, providing once again a government for Ireland, by the Irish, in Ireland. A second law suspended Home Rule for a year or until the end of the war. This was to allow the Ulster argument to be heard again. After the Allies' victory at the Battle of the Marne, no one doubted that the war would be over in months.

Sparks shot hundreds of feet into the air from the bonfire in the middle of Listowel market square. The fife and drum band played their hearts out. People cheered and danced and kissed each other, tossing copies of newspapers into the air on to the leaping flames. The headlines proclaimed, "Ireland's Day of Triumph" and "At Last! Our Own Again!"

Very few people in Listowel doubted that Ireland was again—or very soon would be—her own mistress. Jack Aherne was one, so were members of the local cell of the IRB. They thought the flames might be prophetic.

In Belfast and Derry, there were bonfires too. The youngsters stood around them echoing the words of their elders who drank gloomily in their Orange Lodges.

"No surrender!" they shrieked. "No Pope! No surrender!"

Chapter 2
April, 1916

"So what are you thinking of all this in Dublin then?" Sean Aherne asked his father, pouring him a glass of porter.

Jack Aherne looked carefully around the tavern bar halfway up Church Street in Listowel. There were only two old women sitting in the far corner that early in the morning. He glanced sideways at his son and sipped his drink before answering.

"I'm thinking that it's the maddest enterprise since the rising of '48. And it's probably even madder than that. Trying to hold the Post Office against the entire British Army."

"Aye, Dad, that's what most of the boys in here were reckoning last night."

Jack nodded ruefully. "Sheer madness, so it is. But I'm hearing that even a couple of the local boys are up there as well."

"O'Rahilly's there from Ballylongford."

"And wouldn't he just be . . ."

"And Mickey Mulvihill and Paddy Shortis from Ballybunnion." Sean Aherne pulled himself a glass of porter.

"Just as well the rest of the boys got stood down or else Father O'Riordan would be awful busy comforting a lot of fresh widow women," muttered his father. And then he hesitated for a moment before continuing: "Perhaps he'd have been calling here with his soft words if young Bryan had taken the Dublin road."

"Thanks be to God that he didn't."

"Thanks indeed. And wasn't I warning you when he

joined these Volunteers? And did you pay heed? You did not, Sean, you did not."

"Now, Dad, that's not fair and you know it." Although quiet, Sean's voice bore a note of angry protest: "Not one of us knew the Volunteers would turn to this."

"If you'd listened to your betters."

"Like you."

"Yes, like me, you would have known. If you'd opened your ears and kept your gob shut you'd have . . ."

"You're not in the classroom now, Jacko," a cheerful voice interrupted. It was their friend, Davy Lawlor, the parish clerk and bell ringer at St. Mary's. His use of Jack's nickname broke the tension. Father and son exchanged guilty glances.

"The usual, Davy?" Sean asked quickly.

"Aye, and one for yourselves now. Help you to cool down maybe."

Lawlor, a thin, wiry man, was known, like the Ahernes, as a person with a strongly independent will whose opinion was widely respected.

"The rising?" he went on, passing some money over the counter. "That's what you're blathering about?"

"Aye," Jack replied, smiling. "Enough they should be destroying the fair city without causing trouble in this house."

"Is it that. Blasted fools, so they are."

"They seem so at the moment," Sean interrupted. "But I've been wondering what folk'll be saying of them when it's over."

"Now you're thinking, son!" Jack exclaimed, draining his glass. "If these are the boys I'm guessing they are then they've a deeper game on than anyone's seeing."

"Fenians, you mean?" asked Lawlor. "Are you seeing their hand in this business?"

"Whose else?" Jack replied, gesturing to his son to refill the three glasses. "They've been planning for this since the war started, I reckon."

As usual, there was a kernel of truth in what he said. Within a year of the outbreak of war, more than 130,000

Irishmen—well over half of them Catholics—had joined the ranks on behalf of the British Crown.

The vast majority of those who didn't actually join up served in the National Volunteers. Out of the 190,000 of 1913, less than 15,000 split away to form the "Sinn Fein Volunteers" sometimes called the "Irish Volunteers." Most people laughed at the activities of the diehard nationalists as they went about their drill, still dreaming of an independent Irish Republic. They were jeered and abused, stoned and spat upon. They were considered disloyal by the great proportion of Irish people, a fringe of extremists not worth bothering about.

There were about sixty "Sinn Feiners" in Listowel, drilling secretly with their own shotguns and some of the forty Martini-Henry rifles obtained locally after the gun-running exploit in Howth. Most townspeople knew who they and their leaders were. To Jack Aherne's deepest chagrin, his grandson Bryan remained one of them.

Although the youngster maintained he was still only the flag-bearer Jack had heard enough whispers that Bryan had progressed to carrying a gun. It frightened and appalled Jack. He could see his own father's mistake repeating itself. He talked often to Bryan, attempting to make him realize the danger he was running. The lad listened seriously to his grandfather but always rejected his arguments emphatically.

"What harm are we doing?" he'd ask. "We only drill and march and talk," he'd protest. "The Sinn Feiners are as patriotic as anyone."

The arguments would invariably peter out in the sad, baffled silence which often occurs when equally sincere but different generations are unable to communicate with each other.

Bryan had picked up enough hints from the conversations of his older colleagues to know that the Sinn Feiners were not dedicated to a peaceful solution to Ireland's future. He didn't mind. It added spice to his otherwise orderly routine of school and home. He admired his leaders: the town's doctor, Michael O'Connor, and Paddy Landers, the genial, huge-muscled blacksmith. To him they were men of action.

They appealed to a romantic imagination fed on tales of
legendary heroes. There was just enough of a whiff of
danger in their company to stimulate him without feeling
the slightest fear for his own safety. Life with the Sinn
Feiners was a glorious adventure.

In the months that followed, Jack smelt rebellion in the
air. He read accounts of the Sinn Fein Volunteers drilling
and even practicing mock attacks on public buildings in
Dublin and other large towns. According to the Volunteers,
such exercises were preparation in case Germany invaded
Ireland. The organization went its commonplace way
despite the hostility of many Irish people who had relatives
and friends fighting in the Flanders trenches. And very few
noticed the orders, printed in all newspapers, instructing the
Volunteers how to spend their Easter days off in 1916.

> Following the lines of last year, every unit of the Irish
> Volunteers will hold Maneuvers during the Easter
> Holidays. The object of the maneuvers is to test
> MOBILIZATION WITH EQUIPMENT.

Young Bryan spent days cleaning and pressing his suit
and shining his belt and badges. He was almost in tears on
Easter Saturday when the Volunteers' Chief of Staff, Eoin
MacNeill, suddenly cancelled all the maneuvers, marches
and parades.

What Bryan didn't know was that at last MacNeill had
tumbled to the active presence of the Irish Republican
Brotherhood within the organization's inner sanctums.

MacNeill had known there were extremists who thought
insurrection was the only course, but he hadn't realized until
a few days before Easter that they already had the uprising
planned and poised. When he did, MacNeill agreed reluctantly that it should go ahead in the belief that the British
intelligence officers in Dublin Castle already had wind of
the rising. He feared that the Volunteers might be officially
disarmed and disbanded at any moment whether there was
an uprising or not. And the hard-line Fenians, the inner
members of the IRB, led by Patrick Pearse, told him

confidently that help was on its way from Germany in the form of twenty thousand rifles and millions of rounds of ammunition. These were in addition to the weapons already purchased secretly with the tens of thousands of dollars sent for that purpose by sympathizers in America, members of Clan-na-Gael. To MacNeill, it was a *fait accompli* whether he liked it or not. He agreed to the plan going ahead. His change of mind came with the news that the arms from Germany were at the bottom of Queenstown Harbor after the gun-running ship had scuttled itself following capture by the Royal Navy. The even later news that Sir Roger Casement, a career diplomat who'd been negotiating in Germany on behalf of the IRB, had been captured after landing from a submarine a dozen or so miles from Listowel only served to confirm MacNeill's opinion. The planned rising was doomed and he knew it. He issued the cancellation orders for the maneuvers which were to be the cover for rebellion.

To Patrick Pearse and the Fenians under his control, mainly around Dublin, the cancellation was irrelevant. Pearse believed wholeheartedly in the power of myths to become reality. When he led a hundred or so Volunteers through the entrance of the General Post Office in O'Connell Street, Dublin, a few minutes after midday on Monday, April 24th, 1916, he knew their rebellion had no chance of success. Whether the rank and file men knew it was doubtful.

Pearse announced the new "Republic" from the steps of the building's portico to passing crowds who thought him, at best, an eccentric. Then he read a proclamation from "the Provisional Government" under a fluttering tricolor and, within an hour, the newly-titled Irish Republican Army was busy fighting off units of the British Army, which, ironically, was comprised mainly of Irishmen. The Dublin tenement dwellers welcomed the uprising. It took the police off the streets, allowing them to loot the shops.

In Listowel, each communique from Army headquarters was discussed avidly. They described how the British Army's artillery gradually reduced the rebel positions—and large tracts of Dublin—while innocent people were being shot and killed by both sides. When Pearse surrendered in the midafternoon of Saturday, April 29th, sixty-four rebels had been killed out of the fifteen hundred who had eventually taken up arms, one hundred and thirty-four soldiers and policemen were dead or dying, and at least two hundred and twenty civilians had been sacrificed. The captured Volunteers were reviled by the Dubliners as they were led away to prison. Women screamed, "You deserve to be shot."

Bryan Aherne was inconsolable. He refused to talk to his family, preferring to remain alone in his room. His father tried to comfort him after breakfast on the morning following the surrender, understanding his deep hurt and humiliation, but Bryan would have none of it.

"Well, I've done my damnedest," Sean remarked gloomily when he'd stumped downstairs after his fruitless attempt. "Time's the only healer."

"He'll get over it, son. He's too young to understand," replied Jack Aherne.

"No, you're wrong in that. Bryan can understand well enough what's happened. It's his youth that makes it so hard for him to forgive. He feels betrayed."

Sean gratefully accepted a cup of tea and glanced at his watch. There was an hour before Mass. "Your grandmother often talked of how confused and angry Father was after that fiasco of a rising in '67. I'm supposing our Bryan feels much the same way."

"Will they deport the leaders again this time?"

"They'll be fools if they don't or, at least, take them to gaol over the water. But, perhaps, it's different now."

Sean rubbed the stubble around his chin. He never shaved until minutes before going to the tavern in the morning or, on Sundays like this, to Mass. That way, he reckoned, he spared himself from having to shave again in the evening.

"I see what you're driving at, Dad," he said reflectively. "England's at war with Germany."

"The Irish are at war with Germany as well," Jack pointed out.

"Aye, and that means Pearse and his friends are traitors in wartime. And there's been the gun-running too."

"There could be court-martials not trials, Sean."

"And then?"

Jack shook his head despairingly.

"I pray they don't but the English are fools enough to shoot them. Maybe that's what some of them want anyway. Pearse certainly thinks that everything is reborn in sacrifice. I'm trusting, for all our sakes, that the English understand that."

"They haven't before," Sean replied gloomily.

"And that's the truth."

Jack looked at his watch again. "Are the women ready?"

"Just about, I'm thinking."

"We'll walk down together. I'll just collect your mother."

"Right there. And we'll leave Bryan be?"

"Aye. That'd be best, I reckon. And you get yourself shaved now."

"In the shake of a donkey's tail."

Jack stretched up from the sofa and walked the few paces to the front door. Suddenly, just as he was about to open it, there was a squealing of brakes outside, loud shouting and the pounding of heavy boots on pavement cobbles.

"What the devil?" he exclaimed when the butt of a rifle splintered through a panel in the door a few inches above his head.

"Open up in there!" a gruff voice cried. "Open up! It's the Army!"

The door shivered under another blow. Jack stepped back quickly, alarm pumping through him. He felt his thigh muscles tremble.

Sean leapt out of his chair but the door burst open, crashing back on its hinges, before he could reach it. Two soldiers erupted into the sitting room, rifles swivelling around to cover Jack and Sean.

"Back! Back!" they screamed, pushing the muzzles hard against Jack's and Sean's chests, forcing them to the nearest wall. Two small side tables swayed and fell, throwing china figurines on to the rug. One of the soldiers kicked them out of his way, shattering them into a dozen pieces.

An officer ran, half-crouching, into the room, his revolver outstretched. Upstairs, a woman screamed then began to sob hysterically.

Two more soldiers followed the officer, their dull khaki uniforms contrasting with his shiny belt and jodhpur leggings. They charged through the sitting room, knocking aside the chairs, and hammered open the door to the back kitchen with their shoulders. They knelt at the bottom of the stairway, rifles pointing upwards.

"Where's the rebel sod?" the officer demanded, thrusting his face close to Jack's. His breath smelt of stale brandy and fresh peppermint.

"Rebel? Rebel?" the old man stammered. A rifle butt slammed into his ribs. He gasped and fell to his knees, aware through the pain that the room was filled with even more soldiers. In the distance, church bells began to ring, calling the townsfolk to worship. There was noise everywhere. Shouted orders, splintering chinaware, screaming women, and the bells.

"Where's Aherne?" the officer shouted.

"Which Aherne?" Sean shouted back, forcing himself between his father and the officer.

"The rebel one, you turd!" The officer's voice was high and petulant. He swung the barrel of his revolver at Sean's head.

Sean staggered back, blood flowing from a cut as the metal sliced across his forehead.

"The rebel . . . Bryan Aherne," the officer stormed, lifting his arm as if to strike again.

"Upstairs," Jack mumbled, pointing at the ceiling, fearing that Sean would be hit again. "He's upstairs, but don't harm him. For God's sake, don't harm him. He's only a boy."

"Get him!" the officer barked. He spun away from the two men.

The soldiers took the stairs two at a time. There were more screams, another door banging open, thuds on the floor above. Sean, guessing what was happening, started towards the officer who now had his back turned. Jack saw it all in slow motion.

"No!" he cried. "No, son! Don't make it worse."

The officer whirled around, almost colliding with Sean. He stuck his revolver deep into the tavern-keeper's ample belly. The two men stood there for a moment like a waxworks tableau. Then, Sean lowered his fist slowly, shrugged and turned back to help his father unsteadily to his feet.

The soldiers clattered down the stairs pushing Bryan in front of them. The youngster cannoned into the wall at the bottom and literally rebounded into his escort. They shoved him in the small of the back, sending him tottering into the sitting room. Blood was trickling from his nostrils and lips, staining the front of his collarless white shirt. His face was chalky, shocked, making the blood seem more claret than it was. He staggered towards his father and tried to speak. Sean tried to step forward but was held back by a rifle barrel thrust across his body.

"Holy Mother!" he exclaimed angrily. "What've you done to the boy?"

"Fell off his bed, suh, then down the stairs," one of the soldiers called to the officer, pushing Bryan towards the open front door.

"Get him in the truck," the officer ordered.

"Dad . . . Dad . . ." Bryan sobbed, twisting his head around to look fearfully back at his father as he was frog-marched into the street.

The soldiers retreated slowly, warily, from the bottom of the stairway and the sitting room, rifle barrels still pointing at the two men. When they reached the street, the soldiers broke away suddenly and ran towards the trucks.

Sean and Jack stumbled to the shattered door. They were just in time to see Bryan lifted off the ground by the soldiers and flung bodily through the air and into the back of the leading truck. They recognized some of the strained white faces peering over the tailgate. Dr. O'Connor bent down out of view, obviously to help the youngster. Paddy Landers gave a wan smile through swollen lips. It was clear then that the Army had arrested most of the Listowel Company of the Irish Volunteers.

"Where are you taking the boy?" Sean shouted. "Where's he going?"

"Tralee," the officer called back, jumping into the front passenger seat of his open staff car. "You'll find him there with the rest of the rebels!"

He pulled a whistle from his breast pocket and blew three times. The convoy began to rattle off down Church Street. The officer waved his gloved hand at Sean and Jack as he sped away.

Jack leaned on his son's shoulder, coughing deeply and painfully. The screaming of the women still inside the house filled his ears.

Deep hatred enveloped him for probably the first time in his life. "Oh, the bastards!" he mumbled. "The bastards!"

His eyes focused on drips of blood falling on the cobblestones. They formed a tiny pool between the raised stones. Blood kept dripping and spreading. He could see specks of dust and struggling insects being carried on the spidery, red rivulets. His mind was flooded with the image. He shook his head and gazed into the clear, blue sky. The colors, blue and red, red and blue, mixed together in his brain. Suddenly he realized where the blood was coming from. Sean's face was masked with blood from the cut on his forehead.

"Are you all right?" he asked.

Sean wiped a hand across his face. "A scratch, Dad," he grunted. "Nothing more."

He was still peering down the long, straight street into the slowly settling cloud of dust left by the Army convoy. The trucks had gone. Sean put his arm around his father's waist and started to help him back into the house.

By now, the women had ventured into the front room with the children. Brigid Aherne, with the experience of an elderly aunt, was the calmest. She soothed Sean's wife, Finoola, whose hysterical crying gradually subsided into a bout of hiccups. Her children gazed in amazement at the overturned chairs, the door hanging on its hinges, the lumps of broken china strewn over the usually neat room. Their eyes widened even more when they saw the two beaten men stumble over the threshold. Finoola ran to her husband, wiping the remaining tears off her cheeks with the back of her forearm.

"Water and—hic—rags, Kevin," she called. "Quick now—hic—in the kitchen—hic!"

Brigid quickly placed the chairs upright again and guided Jack and Sean to them.

"The bastards! Oh, the bastards!" Jack continued to mutter.

"Hush, dear," his sister murmured, stroking his brow. "Sit quiet and I'll be sending for your Maude. Sit quiet and it'll soon be better."

A little color returned to Jack's ashen face. He hobbled around the room gripping his bruised ribs and roundly denouncing the arrest of his grandson. "It wasn't necessary," he repeated. "Not necessary to take the boy like that. Not at all."

"So what are we to do about this?" Brigid asked.

"Do?" Jack snorted. "There's not much we can do, is there?"

"But surely they've made a mistake?" his sister persisted.

"Oh, there's no mistake, Aunty," Sean replied bitterly. "The British were after rebels and that's that. They'd take a babbie in swaddling clothes if they thought he was a rebel. That they would."

"And whose fault is that?" Jack demanded, switching the target for his simmering anger.

"Not again, Dad . . ." Sean began to protest.

"Headstrong, that's what you are, Sean," said Jack firmly, ignoring the interruption. "Always headstrong and as thick as . . ."

Then he stopped, noticing properly for the first time the hurt expression in his son's eyes and the white bandage around his temples.

His voice softened. He put his hand on Sean's shoulder,

gently kneading the flesh. "Headstrong you are, and there's no doubt of that, but perhaps not so strong right now, eh? Anyway, not strong enough to bear this silly old curmudgeon."

Sean smiled. He understood.

"Right then," Jack decided. "Let's be dressed and tidied and off to Tralee. We'll have this settled soon enough when we're seeing the proper officer in charge."

But when the family, crowded into Sean's jaunty cart, reached the gates of Tralee Prison nearly four hours later, Jack realized immediately that there were bound to be difficulties. His earlier bravado had been meaningless.

Three ranks of soldiers, bayonets fixed, stood outside the prison gates holding back a crowd of about sixty people, mainly relatives clamoring for information about the arrested men.

"What are they saying?" Jack asked someone on the edge of the crowd.

"Nothing. Nothing at all. That's what."

"Is there an officer there?"

"They've sent for one, the much good it'll do us."

Ten minutes passed before a small door set into the gates swung open. An officer stepped through, hardly glancing at the crowd. Jack recognized him as the one who'd arrested Bryan and the other Listowel Volunteers. A barrage of questions rose from the crowd, all sweaty and dust-streaked in their Sunday-best clothes.

The officer held up his arms, ordering, rather than requesting, silence. The hubbub died away.

"That's better," the officer said. His words carried throughout the crowd. "Now, listen well because I'll be saying this once only."

Jack cupped a hand to his right ear.

"All the men arrested today through North Kerry are here," the officer went on, his voice ringing and clear. "They're being questioned about their activities, their rebel activities, mark you, and that'll take a number of days. Then it'll be up to the Army Commander in Dublin to decide what's to be done with them. Their names will be

posted in your newspaper and police barracks and you'll be
told if they're due to come to trial. There'll be no visits, not
even from priests, so you all might as well return to your
homes. Understand? Good, that's all then."

Before any more questions could be shouted, the officer
saluted, turned briskly and stepped back through the small
door.

Momentarily, the crowd was silent, stunned by the
uncompromising baldness of the announcement. Then the
protests began. Women started to wail noisily, a few
dropping to their knees, crossing themselves, sobbing out
prayers. The soldiers stood impassively.

Jack shook his head in disbelief. He'd always supported
the force of law and order, never believing wild tales of
their brutality and callousness. He felt disoriented, physically and mentally. He knew that later, when he was alone,
he would have to think through his values again.

A terrible despair descended like a rain cloud over
Listowel, making normal life virtually impossible. People
stood on corners, swapping rumors, recounting again and
again how their men had been taken. The town had
dismissed the Sinn Feiners as foolish, possibly dangerous,
extremists. Now, no one dared to criticize them.

Three days after the mass arrests, Ireland was shocked by
the news that Patrick Pearse, Thomas MacDonagh and
Thomas Clarke had been shot at dawn in the yard of
Kilmainham Prison in Dublin. That the rebels had been
refused the comfort of a priest made people shiver with
disgust and horror.

People flocked again to Tralee Prison, fearing that their
menfolk could face the firing squad as well. So tense was
the situation that the Army relented and allowed a deputa-
tion of priests inside to be assured that the local prisoners
were still only being held for questioning.

The Aherne family stayed close together in Church
Street, hardly trusting their emotions to others. Their
anguish deepened with the news of more executions in
Dublin—on Thursday, Joseph Plunkett, Edward Daly,
Michael O'Hanrahan and William Pearse, brother of the

rebel leader; on Friday, Sean McBride; the following
Monday, Cornelius Colbert, Eamonn Ceannt, Michael
Mallin and Sean Heuston; the next day in Cork, Thomas
Kent and then the cruel wait until Friday, May 12th, when
James Connolly was lifted from a stretcher, strapped to a
chair and shot along with Sean McDermott.

The government, which had bowed reluctantly to Army
pressure to allow the executions, announced that the killings
were over.

During the next six weeks, nearly nineteen hundred of the
Sinn Feiners, the Irish Volunteers who'd been arrested,
were transported to internment camps in Britain, particularly in Wales and the Northwest. The others, a thousand or
more, were put into trucks one early morning and driven
back to their villages and towns.

The first the Ahernes knew that Bryan was free was a
banging on the front door while they were at breakfast.

Sinead went to answer it. There was silence for a second
or two, then girlish whoops of joy. At once the house was in
an uproar of laughter and tears.

Bryan was embraced by all the family in turn before his
father, who'd been hopping around the edges of the
welcome, could reach him.

"Son! Son! Oh, my son!" Sean exclaimed, gripping him
tightly by the shoulders.

"I'm home, Dad," Bryan replied, his voice dull with
tiredness. "They've let most of the Listowel Company
home."

"That's good. That's fine," Sean went on, excited sweat
beading on his cheeks.

"Sinead, get your grandad," Brigid ordered, pulling
Sean away. "Leave the boy, will you?" she demanded.
"Can't you be seeing he's near worn out. And you jumping
and hollering like a lunatic."

The room went silent as they saw Bryan still wore the
clothes in which he'd been arrested, the white shirt
encrusted with grime and dried blood. His face was lumped
with yellow and purple bruises, one eye half closed and
puffed.

"Oh God," Sean breathed. "They've proper smacked you, haven't they?"

"They did us all, Dad," Bryan said simply, swaying a little. Brigid pushed a chair under his knees. He sat down heavily.

"What in Holy Mary's name did they do?" Sean asked, anger swelling within him. "Tell me, son."

"Later, Sean. Later," Brigid insisted, taking charge as usual. "Can't you be waiting for the boy to get his breath and strength."

"He's no longer a boy."

Jack Aherne spoke quietly from the doorway. He'd stood there unnoticed, looking at his grandson slumped in the chair surrounded by his family.

"Look at him, can't you? He's a man now, not a boy," Jack insisted.

Indeed, as they looked closer at Bryan, those around him could perceive that the soft features of adolescence had sharpened and set.

"Aye, you're a man now, son," Sean said, a note of pride and wonder in his voice.

Bryan smiled wanly, nodded, then looked toward the door.

"And a rebel, too, Grandad? Am I a rebel?"

Jack smiled broadly, remembering all their arguments about the Volunteers.

"A rebel? Bryan, I'm not knowing about you, of course, being that you're your own man now, but I'm thinking they've turned us all into rebels."

Chapter 3
July, 1917

They'd been gathering throughout the afternoon on the large common above the beaches of Ballybunnion. The warm sun persuaded the bolder spirits to go down to the sands and paddle in the rippling shallows. There was hardly enough breeze off the Atlantic to fluff the crests of the ocean rollers tumbling through the tunnel in Virgin's Rock offshore and into the caves worn out of the cliffs.

Curious children gathered outside the entrance to Cassidy's Health Emporium, tucked below the steep sandy track leading from the top of the cliffs to the beaches. Here, the tourists could soothe their aches and hangovers in a seaweed bath or take an invigorating saltwater shower. The former entailed dunking yourself in a tub of smelly, slippery kelp, then trying to avoid the voracious sand flies until the curious after-smell wore off. The latter involved standing naked in a wooden stall and being sluiced down with seawater through a hole in the roof.

The children delighted in hearing—and imitating—the shrieks of unknowing women who thought the shower was mechanical until Cassidy himself, beaming innocently, peered over the top of the stall to instruct them where to stand so that he could be certain of drenching their nudity with the contents of his bucket.

Many families, including the Ahernes, had decided to make the most of the afternoon, travelling in their hundreds to the tiny seaside resort on the Lartigue monorail train which ran the nine miles from Listowel. The women and children could enjoy a few hours on the beach before returning home, leaving their menfolk to the serious business of celebrating Eamon de Valera's win for Sinn Fein in the East Clare parliamentary by-election.

The sun was poised, sinking hugely orange behind Loop Head across the mouth of the Shannon to the west, before the men—Jack, Sean and Bryan—accompanied their families to the small station. They said their goodbyes, watched them depart on the strange train running on its raised track shaped like an inverted "V," and started back toward the common.

By now, a makeshift platform had been erected there with trestle tables borrowed from Scanlan's Hotel. The Listowel fife and drum band, attracted by promises of free drink, was starting to play, drawing the crowd to the platform, luring the men from the taverns along the potholed track which was Ballybunnion's main, and only, street.

There was a feeling of expectation everywhere which didn't appeal to Jack Aherne, a grim, threatening resolve beneath the drink-inspired revelry. He glanced sideways at Bryan and saw a glint of excitement in the youngster's eyes. The old man prayed inwardly that, on this lovely evening, there wouldn't be any trouble like a week before. Then, the police barracks and some shops in Listowel had been stoned by a gang, purporting to be Sinn Feiners, after the win for Sinn Fein in Longford. The fact that Joe MacGuiness had been in Lewes Jail, in the South of England, throughout the campaign had probably helped his narrow victory, as did the election slogan, "Put Him In to Get Him Out."

"There's too many bottles around for my liking," Jack remarked sourly to no one in particular.

"Bound to be a wee bit of a hooley," Sean said lightly.

"I know these young ruffians' hooleys," his father went on darkly. "They start laughing and end up crying. And, anyway, I thought all Sinn Feiners believed in discipline and proper behavior."

"They're not all Volunteers," Bryan replied, pushing urgently through the crowd, waving now and again to friends. "They might boast they are but they're not really."

"And isn't that just the truth?" Jack sighed. "To hear

them tell it, the whole of Kerry marched into the Post Office behind Pearse."

Bryan laughed, flicking his narrow-peaked cap on to the back of his head.

"At least some of us were prepared to, Grandad," he called over his shoulder, adding with heavy, though affectionate sarcasm, "And isn't that just the truth as well?"

"Get on, you lummock," Jack grunted, prodding him in the backside with his walking stick. "Stop your told-you-so blathering and find my old bones somewhere to rest while I listen to the brayings from the platform."

"Aren't you afeared of what you'll be hearing?" teased Bryan.

"Don't be cheeking your elders, young man," Sean laughed. "Do what Grandad says and clear a space for us old 'uns among your rebel friends. I've a wee bottle in my back pocket that's getting awful heavy."

"A bottle?" Jack gazed balefully at his son, shaking his head in mock reproof.

"The very best of medicine!"

"Is that so? Well, if it's medicine maybe I'll be taking a quiet sip for my legs. Mind you, it'll be just for my legs. I won't be enjoying it."

The three generations of the Ahernes laughed aloud as they flopped on to the grass by the edge of the cliff, to the side of the platform.

"We won't be hearing too much from here," Bryan complained without too much rancor.

"Enough, son, enough," Sean muttered, pulling the cork from a half bottle of Jameson's whiskey. "If it was de Valera I might be listening closer, but it'll be all the puffed-up local gee-gaws spouting away or else I'm Brian Boru's brother."

"And you're not that," Jack interrupted, pulling the bottle out of Sean's grasp, sniffing it and tipping back a quick mouthful.

"Won't your pupils be seeing you?" Bryan asked, still teasing.

"A mouthful never hurt a nun," Jack growled. "And don't all the boys know my preferences well enough by now, having a gobbeen like you as a tittle-tattle in the family?"

The good-humored rebuke made Bryan redden with embarrassment. He should have known that his grandfather never missed anything at school, that he would have guessed that a deal of Bryan's popularity in the classroom had come from his intimate knowledge of "Old Jack's" habits.

For all his brutal experiences in Tralee Prison, Bryan retained an adolescent sensitivity, although he tried to mask it with man-to-man banter. Like the others who'd been arrested after the Easter Rising the previous year, he was still held in some awe in North Kerry. Jack and Sean knew that he played up to the role of "the hard man" with those of his age, the school-leavers entering the humdrum world of menial jobs, if any job at all. Neither of the older men believed that Bryan had been changed much. He hated the soldiers who'd beaten him but not all soldiers. He abhorred the British institutions and systems and policies which had caused so much pain and terror, not the British themselves. His feelings for his fellow Volunteers and Sinn Fein had deepened. They were no longer those of a starry-eyed romantic. They were more mature, more purposeful, mirroring, to a great extent, the change in Sinn Fein itself.

The suicidal uprising, centered in Dublin, had given Sinn Fein and its supporters in the Volunteers, now becoming known as the Irish Republican Army, a clear identity.

In the rebellion's aftermath, Unionists in Ulster agreed that the rest of Ireland could have Home Rule if their counties of influence were excluded. Redmond's Nationalists conceded the principle of exclusion, but only for a limited time. The convention wrangled itself into deadlock over which counties should be excluded before finally sinking into oblivion, helped by leading Conservatives in the wartime cabinet, who said openly that any part of Ireland excluded from Home Rule would remain so permanently.

Even Dublin's leading Unionist newspaper, the *Irish Times*, thought this was nonsense. "In the first place, the country is too small to be divided between two systems of government," its editorial column declared. "In the next place, the political, social and economic qualities of North and South complement one another; one without the other must be miserably incomplete."

The position of James Redmond and, thus, his Nationalist MPs started to become untenable.

Even moderate nationalists realized that Redmond was unlikely to produce Home Rule for all of Ireland, that his negotiations could lead only to partition.

That view was reinforced when Lloyd George succeeded as Prime Minister and promptly brought Sir Edward Carson, the Unionist leader, into his Cabinet. Ironically, the Westminster government helped to fill it by releasing in a Christmas amnesty five hundred rebels who had been held without trial in Britain since the rising.

Among them was a young man from West Cork named Michael Collins, a member of the London Center of the IRB, who'd been in the Post Office during the week's fighting. Collins believed the rebellion's failure was due to poor organization. With the star of the moderate nationalists apparently on the wane, he saw the opportunity for Sinn Fein to establish political respectability. He used the Volunteers to build a professional election machine to campaign in a by-election in Roscommon. On February 17th, 1917, Count Plunkett, a Papal Count, father of Joseph Plunkett, executed after the Easter Rising, was elected on an anti-Redmond Home Rule ticket.

Plunkett declined to take his seat as an MP at Westminster, convening instead an "Irish Assembly"—Dail Eireann—in Dublin. Twelve hundred delegates affirmed that Ireland was a separate nation and called for freedom from all foreign control.

The public's attitude towards Sinn Fein had already become apparent. During the Easter holiday, the IRB flew the orange, white and green tricolor from the ruins of the Post Office with little hindrance. Passers-by raised their hats or waved handkerchiefs at the flag and at what was fast becoming a national shrine. All over Dublin, posters appeared on walls with the message: "The Irish Republic still lives!"

Easter also brought a further bonus for Sinn Fein, the release of another 117 rebels from prisons and internment camps, including the lanky, ascetic Eamon de Valera, who'd been serving a twenty-year sentence after the death penalty was commuted. Michael Collins threw his well-tuned organization behind de Valera in East Clare and the result, with the implicit support of the hierarchy of the Catholic Church, was a third parliamentary win for Sinn Fein.

Roscommon, Longford, and now East Clare, reflected Jack Aherne, his eyes wandering over the crowd on the clifftop. He had to concede that, within less than eighteen months, Sinn Fein had achieved a miracle. Here, before him, was the proof.

The people gathered around the platform were of every age and class. Their headwear, Jack mused, showed that— panamas, straw boaters, homburgs, derbys, common or garden caps—worn by laborers and landowners, shopkeepers and solicitors, potmen and priests. Not all of them, of course, were active Sinn Fein supporters but nor were they opponents. Many, like Jack and Sean, were impressed by the movement's growth, its grip on the public's imagination. Now they wanted proof that Sinn Fein might be able to deliver its promise of coming to some sort of deal about Home Rule.

The band broke into a ragged fanfare as the main speaker scrambled untidily on hands and knees up on to the platform. It was Jack McKenna, the chairman of the county council, who'd led the victory celebrations in Listowel the week before. His speech hadn't improved in the days between, Jack quickly decided. McKenna rambled on, extolling the virtues of de Valera and Collins in particular, and Sinn Fein in general. His audience listened tolerantly, clapping and cheering at appropriate intervals.

"They'd clap if he read them *Alice in Wonderland*," Jack murmured disparagingly. "Sinn Fein'll have to do better than your man here if it's to get my vote."

"Aye, Dad," Sean replied, chewing on a blade of grass. "He's as dry as stale soda bread, so he is."

McKenna could see dozens in the crowd beginning to drift away, some toward the bars, others to the beach. In an effort to hold them, the politician's statements became more wild and inflammatory.

"Those who are not with us are agin us," he shrieked, lifting his arms above his head. "When Sinn Fein takes power, as we surely will, then names will be remembered. Those who've stood astride the progress of Ireland's march to freedom shall be called to account in this life as well as before the Supreme Judge."

"Holy Mary!" Sean muttered. "Your man's going it a bit strong."

"Blathering windbag," Jack remarked. "But some are liking it as fighting talk."

He nodded toward a group of about twenty youngsters at the back of the crowd. They were beginning to argue with some older, better-dressed men near them who apparently shared the Ahernes' opinion of the speech.

Two constables noticed the slight disturbance as well. They'd been standing well away from the meeting, arms folded, enjoying the tranquility of the early evening. As fists began to wave, they started in the direction of the arguing group at a measured, unhurried pace, thumbs in belts, confident that their mere presence would calm matters. They reckoned without being spotted by McKenna.

"And those who grovel for their Judas silver from the British Crown," he declaimed, pointing at the constables, "will be thrice judged and condemned. By the people, by Sinn Fein, and by their Maker. There are some among us even now who profess to be God-fearing Irishmen yet glory in their wearing of the oppressor's chosen uniform. They are no more fit to claim their Irish manhood than . . . than . . ."

The politician hesitated, searching for words.

". . . than . . . than the porkers in the field," McKenna ended lamely. But his words had their effect, desired or otherwise.

The group of young men, all about Bryan's age, gleefully turned their attentions to the hapless constables. Any of their usual inhibitions had been drowned by too many pints of porter.

They encircled the constables, jeering and jostling them. "Porkers . . . porkers . . . porkers . . ." they chanted. Two or three began oinking like pigs.

Even from a distance, Jack and Sean, now standing up to get a better view, could see the constables' embarrassment turn to anger.

"The ruffians!" Jack exclaimed. "They'll be in trouble."

The first blow was struck before he finished speaking. The older constable, grey sideburns visible under his uniform cap, pushed one of his tormentors in the chest, trying to clear a pathway. The youngster retaliated with a wild swing which missed its intended target completely but caught the second constable on the side of the face. Suddenly, everyone started punching and kicking at the policemen. They nearly fell under the onslaught until one managed to clear his truncheon from his belt and began to strike out. The sharp crack-crack-crack of wood on bone sang into the greying dusk.

Instinctively, the people not involved in the fracas surged away from the area, some slipping and falling on the grass in their haste, crying out in alarm. Both police truncheons were whirling, forcing a gap in the crowd. The constables shouldered their way through, both bloodied about the face, and ran bareheaded across the green, heading for the police barracks some two hundred yards away. Their attackers paused for a moment and then set off in pursuit, open waistcoats flapping, screaming their hatred.

"After 'em, lads," McKenna shouted, jumping up and down on the platform, once almost tumbling over the edge in his excitement. "Give 'em a pummelin' for de Valera himself! After 'em! Quick now!"

Jack threw his cap on the ground in disgust and frustration.

"The doltards!" he exclaimed. "Just what they shouldn't be doing, the clods!"

"I'll be stopping it, Grandad," Bryan cried. "I'll get them off."

He raced off across the springy turf, arms and legs pumping.

Sean called once, vainly attempting to stop his son, shrugged despairingly and watched him weave through the panicked crowd before disappearing between the first cabins of the village.

By the time Bryan had caught up with the mob outside the two-story police barracks, it had doubled in size with more inebriated young men anxious to join the police baiting. He battled his way to the front, searching for any familiar faces. Chanting broke out.

"Come out, porkers! Come on out, you porkers, or we'll fry you where you are! Come out and fight!"

There was no particularly vicious intent behind the shouts. Bryan knew they were simply drunken bravado, designed to impress friends rather than scare the trapped police. A small stone lobbed out of the crowd and clattered on to the slate tiles of the roof. A dozen more followed.

"For God's sake, boys!" Bryan bawled, facing directly into the milling crowd. "Go to your homes before there's more trouble. Go to . . ."

"And why should we?" a stocky, fresh-faced youngster protested. "It's fun we're having. Just fun."

Bryan recognized him as Simon Mulvihill, a Volunteer about his own age, a relative of the Mulvihill killed in the Easter Rising.

"There'll be broken heads this night if you don't, Simon," he called.

"A baton charge? With only six of the bastards in there? They'd not be so foolish, Bryan Aherne. Come on and take a shy at the porkers."

"They said we're to cause no trouble."

"Who said?"

"Michael Collins did."

"And where's he?"

"In Dublin, I suppose."

"You suppose . . . well, he's not here then to give his orders, is he?"

Simon Mulvihill ended the shouting match by picking up another stone from the hard-packed earth which made up the village's only street. He waved it defiantly at Bryan before tossing it at the police barracks. This time there was the crash of broken glass in an upper window. The mob cheered and began stoning the building in earnest.

Bryan moved away in despair. He had seen their slack mouths, their wild eyes, their staggering gait. He knew the young men, hardly any of them more than twenty years old, were out of control. What was happening was specifically against the orders of the Sinn Fein leadership. Such rioting could only harm the carefully constructed image of a respectable political organization. It would frighten away the moderate nationalists, the vast bulk of the people who were essential to Sinn Fein's success.

The people of Ballybunnion stood watching from their doorways or their windowsills. The thudding and splintering of stones on brick and slate, the jeering and shouting, followed Bryan as he walked sadly back to the clifftop. He was so deep in thought that he paid little heed to the sudden, flatter crack echoing along the row of small houses and cabins. A woman shrieked. Bryan turned in surprise.

"Jesus, they're shooting!" someone shouted.

Bryan saw orange muzzle flashes at the first-story windows of the barracks. The constables, panicking and vengeful, were firing a volley at the youngsters, trying to scare them off. The front two rows dropped to the ground, screaming, covering their heads with their arms. The others, sobbing aloud with fear, scattered every which way, bumping and bowling into each other in the confusion.

The noise died away with the last echoes of hastily slammed doors and windows and the startled cries of wheeling starlings. The silence was filled with terror and bewilderment and shock. And then it was no longer silence. A scream of excruciating agony pierced upwards from among the piles of young men lying in the street. Bryan rose from his crouching position by a wall and ran towards the sound.

He stepped over people who were just beginning to sit up, some groaning, winded by their falls. Only one lay on his back, hands between thighs, rocking from side to side with pain, mouth wide open in a continuous, high-pitched scream. Simon Mulvihill knelt beside him on one knee, looking down, his fingers stuck into his ears, trying to cut out the horrendous sound.

"Is he hit?" Bryan demanded. "For God's sake, where's he hit?"

Simon didn't reply, just nodded his head, retching bile which dribbled between his lips.

Bryan's eyes slid over the gawky young man lying on the ground. There was no apparent wound in his head, his chest, his arms, his . . ."

"Oh, God!" Bryan gasped. "Oh, Holy Mother! Oh, Jesus!" He felt his throat tighten and dry, his back shiver.

Blood welled up through the wounded man's hands, cupped around his genitals. There was no wound to see, just the blood, pulsing, unending like the scream.

Bryan put a hand out, edging it towards the blood. The man's eyes, staring out of their sockets, saw the movement. He tried to roll his lower body away. His head thrashed from side to side in protest. The scream trailed away, replaced by a single word which had no ending itself.

"Noooooo . . . !"

"It's his cock!" choked Simon Mulvihill, wiping the vomit from his mouth. "That's what the bastard police did. Shot him in the cock. My best friend shot in the cock. The bastard divils!"

"Where's the doctor here?"

"In the bar."

"The bar?"

"At Scanlan's. That's where he was before the meeting, the drunken soak."

"We'll carry your man. Get some others."

Six were needed to carry the wounded man, each step

making him jerk and cry with agony. Blood dripped steadily, marking their progress.

Someone ran ahead to warn the doctor. By the time the bearing party arrived, he'd hastily covered a sofa in the hotel's small front lounge with a white sheet.

The taproom customers lined the narrow corridor to the lounge, clutching their bottles and glasses.

"Who is it?" they asked blearily with the concern that only drunks can muster. "Who's the poor wee fellow?"

"It's young Danny Scanlon," someone answered. "Send word for his ma, will you?"

"Hurry!" urged Simon Mulvihill. "He's hurt something awful. Hurry! There mayn't be too much time."

His prognosis was tacitly confirmed by the doctor's expression after he'd uncovered the wound.

"Bandages . . . sheets . . . anything . . ." the doctor muttered. He was a man of late middle age whose mauve-veined nose betrayed his weakness. "Helped him into the world myself I did," he went on, as he improvised a thick pad to cover the wound. "It's a terrible sin this. Terrible."

Within minutes, the pad was soaked through, scarlet. The doctor waved chloroform under his patient's nostrils and tried to make him swallow sips of laudanum. Gradually, Danny Scanlon grew quieter. Fresh pads were continually pressed to the wound between the legs. They simply soaked up his life-blood.

"Is he to live?" Simon Mulvihill asked.

The doctor shrugged helplessly, gesturing at the ever-reddening bandages.

"Time," he murmured. "Just time."

"There's no . . . nothing?" Bryan interrupted.

"The bleeding, you see, son," the doctor said confidentially. "Not the wound, though that's bad enough. It's the bleeding."

"Perhaps a mercy what with his . . . his . . . shot away."

"Aye, perhaps so. The Lord knows best."

Bryan moved away from the sofa and stood by the door.

A glass was thrust into his hand. He gulped neat whiskey and felt little effect. His brain focused on small details; a patch of discolored wallpaper, the fraying edge on the faded rug, a circle of grease on the back of one of the chairs. Sometime during the next hours, he was aware of his father and grandfather coming to his shoulder.

"Not yet," Bryan whispered, thinking they had come to take him home.

Sean Aherne patted his forearm reassuringly.

"No, son. Not yet. When you're ready we'll be in the bar."

Bryan nodded his thanks.

It took Danny Scanlon hours to bleed to death. Towards four o'clock in the morning his eyes opened. They drifted around the faces before him; the priest, the doctor, his mother, his friends. He smiled slightly. "Oh, Jesus and Mary come against me," he murmured before his eyes closed. He didn't stir again.

The only sign that he had finally died was the doctor straightening up from beside the sofa and stroking a finger and thumb over the young man's almost transparent eyelids, closing them forever.

Bryan crossed himself and pushed his way into the taproom to find his family. It was light outside the hotel when they set off in Charlie Walsh's jaunty cart for home. Knots of people stood around on the grass by the clifftop talking quietly about the night's tragedy. The stones of the castle ruins glinted wet with dew. The houses in the village were curtained and shut. Breaking glass tinkled again and again further down the track leading out of Ballybunnion.

Simon Mulvihill didn't look up at the cart as it swayed and clattered past him. He was too intent, tears streaming down his face, on smashing every window in the deserted police barracks.

"He said he was his best friend," Bryan explained, his voice dull with tiredness.

"Aye," Jack grunted. "It hurts to see someone close die."

"But why him? He wasn't much older nor younger than

me. All he was doing was having some fun. A bit in drink, maybe, but not deserving of that."

"No, not that. Not there," Charley Walsh called back from the driving seat. "No one deserves that. He's a martyr, so he is. The first martyr since the Easter Rising."

"He'll appreciate that, Charley. He really will," Jack said with heavy sarcasm. "So will his mam. We must have martyrs, mustn't we? Martyrs and saints. The land's littered with them, to be sure."

"Do you think they'll remember him?" Bryan asked, jerking a thumb at an old man on the roadside with a donkey laden with two wicker baskets of cut turf.

"Who?"

"Ballybunnion."

"Oh, they will that," his grandfather replied, wiping his dark-ringed eyes. "In a few years, there'll be tell of the lad attacking the police barracks single-handed and falling in glorious battle. Martyrs have to be heroes, Bryan, not beardless boys who die terrified and hurting something awful. If martyrs died like people really do die, why no one would want to be a martyr."

Chapter 4
November, 1917

Bryan Aherne waited an hour after the last goodnights had been called before lifting himself gently off his bed. He pulled his nightshirt over his head, buttoned up the outdoor clothes he was still wearing underneath, and slid a hand under the mattress for his revolver. He tiptoed gingerly down the two flights of stairs from his room, laced up his boots by the front door and slipped noiselessly out into the streets. The lamps had been shut off an hour earlier, at midnight, leaving enough patches of dark shadow under the bright winter moon to conceal his progress for the couple of hundred yards past the darkened police barracks to the gates of St. Michael's College.

The wrought iron gates squeaked gratingly. He paused before going through them, looking around to check that no one was watching. The windows of the college facing him down the drive were dark. The priests, the teachers, were asleep like the rest of Listowel. Bryan leaned against the brick wall by the gates, regained his breath and whistled low the opening bars of "Danny Boy."

A voice interrupted throatily from the shrubbery on the opposite side of the drive.

"Over here. We're over here!"

He darted across the drive just as three figures emerged, crouched, from their hiding place.

"You're late," Jimmy Sugrue muttered.

"My dad didn't come from the bar till late."

Paddy Costelloe, one of the few teetotallers in the Volunteers, if not the whole of Kerry, sniffed disapprovingly.

"Stop the blathering and let's get on," snapped Davy Lanigan. "Your man'll be too fast asleep for us to wake him if we don't move."

Crestfallen by his reception, Bryan nodded and followed his three older companions as they ran quickly across Upper Church Street and into the curving drive of the rectangular Victorian villa directly opposite the college gates. They moved stealthily down the drive, keeping to the edge of the lawn, until they were about twenty yards from the front porch.

"Time for the masks, I'm thinking," Sugrue whispered.

The four Volunteers pulled handkerchiefs from their pockets and tied them across their mouths and nostrils.

Sugrue pointed towards the middle of the lawn in front of the house.

"There," he told Lanigan. "Dig there and make it the proper shape. We don't want just a bloody great hole, remember."

"But . . . but . . ." Lanigan protested. "It's in full sight of the street!"

Costelloe sniffed again.

"Folk'll have to see what's done," he mumbled. "Or there's no gain, is there?"

Lanigan shrugged, hoisted a spade on to his shoulder, and walked on to the grass. He cut through the turf, blessing the fact that frost hadn't yet gripped the earth—it was soft and yielding. The spade bit into the earth as he dug, his breath clouding on the cold air.

The other three walked swiftly to the front door. Sugrue rapped on the glass and banged the knocker while Bryan and Costelloe stood behind him, revolvers in hand. The feel of the cold metal eased Bryan's nerves.

He shivered slightly and wondered whether it was coldness, nervousness or excitement. Although this night's work wasn't exactly blessed by the Volunteers' commanders, he thought, they were bound to be impressed if it went off successfully. Nobody had yet dared to move against Lord Listowel in any way at all so an attack on his right-hand man, his land agent, Marshall Hill, was certain to

cause a stir. It was just the sort of action to bring the young
men to the attention of their officers. And that was precisely
their purpose. Until now, the four inseparable friends had
obeyed orders to the letter, attracting no particular praise
while other Volunteers had undertaken unofficial freelance
operations, winning swaggering notoriety.

Bryan's grip on his revolver tightened when he heard the
bolts being drawn on the other side of the door.

"Who is it?" a man's voice asked.

"From his lordship, Mr. Hill," Sugrue replied, turning to
Costelloe and winking. "We've a message from his
lordship."

A wedge of light broke into their faces. Instinctively,
Bryan checked that his mask was pulled up.

"Yes?" a short bewhiskered man inquired, poking his
face around the door.

Sugrue didn't reply. He simply barged his shoulder into
the door, thrusting it open, sending the middle-aged man
reeling back down the hallway. Surprise flitted across his
face, then anger, and finally terror as he saw the three young
men walk into his house, each with their revolver pointing
at him. Bryan felt almost sorry for the land agent.

"In there," Sugrue ordered, waving his gun in the
direction of the drawing room. Costelloe grabbed Marshall
Hill under one arm. Bryan took the other, pushing their
captive into a high-backed chair near the still-glowing fire.

The land agent's spirit began to return.

"Rogues and vagabonds!" he kept spluttering while
Costelloe tied him to the chair. "His lordship will have your
hides. You'll rot in prison for this!"

"Shut your gob or it'll be shut for you!"

Costelloe's voice, though muffled by his handkerchief,
was laconic, threatening. It ensured a tense silence broken
only when Sugrue ushered Marshall Hill's wife into the
room after rousing her from bed. She held the front of her
dressing gown tightly around her neck. Her hair was spiky
with grips and ribbons. Her face glistened with night cream
and fearful perspiration.

"Swine! Oh, you swine!" Hill exclaimed when he saw

her. He wriggled and strained so vigorously at the ropes binding him that the chair wobbled, then toppled to the floor. The land agent lay on the thick rug, gasping. His wife ran to him, beginning to sob. She tried to lift him but his weight was too much. He thudded back on to the rug, winding himself again.

"Here, missus," said Bryan, hating to see the couple in so much distress. "Leave him to me."

He heaved the chair upright and stood back to allow Mrs. Hill to embrace and comfort the bound man.

"Does bring tears to the eyes," Costelloe remarked without a trace of genuine sentiment or pity.

"Shut up," Sugrue ordered. "We're not here to hurt them."

"Of course, we're not," Bryan chimed in. He realized immediately that he might have sounded too glad that violence wasn't contemplated so he added, as menacingly as he could, "Well, leastways not if you give us what we want."

"My jewels are upstairs," Mrs. Hill volunteered quickly, eagerly. "Take them and be off with you. Mr. Hill's heart won't . . ."

"We're not wanting your jewels, missus," Sugrue stated flatly.

"What then?" muttered Hill, ashen grey and running with sweat.

"We were thinking you'd like to be contributing to the Volunteers," Bryan said helpfully.

"What! What!" Hill exclaimed, indignation and rage overcoming fear. "Contributing to you Sinn Feiners? Help you rebels? You're nothing more than ruffians, just rogues, just . . ."

The words strangled in his throat as Costelloe thrust the muzzle of his revolver against the land agent's left ear and clicked back the hammer.

"Your guns," Bryan interrupted urgently, worried that Costelloe might pull the trigger. "That's all we're wanting. Just your hunting guns."

"In the gun room," Mrs. Hill cried, wringing her hands anxiously.

Sugrue nodded and left the room, returning a few minutes later with a rifle and four shotguns clapped in both arms and with his pockets bulging with boxes of cartridges and bullets.

"Right, boys," he called from the doorway. "Let's away now."

"What about them?" Costelloe asked, waving his revolver at Marshall Hill and his wife. "We don't want them raising the chase."

"They won't be so foolish, what with our man waiting outside till we're away."

Beneath his mask, Bryan smiled at the bluff. He grabbed Costelloe's arm and urged him from the room. But Costelloe wasn't satisfied. His obvious desire to hurt began to frighten Bryan.

"And no doubt these high-and-mightys will have a telephone," Costelloe went on, shaking off Bryan's hand. "Have you thought of that?"

Sugrue laughed. "They have that, but somehow the wires aren't working since I cut them."

Costelloe grunted his satisfaction.

"And by the by," Sugrue continued to the Hills, "I wouldn't be too hasty about telling the police too much. When you draw your curtains in the morning, you'll be seeing a reminder of what could happen if you open your gobs too wide."

"Swine!" the land agent exclaimed again, his anger returning now he sensed his ordeal was nearly over.

"Shush, dearest," murmured his wife, who wasn't as confident.

"Untie him in fifteen minutes, missus. No sooner, mind. Remember our man outside," Sugrue said, backing toward the front door.

The three young Volunteers ran on to the front lawn where Lanigan by now was up to his hips in the hole.

"Leave on, now, Davy," Bryan called. "That's deep enough."

Lanigan clambered up on to the grass and vanished into the night with his friends, all of them, even the dour Costelloe, laughing with relief and self-admiration.

Bryan lay awake for almost an hour when he reached home, remembering every detail of the raid. Just before he went to sleep, the thought came to him about whether it was right that he should have felt so good, so alive, when his revolver had been in his hand and pointing at defenseless people. His mind was too tired to provide an answer.

A few hours later, Marshall Hill parted the curtains of the drawing room.

There, in the center of the prize camomile lawn, was a hole, a grave dug in the shape of a coffin. Mrs. Hill seemed transfixed by the sight.

"Oh, the bastards. The young bastards," Marshall Hill cursed, comforting his wife. The message was clear to him.

The townsfolk of Listowel, walking along Upper Church Street, saw the grave as well. The warning needed no explanations. It was, in fact, becoming all too common.

It needed the detailed view of older men, such as Jack Aherne, to fully comprehend the rising tide of violence and intimidation that autumn and during the winter months leading into the year of 1918.

The youngsters like his grandson could only think of those days as a series of incidents, each more hilarious and daring than the one before. Imperceptibly they were growing used to violence, embracing it as a way of life, as a philosophy. Those of naturally violent natures gloried in the ripening lawlessness. The others, the great majority, came gradually to accept it as nothing out of the ordinary.

The Volunteers were now drilling openly again, better equipped and disciplined than before, usually in the market square or in the grounds of St. Michael's College. Often, when the parades were over, half a dozen of them would toss bricks at the police barracks in Upper Church Street, shout insults, then hare away before any constables dared emerge to give chase.

Farms and houses were raided for weapons. Unpopular landlords had their crops plowed up and their best stock

lamed. They would wake in the morning, as Lord Listowel's agent had done, to find a warning grave on their
land.

Tit-for-tat reprisals began from those opposed to Sinn
Fein. They called themselves "The Black Hand Gang" and
burned down halls used for meetings by the Volunteers or
sent threatening letters to their leaders.

The authorities retaliated by banning all meetings and
parades.

Soon, thirty Volunteers of all ranks were on hunger strike
in Mountjoy Prison after being sentenced for drilling or
making seditious speeches. They demanded the status of
prisoners of war, refused to wear uniforms and smashed up
their cells.

On April 9th, the British Government announced that
military conscription would be extended to Ireland. Lloyd
George forgot all his earlier prevarication and offered
Ireland immediate Home Rule, although with the partition
of Ulster.

He declared ringingly, "When the young men of Ireland
are brought into the firing line, it's imperative that they
should feel they are not fighting for establishing a principle
abroad which is denied to them at home."

The Irish people remembered the tens of thousands
who'd already given their lives voluntarily. They united in
their opposition to conscription and, this time, united
behind Sinn Fein. On April 18th, political leaders of every
persuasion met in Dublin to condemn the British Government.

Their condemnation was echoed at meetings in towns and
cities throughout the country. In Listowel, there hadn't been
such a gathering since the heyday of Parnell and the Land
Leaguers.

The Ahernes rushed their Sunday lunch wanting to be
early in the market square to obtain a good position. To their
dismay, they found dozens already clustered around the
platform outside the Arms Hotel decorated with tricolors
and a large banner stretching overhead which proclaimed,
"No Conscription—Stand United."

Maude Aherne looked anxiously at her husband, Aunt
Brigid and her grandchildren. She worried how they would
endure the crush in the warm spring afternoon. Her son
noticed the expression on her face and understood.

"Wait here," Sean said. "I'll be seeing what I can do
about a better place."

Ten minutes later, Jack, Maude and Brigid sat by one of
the windows on the first floor of the Arms Hotel with four of
the grandchildren grouped around. Sean and Finoola stood
just outside the hotel entrance behind the platform, while
Bryan insisted on going off on his own, saying he wanted to
stand in front of the speakers.

Bryan had another reason for wandering off, a girl with
hair the color of ripened wheat. He prayed she would come
as she said she would. It would be too much to hope that she
would be alone. He caught sight of her, pressed against the
railing of St. Mary's Church, right at the back of the throng.
Her long straight tresses were instantly recognizable at a
distance and even when partially hidden by a wide-brimmed
straw hat tied with red ribbons. It had been the color of her
hair, so unusual in this part of Kerry, that had caught his
attention first during a Volunteers' route march to Ballylongford. She'd watched the ranks of men swing by from
behind the wall of her parents' small dairy farm by Galey
Bridge, three miles from Listowel. She'd smiled shyly at
the young men. All of them ogled her. Only Bryan had
cycled back the very next day. Then, in his own shyness,
he'd forgotten to ask her name until he was on the point of
leaving, when her mother had called her back into the
farmhouse for tea.

"It's Hannah," she'd called after Bryan had cycled away,
his machine wobbling. "Hannah Wilmot."

He needed all his strength and height to shove his way out
of the crowd to where Hannah stood. She, and presumably
her parents, were too intent watching the speakers gather on
the platform to notice his approach.

Bryan coughed, exhaling a deep breath.

"So . . . so you came," he spluttered, pulling off his
cap.

"I said we probably would," she replied demurely.

Her mother, small and round and neat, turned when she heard her daughter's voice. Mrs. Wilmot's gaze was friendly yet appraising.

"Mother," Hannah said coolly, "this is the young man I told you about. Bryan Aherne."

"Mr. Aherne. A pleasure, I'm sure."

"Mr. Aherne's a Volunteer," Hannah said by way of an introduction to her father.

"Are you, young man? Are you indeed? And what might you be volunteering for?" Hannah's father smiled, winking.

Bryan liked Mr. Wilmot immediately. His eyes were, at the same time, shrewd and twinkling, set deep in a ruddy-hued face.

"Well, Mr. Wilmot, anything you might care to suggest," he responded, quickly put at ease by their obvious friendliness. "I'll be volunteering for anything except that," he continued, pointing at the anti-conscription banner high above the platform.

"We'll be discussing that maybe, Mr. Aherne, some other time, but for now I'm thinking the speechifying is about to start."

"Then may I join you to listen?" he asked, hoping that he didn't sound too formal.

"Note the young man's manners, Mother," Hannah's father said dryly, winking at Bryan again. "A town boy for sure."

Bryan realized that he was having his leg pulled but, before he could think of a suitable reply, clapping rippled through the crowd. The main speaker stepped forward to the rail at the edge of the platform, arms upraised for silence. The crowd went quiet, recognizing the town's curate, Father Charles O'Sullivan.

"Fellow citizens," he began, his deep voice reaching easily to every section of the crowd. "Fellow citizens, with all my soul I say it is good to be here, it is good to be alive today when the hour of national redemption is nearer at hand than any of us could have hoped for."

A huge, approving cry rose into the air, lifting the rooks out of their crannies in the ruined keep of Listowel Castle.

". . . Mankind has reason to remember that day when a money-tax imposed by England led to the birth of a nation and the uprising of the American constitution. Mankind shall have as much reason to bless this day when a blood-tax imposed by England has called forth this declaration which, with God's help and an even more sacred human right, shall carry Ireland along the same glorious way of salvation."

Father O'Sullivan's right hand, holding the Bible, shot into the air. The crowd cheered and clapped. Bryan looked quickly at Hannah. She smiled back. The young man felt suddenly very possessive toward her. He was elated at the priest's powerful words. He felt part of Ireland, part of its history, simply being in the market square this warm April afternoon. His attention was dragged back to the platform.

"We accept the passing of this conscription law," Father O'Sullivan roared, "as a declaration of war on the part of England upon the Irish nation!"

The priest waited for fresh cheers to subside before leaning forward confidentially over the platform's single wooden railing. His voice began again softly but grew in pitch and power, until it boomed and battered at the bricks of the surrounding houses and shops and taverns. A horse tethered behind St. John's Church in the center of the square threw up its head, shaking its mane, scared by the noise. The crowd, some open-mouthed, stood transfixed by the oratory.

"I will tell you plainly what the issue is—whether Irish women, the mothers of our blood, the Irish men, the guardians of our manhood, whose sires have proved in many a bloody battle that they were the owners of their own souls—whether Irish women and Irish men are the owners of their own lives and bodies and blood or whether these things are the property of the Cromwellian breed whose names have often been written in blood over the graves and corpses of small people.

"In God's truth, this is the issue—whether we are freemen in our blessed land given to us by God, or chattels to be disposed of by barter; whether we are freemen or pawns to be played off in a game of political strategy; whether we are freemen or a mere human crop to be seized and mown down by military incompetence; whether we are freemen or slaves to be led to the slaughter by hungry capitalists and greedy traffickers. This is the issue which the people of Ireland are preparing themselves today to fight out to the end."

The shout of acclaim from the people of Listowel was so overwhelming, so rousing, that Hannah and her mother pressed their hands to their ears.

"Listen!" Bryan shouted, his lips close to Hannah's ear. "Listen! Have you ever heard such words? They'll have to take heed of us now. Surely they will!"

Hannah nodded her head up and down, eyes laughing, still trying to block out the noise.

Her father leaned over and tapped Bryan on the shoulder.

"Did you hear him? Did you just hear the curate, Bryan? War, he said! A declaration of war!"

"And war he meant if they force us into the army," Bryan shouted back.

All around, people were laughing and hugging each other. The hysteria lasted a full five minutes before the crowd began to regain control of itself. Women patted their hair back into place, men fiddled with their ties and cuffs, a few clearly regretting such open displays of emotion. Family groups started to drift away.

"Come on, Father," said Mrs. Wilmot. "There's the cows to be milked and Hannah has the chickens to feed."

Her husband seemed disappointed at being dragged back to reality. He grinned lopsidedly at Bryan.

"Young man, exposed for all the world to see are the burdens of being a poor farmer. Women and animals wait for no man. You see that? Well, you better be remembering it."

Bryan smiled, shrugging, unsure if he was meant to reply. He'd hoped for more time with Hannah, perhaps a stroll around the town.

"You have to go then?"

"We do that," Mrs. Wilmot replied, firmly, offering her arm to her husband. Hannah stayed silent but the downcast expression on her face told Bryan that she would have preferred to remain a while.

"Well," he said lamely. "Well, it's been . . ."

"We're at home on Sunday afternoons usually," Mrs. Wilmot interrupted, seeing his glum expression. "That's if you'd care to call sometime."

"May I?" Bryan asked eagerly. "May I . . . next Sunday perhaps?"

Hannah grinned delightedly. Her hair shimmered as it caught the sun. Her father smiled his agreement.

Bryan called the next Sunday at the farm at Galey Bridge and on the following two Sundays before deciding that he'd better tell his family about Hannah. Nervously, he broached the subject only to be met with suppressed giggles: they had known about her ever since the anti-conscription meeting. His grandfather's sharp eyes had spotted them together from his vantage point in the Arms Hotel.

"You're not minding?" he asked defensively.

"Mind? Mind? Why should we?" his mother replied, eyes brimming with amusement and love. "We're looking forward to meeting her . . . if you choose . . . when you're ready, of course."

And so, during that summer and autumn, Bryan and Hannah became accepted in and around Listowel as a couple whose families had visited each other and had properly approved the courtship. Not that there was any question yet of becoming formally engaged. They were simply walking together. There didn't seem the time for much more, as events around them moved with increasing momentum.

The groundswell of protest against the conscription law was all that the more militant Volunteer companies needed to step up their campaign of raids and intimidation. Farmers opposed to Sinn Fein, fearing attack, mounted all-night guards over their property, but that didn't prevent their animals being mutilated, their barns being burned, nor the macabre warning graves being dug.

Bryan found himself so involved in the planning and execution of these raids that he scarcely had time for his work, albeit casual, at his father's tavern. His rows with his family grew more frequent as their anxiety increased about his activities, but they were powerless to stop him. He didn't even bother to hide his prized revolver from them.

It was as if he were a person split in two. He loved and respected his family, but in the company of the Volunteers, he was as dedicated as any to spreading fear and chaos. Like thousands of young men that spring and summer of 1918, both in the trenches of France and the countryside of Ireland, Bryan Aherne was being molded by events totally outside his control. There was no going back.

Ironically, the threat of conscription, which had handed so many political cards to Sinn Fein, was shelved as an exhausted German army fell back before the Allies' counter-offensive. But the Goverment in London quickly provided another *cause célèbre* for the hard-line nationalists.

On May 17th, seventy-three Sinn Fein leaders were arrested, including Eamon de Valera. Within months, more than five hundred people in Ireland were in prison. The charges ranged from concealing weapons to offenses such as answering policemen in Irish, and singing songs like "Wrap the Green Flag Round Me Boys." Each arrest was another victory for Sinn Fein.

A voluntary recruiting campaign during these months of arrests and repression still produced more than ten thousand Irishmen willing to fight for the British Crown. But that mattered little during the General Election called for December, 1918, weeks after the Great War ended. Most of the soldiers, loyal to the Crown, never received voting papers because of maladministration. Their absence from the ballot added to Sinn Fein's resounding victory. The Ulster Unionists were badly mauled, gaining a majority in only four of the nine counties to which they laid claim.

For the first time in Irish history, a political party pledged to total independence from Britain had won power. It was swift to capitalize on its supremacy, despite the number of its leaders still in prison.

On January 21st, 1919, Sinn Fein called Dail Eireann, the national assembly, into session at the Mansion House in Dublin. It issued a Declaration of Independence, announced an official constitution, and appointed ministers.

Yet no agreement had been reached with the British Government and British troops effectively controlled the country with the help of British-controlled policemen.

What concerned the Irish more were the killings, a few days after Dail Eireann began sitting, of two constables, shot at point-blank range by four masked Volunteers, acting on their own initiative, at Soloheadbeg in County Tipperary.

There was little else to discuss when the newspapers printed the gory details side by side with the frantic condemnations of the Catholic hierarchy. No one could believe that Sinn Fein would order such a deed. No one could distinguish, not even the learned churchmen, between the public voices of Michael Collins and Cathal Brugha, urging moderation, and their private advice and instructions to the Volunteers firmly under their control. It was no different in Listowel.

"Wasn't it dreadful? Those poor constables . . ." Hannah Wilmot remarked, sitting next to Bryan Aherne on the narrow, lumpy sofa in the front room of the farmhouse at Galey Bridge.

Bryan glanced at the rain pelting against the small, quartered windows. He'd have to borrow a coat from Hannah's father for his return home. It had been clear and cold when he'd set out on his bicycle.

"Hum," he grunted, not really listening. His eyes darted towards the wooden door leading to the kitchen. As always, it was a few inches ajar. He knew Hannah's parents were sitting in there by the warm range, trying not to listen to the young people's conversation, yet with ears pricked for the tiniest rustle of impropriety. At least, he thought, they were better than some parents who would never let their daughter alone in a room with a young man under any circumstances.

He reckoned it was a fair compromise to leave the door open those few inches.

"I said, wasn't it awful bad about those constables?" Hannah repeated, nudging him gently with her forearm.

"Yes . . . eh, yes . . . terrible sad," Bryan muttered.

"Their poor wives and children."

"Yes."

"Do you think they'll catch them?"

"Who's knowing?"

His hand slid over the shiny leather of the sofa. He touched Hannah's fingers. Their hands twined, squeezing. They didn't look at each other for a moment, savoring the contact of each other's flesh.

"Do you think they were Volunteers like the newspapers say?" Hannah asked, her eyes fixed straight ahead on the fringe of the green cloth hanging from the mantelpiece.

"The newspapers say anything," said Bryan, repeating the message he'd heard so often from his commanders.

"But if they were Volunteers?" Hannah persisted.

"They're not!"

"But if they were, you wouldn't help them, would you?"

Her eyes searched his face. Her lips were so near. He bent his head fractionally closer.

"Help them?"

Their lips were inches apart. He could feel her breath, smell upon it the fresh milk she'd drunk at teatime.

"Do things like they did, if they did . . . with guns . . . shoot . . . kill people."

Bryan shook his head, his lips brushing hers for an instant before their hands drew apart.

"Still raining," he remarked, louder, suddenly very conscious of the folded sheets of paper in the inside pocket of his jacket.

Bryan didn't want to show Hannah, her parents, his family, or anyone the current issue of the Volunteers' secret journal, *An t-Oglach, The Soldier*.

This informed the Volunteers that they were now regarded as the army of Ireland; the Dail Eireann claimed the right of "every free national government" to inflict death on the enemies of the state.

Cathal Brugha, the son of a Yorkshireman who'd been christened Charles Burgess, presiding in the Dail in the absence in Lincoln Gaol of de Valera, had personally vetted the secret statement.

"Enemies of the state," it continued, "are soldiers or policemen of the British Government whom every Volunteer is entitled morally and legally to slay if it is necessary to do so in order to overcome their resistance."

"Don't worry about the rain," Hannah said, breaking into his thoughts. "There must be a spare cape somewhere around the farm."

She traced her fingernail across the ball of his thumb. Bryan shivered.

Chapter 5
June, 1920

The small locomotive from Newcastle West and Abbeyfeale, smart in green and black livery, was the obligatory ten minutes late when it puffed and chugged into the station platform at Listowel that sunny June day. If it had been on time it would have upset half the townsfolk who regulated their clocks in the certain knowledge of the noon train's consistently late arrival.

To give him his due, the stationmaster noticed immediately that the locomotive was pulling four carriages, rather than the normal two, and he did wonder why the driver gave three blasts on his whistle instead of just one. His porters were busy opening the first-class doors and hunting down tipping customers with the minimum of baggage.

It was the station boy, Billy Mahony, leaning on his broom, who saw them begin disembarking from the last two carriages, kitbags and rifles slung over their shoulders.

"Look at their uniforms!" the lad exclaimed. "Which regiment would they be from?"

The stationmaster, Henry McGill, did look, face blanching, and then scurried through the ticket gates and off toward the center of the town. On the way, he told everyone he knew about the arrivals. Finally, considering his duty done and sweating profusely under the midday heat, the stationmaster subsided into his favorite nook in the Castle Bar and gulped down a glass of porter before repeating his news to anyone who cared to listen. His alert ensured a good crowd outside the station to watch the men march away.

People gazed curiously at the unfamiliar uniform, the bottle green jacket of the Royal Irish Constabulary, the khaki trousers of the British Army. They listened to some of the men's rough English voices and saw how hard and fit their bodies were.

"It's the new police," someone muttered. "They didn't have enough proper uniforms for all of them."

"They've been in Cork," another said, careful not to speak too loudly.

"And Tipperary. They've been in Tipperary."

"Aye, that's where the name's from . . ."

". . . after a pack of hounds they called 'em."

"Aye, that's right . . . a pack of hounds."

The new police recruits realized they were the center of attention. They didn't mind. After the horrors of The Great War, the mumblings of some Irish peasants miles from anywhere were of little importance. What was important, however, was to create the right impression, to show these ill-dressed clods who the masters were now.

One of them, young with cropped ginger hair, casually unslung his service issue .303 Lee-Enfield rifle and worked the bolt, thrusting a bullet into the breach as he surveyed his new surroundings. The watching crowd heard him say something to his companions who laughed out loud. The man didn't even seem to aim properly. In one smooth movement, he lifted the rifle to his right shoulder and squeezed the trigger.

Crack!!!

The unexpected shot made some of the crowd literally jump with surprise and a woman's shawl slipped to the dust.

In a field across the railway tracks, a small grey donkey shuddered, gave out a single bellow of shock and pain, and then fell over, kicking and struggling, blood spurting from the fatal wound in its side.

The group of police, already becoming known in Ireland as the Black and Tans, or simply the Tans, were still laughing as they formed up into ranks and marched off toward the barracks in Church Street.

A few minutes later, unaware of what had happened at

the railway station, Sean and Bryan Aherne, flanked by customers, watched the men's arrival in the street through the dusty windows of the tavern.

"They look hard men for sure," Bryan commented. "They know their drill. You can tell that."

"The sweepings from the English gaols," a customer broke in. "At least, that's what they say in Cork."

"That's all they could find to do the filthy work," another added.

"You're not surprised at that, are you?" Bryan asked, balancing his half-filled glass carefully on the windowsill before rolling himself a cigarette. "The police hereabouts are scared to move out of their barracks without the soldiers holding their hands."

"And even if that were true, who's to be thanked?" his father interrupted. "They wouldn't be here at all but for the shootings and burnings. It's come to a pretty pass when we have English gaolbirds helping the Irish police. I'm thinking the boys'll have to be looking out for themselves now."

Sean gazed quickly at his son, watching his expression. In public, they never acknowledged Bryan's membership in the Volunteers, the Irish Republican Army. Everyone locally knew as well, of course, but it was never spoken of. Much better, people had decided, not even to mention the organization but just to term its members as "the boys."

"Oh, I don't know, Dad," Bryan said confidently. "I'm thinking that the boys'll be more than a match for them." He downed the dregs in his glass. "The word'll come soon enough how we're to deal with them."

The tavern door flew open. A railway porter burst in, breathless from running, trembling with suppressed excitement and shock. "And did you see what those murdering sods just did?" he cried before he was properly through the door.

"The Tans?"

"Yes, them," the porter continued, pointing dramatically at the men across the street beginning to file into the police barracks.

The shooting of the donkey, described and embellished in

horrified tones again and again that day, June 7th, 1920, soon had its desired effect on the people of Listowel. They were now in no doubt that they were caught up in the events which were transforming their country. Like many they'd still been hoping that they could escape from the dreadful reality. Indeed, they were already building myths as a last refuge from reality.

The Black and Tans had already been dubbed as gaolbirds when—and the facts were perfectly well known—they were merely veterans of The Great War, though understandably battle-hardened and undoubtedly cynical. They'd all had to possess a good character reference from their former military units to be able to join The Royal Irish Constabulary and earn their ten shillings a day. Their reasons for joining might have been more a desire to escape lengthening unemployment queues rather than help preserve the peace in Ireland but their recruitment had been made necessary by the fast-worsening security situation. More and more men were resigning from the RIC as the campaign of terror, ordered and directed by Michael Collins and Cathal Brugha, spread into every village and townland.

Since the killings at Soloheadbeg the previous year, dozens of ordinary policemen, along with magistrates and soldiers, had been callously shot down by the IRA, the majority without even the opportunity to defend themselves. The troops had responded with martial law and curfews but their discipline, like that of the police, had held steady under the utmost provocation. Only in the last few months had it begun to crack.

Politically, there was stalemate. The British Government wouldn't bring in the promised Home Rule Act, promised at the end of The Great War, until the international peace conference was over and went so far as to block the attendance there of an Irish delegation.

Although officially declared illegal at the end of 1919, Sinn Fein progressively filled the vacuum, aided by the sweeping victories of its individual candidates in the local council elections held shortly before the Tans came to Listowel. Michael Collins and Cathal Brugha effectively controlled Dail Eireann, now underground after being suppressed, through supremacy in Sinn Fein and its secret inner circle of dedicated revolutionaries. As the police became powerless, the Volunteers of the IRA took over many of their duties in at least half the country, organizing patrols and even holding courts for common miscreants.

The majority of ordinary people were aghast at this state of anarchy, as appalled and condemnatory as the hierarchy of the Catholic Church which had precipitantly lent its support to the organization behind the chaos. The seeds which had been sown on all sides for so many years were bearing fruit with the arrival of the Tans and the beginning of a backlash from the sore-pressed constables of the regular force.

Sinn Fein clubs and the homes of supporters were being broken up and set on fire just as dozens of police barracks had been previously. The Sinn Fein Lord Mayor of Cork, Tom McCurtain, was murdered in his bed by masked policemen just as their friends and colleagues had been. The forces of authority were striking back. Acts of terror by the IRA were bringing reprisals. The reprisals spawned further acts of terror.

But, until the arrival of the Black and Tans and the shooting of the donkey, the viciousness of events had seemed remote from Listowel. The small market town was far enough off the beaten track, too much a closed community, to have avoided the worst excesses. There'd been the burnings of police barracks in the area, but, by coincidence or design, the buildings had been unoccupied or evacuated without bloodshed.

The only fatality had been a police sergeant, shot during a gun battle when he'd refused to hand over the police payroll to an ambush party not far from Hannah Wilmot's farm at Galey Bridge. But so bravely had he fought, his family had received donations and condolences from the Volunteers themselves, ashamed and upset at his death.

In this part of North Kerry, the violence had been as ritualistic, impersonal and formal as an old-time faction fight. It would soon change. The minuet of death was being danced throughout the land and Listowel would not be allowed to sit it out.

The first indication of what was to come appeared only ten days after the Tans' arrival. Sean and Bryan Aherne were taking a mid-afternoon break from their own bar, leaving Aunt Brigid in charge. Like many other tavern keepers, they preferred to go to another bar for their own refreshment. It gave them an escape from their own, all-too-familiar customers as well as the opportunity to see how a rival's business was faring.

This hot summer day, June 18th, they favored T. D. Sullivan's bar in the middle of William Street, facing on to Market Street, the main road leading west out of town. The streets were quiet, almost deserted, while Listowel basked somnolently in the heat. But to the Ahernes' surprise, T. D. Sullivan's was packed and noisy in contrast to the empty establishment they'd left behind.

"What's this?" Sean joked, seeing uniforms all around him. "Bit early for the policemen's Christmas dance, isn't it?"

Sullivan, busy behind the bar, shook his head worriedly.

"It's no laughing matter, Sean," he replied. "There's real trouble on."

"Trouble? The only trouble they're having is drinking the stuff quick enough. Maybe you're running low . . . is that the trouble?" Sean retorted, not taking him at all seriously. He ordered two drinks and leaned his elbow on the bar, surveying the customers. "Hello, Tommy," he called to Tommy Carmody, one of the constables packed into the bar. Most were arguing excitedly, hands gesturing. "The sun got you all off the streets, then? Who's minding the barracks?"

"Bugger the barracks! Bugger the lot of them!" Carmody shouted, eyes angry, voice fierce.

"I'm for us all resigning," another constable exclaimed in Sean's ear.

"What's all this talk about, Tommy? What's on?" Sean asked.

The constable hesitated for a moment, seeing Bryan

standing by his father, knowing full well his connection with the IRA. Then, he shrugged.

"Well, it'll be out soon enough, Sean, so I'm supposing there's no harm in telling you two."

Carmody paused, looking hard at Bryan.

"Even if the news will have the rebels dancing a jig."

"Come on, man," Sean urged, ignoring the barbed remark. "You've me burning with curiosity so you have."

"Well . . . well, we've just had a meeting down the barracks with Colonel Smith."

"The police commissioner for Munster?" Bryan interrupted.

"Himself and Captain Watson from the Army and some big-wigs I'm not knowing."

"It must have been important," Bryan interrupted again.

"Shut up, son, and let Tommy talk," Sean ordered gruffly.

"That's right, son," the constable agreed. "Shut up or your rebel friends won't be getting the latest news. The fact of the matter is they wanted us to hand over the barracks to the soldier boys. Said we're to combine totally with them. Said we're to take their orders."

Sean whistled through his teeth in surprise. Another constable joined the group, his eyes reddened by drink, tobacco and tiredness.

"And what about the pacification, Tommy?" he asked. "Have you told them?"

"Not yet. Give me time. The colonel said the Crown Forces were going on the offensive."

He looked hard at Bryan again.

"To beat the rebels at their own game. There's to be martial law and then what he called a ruthless pacification campaign. He said that if any innocent people got killed then he would see that we wouldn't have to answer for it. He reckoned the bloody government needed our help."

"And what the fuck have we been doing all these months, I'd like to know?" the other constable said vehemently.

"Needed our help to beat the rebels and if anyone didn't want to help then he should get out of the force."

"Holy Mother of God!" Bryan exclaimed.

"So that's what it's all about," Sean chimed in. "I can see why you're talking of resignations. What did you do when he said that, Tommy?"

"Well, we thought something was up so we'd elected Jerry Mee to speak for us. He stepped up bold as brass and said his piece. You should have seen the colonel's face, being talked at like that by a common or garden constable. 'By your accent,' Jerry said, 'I take it you're an Englishman. You forget you're addressing Irishmen.'"

"That's telling him," Sean breathed, his glass of whiskey untouched in his hand.

"That wasn't all, mind. Jerry Mee took off his cap, his belt and his bayonet and flung them on the table in front of the colonel. 'These too are English,' he said, standing as straight as the road to Tralee. 'Take them as a present from me, and to hell with you, you murderer!' Old Smith went purple. 'Arrest that man! Arrest that man!' he screamed."

"And did you?" Bryan failed to conceal the excitement in his voice.

"Arrest Jerry? Arrest him? Like pig-shit we did. You stand by a man like that, son. In fact we all stood by him. Told the big man that there'd be blood spilled if they laid a hand on Jerry. That finished it there and then."

"And now you're having the celebration, and quite right too!" Sean exclaimed. "It'll cost heavy but I'll be after buying a drink for every one of you boys."

"It's not as simple as that, Sean," Carmody continued. "The drink'll be more than welcome but we've a lot of thinking and talking to do. We came across here 'cos we were fearing what might happen if we stayed at the barracks. They might have called the troops to us and clapped us in our own cells."

"Fat chance," the other constable snorted. "They'll be having my resignation papers and that's all. I'm not killing innocent civilians. I'm a policeman, not a bloody murderer."

"And that's an Ulsterman saying that," Carmody grinned, jabbing his thumb at his colleague.

"Makes no difference where I'm from. Either we're proper policemen or we're not. And, anyway, an Ulsterman's an Irishman, isn't he?"

The mutiny of the Listowel police—and the resignations of fourteen of the twenty-five constables—meant that the town passed virtually under the control of the troops and the Tans. It meant that martial law, declared three days later, would be doubly unpleasant. It meant too an immediate dilemma for the Ahernes and all the other families who had relatives in the Sinn Fein Volunteers, the IRA, or Cumann na Mban, the Volunteers' section for women and girls. Should they go into hiding or brazen it out by continuing their normal lives?

"I've done nothing they can charge me with," Bryan declared firmly that first day of martial law, sitting in the front room at No. 32 Church Street.

"You're sure?" asked his grandfather, leaning back on the narrow sofa, sucking on an empty pipe. "These people mightn't be too finickity about laws now they're in charge. The regular police are different. Taught some of them myself, so I did. They knew us and we knew them. Bit of respect between them and the boys, I wouldn't be surprised."

"We never went for them as individuals," Bryan interrupted. "Sure I've been at a few barracks burnings but no one got hurt. No one. And I've never been in an ambush yet, never fired a gun in anger."

"Of course you haven't," his mother remarked soothingly.

"And I've got rid of the gun," Bryan continued. "Buried it at the farm."

"Hannah's?"

"Uh-huh, but no one, not even her, knows where. I wouldn't let her look."

There was silence for a moment. The grown-ups suddenly realized that only Bryan could make the decision. The old schoolmaster, still a part-time teacher, peered at his grandson, adjusting his glasses to do so. There were lines on the young man's forehead, not deep yet but unmistakable. Bryan's straight, slightly pinched nose gave his face an appearance of firmness and resolve. A lock of black hair tumbling over the broad forehead suggested vulnerability. His hands were definitely those of a doer, a toiler, not a scholar, large and capable, two long fingers stained a little with nicotine. Was one his trigger finger? Jack shook the question from his mind. But another filled its place. How had the boy, his grandson, the son of his only son, come to this?

"You think I should go on my keeping, Grandad?"

"Off on your own? Running? Hiding?"

"Yes."

"Where would you stay, dear?" his mother asked anxiously, reaching out for Sean's hand.

"With friends for a few nights, then move on. Keep moving on. There are plenty of barns around. This weather, it'd be no problem, no hardship."

"Son," said Sean, "don't you think they'd really start hunting you down if you went missing? They'd really think you'd something to hide, something to be afeared of."

His grandfather pulled the pipe out of his mouth. "My opinion is that he should bluff it out. Stay put and not go on his keeping. Keep out of everyone's way for a while. But it's his life, isn't it, Bryan? It's your decision!"

Bryan smiled at him, his eyes reflecting his gratitude. "I'd never harm the family," he said quietly. "You know that, Grandad. If you're troubled because of me, then I'll be away."

"Aye," Sean said pessimistically, glancing sideways at his wife. "If we're troubled . . ." His voice died away.

That evening, at six o'clock, the streets of the town were empty except for patrols of troops, police and Tans. Gradually, Listowel learned to live under the curfew. Friends who came to spend a social evening stayed the night. At first, the novelty was welcome. No one really suffered, not even the taverns. Customers seemed to buy the same amount of drink as they did before in spite of the much-shortened licensing hours.

But soon the restrictions started to become irksome. Occasionally, the equally bored Tans livened up the evening and their drinking bouts in barracks by loosing off shots at any lights showing in houses. This forced the townsfolk to barricade their windows.

At No. 32 Church Street, Sean procured some oily bales of sheep's wool to block the windows and doors, front and back. The smell, particularly that fine summer, permeated everything in the house. The children grew more fractious, pressing their noses to cracks in the barricades, watching troops stroll down to the river at the end of Tay Lane for a swim in the welcome cool of the early evening.

Their irritability and restlessness naturally transmitted itself to their parents. Throughout the town—and Ireland—resentment increased as martial law showed no sign of coming to an end. House searches became a matter of routine, as routine as the milkman calling. The soldiers were immaculate in their behavior but unrelenting in their thoroughness. Once Finoola Aherne, panicking like a disturbed chicken, had to unstack every pan, every piece of crockery in her kitchen to satisfy a search party that she had no hidden IRA messages.

A search by the Tans was altogether different. Precious ornaments and family souvenirs were smashed. Small children were shouted at and frightened. Rifle butts somehow dropped painfully on toes and fingers.

The retribution grew more offensive, if that were possible, as summer gave way to a glorious autumn. Members of a new adjunct to the security forces began to spread into North Kerry. These were called officially "Cadets," part of the Auxiliary Division of the Royal Irish Constabulary. These men were recruited from the ranks of out-of-work British officers. They were paid £1 a day and used mainly for lightning, motorized raids in their Crossley tenders on suspected rebel hideouts. The people of Listowel came to hate the strutting arrogance of the Auxiliaries as much as the physical crudeness of the Tans, marginally preferring the attentions of the regular police constables and the troops.

Their preference became more marginal, however, when District Inspector Tobias "Toby" O'Sullivan was posted to the town in charge of the Crown Forces throughout the area.

The reputation of this burly, stocky man whose semi-permanent smile never quite reached his bleak eyes had travelled ahead of him after his surviving an IRA attack on his previous headquarters at Kilmallock, County Limerick. The attackers had set fire to the building during a five-hour siege by breaking open the roof slates and pouring petrol through. O'Sullivan had managed to escape to fight another day, leaving a sergeant and a constable to perish in the flames. That the constable had been a blood relative, his nephew, had added to O'Sullivan's image as an officer with ruthless disregard for human suffering. Not that there was much such regard by either side in those months.

During one weekend at the end of August, seven policemen and one Army officer were killed by IRA gunmen. One was a senior police officer who'd been implicated in the murder of the Lord Mayor of Cork. The officer died in his home town of Lisburn, not far from Belfast, and forty Catholic homes were burned in retalia-tion.

The flames didn't have to be seen in Belfast for rioting to start there. When order had been restored, twenty people were dead and eighty-seven wounded, most of them from the Catholic minority huddled against the fiercely Protestant majority. Tit-for-tat, it went on.

Soldiers and police were shot. The Tans and Auxiliaries burned entire villages. In some townlands, people slept out in the fields all night for fear of reprisals. But their will didn't evaporate in the way it had in previous rebellions. Terence MacSwiney, the new incumbent as Lord Mayor of Cork, epitomized that freshly-forged spirit following his arrest at a Sinn Fein conference. He chose not to eat for seventy-four days and died in Brixton Gaol in London on October 24th.

Still the terror went on. It increased. Less than a month

later on November 21st, Michael Collins's murder gang
shot and killed twelve British army officers in Dublin. Most
died in their pajamas, in hotel rooms and lodgings, many in
front of their helpless, shrieking wives. Later that same day,
twelve civilians, including a woman and a child, died in a
hail of bullets when police opened fire on a crowd at Croke
Park attending a Gaelic football match between Dublin and
Tipperary. That very night, three men, two of them IRA,
were shot by Auxiliaries in the guard room at Dublin Castle,
the center of British administration in Ireland. It was said
they were riddled with bullets when trying to escape. Not
surprisingly the day became known to both sides as
"Bloody Sunday."

A week later, an entire convoy of Auxiliaries and Tans
was wiped out in an ambush near Macroom in County Cork,
neighboring Kerry. The death toll was seventeen of the
security forces and three IRA men. The horror was
compounded by the fact that many of the Auxiliaries and
Tans were shot and bayoneted, terribly mutilated, where
they lay dying or dead.

The overwhelming presence of the security forces in
Listowel had meant that the Volunteers living there had had
to be extremely careful about their actions. In consequence,
the town had suffered little by way of reprisals. But now,
after such a massacre as Macroom? The worst was feared.
The local IRA commander, Paddy Landers, the blacksmith,
quickly ordered his men to disperse for a few days and sent
messages to the town's tavern-keepers that, on no account,
should they allow the singing of the verses glorifying the
massacre which were being circulated within hours.

> On the 28th day of November
> Outside the town of Macroom,
> The Tans in their big Crossley tenders
> Were hurtling away to their doom.
> For the lads of the column were waiting
> With hand-grenades primed on the spot,
> And the Irish Republican Army
> Made shit of the whole fucking lot!

Bryan understood the orders perfectly. Any provocation could only bring more suffering upon the town. He decided, like the others, that he would spend the next week living rough in the countryside.

Early next morning, the day after the massacre when its full impact was beginning to be felt, his mother and Aunt Brigid filled his rucksack with thick brawn sandwiches, two lengths of cooked drisheen and half a cheese.

"You'll be maybe getting a wee bit cold at night," his father winked, slipping two half-bottles of whiskey in with the food when the women's backs were turned.

"It'll go well, Dad, with the milk I'll be borrowing from the cows," Bryan smiled back.

"Aye, it will that. Now you're certain you'll be safe on your own keeping? You've your cape and your thickest coat and underwear? As soon as you're gone, son, I'll be barricading the house and the tavern. We'll be safe when you return."

The whole town seemed to have had the same idea. Bryan cycled away through streets echoing to the sound of nails being driven into planks of wood fitted over windows of shops and homes. There was no sign of any of the security forces, not even outside the police barracks. Their absence from view struck him as somehow ominous. He decided to head for Galey Bridge to explain to Hannah why he wouldn't be seeing her for a few days. Her mother, however, had different ideas when he arrived there.

"I'll hear of no such thing, young Bryan, sleeping in ditches and such like!" Mrs. Wilmot exclaimed indignantly, crackling smart in her apron, standing by her gleaming, black-leaded range.

"But there'll be barns to sneak into," Bryan protested.

"Barns?" Mrs. Wilmot sniffed disdainfully. "Cold and drafty, if I'm knowing anything of most of them in these parts. No more than lean-to sheds, I'm thinking."

"They'll be all right for a couple of days."

"They'll not be," she insisted, waving a stirring spoon at him. "I can see why you're on your own keeping—and I'm not criticizing you what with those Tans around and awful angry they must be—but if you're to stay in barns, you'll stay here in a proper one. Mr. Wilmot's is at least waterproof, and you can be having some blankets."

"I don't . . ." he began.

"Can he, Mother? Oh, can he?" Hannah asked eagerly.

"Of course he will. That ways, at least we'll be knowing what he's up to . . ."

Bryan shrugged resignedly, smiling.

"But I'll be out cycling during the day," he said, conceding defeat with some inward gratitude. "I'll only be coming here at night. The police probably already know about Hannah and me. They've seen us around together, I'm sure. They might come searching if they don't find me at home. I wouldn't want them seeing me on the farm if they drove past."

"We'll talk about that later," Mrs. Wilmot promised, shaking her head in mock dismay, returning to her pots.

"Come on, Bryan!" Hannah urged gaily. "Let's find a comfortable place for you with the cattle." She led the way into the farmyard.

The chickens, wandering free in the mud, parted ranks before them, clucking fussily, as the two young people walked towards the two-story barn, about fifty yards from the house.

Instinctively, Bryan looked across to the other corner of the yard where the pigs were kept. He'd buried his revolver, securely wrapped in oilcloth, close by the entrance to the sty. As far as he could see, the patchy turf there hadn't been disturbed. He assumed it was still safe.

"Will you be having an upstairs or a downstairs room, sir?" Hannah joked once they were inside the barn.

Bryan gazed along the milking stalls in front of him, filled with black cows standing hoof-deep in manure-streaked straw. They stared limpidly back.

"Upstairs, I think, miss," he replied.

Both giggling, they clambered up the ladder to the hay-loft which ran half the length of the barn. For the next hour, they heaved the bales around creating a hiding place for

Bryan in one corner. To reach it, he would have to climb up and over the bales, but once inside he'd be safe from all but the most meticulous search.

He spent the rest of the day in the farmhouse, looking nervously through the windows whenever a very occasional vehicle clattered by. After an early supper with the Wilmots, he returned to the loft with Hannah, this time with blankets. She held an oil lamp above her head, jagged shadows flitting across her face, while Bryan made final adjustments to his sleeping space.

"Right," he called from behind the bales after a few minutes. "It's as snug as it will be."

"You're sure?" Hannah stepped up on to a bale and stood on tiptoe, trying to peer over.

"Aye. You'd better away now."

His hand waved goodbye above the bales. She leaned forward all she could, just managing to brush her fingers against his. When Bryan felt her hand, he stretched further upwards and clasped it, squeezing for a moment.

"Good night, Hannah," he said, huskily.

"Sleep tight and God be with you," she called from the other side of the bales. "Avourneen," she added in a whisper, uncertain whether she wanted him to hear the endearment, hoping that he might. Although they'd been meeting for over a year, their romance was still delicate and fragile, their physical intimacy rarely more than an occasional fleeting kiss.

Once, when they were embracing, Bryan's hands had slid down Hannah's back and gently cupped her small, giving buttocks. She'd allowed them to remain there for long moments imprinted on his memory before twisting out of his arms, face lowered, her breath audible. He'd begun to stammer a question, disconcerted, and then had fallen silent, realizing she wouldn't, couldn't, answer. Nor could he ask.

Another time, during that past, marvellous summer, he'd joined the Wilmots in a swimming expedition to the River Gale, alongside their farm. Of course, the river had been reduced by the heat to little more than a trickling brook but it was still delightful to feel water moving against limbs. Hannah had insisted on changing into her mother's bathing costume behind some shrubbery and, as she'd stepped over Bryan, lying on the riverbank with her parents, he'd looked up. The sight of the blondish, curly hairs between her thighs, glimpsed through the folds of the overly-large costume, remained with him.

As experienced and hardened as Bryan might have been in other ways, he still possessed the fumbling inexperience with the opposite sex common to most young Irishmen, particularly those brought up outside the larger cities. His courtship of Hannah had progressed steadily, slowly, not dramatically and passionately.

Later that night—he came awake to the sound of shouting, the slamming of metal doors. He shook his head, not sure whether he was dreaming, confused about where he was.

An angry voice, tinged with defiance, cried out, clearly carrying to him in the blackness of the hayloft.

"And what the hell are you wanting at this time?"

The question, outraged, wasn't answered. There were noises, strange noises at that distance, before a woman began shrieking.

Bryan heaved himself over the bales, feeling his way in the dark, hands outstretched, and started down the ladder. The cows scrambled in the straw, disturbed, rising from their sleep.

"Get out of the way or I'll give you the contents of this!" a man's voice shouted.

"Shoot me!" a woman exclaimed hysterically. Bryan, mind clearing, knew it was Hannah's mother.

"Shoot me!" she repeated. And again, "Shoot me! I'd sooner die than be living after him!"

"Bring him out or your man's dead," another man called, his excited voice slightly slurred. The accent was odd to Bryan, his ear pressed against the barn door, unable to find a chink in the wood. It wasn't an Irish voice. Perhaps it was Scots, perhaps English. He wasn't sure. Certainly, the man sounded like he'd had more than a few drinks.

"You've done as much to many a good man!" Mrs. Wilmot answered back, desperation yielding defiance.

"You'll take him up in a box!" the same man threatened.

Bryan pushed lightly against the barn door, easing it open a fraction. He could now look out through the tiny gap.

The front of the whitewashed farmhouse was lit yellow and garish by the headlamps of three Crossley tenders.

Eight Tans in uniform, three swaying perceptibly, stood in a wide arc in front of their vehicles, backs toward him, rifles casually at the port position across their chests.

A smaller group stood within the arc. Three Tans were in a line, rifles aimed at Mr. Wilmot, who was pressed by his own terror against the wall by the front door. Beside the soldiers was a taller man with badges of rank on his shoulder, his cocked revolver at arm's length. Mrs. Wilmot knelt before her husband in the tacky mud, white nightgown rucked and dirt-stained. Hannah stood in the doorway, long hair framed golden by the lamp burning behind her, the outlines of her rounded slimness showing through the thin cotton of her nightdress, the divide between her thighs noticeable. The playing shadows obscured her face. The faces of the Tans were also dark and difficult to see. Bryan realized that the men's features had been deliberately masked with oil or soot or grime.

"Give him to us," the man with the revolver ordered. "Give him up or your man'll be shot through."

"Who? For God's sake, who?" Mr. Wilmot shouted.

"The rebel. Give us the rebel or you're dead!"

"I don't know a rebel!"

"You know Aherne, Bryan Aherne. He visits here. And since he's not at home, he's here! Give him up!"

"Bryan? Is he a rebel?" Mr. Wilmot pretended surprise without much success.

"He's a rebel as well as the murdering corner-boy who fucks that whore of your daughter!"

Mrs. Wilmot screamed. Slowly, she fell on to her side in a faint, nightgown rising above her waist, displaying her nakedness. Her husband knelt quickly beside her. His fingers scrabbled to make her decent. His shocked face, upturned, appealed mutely to the Tans.

"He's not here," Mr. Wilmot said, his tone suddenly flat with resignation. "I wish to God that he was, that he could face you, but the truth is he's not been here for a week past."

A Tan, staggering with drink, loomed behind Hannah in the doorway, thrusting her aside.

"No one," he called. "No one. It's empty."

"Sure?" asked the man with the revolver.

"Certain."

Bryan's mind emptied of everything except the image of his gun lying not ten yards away. He eased the barn door open another six inches, ready to slip through, and then stopped, regaining his senses. What could he do? He'd be shot before he reached the weapon. Even if he did find it in the dark and confusion, how could he use it without causing the deaths of Hannah and her parents?

"You're sure?" The question came again from the man who seemed to be in charge. "We've none of them yet anywhere. This is the tenth or eleventh fucking call and we've no one."

"Not one of the rebel bastards here."

"They'll still pay. Oh, yes, they'll pay or my name's not O'Sull . . ." The man stopped and laughed to himself. "They'll pay all right," he repeated. "Hold the dirty whore there!"

The Tan in the doorway slung his rifle over his shoulder and pinioned Hannah from behind, hands brutally squeezing her breasts, his lower body jerking against her buttocks as if he was having sex. The other men laughed at the pantomime. One tried to cross his legs and almost fell down.

Sounds of breaking and tearing came from within the farmhouse, wood and china, glass and cloth.

A Tan stepped forward, white teeth grinning across his darkened face. He pushed the muzzle of his rifle hard against Mr. Wilmot's forehead, holding him in a kneeling position.

Headlights glinted off the steel blade of a knife, suddenly in the hand of the man who'd held the revolver.

With a lurch and a cry of triumph, he grabbed hold of Hannah's long blonde hair and began sawing at it.

Hannah yelped with pain—Bryan quivered at the sound—but stood straight. The tresses fell around her feet, one by one, until she was cropped like a boy. Jagged clumps of hair stood every which way from her scalp. Tears streamed down her cheeks, glistening in the lights.

Her tormentor stopped, satisfied. Then, faster than the eye could follow, he jerked out his free hand, thumb upturned, and thrust it between Hannah's defenseless thighs. She shrieked once and doubled up, sobbing and gulping in her agony.

"No more than she's had from that rebel sod," the man guffawed triumphantly. "Maybe thicker and harder though!"

The Tans around him burst into raucous laughter.

"Shall we give it her proper, sir?" one asked. "Show her what it's like with real men?"

Hannah's violator shook his head, stepping away from her. He sniffed ostentatiously at his thumb.

"They're sweeter smelling in Listowel," he laughed.

Bryan crouched, retching silently, behind the safety of the barn door. Despite the pain within him, he knew at last that he would be capable of killing another human being.

Chapter 6
January, 1921

The first time they had tried to murder him, the bullet had missed by feet, spattering harmlessly off a wall, panicking the crowd at Listowel Fair. The second occasion had been even more frustrating. The ambush had been perfect but their damp ammunition had refused to fire. Those selected for the third attempt were more than a trifle nervous as they moved to their positions under the overcast, grey-drizzling January sky.

Con Brosnan, Donalin O'Grady and Bryan Aherne walked singly down Church Street, caps pulled down over their foreheads to keep the rain out of their eyes and to hide as much of their features as possible. The young men kept three or four yards apart, pretending to look into the shop windows or bending down to tighten their bootlaces, eyes alert for the first sign of police or troops. Jackie Sheehan kept pace with them on the other side of the street. The ballot had decreed that he should give the signal. The other three carried the guns.

They paused at the end of Church Street, where it bent back on itself and became William Street. Opposite them were two bars, Kennelly's and Broderick's, flanking the narrow entrance to Tay Lane whose cobbles sloped down to the banks of the River Feale. The clock in the window of McAuliffe's, the boot shop, showed twenty minutes to midday.

"Still plenty of time," Bryan muttered under his breath. "Plenty yet." He slid his hand into the right-hand pocket of his overcoat, letting his fingers caress the barrel of the revolver.

There was no denying he felt on edge. The fluttering stomach muscles, the constant pressure in his bowel, told him that. In fact he was surprised that he didn't feel worse. Of one thing he was certain. He had absolutely no qualms about this mission. Since that night at the farmhouse, nearly two months before, the thought of revenge had burned within him, searing away any conscience he previously had about killing.

His local commanders in the IRA knew this. They were loath, however, to issue the order for execution immediately. The assault on the Wilmots, particularly Hannah, and the sack of their home were terrible, but many similar incidents had occurred the same night in Listowel and the surrounding area as the Tans and Auxiliaries had run amok, infuriated by the massacre of their comrades at Macroom.

The early order to disperse from Paddy Landers had meant that none of the IRA volunteers had suffered, only their families and friends. One by one, the Volunteers had emerged from hiding, apprehensive, only to find that life had returned to normal.

As the weeks passed, Bryan, impatient and deeply angry, often thought of exacting retribution single-handed but an incident on New Year's Eve in William Street made that unnecessary.

A group of Tans, viciously drunk in their seasonal celebrations, set upon a young man as he walked home. They beat and kicked him so severely that he died the next day without recovering consciousness. Their victim was the twenty-year-old son of Davy Lawlor, the parish clerk and bell ringer, a man loved and respected throughout Listowel. Some months before Lawlor had refused to toll the church bells at a funeral of a Tan who'd died from natural causes. To retain any credibility, the local command of the IRA had to respond to the atrocity. The execution was decided by a unanimous vote. That two unsuccessful attempts had already been made showed just how inexperienced in such matters the local Volunteers were.

Bryan glanced again at the clock in the window of the boot shop. Its hands had hardly moved. There were still more than fifteen minutes before District Inspector Tobias O'Sullivan of the Royal Irish Constabulary, area commander of the Crown Forces in North Kerry, would walk down this street, turn this corner where Bryan stood, on his way home to lunch with his wife and children. He had taken the same route for the last ten days.

Con Brosnan, who was in the lead, nodded his head slightly in the direction of Kennelly's Bar and moved towards its front door. The other two with the guns saw his signal and followed him. Jackie Sheehan stayed on the corner.

The streets were empty except for three women—one in a wide-brimmed, black straw hat, the others covering their hair with thick, dark shawls—and two chestnut horses tethered to the bollard outside Broderick's Bar, nuzzling contentedly into their feedbags.

Bryan had the impression of time almost standing still as he followed the others into Kennelly's. Every house, every shop, was familiar to him, had been since childhood, yet now he seemed in a strange place.

"Morning, friends," said Kennelly's son behind the bar, recognizing each of them. Bryan looked evenly at him, realizing again the impossibility of remaining unknown and unidentified in his own small town. He didn't worry too much about it, though, believing that no one would inform on them, particularly after what they were about to attempt.

O'Grady acknowledged the greeting.

"Half glasses of porter all around," he ordered. "And then it might be better if you were attending to the barrels in the back."

He folded back his overcoat, allowing the barman to see the handle of the revolver stuck into the top of his trousers.

Kennelly's son nodded his understanding, his hands shaking as he poured the drinks. He waved away Bryan's offer of money and disappeared quickly into the bar's back parlor.

"Not long," said Con Brosnan, moving to a table by the window, swallowing at his glass on the way.

Two elderly men, scarves knotted in place of ties and

collars, shuffled to their feet at a neighboring table and left the bar, their watery eyes registering disapproval of the new customers.

"Long enough," Bryan said, picking up the conversation. "But make the drink last."

"Aye," said O'Grady. "Make it last, Connie boy. It could be you won't be having a drink ever again."

"That's amusing?" said Brosnan, his mouth tightening.

"Not meant to be," O'Grady muttered. "There's no joking now."

"Aye," Bryan agreed. "No joking now."

Their eyes swivelled around each other's faces, trying to draw courage and encouragement.

"Remember he'll be wearing the steel vest," Bryan said quietly.

The three nodded wisely, nursing their drinks. They kept looking through the quartered window at the junction of Church Street and William Street, checking that Jackie Sheehan was still there.

Sheehan himself was literally quivering with nervousness. He'd seen District Inspector O'Sullivan begin walking down Church Street from the police barracks, accompanied, as always, by two Tans, rifles on shoulders. The Inspector's raincoat failed to hide the bulk of the bullet-proof armor underneath covering his chest and stomach.

Now, O'Sullivan had stopped ten yards from Sheehan, chatting animatedly with an elderly man whom the look-out recognized as a retired constable called Dan Farrell. After five minutes, he turned to his escort and waved them away. The two Tans said something—perhaps protesting, Sheehan thought—before returning the way they'd come.

"Well, goodbye then and God be with you," O'Sullivan said at last. Sheehan, stepping from one foot to the other in his nervousness, heard the words quite plainly.

The police officer resumed his walk home, actually nodding in a friendly fashion at Sheehan, one of the very few people on the street.

As O'Sullivan reached the bend at the bottom of Church Street, Sheehan crossed the road quickly, head pulled down

into his shoulders. Opposite Kennelly's, he drew a handkerchief from his pocket, wiping it across his face as if drying
away the raindrops, then hurried away into the market
square.

The three young men in the bar saw the signal. Bryan
suddenly felt an emptiness in his stomach.

Outside, the drizzle had turned into more solid rain. The
three fanned out across the narrow street, only five yards
wide, in front of O'Sullivan, hands in pockets clasping their
revolvers. He didn't even look at them, his attention
focused on a doorway further down William Street. Bryan
followed his gaze and saw a woman and a young child, a
girl aged about ten, waving. The thought registered that
they must have been the police officer's family. He felt no
emotion about them, only again the emptiness within
himself.

They drew their revolvers almost at the same moment,
about six feet from their intended victim.

District Inspector O'Sullivan didn't seem to notice their
presence until a second or so later, when they were even
closer.

He looked into the faces of Con Brosnan, Donalin
O'Grady and Bryan Aherne, faces he vaguely knew, the
ever-present smile on his face, his cold eyes assessing. They
hardly widened when they saw the pointing, aimed revolvers, only grew more quizzical, perhaps even reproving.

Bryan believed he fired first but he wasn't sure since the
three reports were practically simultaneous.

He felt the gun leap in his hand, the muscle spasm akin to
that when a freshwater salmon is hooked.

He was so near to O'Sullivan that he thought he saw the
flesh opening, tearing, under the impact of the bullets. First,
in the side of the neck; then in the middle of the cheek;
finally, at the top of the ear, just under the hairline.

The smile didn't leave O'Sullivan's face. In fact, it
appeared to widen as his features distorted sideways and his
life blood spouted upwards and outwards.

He took one step, still smiling, his eyes emptying of expression, beginning to film over.

Bryan fired again, his revolver by now almost touching the tip of O'Sullivan's nose.

The police officer's head jerked back. His legs shot out behind him, his muscles losing all messages from his shattered brain. He fell to the wet cobblestones, a bubble of air moaning in his throat. His body twitched once, lifting perceptibly off the ground, and then he was still. His uniform cap, bloodied, rolled gently toward the gutter.

"He did forget his head, didn't he?" said Con Brosnan, a note of wonder in his half-whispered remark.

The three young men stood for a second, looking down at the body, revolvers still smoking, in communion with the act of death.

"Toby! Oh, Toby!" a woman shrieked. There was other screaming too. Perhaps a man, probably another woman. Shoes clattered on cobbles, running, slipping in the wet.

Bryan glanced up and saw O'Sullivan's wife rushing toward them, hair streaming, arms outstretched, her pleasant, round face twisted with anguish.

"Oh, Toby, my Toby!" she repeated, her voice rising to a screech. "Toby, what have they done?"

"Mama! Mama!" sobbed her little girl, running a few feet behind her mother, terrified by the sound of the shots, the sight of the blood, the crumpled shape of her father.

"Come on, for fuck's sake," Brosnan grunted. "Let's away, boys."

The three turned on their heels and fled toward Church Street, pursued by the shrieks and sobs of Mrs. O'Sullivan and her small daughter. Bryan looked back over his shoulder once just before he ducked into a side alley. Mrs. O'Sullivan was prostrate over her husband's body, trying to lift his shattered head, blood streaked on her hands and face.

"Jesus! Oh, Jesus!" he panted, the realization of what he'd done beginning to strike him.

"Did you see his head?" O'Grady cried behind him. "Holy Mother, did you see it?"

The alley twisted and turned before it opened on to the town's sports field. They dashed across the open space and into the comparative safety of Gurtinard Woods on the other side.

Behind them, Listowel was in turmoil. The police had rushed to the scene from their barracks only a hundred yards away. An army patrol was there a minute later. Those few who'd seen the murder had already vanished, leaving the pathetic widow and her child alone in the middle of the street with the body.

Two farmers, who'd witnessed the shooting from the windows of Broderick's Bar, had leapt onto their horses, tethered outside, and galloped pell-mell out of town. At first, the police thought they were the culprits and set off in pursuit. Others ran into the market square, revolvers in hand, cursing and shouting. The townsfolk who saw them coming dashed indoors out of their way.

Then, suddenly, there were schoolchildren all over the center of town, returning home for lunch from St. Michael's College and the National School next door. The police and soldiers swore and cuffed them as they milled and swirled about, making movement of trucks and tenders impossible for vital minutes.

Eventually, the army was able to chase the false trail inadvertently laid by the two farmers and set off along the Tarbert road. By then, though, the farmers were safely at home. The troops' confusion was increased by an old woman with a donkey and cart who'd seen the farmers. She deliberately sent the soldiers in the opposite direction.

In Listowel, businesses closed down, windows and doors were locked and bolted; streets cleared of people. Everyone feared what was to come. They waited fatalistically for two hours. Then the Tans emerged from their barracks in twos and threes, infuriated after viewing the body of their slain commander, inflamed by drink, out for revenge.

They walked along Church Street, smashing windows with their rifle-butts. Some thrust their rifles through the broken glass and loosed off bullets into the houses. Others took aim at people visible behind their makeshift barricades and fired round after round. The town echoed to the crackle of indiscriminate firing. Amazingly, not one person was wounded.

For more than four hours, most of the townsfolk lay huddled, terrified, on the floors of their homes, hiding under beds, even in wardrobes, for protection.

Pet dogs and cats still on the streets were shot or bludgeoned to death.

Shops and bars were looted for drink and cigarettes, food and clothes, before the Tans tired of their orgy of destruction.

That night, Listowel was too afraid to sleep, scared of any knocks on the door which might herald more shooting. Most locked themselves inside rooms, clasping their rosary beads tightly around their fingers.

Bryan and his two companions spent their night among the broken-down walls and under the leaking thatch of the old Aherne cabin at Drombeg. It had taken them nearly five hours to reach it, skirting the town, keeping to the hedgerows and copses, hiding from anyone who passed. The three Volunteers were cold, hungry, wet and tired. In their low state, doubts began to surface.

O'Grady was the first to voice the thought uppermost in their minds.

"The swine deserved to die," he said quietly. "He did, didn't he, boys?"

"Aye," Bryan replied wearily. "He did that."

"But is it right that we killed him?"

"Who else?" asked Brosnan.

"But was it a mortal sin?"

There was silence. The young men were as religious as any person of their age and upbringing, which meant that the strictures of the Catholic Church were of considerable influence among them, even if they were sometimes loath to admit the fact openly.

"The bishops keep saying all the assassinations are wrong," Bryan said finally.

"But they supported Sinn Fein."

"They did that, Con, and Sinn Fein is the government, is Dail Eireann, and we're acting under its orders, aren't we?"

"Through Collins and Brugha."

"Aye, we're the proper army, they say."

"They do that," O'Grady agreed, brightening perceptibly.

"There's the rub, though," Bryan added, shaking his head sadly. "The people voted for Sinn Fein true enough, but they didn't vote for all this bloodletting. There's been no war declared, has there? And the orders from Collins are secret, aren't they? They're not passed by the Dail, wherever it's meeting, are they?"

The others were forced to agree, gloom returning.

"What would Father O'Connor say?" asked Brosnan, thinking of Listowel's parish priest.

"Grandad talked to him about the killings the other day, so he did," said Bryan. "Father O'Connor told him the Church only approved of violence in a rebellion when it was against a tyranny ruling by force against what the people want . . ."

"That's the British, isn't it?" O'Grady interrupted eagerly.

"Oh, yes, it's the British all right," Bryan went on. "But the Father also said that the rebellion had to be approved by the whole community if it was to get the Church's blessing as well."

He drew heavily on a rather limp cigarette before passing it to Brosnan.

"There's the problem. Does the community approve or not? The newspapers don't for sure . . ."

"They'll all approve if we get an Irish government in Dublin," O'Grady said.

"Oh, yes, they'll do that. We'll be the heroes then, the real boys, not the murdering corner boys they call us now. Oh, yes, they'll be happy then. But I'm thinking most people want the quiet life, Donalin, my boy. They want change without the trouble. They want an omelette without breaking the eggs."

"Isn't that the truth?" Brosnan echoed.

"But we're sort of doing the right thing?" O'Grady asked tentatively, determined to salve his conscience somehow.

"I reckon," Bryan sighed. He wasn't sure about anything now that the adrenaline had stopped flowing.

"So, at the worst, it's only half a mortal sin, shooting O'Sullivan?" O'Grady persisted.

"Aye, Donalin," said Brosnan, suddenly wearying of all the chatter, preferring to seek solace in his own thoughts. "Only half at the worst!"

"And if your mother wore a mustache, she'd be your father," Bryan murmured under his breath, angry with himself for trying to ease O'Grady's mind with such futile arguments.

Even while he'd been uttering the words, he'd known the truth within himself. No human being deserved to die in the manner of District Inspector Tobias O'Sullivan, but then no young woman should have been treated like Hannah nor a young man beaten to death like Davy Lawlor's son.

He fell into an uncomfortable, broken sleep, reflecting on how easy it had been to kill, how difficult to justify the killing. He didn't feel especially guilty, only changed, perhaps soiled, certainly older by another man's life. Or should it have been death? And was it true that you killed a bit of yourself when you killed someone? He dozed off, his damp cap under his head.

Shivering with cold, they awoke so early that it was still dark. After a brief discussion they decided to strike out for Ballybunnion, hoping for food and shelter during the inevitable hue and cry.

Bryan asked them to wait a few minutes before setting off. He went outside, trying to find the graves he'd often played around as a youngster. The darkness and the thick, matted undergrowth made his task impossible. With a single, regretful glance at the tumbledown cabin, the setting for so many family tales, he followed his friends along the potholed road toward the seaside village.

Their first inquiry on the outskirts of Ballybunnion took them to Simon Mulvihill's cabin where they were welcomed immediately, sat down by a swiftly-revived fire, and plied

with hot oatmeal fortified with poteen. The Mulvihills, of
course, had a shrewd idea of why the three were on the run
but declined to ask questions, preferring the story to be
volunteered in time. When it was, they listened in silence,
eyes hard and gleaming.

Simon Mulvihill set off that morning with messages for
their families and the IRA commanders. In the next ten
days, Bryan, Brosnan and O'Grady were moved around the
village, spending each night with a different family. It was
as if the whole of Ballybunnion wanted to share the burden
and danger of their concealment, realizing that they would
share the punishment if the three Volunteers were discovered.

The Army had instituted a policy of official reprisals,
burning houses after ambushes, destroying whole townlands after murders and interning suspects without trial,
more than a thousand of them so far.

In the circumstances, North Kerry escaped comparatively
lightly after O'Sullivan's killing. Three more companies of
troops were sent to Listowel with orders to enforce martial
law more rigorously. The names of shops written in Irish
were defaced. Indeed, shops were only allowed to open
from ten o'clock until noon on Mondays, Tuesdays and
Wednesdays, and markets and fairs were banned. The life
of the town came to a virtual standstill. Even worse, orders
were issued and posted throughout Listowel that in future
any man, aged between twenty and forty-five years, deemed
to be in suspicious circumstances, armed or not, could and
would be shot where he stood.

The IRA decided its Volunteers could no longer operate
undercover in the town. It was time to establish a permanent
fighting force, a flying column modelled on those already in
existence elsewhere.

Twenty-nine volunteers from the 3rd and 6th Battalions
of the IRA—most of them, like Bryan, already on the run—
met at Derk townland, a mile or so from Listowel, on the
afternoon of Sunday, January 30th. Their first job was to
select a commander. The obvious choice was the only man
with experience in the regular British Army, Tom Kennelly,

a farm laborer. He was elected by a unanimous show of hands.

Kennelly, tall and powerful, unhurried in speech, stood in the center of his men as they sat in the grass. Bryan was overjoyed to be with them. The ten days that he, Brosnan and O'Grady had spent in hiding had been the most boring and depressing of his life. There'd been nothing to do except think morbid, fearful thoughts, worrying about his loved ones. Now, he was part of a group again. Companionship and resolve surrounded him, just as the Volunteers surrounded the new leader of the North Kerry Flying Column.

"Men—friends," Kennelly began, "most of you will have heard of the Three Musketeers. They were soldiers too, fighting against greater numbers, great odds. Well, the Musketeers had a motto which we're going to use. You know it. 'One for all and all for one.' That's how it'll be with us. We've strength in numbers to protect ourselves and to strike at the troops and those bastard Tans. It's not to be an easy life."

Some Volunteers laughed at the obvious understatement. Kennelly smiled, feeling the sense of unity around him.

"No soft pillows for us. We'll live off the land and we'll stay on the move. They won't know where to find us, and, more important, they won't know where we're to attack next."

He paused before continuing, searching their faces, watching their nods of approval.

"Now, the first job is to pool what resources we've got and then decide where our headquarters are going to be."

The Volunteers placed what weapons they had on the grass near Kennelly's feet. It was a frighteningly small arsenal with which to start their campaign. There were seven rifles, four revolvers, eight shotguns and just over two hundred rounds of assorted bullets and cartridges, about ten for each weapon.

Kennelly grimaced when the count was done.

"It's a start anyway, boys," he said, shaking his head ruefully. "We had to start somewhere. The rest'll come

from our own supplies and from the soldier-boys themselves."

The flying column decided to move south of Listowel,
between the town and Tralee, into even more sparsely
populated country, into the comparative safety of the Stack
Mountains, some rising more than a thousand feet above sea
level. Here, the flying column reckoned it was safe from
any surprise attack. And so it proved. Alerted by informants, the army followed them to the mountains, but no
officer was foolhardy enough to go into the mountain range,
to risk ambush among the dark, overhanging crags and the
deep valleys, flaming wine-red and yellow with heather and
gorse.

From the mountains, the North Kerry Flying Column
created a legend of terror.

Those who were believed to be informers were shot and
left at the roadside with warning labels pinned to their
bodies. Many mistakes were made but none admitted. Not
even in the case of a 68-year-old pensioner called Patrick
Roche whose only offense was to sell milk and vegetables
outside Listowel police barracks.

The flying column stole mailbags, searching for letters
from informants. The ripped bags were left in public places
so the message was clear.

They attacked police barracks in the dead of night. One
simultaneous raid was against those in Ballylongford and
Ballybunnion. Usually the Volunteers were driven off in
panic, searchlights playing and machine guns hammering.
But, in Ballylongford, the column succeeded in fatally
wounding a Tan. In reprisal, twenty thatched cabins were
burned down in the small village and fifteen men badly
beaten.

So it continued week after week, month after month.
Attack and reprisal. Reprisal and attack. A Volunteer killed
in an ambush that went wrong; a landowner taken out in his
dressing gown and shot in revenge. The killings were as
merciless as the reprisals. Between the two sides, the
ordinary people suffered.

The Irish Times, appalled like most newspapers, wrote

trenchantly, "The whole country runs with blood. Unless it is stopped and stopped soon, every prospect of political settlement and material prosperity will perish and our children will inherit a wilderness!"

Such concerned views mattered little to the Volunteers of the North Kerry Column. Their lives were full of romance and adventure, so they thought, with the discomfort and danger providing additional spice. They were swaggering heroes, their otherwise humdrum lives long forgotten. They were the defenders of the people, so they said. They didn't add that the people wouldn't have had to be defended against anything if the Volunteers hadn't begun the campaign of terror in the first place. They were reliving the history of the Fianna, the mythical warriors of Old Ireland.

Sometimes, as it often does, reality intruded. Then, the Volunteers reverted to being simply bewildered youngsters afraid for their lives, unsure of their cause, longing to be home and away from it all.

United, the North Kerry Flying Column was a formidable guerilla group. Fragmented, its members tended to be easy pickings for the security forces. And, in early May, 1921, the column was forced to disperse by an outbreak of scabies, known to locals as "the IRA itch." The men were ordered to go their own ways for a week or so, since together they could hardly stop scratching long enough to aim their weapons.

At first, Bryan was tempted to risk a visit to his family in Listowel. They'd kept in contact through intermediaries but he ached to talk to them again, to seek reassurance for what he was doing, perhaps even to receive their blessing.

One night he crept within fifty yards of the bridge over the River Feale leading directly into the town. To his dismay, there were makeshift sentry huts at either end and two soldiers on patrol. He circled the town desperately. Everywhere there seemed to be barbed wire barriers and searchlights. Listowel, in fact, had been effectively sealed off. No doubt there was a way through but he decided the danger of capture was too great.

He laid low for the next few days, living in the dense

undergrowth of a copse off the Tarbert road, eating berries
when his small supply of bread and drisheen was exhausted.
On May 12th, hunger and loneliness forced him into the
open again. He set off for the Wilmot farm at Galey Bridge.

It was a warm day with high, gentle clouds as Bryan
moved cautiously through the scrub at the side of the road
leading east from Listowel. He brushed the back of his hand
against his face, feeling the bristles of his beard, hoping he
wouldn't appear too disreputable to the Wilmots.

The months away from Hannah had proved to him—if
proof were needed—how much he loved and needed her.
When he'd joined the flying column, she still hadn't
recovered fully from the assault. She'd been quiet and
withdrawn, a sadness in her eyes, a bewilderment caused by
the brutal realization of how her body could be used by
men, a feeling of violation and uncleanliness at the very
core of her femininity. Except for her ravaged hair,
permanently hidden by a scarf, there'd been few physical
after-effects. The main problem was the shock in her mind.
Bryan prayed that by now, four months later, she would
have returned to her previous laughing, carefree self. He
still felt guilty that he'd not been with her during her time of
need. That guilt and his desire for her made him hurry on,
abandoning most of his caution.

Suddenly, terrifyingly, a voice called from close by.

"Bryan! Hey, Bryan! Here! Over here!"

His body froze, only his eyes moving, darting along the
hedgerows and deep into the trees beyond. He was
conscious of the beating pulse in his veins. His hand edged
towards the revolver in the pockets of his grubby jacket.

"Over here!" the voice repeated. "On the other side!"

Bryan's head flicked around, his right hand now firmly
clasping the butt of the revolver. He saw the face smiling at
him over the hedge on the opposite side of the road and
relaxed. It was Jerry Lyons, another member of the flying
column.

"Jesus!" Bryan exclaimed, relieved, glad to see a
friendly face again. "And that was a helluva shock you
gave me, boyo, to be sure!"

Lyons laughed, beckoning. Bryan looked quickly up and down the narrow road, saw that it was deserted and scurried across. The two young men patted each other's shoulders, delighted to have company again.

"You're after going to Gortaglonna then?" Lyons asked. Bryan was puzzled.

"I'm making for Galey Bridge."

"Some of the boys are meeting at Gortaglonna."

"What for?"

"Oh, just a wee chat to see if anyone knows the next chorus," Lyons shrugged. "Are you coming?"

"Well . . ."

Bryan was doubtful. Hannah and her family remained uppermost in his thoughts.

"It's not far out of your way. Not far at all," Lyons urged. "We won't be long. Just a wee chat. Any more would be mighty dangerous so close to town."

Bryan shook his head resignedly. He grinned.

"I'll come if you've got a fag, Jerry," he said. "I've been out of them for days."

"Good man you are!" cried Lyons, reaching into his pocket for his battered tobacco tin. He handed it to Bryan and waited until he'd rolled and lit a cigarette before grabbing his arm and pulling him playfully along the side of the field behind the hedgerow.

When they reached the bridge over the gurgling stream just outside Gortaglonna townland, they found three others waiting, concealed at the roadside, the Dee brothers, Con and Paddy, and Paddy Dalton.

Bryan's misgivings disappeared with his pleasure at being with them again after spending so many days and nights alone. They moved into the field next to the bridge, chattering excitedly, quite forgetting all precautions.

They didn't even look up when the lorry rattled over the bridge. And it was too late, much too late, by the time the five young men heard the squeal of brakes.

From the corner of his eye, Bryan Aherne glimpsed the Tans leaping over the side of the lorry, rifles in hand, and starting toward them.

He turned from side to side, searching for an escape. There was none. The Tans had spread far enough across the field to block any retreat.

Dalton flung himself bodily into the prickly hedge. Lyons followed him.

"Take cover!" Paddy Dee shouted, attempting to grab the revolver in his belt, tangling his thumb in his torn waistcoat.

Bryan stood still. His hands rose slowly above his head. At least four rifle barrels pointed directly at him.

"Come on out, lads," he said quietly. "We're done for. Come on out with your hands up!"

His voice was dull and resigned, empty of emotion.

For a split second, his brain held a vivid image of the shattered head of District Inspector Tobias O'Sullivan.

Chapter 7
May, 1921

The Tans were almost incoherent with excitement at their capture. They recognized two of the young men in the field, Bryan Aherne and Jerry Lyons, as undoubted members of the North Kerry Flying Column. Hunting the column had become an obsession with the Tans, allowing them no rest, peace nor safety.

"The buggers!" one Tan shouted exultantly. "We've the buggers at last!"

"Look at the stinking shits!"

"Buggers!"

"Fuckers! Just see the fuckers now!"

Abuse flew from every side.

The five Volunteers, not daring to speak, stood in the middle of the circle of Tans, hands high above their heads, two of them bleeding from bramble scratches. Their faces were grim and set, fearful. Tears ran down Paddy Dalton's cheeks.

A second lorry pulled up. Two inspectors of the Royal Irish Constabulary jumped out of the driving cab and entered the field. They talked briefly to one of the Tans before approaching the prisoners.

When they were about two yards away, they both drew their revolvers from shiny black holsters. The taller inspector was grinning broadly.

He stood in front of Dalton, shaking his head gently like a schoolteacher who had discovered a naughty pupil. He sucked his teeth in admonition. Dalton turned slightly, seeking support from his friends. As he did, the inspector lashed him across the nose with the barrel of his revolver.

Dalton yelped with pain. Blood poured from his nostrils and into his open mouth. He coughed and choked.

"Search the bastards!" the second inspector, an older, broader man, ordered in a matter-of-fact tone.

"Strip!" the Tan bellowed, jabbing his rifle into Con Dee's stomach. "Undress. Take your clothes off. Strip or we'll fucking rip 'em off!"

The Tans became even more excited when they found the revolvers in the pile of clothes.

"So it is them indeed," the taller inspector remarked quietly, almost reflectively.

Suddenly the Tans were all around the naked prisoners, kicking and swearing, punching and spitting, striking out with weapons and fists at the defenseless flesh before them. The frustrations and fears of the past months were vented in their frenzied, vicious attack.

Bryan fell to the ground under the blows, winded, unable to cry out with the pain searing through every limb. He was incapable of defending himself. His arms were wrapped around his lower belly, one hand between his legs guarding his manhood. He felt his flesh jarring and compacting from the blows, sensed an eyebrow tearing open from the side of a boot, slowly almost lost consciousness, drowning under the waves of agony.

"That's enough, boys," someone shouted. "We've other plans for the murdering bastards."

The blows stopped as suddenly as they had begun.

"Here," a voice said from above, throwing his clothes down beside him. "Put 'em on smartish if you don't want any more of the same."

He struggled into the garments, still laying on the ground. He knew his limbs would betray him if he tried to stand.

Dalton and Paddy Dee were so hurt that they were unable to do more than wriggle into their vests and shirts. The Tans laughed and picked them up, one to each arm and leg, and tossed them into the back of the second lorry like stalks of corn. The three others limped after them, still groaning, only to be helped into the lorry with kicks and punches.

"Oh, Mary and Joseph!" Lyons muttered, lying next to Bryan. "We're done for. Oh, Holy Saints come against us!"

Bryan turned toward him, trying to smile through broken, swollen lips. Strangely, he felt very strong and alive although he knew that his body was near to breaking point.

Lyons gathered some of Bryan's apparent inner strength and tried to smile back.

"What now?" he panted. His front teeth had disappeared. Blood spittled from his gums as he spoke, spraying onto the muddy, wooden floor of the lorry.

"Shut your fucking gob," one of the Tans snarled, lifting his rifle and slamming the butt down.

The lorries cranked into motion, jolting and bumping down the road before turning and heading west back toward Listowel.

Back to the police barracks, Bryan assumed, for a night in the cells, another beating, and then to the interrogation center in the Ballymullen Barracks at Tralee. Surprisingly, he didn't feel downhearted. The others seemed in worse shape than he was. He shook his head, trying to clear the singing in his ears. Incongruously, his eyes focused on Paddy Dalton's penis, not six inches from him. Jesus, he thought, it was a fair size. A bawdy rhyme from his schooldays came into his brain.

> Long and thin, goes right in,
> Pleases all the ladies.
> Short and thick does the trick,
> Out come all the babies.

He smiled lopsidely to himself, his mind still spinning. Jesus, he decided, it was a long cock that Paddy had. Bit limp now, but decidedly formidable. He groaned as the lorry jerked to a halt.

"Out, you bastards!" the Tan guards shouted. "Out!"

"Balls," Bryan muttered, still thinking of Dalton's attributes. "Big balls . . ."

"What's that?" one Tan demanded, boots planted either side of Bryan's face.

He didn't reply, lifting himself on to all fours before gingerly standing upright, gazing around, opening and shutting his eyes to see properly. To his surprise, they weren't back in Listowel but still in the countryside and, as far as he could judge, only half a mile or so from where they had been captured.

Bryan, prodded in the back by a rifle, jumped down from the lorry first. He stood by the tailgate handing the others down. Lyons helped him support Paddy Dalton as they were pushed and pulled into the field by the road and then roughly shepherded across that field toward another about forty yards from the lorries. The Tans were intent on taking their prisoners as far away from the road as possible, somewhere out of sight and hearing of any passers-by.

With the last kick and shove, the five young men, two of them hardly conscious, held up by their friends, were pushed through a rickety wooden gate into the field.

The Tans didn't follow.

Bryan looked quickly at Jerry Lyons. His face was ashen with fear, his mouth working, trying to speak.

"Oh, Jesus," Lyons blurted eventually.

Bryan shivered and nodded.

"They're going to do for us!" Lyons went on. His voice rose: "They're going to do for us here and now!"

Bryan turned and faced the Tans. His mind suddenly cleared and calmed when he saw them leaning over the stone wall surrounding the field, about five yards away. Their rifles rested on the wall, barrels pointing casually. Bryan had seen such expressions before on the faces of his own friends in the flying column just before they had shot a retired policeman accused of being an informer.

"You can't do this," Bryan shouted. "There's been no trial." As he spoke, he realized how futile his plea sounded.

The Tans laughed, genuinely amused. "Trial?" one of them called back. "Trial? You fucking murderers expect a trial?"

"They expect a trial," another echoed mockingly.

"Fucking mad dogs don't get a trial," a third exclaimed, his voice flat and cold.

"For pity's sake!" Lyons cried.

"Pity?" the tall inspector replied, pushing aside two of his men so that he could be clearly seen. "You murderers want pity? What pity have you shown? What pity to those you've shot down in the back and in the dark? What pity to Mr. O'Sullivan's wife and his wee one? You can be thankful your women won't see you snivelling here, begging for mercy you don't deserve and mercy you're not going to receive!"

Three of the Tans began chanting.

"Murderers! Murderers! Murderers!"

Bryan plucked at Lyons' sleeve, hoping his friend wouldn't protest any more. He knew it was hopeless. All that could be done was to muster as much dignity and defiance as possible.

"Not like this," Lyons muttered. "For Holy Mary's sake, not like this!"

"Face the bastards," Bryan urged. "Show 'em we're not afraid."

He gazed quickly along the line of his friends.

Dalton and Paddy Dee were bent almost double, moaning still, pink spittle dribbling from their broken mouths, their bare legs spindly and quivering with weakness. Bryan thought that it was a blessing that they were not fully conscious.

Lyons' head was sunk into his chest. His eyes were screwed shut, his lips moving in prayer.

Con Dee, Bryan discovered, was looking along the line just as he was. Their eyes met. Dee shrugged helplessly and half-winked as if in encouragement.

Bryan's mind began to fill with images of his family, of happy gatherings, of Hannah. He sensed an unbearable sadness, felt his throat closing, tears nearing his eyes.

He blinked rapidly and looked straight ahead into the face of a Tan, his rifle now aimed at his shoulder. A dozen rifles pointed over the wall. The Tan directly in front of him couldn't meet his eyes directly and shifted his aim slightly.

Bryan thought that the man was wanting someone else to fire first, that he didn't want to initiate the killings himself.

The seconds passed like minutes. There seemed silence all around. Bryan tried to think of a prayer. None came to mind. He wanted to say something but couldn't.

And then the rifles exploded.

The crashes and flashes echoed so close that Bryan's ears were deafened. But where was the impact, the tearing and shattering of flesh and bone, the overwhelming pain and the darkness?

Beside him, Lyons moaned. A scream of agony strangled, gurgling, in his throat. Bryan saw his arms fly above his head, the dust puffing from the front of his waistcoat, the redness soaking out through the two holes in the blue serge cloth. Lyons fell back and lay still, eyes and mouth gaping wide to the sky.

Bryan glimpsed Dalton and Paddy Dee spinning backwards.

Dalton clasped the side of his head, trying to touch the hole in his temple. Dee bent his arms in front of him as if embracing and pulling the bullets into his chest and throat.

His brother, Con, was beginning to run, horror mingled with disbelief on his face.

Instinctively, Bryan did the same. He ran like he'd never run before, legs pumping almost to his chest. He ducked and weaved, looking once to his left, seeing Con Dee crouched very low.

Bullets crackled and whizzed past and over him. He thought he heard the sounds of pursuit, some shouting and yelling, but he wasn't sure.

Behind him, the two inspectors were trying frantically to restore some order to the Tans. All of them, when firing, had tried to avoid shooting the prisoners who stood straight and gazed balefully ahead, hoping that someone else would be aiming at them. And when Bryan and Con had started running, some of the Tans had hurdled the wall in pursuit, effectively blocking the aims of the rest. Now, they had stopped their chase and were firing from kneeling or prone positions at the figures fleeing from them, more than eighty yards distant.

Bryan, lungs tightening with exertion, risked another

sideways glance. He saw Con Dee stumble momentarily and grab the back of his right thigh. For a second, it seemed he would fall but somehow he continued, limping sideways, dragging his right leg straight behind him.

Ahead of Bryan, twenty yards away, a ditch about four feet deep curved toward a thick copse of trees and overgrown bushes. His stride shortened as he tired. The shooting behind him slackened. He was nearly there, only a few more yards. Bryan wanted to shout in triumph and relief but he'd no breath to spare. He lifted his head in thanks to the sky.

As he did so, a bullet struck him just below his right shoulder blade, tore obliquely through muscles and flesh, skidded off bone and left his body four inches beneath his armpit.

The impact, like a violent shove in the back, sent him tumbling into the ditch.

He tried to move, to lift himself, knowing he couldn't remain where he lay, that he had to reach the copse.

Pain arrowed through his body. His right side was virtually paralyzed with shock. Bryan bit into his tongue, attempting to hold back a cry.

Slowly, he dragged himself along the ditch with his left arm. His nails and fingers dug into the earth, hauling him along, until after what seemed an eternity of pain, he reached the copse and slid under the cover of a large bush, a few yards inside the protective greenery.

He lay there, feeling the blood running down his ribs. He pictured in his mind his heart pumping life-blood through the wound, pumping, pumping away till there would be none left.

"God help me," he whispered, face pressed against the damp soil. "Please, please help."

Bryan knew he had to leave his hiding place quickly or else he would have no strength to move at all. He would simply bleed to death where he lay. If the Tans saw him . . . well, it made little difference whether he died under the bush or out in the open with the sun in his eyes and the wind in his hair. Actually, he decided, the latter would be preferable.

He crawled back into the ditch and pushed himself upright, panting with exertion, gritting his teeth and screwing up his eyes with pain.

To his amazement, there were no Tans in the field any more. He clambered out of the ditch, bent over, trying to stem the blood from the exit wound with his left hand. He was unable to reach the wound in his back at all.

The two police lorries were beginning to move off down the road two hundred yards away. Bryan could just make out what looked like three sacks tied behind one of them. They bumped and jolted on the road surface, raising a trail of dust. He looked up at the sun, working out his position, knowing it wasn't too long into the afternoon.

Galey Bridge and the Wilmot farm must be roughly north from where he stood, he thought. He stumbled off with the sun at his back, praying he'd enough strength to walk nearly three miles, hoping that he would recognize the correct road when he reached it. He sensed that his hold on consciousness was only very slight and ebbing fast at that.

Con Dee was watching Bryan as he staggered across the fields. His leg had been shattered by the bullet which struck him in the right thigh. He'd stopped the bleeding with a rude tourniquet but didn't plan to move until darkness. He was still in a state of shock, horrified by what he had seen.

Once Bryan disappeared into the copse, the Tans had given up the chase surprisingly quickly. Probably, Con reckoned, the two inspectors had become worried about being seen at what, after all, had been a cold-blooded massacre. Instead, the Tans had returned to the three crumpled bodies in the field, apparently holding a discussion about them.

Finally, to Con Dee's horror, they'd produced some rope from the lorries, tied it to the legs of the dead Volunteers and pulled them out of the field.

They had secured the bodies to the back of the first lorry and set off, Con presumed, for the mortuary in the old workhouse at Listowel.

He had turned away, sobbing, as his brother's body had bounced bloodily along the road and out of sight.

At least, Con thought, two of them had survived to bear witness to what had happened.

By the time he had walked more than two miles, Bryan was virtually unconscious. He reeled from side to side of the deserted road with little control over his limbs. The pad which he had made to partially staunch the flow of blood had long ago dropped in the dust. His progress was marked by small splashes of red. His eyelids were almost closed. What he could see of his surroundings continually receded and then grew, receded and grew, throbbing and hazy.

He thought he was on the right road. He turned to look up at the sun, eyes flickering. The blinding orb swooped down, searing him with light and darkness. He cried out once with all his remaining strength and fell, swooning, on to the grass verge.

Hannah Wilmot heard the shout while she fed the chickens in the farmyard. It mingled indistinctly with the cluckings of the birds at her feet. She paid little heed to it, assuming it must have come from the gang of boys who liked to play by the stream near the farm.

She finished her chore and started back towards the house. She stopped by the door, listening. There were no sounds of boys at play, no sounds at all except those of the animals.

"Did you hear that cry?" she called to her father, working across the yard near the pig-sty.

"The one a wee while back? Sounded like someone stepping on a thorn."

"Like someone hurt?"

"Aye. Now you say it, like someone hurt."

"But no one passed the farm going either way. So if they're hurt they're still out there."

Her father looked thoughtful. He leaned his mucking-out fork carefully against the wall of the sty and waved to Hannah to follow him. She patted the scarf around her hair, checking that it was properly in place, before hurrying into the road after him.

They gazed up and down, shielding their eyes from the sun, before walking fifty yards to the bend in the road, peering carefully into the hedges on either side.

"An animal maybe," Mr. Wilmot remarked, shrugging his shoulders.

Hannah nodded. "Probably."

They linked arms affectionately, turning back. They had become very close since their sufferings at the hands of the Tans.

"Listen!" Hannah cried suddenly, spinning around, pulling her father with her. "Listen!"

Both heard the low groans. They ran to the bend in the road and saw the shape forty yards from them. Mr. Wilmot's first thought was whether it was even human. The shape, the person, inched along, flat on the road, limbs moving so slowly, like a giant red-streaked crayfish.

"Holy Mother of God!" Mr. Wilmot exclaimed, breaking into a run.

"Bryan! It's Bryan!" Hannah cried. She knew deep within her that she was right although she was totally unable to recognize him.

In the few seconds they took to reach him, Bryan stopped moving, unconscious again.

One look told Mr. Wilmot that the young man was near to death.

"It is him?" Hannah called, a few yards behind her father, not really needing confirmation.

Mr. Wilmot nodded grimly. He bent down and lifted Bryan around his shoulders and under the knees. His body was light. A trickle of blood ran from his back, soaking into the dust.

Father and daughter looked into each other's faces, hoping beyond hope, worried beyond concern.

"Quick! Take the horse into town," Mr. Wilmot ordered. "Bring the doctor and tell your mam to have some bandages. Quick, girl, there's not much time."

"Can't I stay?" Hannah begged, cupping her hands lightly around Bryan's slack jaw.

"Do what I say, Hannah. Quick, else we'll be burying the boy this night. For God's sake, hurry!"

Hannah ran off, skirts gathered up, weeping silently, leaving her father to carry his burden back to the farmhouse as gently as he could. She clattered past him on horseback before he was into the yard. Their eyes locked for an instant before, without a backward glance, she continued her gallop toward Listowel.

Within an hour, Doctor Maguire's automobile swung through the farm gates with Hannah in the passenger seat.

By then, Mrs. Wilmot had cleaned Bryan's superficial wounds and managed to stop the loss of blood with copious bandages torn from old bedsheets.

"There's no bullet there and nothing's touched his lungs," Doctor Maguire announced after his careful examination. "Those are the blessings but the poor man's taken an awful beating and lost too much blood for my liking."

He stretched upright.

"The bandaging's good," he said, smiling encouragingly at Hannah's mother. "No worse than I could do . . . and probably better at that. Now tell me, do you know what happened?"

The Wilmots shook their heads, moving closer to each other as if seeking mutual strength.

"No need to tell me anything, I'd guess he escaped from the massacre at Gortaglonna. From where you found him, that makes the best sense."

By their expressions, the Wilmots clearly didn't know what the middle-aged doctor was talking about.

"The Tans killed three of the boys," Hannah explained quietly, her face set. "Shot down in a field this very afternoon."

"It's all over the town," said Doctor Maguire. "Shot while resisting arrest, the Tans say. They're viewing the bodies now to find out who they were."

"Will he . . . ?" Hannah gestured toward Bryan, unable to complete her question.

Doctor Maguire tucked the stethoscope back in his black bag.

"If there's no infection, no more bleeding, he should pull through. I've stitched him the best I can and now it's simply a matter of rest and quiet. He's in the Almighty's hands, so he is."

Before returning to Listowel the doctor reluctantly helped move Bryan across the yard and into the barn where Hannah and her mother had prepared the cleanest and coziest spot possible. They had fashioned a small cubicle in the deepest corner of the barn out of bales of the left-over winter hay and pinned blankets to the hay and the barn walls, shutting out any drafts. They laid two mattresses on a flattened pile of straw. Only four bales had to be stacked to shut the space completely from view. It was to be the limit of Bryan's existence for the next seven weeks.

In the first crucial days, the Wilmots took turns sitting by him. Hannah spent every night in the barn, poised over Bryan, watching every flicker of his face in the light of her oil lamp as he struggled for life.

At times, he was delirious, swearing and cursing, shining with feverish sweat. Hannah would wash him and hold his hand until he lapsed again into fitful unconsciousness. Like anyone who nurses a sick person, she came to know every inch of his body, each of its functions. It didn't disgust her, only made her love him more in his helplessness.

When he was out of danger, his eyes clear but weak, the Wilmots arranged for Bryan's family to visit and nurse him.

Jack Aherne sat with his grandson for hours at a time, twice spending the night with him. The old schoolmaster would retell the family legends and, when he judged Bryan to be strong enough, discuss with him the latest political moves and the progress of the IRA campaign.

By now, this late May, Eamon de Valera had returned from America having failed to win recognition for the self-proclaimed Irish Republic following bitter arguments with Irish-American politicians. Once back in Dublin, he was allowed to travel around virtually unmolested on the orders of Lloyd George, the Prime Minister, who knew that he needed the Sinn Fein leader's influence if ever the IRA were to be brought to the conference table.

The campaign of terror, the five hundred soldiers and police killed since the beginning of 1920, had produced the realization in London that only massive repression could end the guerilla warfare. Lloyd George saw that the IRA could not be wiped out without the use of methods which he thought would be wholly unacceptable to the British people.

After all, Lloyd George reasoned, hadn't the recent elections effectively split the country into two, thus dashing the main aim of Sinn Fein and the Irish Republican Brotherhood at its core?

The elections held that May were organized in accordance with the 1920 Government of Ireland Act, introduced as a replacement for the long-promised Home Rule Bill.

Under the Act, there would be parliaments in Belfast and Dublin with clear provision for a Council of Ireland with power to unite both parliaments without reference to the Imperial Parliament at Westminster.

The results of that election had been wholly predictable. Sinn Fein won all but four of the 128 seats in the twenty-six counties of the south. The Unionists won forty of the fifty-two seats in the six counties in the North and Northeast, said to comprise Ulster.

In Dublin, Sinn Fein constituted the second Dail but declined to meet in public as the official Southern Parliament, still preferring to move its meetings around secret locations.

In Belfast, it was different. The Northern Parliament convened with majestic ceremony and a moving address by King George the Fifth.

All that the Irish Republican Brotherhood had plotted and fought for—one Ireland, freed from England—was ashes. It had been politically outmaneuvered. The war, such as it was, might not be lost but it couldn't be won. It was a time for talking, perhaps even a truce.

Such suggestions, reported in the newspapers, made Bryan Aherne doubly frustrated during the tedium of his convalescence. His one aim was to recover his fitness and rejoin the flying column to take revenge on the Tans. That, however, was proving a long process.

He exercised as much as he could, but even seven weeks after the shooting he still became exhausted after little more than an hour's walk around the country roads at nightfall, the only time when it was safe to leave the barn. And all the

while he read of the negotiations which were bringing a
truce nearer. He felt physically sick at the thought that the
war might be over by the time he was fit again. His only
consolation was the hours he spent with Hannah. She made
no secret though of her delight at the prospect of peace.

One Saturday in July, Bryan was woken from his after-
lunch doze in his hiding place by the sound of the barn
doors swinging shut.

He peeked over the bales of hay. Hannah stood by the
closed doors, her face wreathed in a mischievous grin. She
had a newspaper in one hand. The other was hidden behind
her back.

"I thought you said you were going into Listowel with
your parents," he called, wiping the sleep from his eyes.

"I was too but I decided to stay behind when the postman
brought the newspaper."

She walked towards him, long green skirt sweeping the
floor.

"It's a surprise for you," she said, handing the paper to
him. "A marvellous, wonderful surprise!"

He looked at her suspiciously, half smiling.

"Go on then," she urged. "Look at it."

Bryan opened the newspaper, the *Irish Independent*, and
stared at the front page. His heart fell. The large headlines
proclaimed that a truce in hostilities had been agreed the
previous day in Dublin. All fighting was to end from noon
on Monday, July 11th.

His face registered so much dismay that Hannah had to
feel sorry for him despite her own joy.

Bryan turned away from her and threw the paper on the
ground. He stamped on it angrily.

"Why?" he exclaimed. "Why? We were winning. Why
give it up now?"

"Because the people are tired of it maybe," Hannah
replied quietly, seating herself on the hay bales and
swinging her legs. She placed a hand gently on Bryan's
right shoulder. "You almost died," she went on. "And for
what? For what the British had offered us all along."

He struck his clenched palm against his thigh. "We didn't

start fighting to finish it like this," he said. "We've two
Irelands now, not even one, and we're accepting that?"

"They are. Your leaders are. Collins is."

Bryan turned, arms outstretched, appealing.

"But don't you see? Don't you see that those boys—the
two Paddys and Jerry—died for something else? They stood
there and took the bullets because they believed that one day
there would be a republic for all of Ireland. And now we've
a government in Belfast and one in Dublin, believing
different things and both still really under the control of the
British."

Hannah looked solemnly up at him.

"I know." She hesitated before whispering, "I know,
dearest, but it means that you're safe . . . that there'll be
no more killing . . . no more raids . . . no more Tans."

A tear slipped down her cheek. She brushed it away,
adjusting the scarf around her head at the same time.

Bryan suddenly felt very ungrateful. He sensed the depth
of her emotion, knew that she was thinking, caring, about
him. He moved closer to her and put his arms around her
shoulders. "And what are you hiding then?" he asked
softly, his anger and disappointment vanishing as he looked
on her beautiful face. "What's behind your back? Another
surprise?"

She wrinkled her upturned nose.

"Can you smell it?"

"No. Show me."

"And who's the man of the world then?" she mocked,
producing with a flourish a half-filled bottle of whiskey.

"The hard stuff!" he cried.

"For a celebration of peace."

"Your da's?"

"He won't be minding."

"It's been a long time, so it has."

He took the bottle from her, uncorked it and gulped down
a mouthful.

"Hey!" she protested. "I'm celebrating as well."

"You don't drink. Girls don't drink whiskey," he teased,
feeling the alcohol warming him already, its fumes filling
his nostrils.

"I do."

"No proper girls do."

"I do so—and I'm proper!"

He looked at her for a second.

"I know you are," he said huskily. "You saved my life, so you did, and that's very proper."

He handed Hannah the bottle. She took a tiny, apprehensive sip.

"There!" she said, her blue eyes glinting cheekily. "I told you so."

"Then, if proper girls can drink the hard stuff," Bryan interrupted, his voice suddenly serious, "they can also do something else."

She looked questioningly at him, not replying.

He smiled gently and began untying the scarf on her head. "Then proper girls can be forgetting all that happened to them."

"No, no!" Hannah tried to push him away but it was too late. His hands were touching, caressing her blonde hair, now released from its cover, just reaching down to the nape of her neck.

"It's beautiful," he said wonderingly, feeling its softness. "It shouldn't have been covered for so long."

"It's awful," she cried. "The Tans . . . the Tans."

"I know. I know what they did but that's all gone now," he said soothingly. "If it's peace, whether I like it or not, then everything's in the past."

"It's not like it was."

"It's still beautiful. Like the color of ripe wheat."

He pulled her to him.

"Is it really?" she murmured, her face and hair pressed to his chest, feeling his bare skin against her through his half-opened shirt.

"It is that."

Bryan moved his hands, clasping her narrow waist to lift her off the bale of hay and into the confines of his hiding place.

"Have they gone?"

"Who?"

"Your mam and da."

"An hour back. They said they'd be calling on your folks for tea as well."

During the past seven weeks the two families had become very close; it wasn't uncommon for Hannah's parents to leave the young people unchaperoned.

As Mrs. Wilmot had remarked to her husband weeks earlier, "She's seen him as nature intended when he was half-dead, Cathal, done everything for him, and the Tans . . . well, you know what I mean. She's grown up now, so she has, and they're together and that's that, if you're asking me. He's a good boy and when all this is over . . . well, they're as good as man and wife, so they are."

Mr. Wilmot had to agree. "He's from a good family, that's true. Mona . . . ah, you're probably right. She's a sensible lass."

Ironically, the relationship between Bryan and Hannah had grown less easy the more they were left alone. Bryan, for one, sensed a growing tension between them.

Perhaps, he sometimes thought, it was because of all she had done for him during those days and nights when he had wavered between life and death, needing total nursing. From the odd, unexplained remarks she had made, he guessed that his body held few secrets or mysteries for her.

During the past few days the tension had become almost unbearable. He seemed to shiver every time any part of their bodies touched accidentally.

They sat next to each other on the mattresses, their backs pressed against the hay. They didn't speak. Bryan felt that the whole barn, the whole world, had shrunk to this tiny space.

She offered him the bottle, tilting it towards him. He took another gulp and watched while she sipped at its neck. He noticed she didn't wipe it after he had drunk. He eased the bottle from her grasp and put it down away from them.

"You've had enough?" she asked.

"For the minute."

Bryan slid his hand into the space between them, hoping

to find her hand. When he did so, he hesitated for a second before actually holding it.

To his surprise, Hannah immediately squeezed his hand, scratching a fingernail across his palm.

"Well, are we celebrating?" she whispered.

"What?"

"The truce . . . you alive . . . us . . . anything?"

"I suppose so."

"Only suppose so?"

Hannah turned her head towards him, lips slightly parted. The pink tip of her tongue moistened them. They shone in the gloom at the back of the barn. One of the horses whinnied in the stalls a dozen yards away.

Hannah had heard enough of Bryan's feverish ramblings to understand his inexperience with the opposite sex.

She leaned sideways toward him, pressing into him, slightly uncertain herself. Their lips met, softly at first and then harder.

They broke apart, breathing heavily, smelling the sweet whiskey fumes in each other's mouths.

"When I could, I wanted to say . . ." Bryan stammered.

"Yes . . . ?"

"Well, we'll marry, won't we?"

She nodded, smiling. She offered her mouth to his again, her eyes open until the very last split-second, watching his eyes grow wider and deeper.

As they kissed, her mouth opened under his allowing their tongues to touch.

Bryan's hand shifted toward the front of her white lace blouse, brushing across her nipples. It hovered for a moment, undecided, before moving boldly to her left breast. Hannah moaned deep in her throat. He felt an explosion of her breath in his mouth. She pushed him away from her, twisting, and then relaxed, allowing his hands free passage over her outer clothing.

Their embraces became more frenzied. They tumbled full length on to the mattresses on the straw. Hannah's skirt hitched up above her knees. Bryan's hands became more searching and demanding.

"Careful. Be careful," she whimpered against his throat as his fingers caught in the opening of her blouse. He stopped for a moment and then tried again to undo the tiny, delicate pearl buttons.

She uttered a deep sigh.

He looked down at her face, framed by her tumbling hair. Her eyes were grave, appealing, unsure.

"You do love me?" she asked.

"I do so, mavourneen."

She paused and sighed once more.

"Then wait," she said, suddenly decisive. She squeezed from under him and got to her feet.

"No, don't look," she ordered as she stood behind him. "No, don't look," she repeated. "Don't look! Don't turn round!"

He thought she was leaving, clambering back over the bales. His face pressed against the mattress, sniffing the familiar smells of the barn, waiting to be alone again.

Bryan heard movements behind him and turned his head.

He rolled over onto his back and looked up.

Hannah stood sideways against the wall of hay. The green skirt which she had removed was held shyly up to her neck.

Slowly, she lowered and spread her arms wide. The skirt billowed down on to the pile of clothes already at her feet.

For long seconds, the soft light filtering into the barn played its shadows across her nakedness, touching a pointed nipple, dappling the small triangle of curls, caressing the curve of her buttocks.

Before Bryan could raise himself on to his elbows, Hannah knelt and bent over him, her breasts swaying gently.

"I love you," she said simply. Her mouth closed over his. His hands slid around her, marvelling at the smoothness and roundness.

Their love-making was swift and fierce. Bryan tried to be considerate but the fact of being inside her, above her, with her, swept everything away. She clung to his neck, panting against his ear.

When it was over, as he began lifting himself away, Hannah's arms circled his back, pulling him close again.

He looked down at her, stammering an apology, hoping he hadn't hurt her, hadn't been too rough.

"Don't be sorry. I'm not," she breathed.

"It was . . . it was all right for you?" he asked tentatively.

Hannah smiled contentedly up at Bryan, her eyes glistening.

"We'll be married . . ." he began.

"Aye, avourneen . . ."

". . . as soon as possible."

"Aye . . . he'll need a da."

"Who?"

Hannah pointed down between their bodies, her fingers brushing against him, feeling him instantly lengthen and thicken, feeling his seed deep within her.

"He will," she murmured.

Chapter 8
February, 1922

The cobblestones in Church Street were so greasy from the
overnight rain and the February dampness in the air that
Bryan Aherne had difficulty in keeping his feet.

"Are you sure you want to come along?" he asked his
wife anxiously, sliding his arm gently around her thickened
waist.

"Of course, silly," Hannah replied, smiling up at him
from under her new, pink cloche hat. "It is a day of history,
isn't it?"

"It is that, dear, but just you hang on tight to me. Don't
want you slipping up."

"No dear," she sighed, wondering why men became so
fussy at such times.

Bryan maneuvered her past the people in the street,
nodding greetings here and there, hoping they realized from
Hannah's shape that she, as he put it affectionately, carried
all before her, now seven months pregnant.

Most of the Listowel folk, of course, knew perfectly well
about Hannah's condition. In fact they knew most everything there was to know about the young married couple
who had moved into the neat, terraced cottage in Courthouse Road.

After all, they said to themselves, justifying their
inquisitiveness, wasn't Bryan Aherne one of the real boyos,
the hard men, in the town, if not the whole of Kerry?

Bryan was regarded with considerable awe. His part in
the murder of District Inspector O'Sullivan and the escape
from the massacre at Gortaglonna were in the repertoires of
local ballad singers. Both incidents had been elevated into

117

the realms of myth, glorifying killing and bravado, omitting pain and fear.

"Great morning, Mr. Aherne," a young boy called, brushing past Bryan, touching his cap to Hannah.

"It is that, praise be," Bryan replied automatically.

"Who's that, dear?" Hannah asked, noticing that the youngster had immaculate puttees wound around the lower half of his trousers.

"Don't recognize him," Bryan grunted. "One of Davie Carroll's Fusiliers, I'd bet."

Hannah said no more on the subject, knowing that Bryan was particularly irked about how many of the town's young men were trying to give the impression that they had been active in the Tan War, as it was now termed.

It had become the vogue to dress in puttees or gaiters and long raincoats, the style of the North Kerry Flying Column.

Davie Carroll, the town's leading draper, had done a roaring trade in such items, and thus the contemptuous nickname of "Davie Carroll's Fusiliers" for those who wished to appear what they were not and never had been.

Their masquerades, their play-acting, Bryan thought as he walked along, were only a small part of Ireland's sickness that late winter. After the truce and the treaty signed five months later, the country was confused, fearful and divided. And that mood had undoubtedly spread to Listowel.

But this day political differences would be put aside, he reckoned. It was likely to be a day for drinking and the telling and retelling of the old and not-so-old legends for most, if not all, the townsfolk.

The crowds grew thicker when Bryan and Hannah turned into William Street and reached the junction with Market Street. People on the edge of the narrow, uneven pavements moved courteously aside to allow Hannah an uninterrupted view of the convoy of trucks and tenders parked, engines idling, further along the street.

She had expected the onlookers to be happy and excited. Instead there was a distinct feeling of tension everywhere.

The low murmur of conversation around her died away

completely when dozens of Tans and Auxiliaries began streaming from their barracks and boarding the vehicles in the convoy.

Hannah felt Bryan's protective hands suddenly tighten their grip on her shoulders. An irrational pang of fear made her legs tremble. She winced as the baby moved inside her womb.

She wanted so much to shout, to scream at the men in green and khaki. Obscenities, awful words, formed in her brain. Her fingernails pressed sharply into her palms. She saw herself for an instant dashing forward into the street and lashing out with hands and feet at the grim faces. But Hannah did nothing, said nothing. Neither did anyone else.

The spectators watched sullenly, nursing their loathing and bitterness, even luxuriating in the depths of their hatred for these men whose presence had hovered over the town like a malevolent spirit for more than eighteen months.

Smoke from ten exhaust pipes billowed and hung in the air as the drivers revved up the engines. A young officer wearing a fawn trenchcoat stood up in the front seat of the leading tender and waved the convoy forward.

The vehicles rumbled and rattled through the gauntlet of silent hostility. Hannah looked closely into the passing faces but did not recognize any of them.

A single, vehement curse rang out above the noise of the engines. "May you rot in hell forever!" By then, though, it was too late for others to join in.

The convoy turned into Market Street and headed away from the crowds, safely on its way to Tralee and the beginning of the evacuation of the British forces from Listowel and Kerry.

Listowel came to life again. The crowd began dispersing. Some people stood together in small groups for a while, talking quietly, rather disappointed after what was supposed to have been an occasion to remember, perhaps let down by the strength of their emotions and expectations. The others hurried off to their homes, the shops or the bars.

"Well, they've gone, haven't they?" Hannah remarked as she and Bryan started toward home.

"Aye, and good riddance!"

"Did you really hate them?"

"Yes. Did you?"

"But I didn't recognize any of them, dear."

"Nor did I."

"I felt baby move when they came out of the barracks."

"I'm glad they've gone before he comes into the world."
Bryan hugged Hannah close for a moment.

"You know, I'd have taken a shot at them if I'd my gun."

"I would've as well. I really would, Bryan."

"Your gun?"

"Well, yours . . ."

They laughed together, knowing how much Hannah
hated the sight and sound of firearms, even her father's
ancient crow-gun.

"Are you off drinking now?" Hannah asked mischievously when they reached the corner of Courthouse Road,
near the top of Church Street.

"You know I said I'd meet Grandad Jack in the tavern."

"Well, while you men are jawing, I'll pop around to
Forge Lane and keep Grandma Maude company."

"You mean you'll have a good gossip?"

Hannah looked exasperatedly at him.

"Why is it men hold discussions and women gossip?"

"Cos you do and that's why," Bryan smiled, bending
slightly to kiss her cheek. "See you later."

"And not too much, mind you," Hannah called sharply
after him. "Or you'll have no bed nor tea tonight."

Bryan gave an exaggerated shrug of his shoulders, waved
and crossed the street toward the family's tavern where his
grandfather was already waiting for him, seated as usual at
the table nearest the bar.

Jack Aherne had been treated kindly by his sixty-nine
years. His mind was clear and retentive, his back straight,
his eyes as observant as ever they'd been in the classroom.
Only his legs gave him trouble, allowing him to walk, at
best, a few hundred yards before a necessary rest.

"Any trouble, then?" Jack asked, pipe between clenched
teeth, when Bryan had placed two frothing glasses of porter
on the table.

"Not a whisper, Grandad. They seemed as happy to leave as we were to see them go."

"Hardly surprising, young Bryan, is it? They didn't have much of a time here, did they? Not during the troubles and not since the truce, did they?"

The old man was thinking of the numerous gunfights between the Tans and the IRA Volunteers in North Kerry during the past months of supposed, declared peace.

"Old scores," Bryan mumbled, totally unrepentant that he had taken part in, even organized, some of the incidents. "Pity is, we didn't kill any of them, let alone wound them."

"And what about that police sergeant shot down on the green at Ballybunnion?"

"Nothing to do with us, Grandad. Nothing. Truthfully. Simon Mulvihill was only settling personal accounts for Danny Scanlon."

"Was he now?" Jack said sarcastically. "Well, that makes it fine and dandy then!"

"You remember Danny Scanlon and what happened?"

"I do that . . . hot outside the barracks in the riot . . . straight through his wedding tackle . . . I remember, but I'm also remembering how long ago it was. Five years is a mighty long time waiting to settle that blood debt." Jack Aherne's voice was bitter, his eyes angry. "If you youngsters want it like that, why they'll be backshooting all over Ireland for generations to come!"

"It's not that way, Grandad. You know that. Calm down. Calm down, please," Bryan pleaded, worried that they might be overheard.

Jack paused, gazed around the bar, then nodded resignedly. He emptied his glass and pushed it toward his grandson.

"Bring two more," he ordered. "They'll cool us down. And don't be worrying. I'll pay."

Almost simultaneously, grandfather and grandson broke their silences.

"I'm sorry," Bryan began.

"So what happens now they've left?" Jack interrupted, tamping down his pipe before relighting it.

"You haven't heard, Grandad?"

"When does it happen, Bryan?"

"I thought you'd heard. I knew you would have!"

"The Tans leave and you IRA, you Republicans, move in? Is that it?" Jack asked.

"Yes."

"Does anything change then?"

Bryan paused before answering.

"You know as well as I do, Grandad, what's happening."

"Does that make it right . . . your boys taking over from the Tans?"

"Who knows? But what else can we do?"

"Aye."

They were silent again, both considering the political events which were dividing their small market town as well as their country, or rather twenty-six counties of it.

The new Irish Free State was to have its own parliament, its own constitution and its own army and navy. Militarily, all Britain wanted was the use, if needed, of four sea ports.

But the Irish delegation at the conference had been completely outclassed on the question of Northern Ireland by the British negotiators.

If the Northern Ireland Parliament asked to stay out of the Irish Free State within a month of the treaty proposals becoming law, then it could do so. It was, of course, a foregone conclusion that such a request would be made. But then, under the British scheme, a boundary commission would begin work considering the border between North and South.

On this issue, Lloyd George used all his cunning to find agreement.

He led Michael Collins to believe that the boundary commission would hand a good deal of Ulster back to the fledgling Free State. Collins hoped in turn that this would make Northern Ireland stillborn, not viable politically nor economically.

At the same time, Lloyd George gave the Ulster leader, James Craig, the impression that hardly any boundaries would change.

Within months, those understandings—or rather misunderstandings—were to cost hundreds of lives, many of them totally innocent.

The debate in the Dail was filled with bitterness and acrimony before the treaty was approved by the 121 representatives with a majority of only seven votes.

De Valera resigned as President and went into opposition, being replaced by the ailing Arthur Griffith. Strong differences emerged between those, like Collins, who regarded the treaty as a first step toward a full Irish Republic, and those, like de Valera, who saw in it the betrayal of all for which the IRA had fought its guerilla war.

But Collins, as before, controlled the Irish Republican Brotherhood. He threw its weight and influence behind the treaty, however much he disliked the necessary compromises within it. This gave him tentacles spread throughout the IRA but they were not enough to win anything like total agreement for his view.

The IRA split into two. Those who supported Collins and the treaty were swiftly issued with green uniforms, arms supplied by the British, and transformed into the Free State Army. Those against the treaty hid their weapons and pondered the next move.

In Listowel, after much heart-searching and anguish, sixteen of the North Kerry Flying Column, originally members of the 3rd and 6th Battalions of the 1st Kerry Brigade, IRA, decided to join the army. Fourteen, including Bryan Aherne, gave their allegiance to the anti-treaty Republicans supporting de Valera.

Both factions actively canvassed support and new recruits. Both had equal success. North Kerry, like Ireland, was tearing apart like a sheet of tissue paper between the Free Staters and the Republicans.

And in the six counties of the northeast, now officially Northern Ireland, the eternally fragile peace between the Protestant majority and the Catholic minority ruptured into vicious sectarian warfare.

The Republicans within the formerly united ranks of the IRA realized that they would soon have to make their first

move, that the bloodletting was likely to spread throughout
the island.

Their opportunity came as the Auxiliaries and Tans
started to be evacuated, the first of the British forces to
leave under the terms of the Anglo-Irish Treaty.

What happened in Listowel almost exactly mirrored
events in the rest of Ireland. As Bryan Aherne and his
grandfather sat in the family tavern in Church Street around
midday on February 14th, 1922, groups of anti-treaty
Republicans stealthily took over armed occupation of the
emptied Tans' barracks in the market town, in Ballybunnion
and Ballylongford.

Jack Aherne had a fair idea of what was happening and
persisted in questioning his grandson.

"So where does it all lead?" he asked, none too gently.
"If I knew, if I'd heard what your boys were planning to do,
surely the Free Staters would have known as well?"

"A bit late now, I'm thinking," Bryan grinned, perhaps a
trifle smugly. "We beat them to the punch. Now we have to
hold the line while the politicians sort it out."

"Politicians?"

"Mick Collins and Dev and the rest."

"Do you really think they will . . ."

"Yes . . ."

". . . because if you do, you've more belief than
you've the right to."

Bryan shook his head tiredly, dispiritedly. "They have to,
Grandad, don't they? For Jesus' sake, they've got to. I don't
want any more killing. Oh, yes, I fought the Tans and
whatever. You know that. So does everyone else. But I'd
never tell anyone else but you that I'd probably damned my
soul because of it, because of the killing I did. I don't want
any more killing." He paused, his eyes circling the bar,
taking in the customers. He reached into his jacket pocket
for tobacco and cigarette papers. "Sure, I don't like the
treaty, Grandad. Nor do you, if you say what you mean."

Jack's voice was stern, resentful that his integrity might
be questioned. "Don't ever be thinking, young Bryan, that
I'm not with you in everything, with all your thinking,

excepting, that is, your methods. Those I don't like and never have."

Bryan grimaced, reddening a little on his cheekbones.

"So what do we do? Nothing? Let it pass by default? After all the blood? Just let it pass?"

His grandfather slammed his glass down on the table, becoming deeply angry.

"The treaty was voted on and passed by the Dail," he argued. "Or aren't you believing in democracy? Is that what you're about? Is that what you're about just like the rest of them? The people have to accept what you lot want come what may? Is that what it is? Heads we win, tails you lose? Is that what it is?"

"No, no . . ." Bryan protested, temper rising.

His father, who'd just arrived in the tavern, leaned over the bar, guessing already the subject of the argument, the familiar subject between the two.

"Come on, Dad," Sean Aherne urged, tongue in cheek. "Let the boy be. We've enough problems without a scrap in here."

"It's no scrap, son," his father snapped back. "We're talking—or trying to—about democracy . . . at least, the Irish version of it. That's no joking matter these days, is it? Or is it?"

"And sure, what was all the fighting about if it wasn't democracy?" Sean replied.

"Sure it was, Dad," agreed Bryan.

Jack Aherne rose dourly to his feet: "Don't you realize that now we've a proper Irish Parliament again, we've to settle differences without the gun? If Irish are to fight Irish over what this word means and that doesn't, why, then, there's little hope for us—nor should there be—for generations and more. The politicians will always be pandering to your man with the biggest gun and that's no good for the rest of us—the old folk, or you'll excuse the expression, the women, the children, the ordinary, wee people—who just want to live their lives the best way the good Lord allows us."

"Oh, Grandad, it's not . . . you know it's not," Bryan began again.

"Anyway, I'm away now, having served my purpose as a decoy."

Bryan placed his hand on his grandfather's forearm, attempting to restrain him, but the old schoolmaster brushed it aside and walked stiffly to the door.

"Grandad!" Bryan appealed. "Grandad, please come back."

At the tavern entrance, the old man turned, wagging his head ruefully. "Here endeth the first lesson," he called, the merest suspicion of a twinkle in his eyes. "And God be with you." He gave a little hop, half twirled his walking stick and went through the door.

The next morning, Bryan Aherne, and most of Listowel, awoke with a hangover to discover that the town was split into two armed camps.

During the night, the Free State Army had rushed 250 troops from Tralee to garrison and fortify the old workhouse at the end of Market Street, by the junction of the road to Ballybunnion.

By midday, the troops were nervously patrolling Listowel. The anti-treaty IRA responded immediately by sending out its own patrol, using some of its most experienced men.

The two groups edged cautiously, watching each other carefully, yet trying to pretend that the other wasn't there.

Bryan wore his revolver in a holster at his waist, the flap conspicuously unbuttoned, as he led the IRA patrol with Con Dee at his side, his rifle in the crook of his arm. Three others trailed behind, carrying Lee-Enfield service rifles captured in raids on police barracks.

They all knew that the patrol was simply a show of strength designed to prove that the IRA wasn't cowed by the official government's troops, was still a force to be reckoned with in the town.

Around and around Listowel they went following each other, first one in front, then the other, through streets and alleys rapidly emptying of people who had sensed the danger themselves.

"We can't be going on like this, Con," muttered Bryan Aherne to his second-in-command out of the corner of his mouth. "It'll be dusk soon and then heaven knows what'll happen in the dark."

"Aye. I'm so jumpy I'd shoot at moonbeams. What I'm needing is the hair of the dog, not all this nonsense walking around with a loaded gun."

"Amen to that."

"Besides, someone could be awful hurt. Those Free Staters look like they know one end of a rifle from t'other."

"And don't I know that. We helped train a few of them."

"I'm guessing so."

"So what do we do?"

"Don't be asking me. You're the officer, and anyway, the old leg's beginning to gyp me."

"That's an awful help, Con!"

"Well, we could just go home, after all."

"No. That'd be losing face. The big man wouldn't be liking that."

"Well, what then?"

Bryan looked across the opposite side of the market square where the army patrol was standing, seemingly deep in discussion. Their officer gazed back at him.

"Let's take our own route," Bryan suggested. "And if they . . ." He jabbed his thumb at the huddle of green uniforms. ". . . don't follow us, we'll go around the town once on our own and then home. That'll show we're not worried about them, won't it?"

Con Dee and the others didn't need a second bidding. With a new spring in their step, the IRA men wheeled out of the market square and began their fifth circuit of Listowel's near-deserted streets.

This time, without the irksome presence of the Free Staters, the atmosphere was more relaxed. They exchanged greetings with the few people still around and waved jauntily to those peeking nervously from behind their curtains.

The afternoon became darker, colder and damper. The patrol increased its pace, anxious to be on the way home, preferably after a stop in a warm, friendly bar.

"Back to the square and that's it, boys," Bryan announced over his shoulder, hurrying down Charles Street, alongside the courthouse, ready to turn right into William Street.

"And maybe a wee jar or two with the officer?" one of the patrol called cheekily.

Bryan turned his head, about to answer before he reached the corner of the street.

"No sodding cha . . ."

The riposte choked away into a gasp. He cannoned into someone coming the opposite way around the corner.

"What the fuck?" he spluttered.

"Jesus!" cried Con Dee, already starting to crouch into a firing position by the wall.

"It's them!" a voice shouted in alarm.

Suddenly, the street corner was filled with a confused mass of men, feet and weapons tangling and jangling together, as the Free Staters' patrol collided with the IRA men.

Bryan heard the click of a rifle bolt behind him.

"No, no," he screamed. "Don't fire! Don't fire!"

Automatically, though, his hand darted toward the butt of his revolver.

"Hold your fire, for Christ's sake!" the man beside him frantically ordered.

They looked into each other's faces at close range for the first time.

"Paddy Murphy, as I live and breathe!" Bryan exclaimed.

He realized immediately that the Free State Army Officer he'd bumped into was an old friend from the North Kerry Flying Column and the 1st Kerry Brigade, IRA.

"Well, well, if it isn't the bold boyo himself," Murphy replied, smiling hesitantly at Bryan.

"So it's you, Paddy, we've been following around. I should have known."

"Should have known? Why?"

"By your ragtail formation, of course," Bryan joked. "Call yourself an army . . ."

"And wasn't I saying the same about your wee mob of amateurs?" Murphy's grin broadened.

Bryan blew into his cupped hands. "Jesus, it's perishing," he complained, his eyes flicking around his men and the Free State troops. They were lowering their weapons, smiles of recognition on their faces.

"It is that," Murphy agreed. "Haven't seen hide nor hair of you for months."

"Not since the split up."

"Well, how are you then?"

"Middling, Paddy. Just middling."

"And the wife?"

"Two months to go."

"You should be indoors."

All around them the men were chatting together, swapping cigarettes and matches.

"Aye, you've something there, Paddy. But, as the man says, orders is orders."

"Aye." Murphy scratched his gingerish hair. "That's the rub, isn't it? Orders."

"What are yours?"

Murphy looked doubtful for a moment, then shrugged: "Just to make sure your Republicans aren't taking over any more of the town."

"Just five of us? Chance'd be a fine thing!"

"So what are you doing then?"

"Simply watching what you're up to. That's all."

The two men gazed at each other for a second before bursting into laughter, both seeing the black humor of the situation.

"Is it a private joke, then?" Con Dee asked sarcastically.

"No . . . no . . ." Bryan coughed, wiping tears from his eyes. "It's just so stupid . . . so fucking stupid . . . that's what's so funny. We've been spending the afternoon watching these boys watching us and they've been doing the self-same thing."

Murphy nodded. "A bloody pointless exercise, that's what," he guffawed.

"Shall we pack it in?" Bryan suggested.

"Why not?"

The two officers shook hands.

"A drink sometime maybe, Bryan?" Murphy asked.

"You know where to find me, Paddy."

"I do that. Indeed I do," the Free State officer replied, giving Bryan a mock salute.

"Come on, boys," ordered Bryan, "the first drink's on me and then we're away to our homes."

That night, after supper, he held Hannah tightly in his arms as they lay in the warmth of their bed.

"I think it'll be all right, mavourneen," he whispered, face pressed into her sweet-smelling hair.

She shifted her position, trying to be more comfortable. Her back pushed against him. His arms circled her, gently holding her breasts.

"All the men with guns though," she worried, voice half-muffled against her pillow. "Guns and men all over town."

"They're old friends really. Sure, they've different points of view but they're not wanting a fight. Leastways I don't think so. Why, old Paddy Murphy greeted me like a long-lost brother. All of us have been through a war together. We're not wanting another one."

His hands slid under her nightgown, running across her smooth flesh. Their lovemaking was less frequent and more sedate because of her advanced pregnancy, but no less passionate nor mutually satisfying for that.

Hannah lifted herself a fraction, offering her body. Bryan slid into her.

Later, not much later, as they drifted off to satiated sleep, his mind wandered back over the past months. They had been overwhelmingly happy together. His decision to move into Listowel rather than live with the Wilmots at Galey Bridge had been the right one. They might have been stifled under the concern of Hannah's parents for their only child. As it was, Mrs. Wilmot visited them twice a week, full of ideas and suggestions.

Nor was he overfond of being so near his own family. His parents were always calling around. It was something he was obliged to accept for the time being, in return for their financial help in renting the house in Courthouse Road and the virtual sinecure of his part-time job at the tavern.

Soon, Bryan knew, he would have to find a proper job. Fatherhood demanded that. But it would have to wait until the tensions had died away and Ireland had finally decided what it wanted to do about the treaty; until then perhaps, he could be released from his commitment to the anti-treaty IRA.

This proved a longer process than he had foreseen. The Republicans and the Free Staters in Listowel maintained the unspoken truce of old IRA comrades but continued their patrols, even strengthening their numbers. The mood of foreboding grew almost daily.

Most of the country, whatever their allegiance, shuddered when de Valera proclaimed that if the treaty was ratified, the IRA, "in order to achieve freedom, would have to march over the dead bodies of their own brothers."

"They will have to wade through Irish blood!" de Valera warned chillingly.

As the fear grew, so did the anarchy, particularly by the anti-treaty Republicans, desperate for money and equipment to be able to face the government troops.

Post offices were held up and robbed; goods were stolen from trains; people were terrorized into subscribing to so-called collections. Once again, old scores were settled. The lifeless body at the side of a country road became a familiar sight. It was as if the entire country was talking itself into a war that no one, except the zealots, wanted.

Not that that mattered a jot in the Aherne household in Courthouse Road on the morning of April 14th, 1922, with Bryan running for Annie Cahill, the midwife, after Hannah had shaken him awake.

"Baby's coming," she said, her voice trembling, her eyes calm.

"Oh, God!" Bryan cried, leaping out of bed and pulling his trousers over his striped nightshirt, stubbing his toe against the brass bedstead in his hurry.

"Be careful, gosseen," Hannah exclaimed. "You'll be

falling out the window next and then where'll we be? There's time yet."

Indeed, Bryan had another four hours of anxious waiting in the kitchen, boiling kettles, fetching towels, trying to shut his mind to Hannah's occasional moans from above, before he heard a sharp slap followed by a thin piercing wail.

He ran to the foot of the narrow staircase, combing his hands nervously through his hair.

"It's fine they are," Annie Cahill suddenly called, her beaming face appearing around the turn of the stairs. "Come and say hello to your wee son! It's all done. It's a proud man you should be."

Hannah smiled palely up at him when he stepped into the room, her hair still damp with perspiration. He bent over the bed to peck her cheek and look more closely at the swaddled baby, at his son's tiny, mottled red face, wisped with dark hair, eyes tight shut.

"He favors you," Hannah said quietly, smiling to herself.

"Now be off with you and tell your folks," Annie Cahill ordered briskly. "There's some women's work to be done yet. Be back in an hour though. I've another confinement due any time."

"I'll be sending Mam and Grandma Maude," Bryan whispered to Hannah. "Love you," he added.

Her tired eyes, dark ringed, glistened up at him. "Not too much celebrating, mind," she murmured, gazing at her baby for a second. "Remember you're a da now."

After taking the news to Forge Lane and No. 32 Church Street, Bryan headed for the tavern, reckoning he deserved a good drink after the morning's anxieties of fatherhood. He really did feel proud, prouder, he thought, than he had ever been. A firstborn son, he decided, really proved he was a man at last.

Bryan's huge beam told his father immediately of the successful birth. He could hardly stop his son talking after he had burst forth with the good news.

Sean Aherne reached for the whiskey bottle to pour drinks for everyone in the bar.

"To the wee one, God bless him and keep him all his days and may he die in Ireland," he toasted, gulping the whiskey down and refilling the glasses.

"It's a marvellous feeling, Dad, isn't it?" Bryan enthused.

"So it is, son, but I'm wishing it'd come a better day."

"A better day? Why? What's happened?"

"It's in the newspaper. Last night the Republicans took over the Four Courts in Dublin as their military headquarters. Threw down the gauntlet to Mick Collins and the government."

Bryan was silent. He emptied his glass, the spirit burning in his throat.

"Slainte," he said automatically.

"What's that?" his father asked over the increasing hubbub in the tavern. "If you ask me what it means, Bryan, I'll be telling you. It means fucking war, son. That's what it means. Civil fucking war!"

"Slainte," Bryan repeated, not quite hearing his father.

Chapter 9
June, 1922

The sunlight played on the dull grey walls of a town holding its breath. It glinted and sparkled on the dozens of rifle barrels poking out of second-floor windows on three sides of the market square. It danced through the dusty glass of the Listowel Arms Hotel in the lower corner of the square, forcing the troops of the Free State Army to shield their eyes, making them feel even more isolated. It warmed Bryan Aherne's face as he strolled around the square with Brigadier Humphrey Murphy, commanding the Republican forces in the area and in charge of Listowel.

"There's been a good job done here, Aherne," the brigadier said, stopping by the entrance of St. John's Church to survey the surrounding buildings.

"We've everything except the hotel," Bryan replied. He swept his arm around the square. "All those houses from the hotel to the hardware shop on the corner. Those two bars, Leah's and Danahar's, on this side and the National Bank over there. No one can enter or leave the square without coming under our guns."

"The machine guns?"

"Two of them here in the square and the other two in those bars in Market Street I showed you, Griffin's and Moroney's."

"Good. That was a fine capture, so it was."

"It was that," Bryan agreed.

Brigadier Murphy allowed himself a smile bordering on self-satisfaction.

"I think we can safely be saying, Aherne, that we can

hold this town," he said. "And if we hold here, we hold North Kerry. How are you deploying the men?"

Humphrey Murphy liked using such phrases to remind those under him that he'd once held a less exalted commission in the British Army.

"Twelve hours on duty, twelve hours off."

"They're happy?"

"They're surviving. There's not much they're having to pay out of their own pockets. The locals are being very generous."

"Good. And the Free Staters?"

"Miserable and frightened, I'm thinking."

"They've not much, have they?"

"No, not much. The workhouse. Clancy's in William Street, Latchford's Mill and, as you see, the hotel over there. Not much at all."

"Well, Aherne, at least no trouble so far, thanks be."

"No. We're allowing them only one small patrol car a day for exercise and provisions. Otherwise, they stay where they are. Mind you, the boys still talk with them through the windows next door."

"Hard to stop?"

"Don't want to really, Brigadier. Many of them are old friends, after all. It's been a bit tense at times but nobody's fired a shot yet."

"I wish I had more confidence, Bryan, that they never will," Brigadier Murphy said, deciding to become informal, heading determinedly for a closer inspection of his forces manning the Castle Bar, trusting to the owner's hospitality.

As Brigadier Murphy ducked through the bar door, he removed his wide-brimmed, high crowned hat, one side pinned in the style of the Anzac troops of the Great War.

Bryan, following, felt rather strange and unmilitary in his normal rather shabby, everyday suit with a mere holster buckled around his waist. But then, he reflected, everything felt strange these days, had done for weeks past.

The results of the election for members of the first Dail of the new Irish Free State, announced only three days later, on June 24th, added to the feeling.

That 94 of its 128 members were in favor of the Anglo-Irish Treaty served only to heighten the dream-like unreality of what was happening. The democratic voice had spoken but, as before, was rejected by the minority who didn't care for its clear message.

Ironically, Michael Collins, the head of the Provisional government striving day and night to keep the Free State intact, provided the final catalyst himself.

As he had done many, many times before, Collins ordered the death of a man. This time his target was Sir Henry Wilson, lately Director of Military Operations at the War Office in London, now advising the Northern Ireland government on matters of law and order.

The murderers, Joseph O'Sullivan and Reginald Donne, were captured swiftly, mainly due to O'Sullivan being handicapped by the loss of a leg at the Battle of Ypres. Before their trials and executions, they revealed their memberships of the IRA.

An outraged British government mistakenly assumed that the killing was at the behest of the anti-Treaty Republicans. They immediately ordered the commander of the British troops still in Dublin, General Macready, to attack the Republicans' headquarters in the Four Courts. He advised wisely that this would only unite once again both Irish factions against the British.

Thus, Michael Collins, who'd ordered the murder in retaliation for the Catholics' sufferings in Northern Ireland, was given an ultimatum to bring down the Republicans himself or otherwise the entire treaty would be abrogated. He played for time by asking London to provide proof of the Republican links of the two gunmen in custody. Since, as the real instigator, Collins knew that there were none, he gained a short respite. It couldn't and didn't last.

At seven minutes past four on the morning of Wednesday, June 28th, 1922, the first muzzle flash lit the Dublin sky. The shrapnel shell, from one of the two British field guns borrowed by Collins, exploded near the outer walls of the Four Courts, ripping into the masonry, shattering windows.

It was one of the better shots by the inexperienced Free State gunners just across the River Liffey.

The Republicans could do little except loose the occasional, hopeful fusillade, huddle in the safest depths of their headquarters, and rue their rejection of Collins' surrender ultimatum.

The pounding barrage continued for nearly two days.

Early on June 30th, a white flag fluttered amid the smoking rubble of the great building. Rory O'Connor, leader of the Republicans, stumbled out of the ruins and into captivity with his executive committee and more than a hundred IRA men.

Their surrender after such futile, though brave, resistance lanced into the abscess of bitterness which had been welling and suppurating for months.

The news of the fall of the Four Courts reached the Republicans in Listowel by telephone at breakfast time that pleasant Friday morning.

At first, no one knew quite what to do. The wiser and older barricaded their doors and windows. The bolder and more inquisitive risked a walk through the streets but soon scurried home after listening to the clicking rifle bolts and angry recriminations coming from the Republican positions.

Bryan Aherne tried to calm his men from the command post above the hardware shop at the corner of the market square. "Wait for orders!" he urged. "For Jesus' sake, we must wait!"

His men reluctantly obeyed his instructions, their tempers and nerves on edge. The minutes of ominous silence ticked away. Suddenly, a cheer rolled into the market square from the windows of the Arms Hotel. The Free State troops, completely isolated there, cheered once more, reacting to the fast spreading news of the Four Courts' surrender, their side's first victory.

The listening Republicans grimaced sullenly. A few brought their rifles to their shoulders, aiming towards the noise.

Bryan, realizing the provocation, dashed to the nearest window and leaned out. "Hold your fire!" he bawled. "No firing without my word!"

A sneering voice bellowed back, interrupting him as he started to repeat his orders, "You fucking rebel! What's the matter? Afraid you'll be tasting the same metal as your friends in the Four Courts? They soon gave up, didn't they?"

The few insults from a Free State Army soldier were all that was needed.

Rifle fire began to crackle from the enraged Republicans. Bullets slapped into the hotel facade, splintering plaster and brick into puffs of dust. Shards of glass smashed to the pavement.

For thirty minutes, the antagonists blazed away at anything that moved and everything that didn't.

The town rang with gunfire, the air cracking and whizzing with hundreds of rounds of ammunition, the four light machine-guns chattering in deadly conversation with each other.

"Stop firing!" Bryan shrieked. "For fuck's sake, stop it!"

His orders were totally ignored and, as the acrid cordite smoke bit into his nostrils, Bryan too succumbed to the general hysteria. It didn't matter that there was hardly ever a clear target at which to aim. The feel of the revolver bucking and humping in his hand was enough.

Gradually the hysteria ebbed. The shooting slackened. Any attempt, Bryan knew, to storm the Free State defenses head on would inevitably mean heavy casualties. He considered burning them out but swiftly rejected that course. A fire would be difficult to contain. He thought of Hannah and their little son, Joseph, of his parents and grandparents on the periphery of the battle. The flames might even spread to their homes.

Around ten o'clock, a messenger arrived from Brigadier Murphy, who was directing the action around the corner in Market Street. The scribbled note ordered Bryan to try for a parley with the Free State troops in the hotel.

Without much confidence, Bryan pulled off his white shirt and tied it to a broomstick taken from the hardware shop below.

Gingerly, he pushed the makeshift flag of truce out of the window, waving it up and down.

The sporadic firing in the market square died away when the Republicans saw the signal although the crackle of shots could be heard from other parts of Listowel.

Bryan poked his head over the windowsill.

He looked quickly to his right along the front of the houses and shops toward the hotel, hoping for an answering flag of truce. Instead, to his horror, Bryan saw a Free State soldier leaning out of a window, rifle aimed directly at him.

"Jesus!" he cried, pulling his head back into cover.

Two shots rang out. The broomstick jerked in his hand as the bullets ripped through the shirt.

A third shot cracked across the square. Bryan heard a wail of fearful agony followed by a soggy thud. A Free State soldier lay on his back in the gutter, legs twitching. A spreading redness across the front of his jacket showed where the Republican bullet had struck.

"God's mercy," Bryan whispered.

"It's Eddie Sheehy," one of his men at another window said quietly.

"You know him?"

"His mam lives next to us. We went to school together."

"Poor silly fucker," another man said, shaking his head sadly.

"There's another white flag!" someone called excitedly.

"Where?"

"By St. Mary's."

A young priest had stepped through the doors of the Catholic Church, holding over his head what looked like a white altar cloth.

The firing stopped while the priest walked without hesitation over to the dead soldier and knelt to administer the last rites.

When the priest had finished, he spoke for a few moments to one of the Free State soldiers in the hotel's downstairs window. Then he glanced up at the windows of the buildings held by the Republicans before walking along the pavement and stopping directly below Bryan.

"Are you in charge here?" he called up.

"Who's wanting to know," Bryan replied.

"I do. I'm Father Troy."

"Well, Father?"

"Can't you be stopping this slaughter?"

"We tried but they fired on our flag of truce, so they did."

The priest, not much older than Bryan, dressed in a shabby black suit, spread his arms in a gesture of appeal. "Will you try again, for the Lord's sake, if I guarantee the Free Staters will respect the flag this time?"

"Aye, if you can."

"They will. They promised me they will."

Bryan leaned a little way out of the window, ready to duck back. No shots came. He waved his shirt again. Another shirt answered from the hotel. He lifted himself into full view.

"God bless you!" the priest cried. He flinched suddenly as a stray bullet from the shooting away from the square slapped into a wall about twenty feet from him.

"Be careful, Father," Bryan shouted. "The bullets won't be respecting your collar."

Father Troy smiled ruefully.

"And isn't that the truth?" he called back. "Will you keep the truce while I'm away stopping the others in this madness?"

"If they will."

"They will."

"I'm praying so, Father, for everyone's sake. And, by the by, you'll be wanting the brigadier above Griffin's in Market Street. He's really in charge."

The priest nodded, waved the white cloth once and hurried out of the square.

His progress along the street could be judged by the way the shooting gradually died away. Within fifteen minutes, it had ceased altogether.

For hour upon hour, the men on both sides stayed tensely on alert while Brigadier Murphy parleyed with the Free State commander, Tom Kennelly. Just before five o'clock, the two leaders walked into the market square with Father Troy between them, white cloth still held aloft.

"They've surrendered," the brigadier called to Bryan. "It's all over here for now. The boys can stand down."

"Thank the Lord," Bryan murmured as his men cheered and slapped each other on the back.

Bryan left his position and went down the stairs, through the hardware shop and into the square. The priest was standing by the dead soldier. He made the sign of the cross above him before covering the body with the altar cloth.

"Shall we be guarding them?" Bryan asked Brigadier Murphy, nodding toward the Free State troops who were emerging from the hotel, carrying their weapons.

The brigadier shook his head.

"No need," he said quietly, looking around to ensure that Kennelly was out of hearing. "They know they're licked. Just keep a close eye on them."

Under Kennelly's orders, the Free State troops stacked their guns in the square and then formed up into three ranks. Four of them carried Eddie Sheehy's body into St. Mary's Church.

Brigadier Murphy waited until they had disappeared from view before addressing the captured soldiers. Kennelly stood by his side, shoulders slumped despondently.

"Lads, you're all as brave men as any commander in the field could possibly want to lead. You fought like Irishmen should and you shouldn't be ashamed that you've had to surrender. Commandant Kennelly here made the only possible decision."

The brigadier turned to Kennelly, smiling sympathetically. They shook hands.

"You were outnumbered and outgunned and there's the end of it," the brigadier continued. "I'm only glad that but one of your comrades died."

Kennelly leaned towards him and whispered a few words.

"And I'm told, one of you was wounded as well."

Brigadier Murphy paused, gazing around the square filled with men, faces dark with cordite powder, grime and nervous exhaustion.

"The war no one wanted has begun," he declaimed solemnly. "All of us, I'm sure, will fight according to our consciences. But now the war is upon us, some might see the issues differently than before. All around you . . ."

He gestured towards his own troops.

". . . are men who fought the British in the name of old Ireland. Many of you risked your lives gloriously as well in that struggle. Many of your brothers and friends gave their lives."

The brigadier pointed dramatically toward the Free State soldiers at ease before him.

"Do you really want to fight against your old comrades? Are you really going to split this brave country of ours in two? Won't you be joining us and finishing the battle for the Republic begun by the Easter Martyrs and the martyrs before them?"

He lowered his voice, speaking almost confidentially. Bryan, twenty yards away outside the Arms Hotel, strained to hear.

"Commandant Kennelly has agreed that as part of his surrender I can ask you to change sides, to rejoin your Republican friends of old. He's assuring me that there'll be no dishonor in this nor any rancor held against any man who does so. What do you say? It'll be your last chance before you go into captivity. Any man now who'll join us on our road to victory and the true Republic . . . well, let him fall out and shake hands with his new comrades. What about it, boys? Who'll fight for the true Republic?"

He folded his arms across his chest and waited.

The Free State soldiers looked around at each other. Some shook their heads immediately. Others whispered together. A few shrugged their shoulders and broke ranks and walked over to those they recognized among the Republican soldiers. In all, fifty accepted Brigadier Murphy's offer. The other two hundred were marched off the next day to Tralee and detention in Ballymullen Barracks.

Within a few days, most of the Republicans had also left on their way to help garrison Limerick where the confrontation between former friends was potentially even more explosive.

Paddy Landers and Bryan Aherne remained in charge of the fifty men still holding the police barracks and courthouse.

The townsfolk of Listowel sensed, rightly, that they'd been spared the worst.

In Dublin, the Republicans' resistance hadn't ended with the fall of the Four Courts. Fighting went on for nearly a week in the capital of the new state, artillery, machine guns and grenades effectively destroying the property in O'Connell Street opposite the buildings ravaged by the British bombardment during the Easter Uprising. The battle was hopeless and the Republicans knew it.

Eventually those still alive surrendered after repeated appeals from priests. The Free State troops led the Republicans off to prison as they emerged one by one through the dust and rubble.

Within five weeks, any pretense that the anti-treaty forces had a chance of winning was gone. Collins sent battalions of newly-recruited men—some former members of the United States Army—in a drive southwest from Dublin, at the same time landing units from the sea behind the Republican lines.

On the morning of August 3rd, Colonel Michael Hogan led ashore more than two hundred Free State troops at Tarbert, on the southern banks of the River Shannon. The few "Irregulars" in the small port decided that discretion was preferable to valor and fled inland, leaving the local coastguard station in flames as a gesture of defiance.

The Free Staters advanced unopposed through North Kerry on their way to Listowel, ten or so miles to the south. Their overwhelming superiority made resistance pointless.

As reports of their progress reached the market town, Bryan Aherne's depression grew. He knew that if the Republicans made a stand, then the main loser would be Listowel itself. For an hour, he, Paddy Landers and Con Dee talked of various strategies which might halt or slow the Free Staters—a series of ambushes, perhaps—but by early afternoon they accepted the inevitable. They would retreat southeast to Abbeyfeale, leaving the town undefended. While the Republicans gathered their equipment and "requisitioned" £1,658 in notes from the National Bank in the market square, Bryan hurried home to give Hannah the news.

"How long will you be away?" she asked dully after he'd told her. She stood by the fireplace, baby Joseph cradled in her arms, pressed against her white apron.

"Not long," Bryan assured her.

He stepped toward Hannah, wanting to hold her and his son, but she turned away.

"How long?" whispered Hannah, automatically patting the baby's back to bring up his wind.

Byran breathed in the baby smells pervading the small home, the odor of milk, powder and drying nappies. "Not long," he repeated quietly. "A month or two at most. The fighting won't last. Mick Collins'll settle it quick enough now his army's front and back of us."

"You've lost?"

"Aye, I'm reckoning so." To his own surprise, Bryan felt neither disappointment nor anger in conceding defeat. Perhaps, he thought, it had always been an impossible dream. Perhaps it always would be.

"I'll be going back to the farm," Hannah said flatly. "We'll be safe there."

"Safe?"

"From your friends in the proper army or, rather, the people you used to call friends. They'll be after looking for you."

"They'd not be hurting you."

"It'll be safer."

"Aye, it may be," Bryan conceded reluctantly. "But this is your home."

"Only when you're here."

"Oh, Hannah!" he exclaimed, made guilty by her deep unhappiness. He slipped his hand around her narrow waist and pressed her back. He hoped she wouldn't feel the revolver belt strapped around his waist. "I'm sorry. I'm sorry, mavourneen."

"Why should you be? You've always been fighting for something, haven't you? We've always come second."

"You haven't. You haven't."

She twisted in his arms to face him. Tears streaked the dusting of powder on her cheeks. "Just for once, Bryan Aherne," she said bitterly. "Just for once, will you be after telling me why the fighting? Just be telling me so I can be explaining to babbie when he's old enough and asking what his da did in his awful short life."

"You're thinking I'll be dead?"

"And why not?"

Bryan gripped Hannah around the shoulders and almost forced her to sit down on the narrow sofa. He knelt before her on the rug, his arms embracing her and their son.

"Don't be thinking that," he pleaded. "Don't be."

"And are you so special then?"

"I'm not . . . but I'll not be doing anything reckless. I've both of you to live for."

"Then, why? Why all this?"

"Because . . . because . . ." He hesitated, shaking his head slowly, before the words came in a torrent, words half remembered from IRA pamphlets and indoctrination lectures, words that sounded angry because of Hannah's use of emotional blackmail.

"Because what I'm wanting is for you and Joseph and all my family and the families of Ireland. It's not for me alone, Holy Mary knows, it's not for me. If this country is to be free—truly free—then its affairs must be changed. That's what we're meaning by the Republic and our need to fight for it. The Republic is the very symbol of what we must be having. It's not enough that Irishmen should form a government in Dublin. It never has been. What's important is how we're governed. It's not enough that an Irish landlord should replace a British landlord. There should be no landlords. Don't you see the land is ours, belongs to everyone? Don't you understand that no one man should have the right to control this or that part of it? It's not enough that our business houses should be run by Irishmen instead of Englishmen, each growing wealthier in turn from the sweat of their workers who produce their riches but have no share in them. Don't you understand that a country's wealth belongs to all its people and should be shared equally among them? It's not enough to change British privilege for Irish privilege. There'll be no privilege in the Republic, not of position, land, wealth, health or education. Doesn't your heart tell you that the Free State is just another name for part of the British Empire with all the evils of imperialism and privilege and decadence that that contains? It's not the Republic of Pearse and the Martyrs. We've simply exchanged one set of masters for another. Don't you believe that in the Republic the only masters shall be the people, with all having equal rights—Catholic or Protestant or Jew—as well as equal opportunities? What we have now only maintains the old social and economic system and brings us nothing. You ask why the fighting, Hannah? Then I'm telling you that there'll always be fighting until there's the Republic. Not a republic. The Republic. That's what the boys died for, standing alongside me in the field at Gortaglonna. Ireland may be the country of dreams and dreamers, but at least they're dreams worthy of your own life and at least there are plenty of dreamers prepared to sacrifice that. While there are, there'll be fighting and bloodshed. And if, one day, there's no one ready to die for the Republic, why then Ireland'll be no better than Britain and the Irish people no better than the slaves of imperialism that they've always been and not deserving to call themselves Irish . . . not deserving at all, God help them.''

Bryan's passionate, jumbled words ended as hesitantly as they'd begun.

Hannah listened, eyes widening, trying to comprehend his whirling thoughts about the Republican philosophy.

"And will this fighting make a better life for Joseph here?" she said finally, turning the gurgling baby toward Bryan so that he could look fully into his chubby face.

"I've said it will," Bryan said gently. "Believe me, it will."

"But what you've been saying sounds an awful deal like

what those terrible men in Russia are saying and you know what the Church thinks of them."

"Communists, you mean?"

"Aye, like them."

"They only believe in what Jesus Christ himself basically preached."

"Then why does Father O'Connor call them the servants of the anti-Christ?"

"Because he's not understanding what they're trying to achieve."

"You're knowing better than the Father?"

"No."

"And they're killing people as well," Hannah said reflectively. "And most people don't want killings."

"Nor do I."

"You're fighting, aren't you, and people are killed in fighting?"

Hannah started to sob, realizing the futility of it all. The baby, sensing the distress and tension around him, began to cry too.

"Oh, Jesus!" Bryan exclaimed. "I've not the time for all this now. No time at all."

He went upstairs, pushed a few clothes into his old rucksack and returned downstairs and took half a loaf and a hunk of cheese. All the while, the baby howled and Hannah sobbed.

Flooded with misery, Bryan walked to the front door. "I'm off then," he called. "I'll be at the farm when I can."

There was no reply. He opened the door as noisily as he could, rattling the latch.

"Bryan! Wait, Bryan!" Hannah shouted suddenly. Her slippers pattered across the sitting room and then she and Joseph were in his arms. Bryan felt the wetness on both their cheeks as he held them close.

Hannah's voice whispered, bedroom soft, against his chest, "You can't be going like this."

"No. Nor could I," he replied, relief surging through him. "No, I didn't want to."

"You have to do it? You're certain? Whatever anyone thinks?"

"I have to."

"Then go with our love and blessing."

She lifted her lips to his. Their long kiss stifled for a moment each other's uncertainty and fear.

"Take care, avourneen," cried Hannah as he swung down the street.

"I will that," he called back.

"For both of us," she murmured, waving him out of sight. She turned back into the house, still speaking as if the baby could understand her every word.

"They'll not be learning that all we're wanting is peace and quiet, a house to call home, and someone to love. They'll not be learning that, will they, babbie? And will they ever?"

Joseph Aherne belched sleepily, ready for his afternoon nap.

Outside, flames began to lick into the sky over Listowel from the fires set by the retreating Republicans in the police barracks, the courthouse and the workhouse.

The gathering pall of smoke was visible a mile away to the advance scouts of the Free State Army.

Chapter 10
January, 1923

On a raw morning, Kevin Christopher O'Higgins, Vice President of the Executive Council in the first Dail and Minister for Home Affairs, looked imperiously down from the second-floor window of the Arms Hotel at the crowd of three hundred, held back by a rank of Free State troops, bayonets fixed to rifles.

"People of Listowel," he announced, "I speak to you at a time when the future of our beloved country is at stake. The question," he continued in a Queen's County accent, "is whether Ireland is to be a nation governed by constitutional principles or whether it is to be a mob dictated by an armed minority. To resolve that question, the nation is entitled to act on its own intuition of self-preservation. My friends, that nation's life is worth the life of many individuals."

Hannah Aherne shivered when she heard those words.

There above her was the man whose sworn aim was to hunt down Republicans like her husband; a man who, with the military, had instituted and implemented the death penalty, without proper trial, for anyone found in possession of a gun; a man who'd authorized the execution without trial of his life-long friend, Rory O'Connor, the anti-treaty Republican leader captured at the Four Courts in Dublin six months before.

"I venture to say," O'Higgins added, his sharp voice carrying against the wind, "that this country of ours has more heroes to the square mile than any equivalent country in the world. That is, if you're foolish enough to name as heroes those in militant opposition to your constitutionally elected government."

"They are heroes. They are," Hannah whispered to herself.

"Sshh," hissed Jack Aherne beside her.

Hannah blushed slightly, looking around to check that no one else had overheard.

"It would be a generous estimate to say that twenty per cent of that militant opposition is idealism. It would be a generous estimate also to say that only twenty percent of it is crime. And between those twenty per cents, there flows sixty per cent of sheer futility. We are presented in Ireland with a spectacle of a country steering straight for anarchy and chaos. If this country fails to get through, if this country fails to win out to democratic government, that will be unfortunate."

O'Higgins' voice was quieter now, but no less lacking in determination and resolve. The crowd stood like statues.

"I do not think that any of us hold human life cheap. But when you must balance the human life against the life of the nation, that presents a very different problem. When the nation is threatened, as it is now, then human life does become cheaper and the fate of individuals of less importance. If the nation's survival demands blood, then blood it shall have."

The statement was so bold, so chilling that Hannah heard Bryan's grandfather draw breath in surprise.

"There can be no turning back, people of Listowel," O'Higgins concluded. "You have seen what measures the nation is prepared to adopt, and, indeed, has adopted to preserve itself. Those in militant opposition have a choice. To surrender or to continue their futile fight. Let them make their choice. But also let them clearly understand what the consequences of a wrong choice shall be."

Hannah suddenly felt trapped in the crowd by her own panic at the politician's message. There was no doubt any longer in her mind that those carrying weapons against the Free State Government were doomed. O'Higgins had been unequivocal. There would be little mercy for such as Bryan and his friends.

She pushed blindly through the dispersing crowd, away from Kevin O'Higgins, away from his stony words.

"Hold fast, lass," the old schoolteacher called, having difficulty in keeping pace with his grandson's wife. He put a hand on her shoulder, drawing her back toward him.

Without warning, Hannah turned and flung her arms around his neck, bursting into tears. "Oh, Grandpa!" she sobbed. "What's to become of us? Bryan'll be dead by the Free Staters. I know he will. They'll get him in the end, so they will."

"Hush, hush, child," Jack Aherne murmured, patting her hair. "Not here. They're all after watching you."

"I'm not caring," Hannah wailed, lifting her face to look into his wise, calm eyes.

"I know you're not, lass," he smiled reassuringly. "But just be thinking what your tears are doing to my nice clean shirt your Grandma Maude ironed only this morning."

He reached into his inside pocket and produced a white linen handkerchief.

"Here," he said. "Dry your eyes and let's be home to see how your wee babbie's faring."

She nodded, gulped back her sobs, trying to smile a watery smile at the same time.

"And what was so terrible about your man?" Jack asked lightly when they were halfway to his home in Forge Lane where Hannah had left baby Joseph.

"Just his words and the way he was saying them."

"And sure and what was so new about that? He's been putting it in the newspapers for weeks past."

"But it's the way he spoke . . . you know . . . here, in the flesh."

"Aye, he looks an awful hard man and there's no mistaking he means business. I wouldn't fancy being on my own keeping with him after me."

"And isn't that how Bryan is? He's a gun and you know what the Free Staters'll do to him if they catch him."

"Don't be worrying. If the Tans couldn't get your Bryan, I doubt if this lot will."

Jack Aherne put as much confidence into his voice as he was able, trying to hide an emptiness of fear within himself. He looked sideways at Hannah. She was biting her lower lip.

"You're right, of course, Grandpa Jack," she exclaimed. "They'll not be taking my . . . our Bryan."

Her voice was bright but her eyes were heavy with threatening tears and ever-present foreboding, an emotion constant to her in these days of Civil War, in its last, most horrific stages.

The Republicans opposed to the Anglo-Irish Treaty had ceased to exist as a force of any subtance after the Government offensive the previous August.

Cork and the other remaining large centers of population in the south and west of Ireland had fallen to the Free State Army within a matter of weeks.

Ironically, Michael Collins had not lived to savor the victory, if any event in a civil war can be termed as a victory. He had died, like so many of his proxy victims, with a bullet through the back of his head in a roadside ambush during the offensive.

The mopping-up operations were now being conducted by his successor as President of the Executive Council, William Cosgrove, and Kevin O'Higgins.

Their orders allowed virtually no quarter. Nor was any offered in return.

Few bolt holes used by IRA men in the Tan War were open to them any longer in their guise of anti-treaty Republicans. The ordinary people were loath to give sanctuary or even food except in pockets of support. And if hiding places were still available on the lands of friendly farmers or landlords, they also held the terrible danger of being known to a fugitive's former comrades, now wearing the green uniform of the Free State Army.

Many a Republican had thought himself safe for the night in his secret place in a hay rick or barn until he had found himself blinking into the light of a lantern and the barrel of a rifle held by someone who had served alongside him in his old IRA unit. Loyalty to the Free State often meant treachery to friends, even blood relations. There was no mercy.

Sometimes, the fugitive died where he was discovered. Sometimes, he was interrogated with the aid of hammers and lighted cigarettes before being shot in a ditch. And quite often he was used as a human metal-detector to clear a road mined not many hours before by his Republican colleagues.

Each new tale of horror reaching Hannah at her family's farm at Galey Bridge increased her fears. In her nightmares, she would see Bryan dying every imaginable death at the hands of the Free State Army. She would wake wet with perspiration, staring into the dark with the awful images vivid in her brain.

Since Bryan had left Listowel with the other Republicans five months before, he'd managed to visit her and Joseph on only three occasions. Each time, he had stayed just the night but those short hours together had been some of the most precious of their marriage.

After passionate and repeated love-makings in Hannah's narrow bed, they had lain awake whispering quietly about their childhood memories, their hopes for the future, their feelings for each other.

All the time, though, Bryan had refused to tell her about his activities in the Civil War and how he was surviving on the run. The less Hannah knew the less she could divulge, however unwillingly, if the Free Staters ever came to interrogate her.

She could guess that her husband was virtually living off the land by the feel of his thin body under her caresses. His ribs and shoulder blades seemed ready to burst through his skin. The black rings under his eyes told of nights sleeping rough. His nicotine-stained fingers with nails bitten to the quick showed the nervous stress of his existence.

On his last visit, just before St. Stephen's Day, she had noticed that he had developed a nervous tic high on his left cheek. She had begged him to stay longer—a day or two, perhaps—but Bryan insisted on slipping away in the half-darkness of early morning, saying that any delay might bring his capture and the chance of harm to herself, their child and her parents.

The ecstasy and relief of each of his visits had soon faded to be replaced by loneliness and nagging fear. Hannah found her parents relatively unsympathetic to Bryan's plight, urging her to persuade him to give up the hopeless fight. Thus, she found herself seeking comfort and reassur-

ance from Bryan's parents and grandparents. And, as the
weeks of worry continued, she discovered a particular
affinity with Jack and Maude Aherne and Aunt Brigid.
Their serenity in old age and apparent acceptance of God's
will in all things helped soothe her troubled mind. In their
company, Hannah could stop brooding, for a few hours at
least, about her husband's fate.

In fact, Bryan was near the limit of his endurance. The
Free State Army's advance had decimated the Republicans
in North Kerry. It was impossible for them to act as a unified
force so they had split into small groups which, one by one,
had been picked off by the government troops. They had
fled into the Stack Mountains between Listowel and Tralee
just as they had done in the days of the flying column. Now,
however, the rocks and crags and valleys were not so safe.
Their pursuers, led by Tom Kennelly and Paddy Murphy,
knew the old hiding places from their own service with the
column and harried the fugitives without respite. Eventually, Bryan and his companions had been driven out of the
mountains and toward the coastlands running down to Kerry
Head, above Ballyheighe Bay, north of Tralee.

By April 1923, Bryan's unit numbered only four, including himself. The others, a dozen or more, had vanished to
their homes after burying their weapons, preferring the
dubious mercy of the Free Staters to the harshness of life on
the run.

The unit had to content itself with occasional skirmishes
with small Free State patrols which usually consisted of a
few shots fired at long range and then a dash to safety. Most
of their time was taken up with finding food and shelter, an
increasingly difficult task as more and more of the population shut their doors to the Republicans.

Bryan's unit was lucky to some extent, though, because
one of them, Jinty Fleming, had a widowed sister living in a
cabin at Ballynaskreena, a mile from the dark impregnable
cliffs confronting the Atlantic near Inshaboy Point.

The four of them would travel inland for their forays
against the Free Staters and then retreat to the coast where
they knew they could find a hot meal of sorts and at least
one night's sleep under a dry roof.

By April, Bryan had virtually decided to give up, to set just one more ambush and then disband. He did not know whether to surrender personally to someone like Tom Kennelly, his old commander in the North Kerry Flying Column, or whether simply to hide out near Listowel until the Civil War formally ended.

They were returning one evening to the cabin after an abortive attempt to mine a road used frequently by a Free State Army cycling corps. For some reason, the troops had not followed their usual route and after two hours and no sign of the soldiers, Bryan decided to blow up the mine by rifle fire.

They walked back toward their refuge in single file, rifles slung across their backs, disconsolate and tired.

"Come on, boys," Bryan urged as they neared the small cabin. "We'll crack a bottle of the hard stuff if you like and drown our sorrows."

"Fuck that!" said Jinty Fleming, a small, wiry man, normally full of optimism and humor. "I'm thinking it'll be better for us to drink some fucking rat poison."

"With our fucking luck," Paddy Swift grunted behind him, "the fucking rats'll have drunk it first."

"And fucking enjoyed it too!" Tom Reagan added.

The four laughed humorlessly.

"Nearly there," Bryan called from the front.

"Thanks be," Swift panted rotundly.

"You'll be skin and bone soon," Reagan joked. "Your mam'll not be recognizing you, Paddy."

"For Jesus' sake," Bryan exclaimed. "Will you be quiet!"

The four quickened their pace, anxious to be indoors, feeling on their faces the first drops of rain from which they knew there would soon be a torrential downpour, an almost nightly occurrence in Kerry at that time of the spring, a season known locally as "scoriveen," "the rough weather of the cuckoo."

In the distance they could hear the Atlantic breakers pounding away at the base of the cliffs.

Bryan was only twenty yards from the cabin, whose

beckoning light was shining around the edges of its ill-fitting door, when he stopped suddenly.

Another sound had reached his ears.

He thrust out his hand, signalling the men behind him to be still. He cocked his head, listening intently, unsure of what he had just heard from the darkness ahead.

"What's the . . . ?" Fleming began to whisper.

"Shut up!" Bryan muttered.

A second later and the sound came again, borne on the wind from the ocean. A definite clink of metal upon stone. Paddy Swift heard it too and, for all his bulk, dropped noiselessly to the ground. The others immediately did the same. They were only too familiar with the noise made by a rifle butt against a loose pebble.

Bryan gestured again and the four of them slid into the shallow ditch beside the track. Fleming's rifle clattered against stones lying under a broken wall.

Immediately, the beams from half a dozen powerful torches pierced the night, searching toward them. Somewhere behind their blinding glare rifle bolts clicked.

"Can you see 'em?" a voice called.

"Not yet. They're not far though."

The beams crossed and recrossed, probing and sliding across the uneven ground, illuminating the steadily falling rain. A voice called again: "Come on out, boys! We know you're there. You're surrounded. Come out with your hands up and there'll be no harm to you!"

Fleming's fingers jabbed into Bryan's leg.

"Let's fuck off," he whispered fiercely.

"Where, for Jesus' sake?"

"Out of this bastard ambush!"

A rifle cracked and flashed to the front and right. The bullet whined harmlessly over them. More rifles began firing. From the muzzle flashes, Bryan saw that they were, in fact, encircled.

Suddenly, behind him, Tom Reagan began firing back, aiming at the flashes in the darkness.

"Shit!" Bryan exclaimed, not bothering to lower his voice. He shouldered his rifle and returned fire as well.

The torch beams converged on the four men crouching by

the wall. Bullets from the Free State troops began whizzing and snapping off the stones around and behind them.

Fleming scrambled on all fours alongside Bryan.

"We'll be massacred here!" he cried. "Let's away now."

"We're surrounded, fuck it!"

"Not if we go down the cliffs."

"In this weather?"

"I know it blindfolded. Come on else we'll be plugged where we are."

Bryan shrugged. The only alternatives were surrender or death, perhaps both.

"You lead then," he told Jinty Fleming. "And you better know what you're at!"

"Right. Over the wall," Fleming ordered. "We'll have to run their fire."

The four of them scrambled over the wall, stones collapsing about them, bruising shins and elbows, and began running across a field.

They crouched low, rifles thrust before them, firing at the flashes all around. The rain beat into their faces, chilling and spiky, soaking through their thin, torn clothes.

"Watch ahead!" Bryan screamed at Fleming, noticing the flash of a rifle directly in front.

"At him, boys!" Fleming shouted back, fear lost in the exultation of mortal danger.

Their weapons jumped in their hands as, somehow, they fired and reloaded, feet tripping over the sodden tussocks in the field.

Ahead, someone screamed in agony. The shooting all about them seemed to grow quicker and fiercer. People were cursing at the top of their voices. A whistle blew shrilly. Torches weaved and bobbed as the Free Staters gave chase. The sounds of the waves below the cliffs became louder.

"Stop! Stop!" Fleming shrieked, flinging both arms out, but Bryan's momentum carried him on, and the two collided, desperately trying to keep their balance, swaying together on the edge of the cliff. When they looked down they saw the phosphorescence of the breaking, swirling waves.

Following Fleming, they dropped to their hands and knees and crawled along the edge of the cliff.

They crawled for perhaps twenty yards before Fleming found what he was seeking, the start of a narrow path leading steeply downwards. The sounds of pursuit behind were drowned by the angry seas below.

"On your bums," he whispered. "Slide easy but hang on for your life! It's mighty slippy."

Down and down they went, the path nearly vertical in places, their fingers and heels digging into the wet mixture of soil, sand and pebbles. Once, they seemed to be hanging directly over the sea foaming and beating against the outcrop of rocks below.

"Watch it! Be careful!" Fleming called after almost two minutes of frantic slipping and slithering, their fear and exertion mingling perspiration with the rain plastering their faces.

"We're nearly there!"

Seconds later, Fleming vanished from sight.

Bryan was left with his legs dangling over a ledge with, apparently, nothing between himself and the sea.

"Drop down!"

Fleming's order came out of the blinding, stinging rain.

"What? Where? Jinty, where, for God's sake?" Bryan called. "I'm not seeing a thing."

"Just drop. There's a ledge below. Just drop. I'll be catching you . . . maybe." Fleming laughed gruesomely, regaining his usual humor now he considered himself safe.

Bryan sucked in a deep breath, closed his eyes and pushed himself over the edge.

Although the fall was shorter than he had expected, his knees still gave way with the impact on rock.

Fleming grabbed him and pulled him into the stygian darkness of a cave, its mouth high enough to be entered without stooping.

Paddy Swift and Tom Reagan quickly followed. All four rested against the wet rocks of the cave walls.

Once or twice, a curtain of spray lashed across the cave entrance but they were so wet already that they didn't bother to move away.

"What now, Jinty?" Bryan asked after a few minutes. "We'll perish with cold where we are."

"Don't worry," Fleming replied cheerfully. "Just follow me. Hang on to my arm."

He led them ten paces back into the cave and around a slight bend.

"Right. Here we are," he announced. "As far as we go."

"It'd be fine," Bryan said sarcastically. "If only we could see where the fuck we were."

"Hang on," Fleming replied grumpily. "Just hang on."

The others listened while he scrabbled around the cave, swearing loudly when his knuckles scraped painfully against rock. Then they heard the sound of matches striking, before a flickering, yellow light suffused the cave. Fleming lifted the stub of a candle and held it above his head.

"There!" he said proudly. "Have a look at the safest hide-out a man ever had."

They could see that they were standing upright in a squarish cave about six feet wide and five feet long, its roof a comfortable foot higher than Bryan, the tallest of them. Its deep brown walls were shinily damp. Water plopped down steadily from several parts of the roof. In one corner, presumably the driest, there was a small pile of sacking.

Bryan nodded, half-doubting, half-approving.

"Where did you get all this luxury, Jinty?" he asked. "Candles and bedding?"

"And sure haven't I been using this place since I was a wee 'un. Came in mighty handy when the Tans were around, so it did."

"I can imagine," Swift said drily. "So what do we do now?"

"Wait for the Staters to get tired of looking for us. That's what we do."

"Won't they find us?" Bryan asked.

"They might and then again they might not. And if they do . . . well, you'll see at first light what problems they'll have."

The four of them spent the night huddled together for

warmth, the sacking wrapped around them. In the early morning, when the sky was turning from black to grey, Jinty Fleming led them to the entrance of the cave.

"Holy Mother, Jesus and all the Saints!" Bryan exclaimed, truly awed, when he gazed out at the landscape above and beneath the cave.

At the foot of the cliff, long ridges of rock ran out, finger-like, to meet and split the foaming breakers. The cave was clearly a mixture of a rock fault and a small hollow beaten out of the cliff by the wind and rain of centuries. It stood ten yards above the apex of a horseshoe-shaped creek with high lichen-covered boulders flaunting their invincibility above the dashing sea. Above, ledges of rock jutted and arched out, effectively shielding the mouth of the cave from all but a few dangerously exposed parts of the clifftop.

The position, Bryan realized immediately, was totally impregnable except from the narrow path or from the ridges of rock within reach of the breakers.

Fleming pointed down to the huge boulders running out from the creek.

"That's our way of escaping if they should be finding us," he remarked. "At the end of them . . . see, there . . . there's another path winding round the cliffs to the next headland. It's difficult but I've made it before."

"In daylight?" Swift asked dubiously.

"Yes."

"Not in the dark?"

"No."

"We'll see when the time comes, if it should," Bryan said. "Right now I'm just wishing we had some food."

"How long do we wait?" Reagan asked seriously.

"Until we're certain the Staters have gone," Bryan replied tersely.

The four sat in the cave entrance watching the breakers below, marvelling at their power and rhythm, drawing the salt-tanged air into their lungs, trying not to think of their hunger.

Then all at once, a shower of pebbles clattered on to the narrow ledge in front of them.

"Jesus!" Fleming exclaimed, jumping up and reaching for his rifle. "Someone's coming!"

The others scrambled for their weapons.

But before Bryan could give any orders, Fleming and Reagan had stood on tiptoe, thrust their rifles over the overhanging arch of rock and fired upwards.

The Free State soldier sliding down the path from the clifftop grunted like a stuck pig, rose to his knees, one hand reaching for beardless cheek, and tumbled headlong down the path and over the edge.

A drawn-out scream echoed against the cliff-face while he turned in mid-air, frightening the birds who fluttered off their nests, mewing and screeching. Their cries continued, a requiem for the hapless soldier as he smashed onto the jagged boulders at the water's edge.

The sea gathered up his limp, shattered body, cradling it, rolling it back and forth gently, drawing it through the pinched mouth of the small creek and into the boundless ocean.

"There's another!" Reagan cried, working the bolt on his rifle, forcing another bullet into the breech. He and Fleming fired again.

The second Free State soldier was by this time scrabbling back up the path to safety, digging frantically into the earth for a hold.

He arched upwards when the two bullets ripped into the back of his green uniform jacket and was dead before he, too, tumbled down the cliff, spinning and twisting in the air, bouncing sickeningly off the boulders and into the spewing foam.

As Bryan watched the two soldiers fall to their deaths, he realized that something quite irrevocable had occurred in his life. He was now committed, as were his companions, to the final fight. He could find no words of reproach for Jinty Fleming or Tom Reagan.

"Inside!" he cried. "Get inside! There'll be hell on earth let loose now!"

It took some minutes for the Free State troops at the top of the cliff to fully appreciate what had happened.

The commander of the cycling corps who had laid the

ambush, Bryan's old comrade, Paddy Murphy, had merely
sent his two soldiers on a reconnaissance down the path. As
far as Captain Murphy was concerned the fugitives had
vanished. The path was one of the last places for a routine
check before calling off the search.

Now, he was both angry at his men's deaths and excited
that at last he could get to grips with an elusive prey. He
wasn't even sure who was in the cave. Jinty Fleming was
one, he knew from interrogating the Republican's sister. But
the others? She wouldn't say. The original information
about four armed men frequenting the Fleming woman's
cabin had been too sketchy to give any further clues about
identities. Perhaps, Murphy thought, the others could be
important? Perhaps one of them was even Eamon de Valera
himself? After all, the Republican leader had been reported
to be skulking around the West.

Murphy's first action was to send his junior officer into
Ballynaskreena with instructions to wire divisional headquarters at Tralee that, as Murphy termed them, "prominent
irregulars" were in the cave and that reinforcements were
needed.

Next, he gathered his senior men around him and worked
out a plan of attack. Clearly, an assault down the cliff was
tantamount to suicide. Other tactics were needed.

In the cave itself, forty or so yards below, Bryan and his
companions grimly readied themselves for battle. None of
them had any illusions about their chances of survival. In
daylight, they were trapped, unable to move. They would
have to take what was coming.

Bryan did tentatively offer an alternative. He felt, that as
leader, he was honor bound to do so.

"We could be showing a white flag," he suggested.
"Maybe they'd take us prisoners."

"Fat chance," Swift grunted, his round, freckled face
set with grave determination. "They'll pot us like clay
pigeons!"

"I was only thinking last night we'd had too good a run
for our money," said Reagan.

"Aye," Swift added, grinning maliciously at Bryan.

"And now we've nowhere else to run to, even if we were wanting to."

"Maybe, before those soldiers, we could have given up," Fleming said. "But they'll be awful mad now, I'm thinking. Awful mad."

"Can you be blaming them?" Bryan replied. He squinted out to sea through the sights of his rifle.

"You're saying we did wrong?" Reagan asked bitingly.

"No . . . no . . . I'm not saying that, Tom. I was only thinking there'll be some weeping mothers before this is over," Bryan said simply, moving to the cave entrance.

An image of Hannah breast-feeding baby Joseph flashed into his mind. He thrust it away, irritated at his own sentimentality.

From above he heard shouted orders, indistinct in the moaning wind of "scoriveen," followed swiftly by the clatter of pebbles falling on to the ledge.

"They're here!" Bryan shouted, lifting on to his toes and peering over the protective arch above the cave. The others dashed to join him.

To Bryan's amazement, all he could see was a wall of orange and black flame trundling down the path toward him. It took a full second for him to realize that, in fact, the Free Staters had set light to bales of hay and pushed them over the cliff.

"Holy Mother!" he shouted. "Back, boys! Back into the cave!"

He cannoned into his companions as he dropped down. Jinty Fleming had to grab Reagan by his jacket lapels to stop his teetering over the narrow ledge.

They cowered at the back of the cave. The flaming bales, parcelled with sods of turf, slid over the arch and hit the ledge just outside. Most disintegrated and continued their blazing way to the rocks below, again disturbing the gulls and cormorants.

But two of the bales wedged themselves into the mouth of the cave, spitting red-hot sparks and billowing smoke.

The onshore wind drove the smoke into the back of the cave, blinding the fugitives, cutting deep into their throats and chests.

"Oh, Jesus!" Bryan choked, eyes streaming and raw.

"We're suffocating," wailed Paddy Swift, burying his head in his hands, twisting back into the cave walls.

"Hang on!" Bryan cried.

He grabbed one of the pieces of damp sacking, pulled it over his head and crawled towards the cave entrance, now invisible in the smoke and flame.

With his rifle barrel outstretched, he pushed and prodded at the burning bales, shoving them inch by inch out on to the ledge. Sparks singed the hairs on the back of his hands.

Finally, when he thought his lungs would burst, first one bale and then the other toppled away toward the rocks below.

Within a minute, the keen wind from the sea had chased the smoke from the cave. They were safe again for the time being.

In the next eight hours, however, while daylight held, the Republicans had to resist three more attempts to smoke them out or, perhaps, burn them alive. The Free Staters used burning hay once more before throwing down blazing bedsheets, presumably gathered from nearby cabins, soaked in oil, tar and a sulphurous compound.

Some of the local people watching from the clifftop thought at times that the very cliff itself would be consumed in the raging flames and their cloying, clinging, creeping smoke.

But, to everyone's amazement, the wind miraculously changed direction and blew the flames out to sea.

Captain Murphy was as baffled and frustrated as the fugitives were surprised and thankful.

That night, the Free State Army officer placed snipers in positions along the top of the cliff where they could gain a slight view at an extreme angle of the cave entrance.

Then, by rope, he lowered a lantern hoping to illuminate an unsuspecting target.

Paddy Swift showed himself for just long enough to place a bullet through the lantern before the snipers could sight him properly.

It was stalemate.

That night, the Republicans slept reasonably well in their

cave, perceptibly warmed by all the flames which had danced around them during the day.

They were woken at first light by the crash of a grenade detonating by the ledge. It was the first of many. The Free State troops hurled down mines as well as grenades and constantly peppered the entrance with bullets from a machine-gun position established on the clifftop. Some bullets whined and cracked inside the cave, ricocheting from wall to wall.

The Republicans huddled at the back, unable to speak in the cacophony of violence, ears deafened by constant explosions, terrified by the hissing, whirling splinters of rock.

To make their ordeal worse, an onshore gale began to blow, driving the sea into a frenzy, smashing great spumes of spray up the cliff-face, drenching the cave. Soon, inches of salt water slopped around the Republicans' refuge.

By late afternoon, Bryan was ready to concede defeat.

The bombardment had slackened off with grenades exploding at only ten-minute intervals. Even those were warnings of what would come when the onslaught was renewed.

It was a miracle that none of the four had been injured so far by bullets, shrapnel or rock but their physical damage could hardly have been greater.

Nerves were in shreds. Bodies ached with damp, cold and hunger. Eyes were bloodshot and raw from lack of proper rest and the continual barrage of salt spray piercing inwards to every cranny of the cave.

Their safety matches were sodden.

They faced the night without light, without a comforting cigarette.

The four looked at each other, despair in their haggard, unshaven faces. None of them wanted to be the first to state the obvious.

"We'll have to go," Bryan said finally flatly. "We can't be taking this any more."

"Surrender, you mean?" asked Fleming dully.

"Whatever you want. Whatever you think best. We're all equal now. There are no more leaders."

"What are you wanting then?" said Swift, his hunger so acute that it no longer pained him.

"It's not for me," Bryan replied. "We either give up . . ."

". . . and get murdered," interrupted Reagan.

". . . or we try Jinty's escape route."

"It's a chance anyway, isn't it?" Fleming said eagerly. "One way we're certain dead. The other, we've at least a chance."

"You're agreed then?" asked Bryan. "An escape?"

"Aye," the three chorused wearily.

They waited until late into the evening before setting off, leaving their rifles covered with sacking in the furthest corner of the cave.

The night was dark and without stars. The gale had abated. But the sea was still in torment when they crept out of the cave and lowered themselves gingerly over the edge.

They slid as noiselessly as they could down the steep incline of the cliff-face until their boots crunched into the thin strip of pebbles at its base. Any sounds they made, Bryan reckoned, would be masked by the grinding surge of the breakers dragging the shingle back and forth.

The four stayed close together in the impenetrable blackness of the great cliff's shadow.

Jinty Fleming led them on to the first of the large, flat boulders curving out into the ocean.

At first, it was easy going, jumping from one boulder to the other, but soon the rocks became slippery with seaweed. And then they came to the boulders washed by the breakers at low tide. The possessive, seeking sea lapped and tore at their precarious footholds.

First Fleming, then Reagan overbalanced and splashed up to their thighs in the icy water. Each time, they were hauled back on to the ring of boulders which would eventually lead, they hoped, to safety.

By now, the four of them were freezing and exhausted. Fleming was becoming increasingly distressed, taking the brunt of the wind and the waves.

He paused more and more often, gazing this way and

that, clearly uncertain of his way in the darkness lit only by the sea's murky phosphorescence.

"Are you fine, Jinty?" Bryan shouted from the back. "Can we be making it?"

He wasn't sure that his voice carried against the elements. He looked around and thought he saw, high up, the glowing fires warming the Free State Army troops on guard on top of the cliff. They vanished when the clouds moved again. The blackness descended.

Jinty Fleming half-turned. In profile, Bryan could see him mouthing some words. Then he leaned, bent sideways and toppled off the boulder and into the breaking waves. He uttered no sound, simply lifted an appalled, white face, upwards, eyes closed, before disappearing from view, before the ravenous sea closed over him.

Bryan spun around instinctively, looking for an escape from what he now saw was a death trap. There could be no escape in this darkness, in this weather. He didn't think of Paddy Swift and Tom Reagan, men who had shared so much with him. He thought only of self-preservation in this wilderness of wind and sea and spray.

When he turned back to the two men still in his charge, they were no longer there.

The breakers had dragged them down, without a sound.

Suddenly, above and to the side of him, a searchlight beamed out from the top of the cliff, cutting through the night.

Its single tentacle reached out to Bryan and embraced him as he stood motionless amid the torrent.

He was so weary and so cold that he hardly felt the sniper's lucky bullet rip down through the rib cage on the right side of his chest.

The crushing impact pushed him sideways into the sea. For a second, he panicked, trying not to take the water into his mouth, attempting to keep breathing.

The effort was too great.

He only had time to wonder why the stars had appeared in the sky. One of them had the face of his wife, smiling.

Chapter 11
April, 1923

In the morning, when the Free State Army soldiers looked over the cliffs near Ballynaskreena, they saw two bodies rolling in the swell of the horseshoe-shaped creek.

They knew that their sniper had probably hit one of the Republicans. The second body suggested to them that all the fugitives had been trying to escape when disaster overtook them. But they remembered what had happened on the first day of the siege and were loath to descend the cliff.

Eventually, Captain Paddy Murphy ordered the launching of a boat from the inlet just around the headland. Five soldiers were rowed around to the head of the creek, directly opposite to the cave. Two of them held iron shutters for protection.

They waited nervously for a couple of minutes, backing oars, but all was silence except for the waves, the sighing wind and the seabirds' cries.

Machine-gunners and snipers on the clifftop covered what little they could see of the ledge outside the cave while the boat maneuvered into the creek and came alongside one of the bodies.

Only then did the tension relax. The troops knew that the siege of Ballynaskreena Caves was over. They cheered with delight and congratulated each other as the bodies were landed at the base of the cliffs.

Ropes and blankets were lowered down the cliff-face. Amid joking and ribald remarks, the bodies were secured and hauled to the top, banging limply against the rocky outcrops.

They were laid on the grass and the coverings pulled from their faces. Captain Murphy looked at Jinty Fleming's cut and bruised features impassively, wondering who the dead man was. He decided to show the body locally for identification.

He moved to the second body. At first he didn't recognize the swollen, yellowish face with open mouth and staring, salt-rimmed eyes. Then he gagged with nausea and turned away to vomit his breakfast on to the ground.

The excited chatter around him was stilled.

"You're knowing him, sir?" someone asked quietly.

Captain Murphy nodded, wiping his mouth with a handkerchief. He gazed down at the body again.

"It's Bryan Aherne from Listowel."

A soldier whistled through his teeth. "One of the big 'uns, eh? Jesus, he looks so young."

"He does that," the captain replied. "But he's been fighting an awful long time. Since he was at school, I hear tell. He was in gaol too and then at Gortaglonna."

"Aye, a miracle that was."

"Yes, he's fought all the way for the Republic. You have to give him that, the Lord have mercy on him."

"Amen," the soldiers muttered in unison.

"Was he a friend of yours then, sir?" one of them asked curiously, sympathetically.

Captain Murphy straightened up.

"At one time, he was close . . . when we were together in the flying column. But you can't have friendships in a civil war. I won't be remembering him as a friend: I've been chasing him too long for that. But, by God, I'll be telling my children about him. You can't be forgetting a soldier like he was."

He clicked to attention and saluted, standing motionless by the body for nearly a minute, the ocean breeze ruffling the skirts of his trenchcoat.

Later, the soldiers placed Bryan's body carefully in the back of a truck, covered it with a tricolor and took it to the mortuary in the old workhouse at Listowel.

Captain Murphy himself drove out to Galey Bridge to

break the news to Hannah. She didn't cry, merely clasped Joseph tighter to herself.

She didn't speak during the journey to the mortuary, just listened as the captain outlined what had happened at Ballynaskreena.

She didn't flinch even when they asked her to formally identify her husband, simply nodded and stepped up to the coffin.

Baby Joseph, a year and a bit old, wriggled in her arms as she looked down at Bryan.

Captain Murphy moved beside her, offering to take the child. Hannah shook his hand away angrily.

"Let him see his da," she said bitterly, thrusting the baby over the coffin. "He'll have precious little else to remember 'cept his dying. And I won't be letting him forget who caused that."

Joseph began to cry.

Hannah left dry-eyed, a deal of her weeping done in the months of anticipation of this day and this scene. She refused to hold a wake and buried Bryan in Listowel graveyard two days later.

The same day, April 27th, 1923, Eamon de Valera signed a proclamation on behalf of the "Republican Government," ordering a suspension of all offensive action by the Irish Republican Army.

BOOK
TWO

Chapter 1
January 11th, 1971

A foghorn sounded mournfully from the murk of Belfast Lough. Flurries of snow whirled off the Black Mountain looming above the city and whipped stingingly down the mean little terraces huddling between its dark shadow and the curving shore of the lough, dominated by the shipyard's huge mobile crane.

An occasional car drove cautiously through the yellow-streaked slush, bumping over one of the ramps built into the road at strategic intervals. The driver deliberately didn't look up at the firing slits in the Army sentry posts, standing like children's tree-houses by the ramps, covered with brown and green camouflage nets and wire mesh to stop a well-directed nail or pipe bomb. He didn't want to appear too interested in the dark gun barrels which moved fractionally to cover his progress until he was out of sight. Menace so pervaded his life that, for life to be at all bearable, it had to be ignored.

Above him, watchful, the soldiers stamped their feet to keep passably warm and offered a year's pay to be anywhere other than the capital of Her Majesty's Province of Northern Ireland on this freezing night.

The boredom of barracks in West Germany, the humidity of Hong Kong, the drill sergeants of Aldershot and Catterick Camps, the insects of Belize, were preferable to Belfast. And the cramped billets in drafty halls and over-crowded police barracks were infinitely preferable to those isolated vigils, peering into the night, nerves stretched, watching and noting every movement in a city divided against itself by centuries of hatred and blood.

A light flashed on the switchboard of the information room on the ground floor of Army headquarters in Thiepval Barracks just outside Lisburn.

The duty information officer leaned wearily forward, picked up the phone and flicked down a switch. It was a friendly journalist, someone who could be trusted, not hostile to or questioning of the Army's job.

"Hello, old boy," the information officer murmured. "Don't you fellas ever sleep?"

"Just a final check, old man."

"What was the last number then?"

"Thirty-six."

The information officer ran his finger down the list of numbered entries for the day's incidents. There had been one more since that particular journalist had called a couple of hours earlier.

"Right, old boy. Just one. Thirty-seven. Not much, I'm afraid. Bit of stoning in Cupar Street after a Saracen ran over someone's dog. All quiet now though."

"Prod or Taig?"

"What, old boy?"

"The fucking dog! Protestant or Catholic?"

The information officer flushed momentarily before he realized the journalist was joking.

"Doesn't say, old boy. Sorry," he laughed.

"Must be Jewish then . . . and tell your boys always to get the fucking religion otherwise we're all up the pipe in this last outpost of Western civilization."

"Too true, old boy."

"Anything else in the wind?"

"Quiet as the grave. They won't be out on a night like this."

The information officer suddenly remembered a conversation he'd heard around the bar in the officer's mess. "Hang on," he added. "There might be something early afternoon so keep in touch."

The journalist's slightly slurred voice sharpened with interest.

"What's that?" he demanded.

"Can't say yet."

"Come on, old man. Give us a clue."

"Can't really. Not yet. Don't know much about it myself but they're quite excited upstairs about some capture they've made."

"Arms?"

"Don't know. Really, old boy. Just keep in touch, there's a good chap. I'm only giving you a word to the wise."

The journalist sighed, not unduly disappointed. He had more pressing business than cross-examining a friendly contact.

"Okay, old man. Thanks for the tip. Sleep tight."

"In this bloody office with every newshound from here to Timbuctoo around my neck? You must be joking!"

"Just think of the overtime, old man," the journalist guffawed, putting down the receiver on the phone on the reception desk in the Midland Hotel, next to York Street railway station, near the center of Belfast. He winked familiarly at the girl behind the desk, picked up his glass of Bushmills Black Label whiskey and sauntered across the hotel's lounge toward a discreet table in the corner.

There he resumed his courteous, though unnecessary, wooing of the pretty wife of a faraway merchant navy officer, affectionately nicknamed by more than one of his colleagues as "The Glengormly Gobbler."

At Army headquarters, the information officer, slightly refreshed by his latest conversation, put his feet up on the nearest desk and carried on reading a green-covered booklet, issued by the Ministry of Defense, entitled "Aid to Civil Power."

It was the distillation of Army wisdom gained in emergencies from India to Kenya, from Aden to Cyprus. The booklet laid down the guidelines of how soldiers should behave when dealing with, for instance, rioting civilians. Its advice was academic and useless to the Army in Northern Ireland. New rules had to be learned, ever since the province's Prime Minister Major, James Chichester Clark, had officially asked the British Government on August 14th, 1969, to send the Army to the aid of his government, to aid the civil authorities. After weeks and months of rioting between Catholics and Protestants, that well-meaning farmer turned somewhat unwilling political leader had decided that the police could no longer cope with the extreme situation of civil unrest which was being fanned and exploited by a hitherto almost extinct Irish Republican Army. However, the information officer on night duty found the booklet's contents reminiscent of the great days of Empire, of long-lost certainty and confidence and conviction, when the enemy invariably had black, brown or yellow faces.

Not far across the road from Thiepval Barracks, down a cul-de-sac of identical houses, Major Stephen Gates, Senior Ammunition Technical Officer (SATO) of the Royal Army Ordnance Corps in Northern Ireland, stirred fitfully in the front bedroom of his two-story married quarters. He eased his arm across the back of his wife, Elizabeth, neither of them yet fully asleep, both conscious of the presence next door of their youngest daughter, Mary.

The major clasped a gentle, if unusually large hand around his wife's right breast and pressed his lower body against hers. These days he found it difficult to fall asleep straight away, always waiting for the telephone to summon him to give advice about a difficult bomb discovered by one of his Explosive Ordnance Disposal (EOD) units.

Apart from the problems of bomb disposal, he was also wondering about the interview planned for next morning with the man captured by 1st Battalion of the Parachute Regiment.

From previous experience, he'd found that such interviews with known bomb-designers like Seamus Aherne always caused frustration and disappointment. His scientific skills allowed him to deal well enough with their explosive devices. His personality, however, often abrupt, sometimes arrogant, rarely helped him understand their motivations, despite his own family's distant Irish connections. After the interviews, the major knew, he invariably drank two too many pints of Bass bitter in the mess, which inevitably led to a whiskey or three. But his position as the senior bomb disposal officer demanded the interview and he was never one to shirk his duty, however unpleasant.

The ways of a terrorist bomber also occupied the mind of Edward S. Aicheson as he pushed through the heavy plastic doors leading to the children's medical ward in the Royal Victoria Hospital, on the corner of Grosvenor Road and Falls Road in Belfast.

The young surgeon had stayed on late, rather than returning to his rented flat in the suburb of Dunmurry, to monitor the condition of the two-year-old boy rushed to the hospital that evening after the explosion in a car in Bedford Street, just outside the local, fortress-like headquarters of the British Broadcasting Corporation.

He walked quickly up to the night sister's dimly lit desk in the middle of the ward.

"How's he going?" the surgeon asked softly.

"The wee 'un from the bomb, sir? He's holding his own. Staff Nurse Anderson's with him."

"I'll take a look." The nasal tone of his Massachusetts voice cut through her broad Ulster accent. The surgeon pulled aside the flower-printed curtains and gazed down on the small figure lying motionless in the high-sided cot. For an instant, rage seared through him as he saw the bandaged head and the tiny face, parchment pale and pitted with angry specks of gravel and glass.

"He's quiet, sir," the staff nurse by the cot whispered.

Aicheson nodded and leaned over the boy, noting his shallow breathing and the slight tremor in one of the small hands lying outside the coverlet. He gently rolled up one eyelid and then the other, peering into the boy's pupils. He was deeply unconscious. The surgeon grimaced. Was it brain damage needing surgery, or merely a deep concussion, serious as that might be in one so young?

That had been Aicheson's concern ever since the boy had been admitted. The superficial injuries caused when the explosion flung him and his mother through the window of the Chinese restaurant had been quickly cleaned by the nurses in the casualty department. They would heal in time. The worry had been the slight sign of pressure on the boy's brain shown by the first X-rays. There would have to be further tests in the morning. For now, Aicheson decided, rest and quiet would do the boy as much good as anything.

"Tell Sister of the slightest change, Staff," he said.

"Of course, sir."

Immediately, Aicheson realized he might have sounded tactlessly patronizing. The nurses at the hospital were among the most experienced in the world. They had to be to cope with the appalling carnage brought daily to the "Royal Vic."

"Of course you will, Staff," he added with a half-apologetic smile. "Good night."

Edward S. Aicheson, graduate of Harvard Medical School, intern and then surgeon at Peter Bent Brigham Hospital on Huntington Avenue in Boston, drove home, tired and despairing of human nature.

For the umpteenth time, he asked himself how any person could knowingly plant bombs which caused such indiscriminate and dreadful hurt to ordinary, innocent people like the little boy he'd just left. What kind of men and women were these?

He thumped the steering wheel of his car angrily. "The bastards!" he cried out loud. "Just who the hell do they think they are?"

Not ten miles away, in his basement cell at Holywood Barracks, a slightly different question of identity was keeping Joseph Aherne's son Seamus from much-needed sleep. He was wondering exactly which two IRA men had been killed when their Cortina car exploded by the BBC while they were trying to deliver their bomb to its target.

He shuffled through mental photographs of members of the Active Service Units of the three IRA battalions in Belfast. After a few minutes he decided it was fruitless trying to guess who the unfortunates might be. He knew that he'd be told soon enough if that sergeant had been telling the truth and his next sleeping place was really to be the Republican wing of Crumlin Prison. His fellow inmates would know. Seamus just hoped the bomb's premature explosion hadn't been caused by a fault in his design. The vast majority of bombs in Belfast at that moment had been made—and were being made—from his blueprints.

Seamus was fairly cynical about how blame was apportioned by the IRA's hierarchy whenever a bomb went wrong.

He, as designer, was top of the carefully worked-out pyramid of responsibility. Below him were the bomb electrician who wired the circuitry to his instructions and the bomb carpenter who built the wooden or metal container, designed to make the task of the bomb disposal officer as difficult and dangerous as possible. From them, the half-finished bomb would be passed on to the bomb officer whose job was to supply and insert the explosive. He would pass the completed device to the bomb-layer, responsible for getting it to the target. But Seamus knew that at the base of the deadly pyramid and the most expendable were the youngsters recruited to steal and drive the vehicles carrying the bomb.

Seamus guessed it was the latter who'd died earlier that night. It usually was.

The IRA's formal committees of inquiry, court-martial and memoranda would undoubtedly push some of the blame for the disaster back up the pyramid to the designer, even if he had been in Army custody when it exploded.

He sighed at the thought.

Chapter 2
January 12th, 1971 (a.m.)

Major Stephen Gates sat at the desk in the interrogation room in the basement of Holywood Barracks perusing the slim, orange file containing all the intelligence and background information that the Army and the Royal Ulster Constabulary had gathered about Seamus Aherne.

Beside him, Captain Charles Briance, a young Ammunition Technical Officer recently posted to Northern Ireland, leafed through the preliminary report supplied by the officer of the 1st Battalion Parachute Regiment who'd detained Seamus.

"Anything there?" the major grunted, brushing an errant lock of pepper-and-salt hair back off his forehead.

"Not a lot, sir. Picked up watching that bomb scene in Botanic Gardens. Smart piece of work by the patrol sergeant . . ."

"Cheeky sod!"

"Sir?"

"Presumably trying to see how we dealt with his brutes."

"Presumably."

"Shouldn't have been so nosey, should be? Has he said much?"

"Not a lot. Seemed a bit surprised that we had a snap of him from his days at the Irish Post Office training school at Dublin Castle."

"Uh-huh."

"Mentioned his father apparently. Asked for a call to him."

"Joseph Aherne?"

"Affirmative."

"Well, old Joe's in my book of words too. Into bombs from way back when. In and out of internment like a yo-yo."

"Hardly a surprise, sir."

"Runs in the family."

"Not an offense though, is it?" the young officer said tentatively.

"Don't be naive, Charley," the major replied wearily, striking a match to light a slim Panatella cigar. He blinked his pale blue eyes as the pungent smoke curled around his face. "We've known about Aherne for a year or more from the usual sources. He's not much good at present but with his technical training from the Post Office and the right instructor he could be a proper pain in the you-know-what. That's why he's got to be nipped in the bud now."

"Of course, sir. Shall we have him in?"

Captain Briance walked to the door, straightening the sleeves of his olive-green pullover. On his right sleeve, as on the major's, was the tiny flash of orange and yellow flame rising above a black circle that identified them as bomb disposal officers.

The captain opened the door and gave an order to the sergeant outside.

"Just wait one," the major called from the desk. "Let's have the sarn't in."

"Suh?" barked the NCO standing at attention in the doorway.

"At ease, Sarn't," murmured the major. "Tell us what the skull's been like while you've had him."

"Bit pushy at first, suh, if you know what I mean. Usual guff about his rights when he got over his first fright. He's settled down now . . . good as gold really. Hasn't had much sleep, of course, suh."

"I see. Do you think he'll talk?"

"Not really for me to say, suh. I can tell you though he doesn't like being hurt."

The major looked up sharply, lips pursed around the glowing cigar.

"Hurt, Sarn't?"

The sergeant reddened slightly. His eyes fixed on an imaginary dot on the wall above the officer's head.

"Stumbled once or twice when we picked him up, if you know what I mean, suh."

Major Gates shook his head slowly from side to side, glaring from under heavy eyebrows. "Yes, I do see what you mean," he said with deliberate irony. "Fetch him along now and make sure he doesn't stumble again."

"Suh!"

The sound of the sergeant's boots clacked away down the corridor, a door clanged open, and then the boots returned, accompanied by the scuff of a softer tread.

"Aherne, suh," the sergeant boomed, propelling his prisoner into the room before shutting the door and resuming his vigil outside.

Major Gates surveyed Seamus's laceless shoes, the unbelted trousers he was holding up with his hands, and his unshaven face and tired eyes.

He saw a dark-haired young man with thin, symmetrical features that gave an impression of experience combined with youthful vulnerability. His eyes met the prisoner's and held them for a moment, before he looked down to his file again.

"Sit down, Aherne," the captain muttered, embarrassed as always at meeting an enemy face-to-face.

Seamus lowered himself wearily into the chair in front of the desk, not once taking his eyes off the stockily-built major with his ruddy, outdoor complexion.

"I'm Major Gates, SATO, and this is Captain Briance, one of my ATOs."

Seamus opened his mouth to reply. The major interrupted coldly.

"Just shut up, laddie, for the moment. I'll tell you when to talk. Right?"

Seamus nodded. The major's authority was so clearly paramount that, for a split second, he thought he was back before his old headmaster at the National School in Listowel.

"Now, young Seamus, you probably realize that we

know all about you and your little tricks. We've been trying
to meet you ever since you arrived on the scene here—when
was it? Fifteen months ago? . . . but we've waited patiently for the pleasure and now here we are. Do you know
I've a ruddy great map in my office with lots of little pins
stuck into it? They're colored green just for you and your
bombs, laddie. Every last one of them. Your handiwork is
quite unmistakable, you know. Very neat way with the
wiring you have, just like they taught you to wire telephone
bells at Dublin Castle. Very good. And your bomb officer?"
The major shrugged. ". . . well, he really should try to
find some new explosive. That Quarrex stolen from the
Enfield munition factory is much too obvious. As soon as
we see that sandy muck, we offer up a small prayer of
thanks to you and your Third Battalion quartermaster."

Seamus shook his head, truly puzzled.

Major Gates smiled knowingly, perhaps patronizingly.

"Once we discover whose little device we're dealing
with, the rest is kid's play. By the book, that's your work,
laddie, and by the book is how we kill the brutes."

There was silence full of unspoken thoughts. Seamus
lowered his eyes.

"Ever thought of building bigger and better bombs,
laddie?" the major asked, a perceptibly harsher tone in his
voice.

"I don't . . ."

"Shut up, young Seamus, and listen to your Uncle
Stephen, will you? I'm just asking if you've some more
designs you're working on."

Seamus shook his head again, becoming somewhat
baffled at the direction of the questions. He hadn't expected
such a conversational, roundabout interrogation.

"Not even those new pipe bombs your boys are tossing
around. Very nasty, they are. Very unstable. Put in the old
co-op mix—your dad used to call it Pax, I wouldn't be
surprised—stick in a fuse, crimp one end and away you go.
Bit dangerous though, isn't it? Quite a few have lost their
fingers and hands, haven't they? Quite a few wingies on
your company's pension scheme, aren't there?"

"I don't know anything about these!" Seamus blurted out, needled that he should be connected with such notoriously shoddy devices.

Major Gates leaned back in his chair, face wreathed in cigar smoke and a benevolent smile.

"Good boy," he sighed. "Just knew you could be relied upon . . ."

"What do . . ."

"Nothing, laddie. Thought all along the pipes couldn't be your work. Shipped up from the south like the nail bombs, aren't they?"

The certainty in the major's voice, its very confidence, his own uncertainty, made Seamus begin to nod his head in agreement before he could stop himself.

"I'm not saying anything," he said defiantly, angry at having been tricked.

"No need, laddie. A nod's as good as a wink, isn't it, Captain Briance?"

"Indeed it is, sir."

"I don't know . . ."

"Shut up, laddie . . . tell me, are you religious?"

"Yes," Seamus replied without reflection. A clear image of Monsignor O'Sullivan came to him, standing before the altar of St. Mary's Church in Listowel, the sun shadowing a cross down the nave. Before he could think about the switch in questioning, the major spoke again.

"No, I mean religious religious, young Seamus," Major Gates persisted. "God knows, I'm a padre's man myself but I doubt if I'd claim I was religious."

"I'm a member of the Church."

"And you believe in the Church's teachings? Say, your Church's?"

"Indeed and why not?" Seamus replied, somewhat bewildered.

"In the sanctity of human life?"

"Oh, Jesus, do we have to go into this?" Seamus exclaimed, genuinely offended.

"Why not, laddie? This is all about religion, isn't it? Protestants against Catholics? Paisley versus the Pope?"

"We're not against Protestants. No way are we."

"Why are you killing and maiming them then?"

"We don't."

"But you do. You know you do."

"Not deliberately."

"That makes the difference, laddie?"

"Yes. The IRA are only against the forces of British imperialism."

"Imperialism? That's balls, laddie! You mean you're against us and the RUC?"

"Yes. No one else."

"And what happens to those who get in the way?"

"That's unfortunate. We don't mean to hurt them."

The accents beat against each other like tennis balls in a fast doubles rally.

"But if they are hurt?"

"Fortunes of war."

"What war? Have we declared war? Has the Irish Government? Have you?"

"We have."

"Bit one-sided, isn't it? We came in here with your people, your Catholics, cheering us to the rooftops. We were the great protectors. Now, suddenly, you say we're the enemy."

"You are. You're the occupying forces."

"But we've always been here. Just like the Protestants have."

"You're in part of Ireland. You're keeping the Border!"

"When did the pure Irish ever run Ireland? Hundreds of years ago. It's like us English saying to the Americans, 'Sorry, we've decided we still run your country.' It's like the Red Indians telling the Americans to give them the whole continent back. It's like the Aborigines saying they own Australia. Or the Maoris, New Zealand. For a people who seem to live in history, you're pretty poor on the subject. History, as they say, having writ, moves on, brother!"

"What's this about, anyway. You're talking rubbish. I don't have to . . ."

"You do what you're told, young Seamus, or you might

stumble some more against the toe-end of a filthy big army boot."

Major Gates was conscious of the captain's surprised, sideways glance. He lit another cigar, not taking his eyes off Seamus.

"Recognize these names—Frankie Sharpe, Donal Card, Alby Walsh?"

The question speared into Seamus's brain. He ran a hand through his dishevelled hair, trying to gain time, his mind exhausted, whirling at the change of direction.

"Of course, you do, don't you, laddie?" the major persisted.

"No."

"Oh, is that so?"

The major slowly picked up some photographs from the file on the desk, their backs to Seamus, and peered at them closely.

"You're sure?" he asked again. "Mind you, it's not the best likeness but I'd have sworn it was you, Seamus, going into the Collins club in Andersonstown with our Frankie."

"I don't . . ."

"You know our Frankie, don't you?" Major Gates went on casually. "The big man in the Rodger McCorley branch—Cumann, don't you call it?—of Sinn Fein in the area. Before he split with the official IRA, of course."

"I don't . . ." Seamus began to repeat but again he was interrupted.

"Of course not. You wouldn't would you, laddie? Not a good religious boy like you."

Seamus, brain numbing with confusion, hardly able to think logically, held up his hands, palm upwards and outwards, as if surrendering.

The bomb disposal officers looked quizzically at him.

"May—may—may I say something, for Jesus' sake?" the young man stammered.

The major shrugged. "Go ahead, laddie."

Seamus thought for a moment, sucking in a deep breath of stale air mingled with cigar smoke. "It's clear you think you know everything there is to know about me," he said.

"You've me down as someone who helps the bombers and nothing's going to change your mind, is it?"

"It'd have to be good," Captain Briance said drily.

"A southern Irishman up here," Major Gates interrupted, flicking through the file. "A man with your Republican background; the whispers in the pubs about you and your bombs; the photographs of you with known Belfast IRA; getting arrested at the scene of a bomb incident . . . Yes, it'd have to be good, young Seamus. Bloody good!"

"In other words, you're just playing cat and mouse with me. Nothing I say is going to convince you that I've sod all to do with this. All you want is for me to shop my friends . . ."

Major Gates rubbed his hand over his firm, jutting jaw.

". . . and I wouldn't be doing that even if I was who you say I am and I'm fucking not."

The major sighed as if Seamus's use of swear words distressed him.

"Just once more," he said quietly, "I'm interested really. If one of your bombs kills an innocent Protestant, say a little boy, can you go to your priest and ask forgiveness in the confessional?"

"I could ask."

"Will he grant it?"

"Most would."

"Most?"

"Yes."

"But how? You've taken life, innocent life."

"I wouldn't have meant to. And I'd be truly sorry that it had happened. And I'd ask forgiveness and accept a penance . . . Jesus, why am I telling you this?"

The major leaned over the desk and offered Seamus a cigar from the brown packet.

"I see you smoke from the color of your fingers. You better have it now before you head for the Crumlin. I don't think they'll be having them there."

He took out a box of Swan Vestas matches, throwing it to Seamus who lit the cigar.

"Last one, laddie?" Major Gates said, almost apologetically, when Seamus had taken his first puff of the cigar, coughing once as the smoke reached his lungs. "This is hypothetical. You know what that is?"

Seamus's look was sufficient.

Captain Briance, a non-smoker, rubbed a surreptitious knuckle across his right eye, discomfited by the smoke filling the room.

"Say, if the Pope declared that he'd excommunicate all members of the IRA. Say, if he announced that it was a mortal sin for anyone to belong. Do you think it'd make any difference to you?"

Seamus puffed on the cigar again, admiring the glow at the tip, the way the grey ash still clung.

"No," he replied after a second's silence. "It wouldn't make any difference."

"That's what I . . ."

"Because His Holiness would never do it."

"And that's what I thought as well."

They looked at each other. Major Gates leaned his right elbow on the desk and covered his eyes as if in prayer.

"We'd protect you if you talked," the officer said quietly. "You could leave the country with a new passport and maybe enough money to start somewhere else—Australia, New Zealand or the States even."

Seamus felt his left eyelid begin to quiver. He couldn't stop it. He shook his head, rubbing the eye, trying to rid himself of his tiredness and confusion. He smiled bitterly.

"You really don't know, do you? If I was telling you anything and then skipped, I might be safe for a year, maybe two, but they'd be finding me. They've friends wherever there are Irish, and that's about everywhere since you fucking Brits ruined this country. I'd have no chance. None at all."

"And what about your chances if we picked up the boys who've been calling around to your place in Andersonstown to see where their favorite bomb designer has vanished to? They might even get the idea that you'd shopped them. They'd be wrong, of course, laddie, but mistakes can happen. And in your case, I promise you they will."

Seamus slumped down in his chair, trying to evade the major's piercing stare. He was trapped and he knew it. He looked up at the ceiling, allowing the intensity of the mesh-covered light bulb to burn into his brain. "No names," he whispered. "No names, not one at all."

"All right then," the major continued, his voice low and insistent. "Who's your instructor?"

"Instructor?" Seamus grinned. "I go by the book just like you said. The American Army manual. It's all in there."

"Smuggled in?" asked Captain Briance, clearly surprised.

"No way. You just fucking buy them in Dublin. Most bookshops have them."

Major Gates coughed, flushing angrily at the captain's ingenuousness, knowing the answer was true.

"Right, laddie," he said menacingly. "Your last chance. Where are the bomb factories? Where are the bombs armed?"

Seamus bit his lip and then sighed deeply.

"I'm only knowing one and that's all you're having. Nothing else. Okay?"

"You're hardly in a position to bargain, laddie, but all right . . . just one thing . . . for now." Major Gates put both hands on the table, locking the fingers tightly together.

Seamus hesitated for a moment before muttering the address of a house off Cromac Street in the Markets district of West Belfast.

"What is it?" the major asked calmly, trying to keep his inner excitement from showing in the question.

"A factory. They've a weekly delivery of the stuff . . ."

"Explosive?"

"Aye . . . and I'm not knowing where that comes from!"

"How much?"

"Depends on what they're making."

"You haven't been putting much in the brutes recently."

"Maybe they're saving it up. I'm not knowing either way."

In fact Seamus did know but he wasn't going to tell about the plan, involving a large bomb, to ambush an Army patrol guarding a BBC transmitter in County Tyrone.

The major nodded, unsure. He thrust back his chair and stood up. "Show me," he ordered, walking over to the large street map of Belfast, colored orange and green, which had been on the wall during Seamus's first interrogation.

Seamus shuffled over, one hand holding up his trousers and gripping the cigar at the same time. With his free hand, he ran a finger over the map until he reached the street he'd mentioned, hard by the city's docks. The area on the map was colored green, denoting a Catholic enclave.

"Number Four, you said, laddie?"

The young man looked sideways at the major. He smiled faintly. "If you like . . . but I thought I said Number Seven."

"Right. Sit down again," muttered Major Gates.

"Now, young Seamus," he began when he'd resumed his seat. "If you've told the truth, we'll keep our side of the bargain. We'll let it be known that you said nothing, that you were a proper little hero. But if you send us on a wild goose chase, then . . ."

The major shrugged his shoulders.

Seamus nodded, understanding the implied threat. He wasn't too worried since he'd given a correct address, although it was for a bomb factory which was due to be moved elsewhere shortly.

In all probability, he thought, the Army would find an empty house with enough traces of explosives to satisfy the major that he'd been telling the truth.

The major slapped the file on the desk. "Come on, Captain," he said impatiently. "We've heard enough."

"And me?" Seamus ventured.

"You? You'll be off to the Crumlin like you've been told."

"On what charge?"

"Nothing to do with us, young Seamus," the major replied, adjusting his black beret.

"The RUC'll be going into your place in Andersonstown about now, I should think. They'll probably find a detonator under the mattress, I wouldn't be surprised. Possession of explosive material contrary to the Act, I suppose. That sort of thing, anyway. You know the score, surely?"

"But there isn't any!"

The major tapped the side of his prominent, rather hooked nose with a finger. "Who knows what they'll find, laddie. I don't. It's nothing to do with us. We're just army . . . not police."

Seamus lifted his head to the ceiling as if in supplication, then leaned forward to stub the cigar out in the metal box serving as an ashtray.

"Don't do that," Major Gates called from the door, half-opened by Captain Briance. "Don't waste it. The sergeant will let you finish it."

His voice fell to a whisper, barely reaching Seamus.

"After all, laddie, never let it be said that the British Army never rewards its informants!"

He flicked his stick against his beret in a mock salute before gently shutting the door.

Seamus sat there with the cigar in his right hand, its smoke turning sour in his throat. He stubbed it out viciously on the desk top.

"Was that really necessary, sir?" Captain Briance asked earnestly as the two officers walked out into the icy air of the barracks' parade ground and headed for their Land Rover.

"The last crack about informants, Charley? Yes, it was necessary. Keeps the skull on tenterhooks, you see. Reminds him of what he's done. Maybe he'll talk some more."

"Do you really think so?"

"Frankly, no . . ."

"And all that religious chatter, sir? I thought we were supposed to stay off that."

"We're supposed not to do many things, Charley, but we have to if we want to stay in this fight. The religion's an old trick. Used it in Cyprus. Keep switching from bombs to

some subject near their hearts like religion or their families.
Makes them lose track of the real questions. Funny, they try
to be truthful about personal matters then find themselves
doing the same about their other activities. You'll get the
knack when you've handled one or two skulls on your own,
Charley."

They reached the vehicle. At the wheel was the major's
personal driver, Corporal Arnold Green, a genial, over-
weight man in his mid-thirties.

The two officers scrambled into the back seats and
clipped on the specially-adapted seat belts.

"Where to, suh?" asked the corporal, his voice nasal
with a thick Midlands accent.

"Home, Green, and put the light on. We're on our way to
put a bomb under some skulls . . . we hope."

The driver grinned broadly as he started the vehicle and
switched on the siren. These were the sort of journeys he
liked. Despite his overhanging belly and permanently
rumpled appearance, he was a driver whose reactions would
have been envied by many professional racing men. The
Army, despairing of ever making him an infantryman, had
discovered Green's latent skills and put them to their best
use.

The Land Rover screeched left out of the barracks and
hurtled down Holywood Road toward the M1 motorway
leading to Lisburn. Even though the siren forced other
drivers to the side of the road, it wasn't enough for Green.
He jumped traffic lights and even drove straight over a small
grass-covered roundabout. Behind him, he left motorists
with palpitating hearts and shattered nerves.

"Quite successful, don't you think?" Captain Briance
said loudly, bouncing in his seat, as the Land Rover slowed
a trifle to negotiate the city center traffic.

"Better than I could have hoped for," the major replied,
twisting sideways in his seat to watch an Army foot patrol
wend its way through the shoppers. The Land Rover
skidded around a corner by the City Hall, sternly Victorian,
narrowly missing two elderly ladies hovering on the edge of
a pedestrian crossing.

"Christ, Green, watch it!" The major interrupted himself for only a second, quite used to his driver's near-misses. "A good address and confirmation of our theory that the pipes and nails were coming from the south."

"Do you trust him then?"

"The skull? Funny, I was just thinking that. Maybe he was just too eager to tell us things, though I think he'd rather talk to anyone other than the Paras. Did you see that sergeant? Built like a brick shithouse. Wouldn't like to meet him on a dark night. I'd say our Seamus had principles but he's also very scared of what his own mates will do to him. Probably heard some grisly tales from his old dad. I'd say it's a fair chance he's giving us some real gen."

"So what's the next move, sir?"

"Tricky one that," the major replied, his voice competing with the vehicle's rattles at high speed and the wailing siren. He saw that they were well on to the almost deserted motorway.

"Shut the ruddy noise off, will you, Green?" he shouted to his driver. "Can't hear myself think . . . that's better."

He turned again to talk to the young captain, still on the familiarization part of his posting. Major Gates believed his ATOs in Northern Ireland should be eased carefully into their dangerous work of defusing bombs.

"Yes, it's tricky, Charley. The brigadier, bless him, wants to make an announcement about capturing the skull. You know the sort of thing . . . 'Army smashes bomb ring' . . . that kind of guff . . . But if we do, we might alert the skulls using the bomb factory and they'll clear the place. Yet again, if we tell the press boys once we've the factory under surveillance, then the publicity might drive the skulls right into our hands. That's one thing to learn, Charley. The press can be a bloody nuisance but it can also be a great help if we manipulate them tactically. That's one lesson I soon got under my vest when I arrived here. The skulls were playing tunes on us because we didn't have the press properly organized. Now we have, they're a jolly useful adjunct to intelligence."

"You mean, we lie to them, sir?" Captain Briance asked.

"Good Lord, no!" the major replied indignantly. "No need to do that. But there are a few key journalists—particularly on the box and in the quality papers—who get very private briefings; they get little tit-bits about the skulls which cause mayhem all over the place. You know, we might pick up so-and-so . . . well, they might be told that chummie was living with a girl we suspect to be a leading skull as well but that she escaped our net. If chummie's married with his wife and kiddies south of the Border, that sort of gen in the papers can cause quite a deal of grief. Good psychological warfare that. Our skulls don't like their right hand with a rosary in it to know that their left hand's up some female's knickers!"

The two officers laughed. The corporal gave a lewd chuckle which seemed to come all the way from his ample belly.

"Shut up, Green!" the major said evenly. "We all know where your brains are."

"Nearly there, suh," Corporal Green replied, in fine humor after his hair-raising drive.

"And when we are, make sure this heap of yours is cleaned, Corporal. I'll want to see my face in the polish or you'll be driving a dustcart," the major warned gruffly.

"Suh," said the corporal without resentment, knowing that, in reality, the major regarded him as almost indispensable to the bomb disposal operation, often bragging affectionately about his skills as a driver to other officers in the mess. Green reciprocated the admiration in his tales about the major.

When they reached Army HQ Major Gates vanished into his filing cabinet of an office and made three telephone calls before reporting to the senior officers manning the operations room along the corridor.

Ninety minutes later, he joined the weekly general operations meeting in the conference room on the second floor, overlooking the helicopter landing area and the sports fields.

He looked around the rectangular table at the half-colonels, colonels and brigadiers, all superior in rank to himself, red brevets on their shoulders.

He was quite at home. He knew that they held greater power over a greater number of soldiers than himself. But he also knew that these men envied, perhaps feared, his own nerve and expertise in walking up to a bomb and defusing it. He played often on the buccaneer, one-man-to-a-bomb aspect of his job to get his way. He was usually successful. The GOC invariably treated his problems with some deference.

"If we raid the place tonight, Stephen," the general asked, "what do we win? What do we lose?"

"I would think everything and nothing, sir. We have to go as soon as possible. I'm pretty sure the skull's telling the truth as he knows it at this moment in time. And with the proper publicity, we might get the bonus of other skulls flooding into the area."

The general, a florid, square-faced man with curly hair parted down the middle, winced. "Please just call them the enemy," he said, a trifle testily. "I had this problem of different names in Aden. Just call them the enemy and then we all know, don't we?"

"As you wish, sir . . . anyway, I think we can draw them in if we time it right. Might have a bigger bag than we hoped."

"It'll give us the chance for a thorough sweep through the Markets area, sir," volunteered the officer commanding No. 42 Heavy Brigade (Royal Artillery), the unit holding responsibility for the center of Belfast.

"You can always lay on a sweep if you want one, Frank," remarked the GOC.

"But without good reason it always causes resentment. We're usually on the streets half the night afterwards with the rioters—as are your chaps, Fergus."

The district inspector of the RUC liaising with the Army, a grey and wise man, nodded agreement.

"It's always different, sir," the policeman said quietly, "if we can give the locals a reason, like a bomb."

The general lit a menthol cigarette, all his wife allowed him ever since the luncheon at the Palace where his nicotine-stained fingers, according to her, had drawn disapproving glances from Prince Philip.

"And precisely how do they know there's a bomb situation?" the general asked. "How do they know it's not a phoney?"

"Oh, they're pretty wily, sir," said the brigadier commanding No. 42 Heavy Brigade. "If they see SATO and his EODs, blue lights flashing, they reckon we're not fooling about."

"Any press releases to coincide?"

The chief information officer smiled rather secretively like someone in possession of mysterious skills.

"No problem, sir. Bell of the BBC and Seymour of ITN are both in town. Both frontline chaps. I'll let them know too late for the network early evening news which'll guarantee the local news on BBC and UTV will run it as their leads at six o'clock."

"Sure, John?" asked Major Gates.

"Well, if not at six, very shortly afterwards. It won't be their end item for sure!"

"And what do we say?" asked Major Gates.

"Simple as you like. A major breakthrough in smashing the bombers? Army questioning bomb ring leaders?"

"Not that!" interrupted Gates. "Keep our sku . . . man out of it for me. He could be valuable."

"What about us then?" asked the RUC officer. "What do we do with our friend who's talked so much."

"Anything found in his lodgings?"

"Enough for a charge, they say," the RUC man replied enigmatically. "They weren't too specific though."

"Well, pick him up from Holywood," suggested Major Gates, "and hold him incommunicado in the Crumlin remand wing till you get the wire. He could do with some more questioning before any charge."

"You don't want him connected?"

"Not if possible. Keep him totally under wraps. Let's say the operation in the Markets area follows a long observation job. Why not say it's down to the RUC. For God's sake, Fergus's boys need some encouragement after what they've been through."

"So what do I tell Bell and Seymour before six o'clock?"

"Just tell them something big's happening which might smash a bomb factory. Tell them to bring the cameras to the east end of Cromac Street and we'll look after them. They'll give their local newsrooms enough to get their teeth into before they rush out."

"Can you provide the men, Frank?" the general asked the brigadier commanding No. 42 Heavy Brigade.

"No problem, sir. It sounds a good 'un to me. Let's see who we flush, eh?"

"Right!"

The GOC made a few notes on his pad and then looked up.

"Stephen, you've got your operation. Hope it works."

Chapter 3
January 12th, 1971 (p.m.)

Glistening wet tarmac reflected the knowingly winking red and blue lights of the Army and police vehicles parked in the tiny side streets surrounding the Markets area of West Belfast.

Messages crackled back and forth on the radio sets.

Soldiers and policemen, rifles and submachine guns at the ready, protective flak jackets buttoned high, redirected the late rush hour traffic into a tortuous detour avoiding the area. Firmly and politely, they parried the inevitable questions from office and shop workers on their way home.

"No, nothing happening. Just a routine check," they'd say in accents which were a vocal map of the United Kingdom.

A few men who'd spent the afternoon between bar and betting shop were moved along with less tact. One drunk went off into the drizzly darkness whining like a hurt dog after a rifle butt on his toes ended the argument he was trying to pick with a young soldier.

Three television film crews huddled down into their dark anoraks, almost invisible against the soot-grimed walls of a tall Victorian warehouse, wondering if they'd be back in their hotels before dinner finished or whether they'd have to survive yet again on curled sandwiches from the night porter.

"Sod this for a lark!" one cameraman remarked morosely, adjusting the 16mm Arriflex camera on his shoulder, forgetting the overtime pay he was due.

"Too bloody true, mate," agreed the sound recordist.

The lighting technician started rubbing his hands together

to keep them warm and accidentally switched on his portable light, his "handbasher."

The strong beam flicked across startled, white faces of the security forces, now perfect targets for any sniper lurking in the deep shadows.

"Turn that fucking thing off!" a policeman roared.

The gloom descended again. There wasn't much excitement and the atmosphere was more one of tight-reined fear and deep-down tiredness.

"Oscar One calling Felix. Over," the radio called. "Come in, Felix."

Major Gates, standing by a Land Rover, pressed the switch on his radio.

"Felix receiving Oscar One. Over," he said, using his new call-sign of the cartoon cat who always walked backwards. He'd thought that more appropriate for bomb disposal than the previous call-sign of "Jelly Baby."

"Area secured, Felix, Over."

"Any skulls, Oscar One? Over."

"Possible three sighted at scene. Over."

"We'll move then, Oscar One? Over."

"Affirmative. Out."

They'd been waiting for more than an hour since the local news bulletins on television and radio had briefly reported the setting-up of road blocks near the Markets area. The information released by the Army Information office had been designed to set IRA alarm-bells ringing, but was so deliberately vague and noncommittal that, hopefully, no one determined to enter the area would be totally scared off.

All the while, the suspected house off Cromac Street had been kept under surveillance through night binoculars. Now, with people apparently at the house, the sweep could begin. Whatever there was to find, would be found.

Men of the Welsh Guards, faces blackened, moved silently into the narrow cobbled alleys to reach within a thirty yard radius of the house named by Seamus Aherne. They clambered over walls leading to the small yards serving as gardens in these "back-to-backs" and negotiated past dustbins and rusting bicycle and pram frames to enter the kitchen doors.

The startled occupants, most finishing high tea and watching television, were told that there was an unexploded bomb nearby. They were hurried into warm clothes and led quietly out of the area, across Ormeau Road to the public swimming baths where policewomen had arranged temporary accommodation for them among the changing cubicles.

An officer's whistle shrilled into the night when the evacuation of the houses had been completed.

In counterpoint, dustbin lids began clattering rhythmically as the people in the Catholic enclave signalled to each other that the troops were coming.

"Go!" ordered Major Gates, slapping the hood of his bomb disposal team's Land Rover.

The vehicle, carrying Staff-Sergeant Blundell and Corporal Jefferson, his assistant, hurtled down the narrow streets, headlights blazing, and screeched to a halt behind a "pig," an armored troop carrier, blocking one end of the evacuated street.

Two groups of six soldiers started edging towards the target house from either end of the street, keeping well into the shadows and walls of the houses on the same side. They were covered by four marksmen with light-intensifying sights on their rifles.

Soldiers in groups of three began to search the houses in adjoining streets.

They hammered on front doors and barged in once they were opened. One man would stay with the family while the other two went quickly through the house, opening drawers and cupboards, looking into attics and under beds—often knocking over and breaking furniture and prized ornaments in their haste.

Those who were slow to their front doors, sometimes the elderly, had their locks kicked in. Women screamed and sobbed with fear and shock. Men cursed with anger and frustration. The soldiers paid little heed.

Overhead, a small Army helicopter circled, noisily, insistently, its powerful searchlight flicking and darting through the steady curtain of rain.

All was noise and frightened confusion, shouts and pounding boots.

A voice magnified by a loud hailer sliced through the skein of sounds. "You in Number Seven. Come out with your hands raised. The house is surrounded. Come out now!"

A light in the front room of the house flicked off.

For a moment, the street was in almost total darkness until a searchlight stabbed out from one of the "pigs," lighting the front of the house as bright as day.

The soldiers dropped to the uneven pavement and wriggled on elbows and knees until they were only two dozen feet from the front door.

A window shattered in the upstairs of the house, glass tinkling on to the streets below. The soldiers at the front and back heard a woman cry out, seemingly protesting. Instinctively, they hugged closer to the wall and pavement.

"Crack . . . peeww! Crack . . . peeww!"

Two revolver shots echoed along the street, bullets whining off the concrete pavement, yards away from the troops.

Another shot, flatter and faster, cracked out, its firer's position in the window clear from the tiny flash of flame. The bullet clanged and ricocheted off the side of the armorplated "pig," not feet from the bomb disposal team.

"Three rounds CS! Fire!" shouted the captain sheltering behind the vehicle, directing the raid.

A sergeant spun around the nearest street corner, raised his weapon to his shoulder and fired. Immediately, he pulled back into cover to reload.

"Thummm . . . !"

One grenade round of CS (Composition Smoke) gas smashed harmlessly against the outside wall of the house, falling into the gutter, billowing its fumes.

"Thummm . . . !"

Another gas grenade.

"Thummm . . . !"

The third grenade followed the second into the house, crashing through a window.

Within a few seconds, the soldiers could see the smoke begin to drift out. They heard someone coughing, a man shouting obscenities, a woman screaming shrilly. The smoke with its irritant chemical compound, fret-sawing at throats and eyes, continued to billow out of the house.

"Marksmen, ready! Prepare to return fire!" the captain shouted. "Fire on definite target!"

The soldiers, picked as battalion marksmen because of their natural reflexes and ability with a weapon, peered through their sights. The east wind blew the CS gas into the faces of those at the furthest end of the street. They lowered their weapons, eyes smarting, unable to see clearly.

One of the marksmen at the other end of the street detected a solid shape moving behind the curtain of smoke. He waited a split second to be sure, then squeezed the trigger.

A man, his back to the street, slumped through the broken upstairs window, twisted slightly in mid-air and thudded to the pavement.

The second marksman at that corner, rigid with concentration, saw the dying man as he came through the window. His high velocity bullet, fractionally off target, smashed into the upstairs room.

"Kerrumpp . . . !"

The fireball of the explosion billowed outwards and upwards, fierce and yellow black and frightful and orange.

The ground shook.

Soldiers lying on the pavement were lifted six inches into the air, choking for breath, lungs frozen with shock.

Almost in slow motion, the walls of the house, front and back, lifted off their foundations and buckled outwards with the explosion's force, dragging the walls of the adjoining houses with them.

Windows for two streets around shivered out of their old putty surrounds and sharded on to the pavement.

Inside the house itself, the people who'd been trying to evacuate the bomb factory were ripped limb from limb.

The energy waves entered their mouths, trying to suck breath, and took the tops of their heads away. Their arms and legs were torn from their trunks, and, finally, in those micro-seconds of carnage, their flesh was ripped from their very bones and scattered this way and that.

On the perimeter of the search area, fifty or so yards from the explosion, Major Gates felt the shock waves travel up through the soles of his boots to punch him, as a boxer's punch, in the solar plexus. He bent forward, struggling to keep some breath in his body.

"Felix One to Felix Two! Come in, over!" he coughed into his two-way radio, still searching for breath. And again, "Felix One to Felix Two! Come in!"

There was no reply, simply the crackle of static noise.

Other radios uttered half-strangled messages as troops and police, winded and shocked by the explosion, tried to report back to their superior officers.

Major Gates was conscious of passing a woman at one house. She stood on the front step shrieking hysterically and pointing, index finger quivering, towards the plume of fire in the sky.

Major Gates skidded around the last corner and cannoned into a soldier who was staggering about, rubbing dust-filled eyes, slightly concussed. "Fucking hell! Fucking hell!" the soldier kept repeating with changing emphasis on the same two words.

"Blundell!" the major called, moving towards the scene of devastation. "Staff-Sarn't Blundell!"

Suddenly, to his horror, he saw four soldiers begin picking their way through the pile of rubble which was all that remained of the bomb factory and the two houses either side of it. "Get back!" he screamed. "Get the hell out of it, soldiers!"

The privates turned and saw a stocky, dust-covered figure waving his arms frantically at them. They stood still for a moment.

"I'm SATO," Major Gates bawled. "Move back to cover. The area's not cleared! Move!"

There could be no mistaking his authority. The soldiers withdrew around the corner shouting to others to do the same.

"Well, that was a bang and a half, sir," a voice said quietly behind the major.

"Blundell!" sighed Major Gates with relief. "And just where the . . . where have you been?"

"Seeing to Corporal Jefferson, sir. When the roof fell in, he was lying under the pig. Got a crack on his head when the shock wave lifted him."

"How bad?"

"Couple of aspirins and an early night."

"Serves him right for lying under pigs, what? Anyway, for one ghastly minute, I thought you'd moved in."

"Without telling you, sir?" asked the young staff-sergeant matter-of-factly.

"Of course not, Blundell," the major said reassuringly, smiling.

The staff-sergeant began slapping the dust out of his combat fatigues, then took off his rimless spectacles and wiped them with a handkerchief.

"Christ!" the major muttered. "I almost had heart failure when the brute blew."

"So did we, sir. Thought the whole street was going."

"How much do you reckon?"

"Good 100 lbs. Maybe more. They wouldn't have felt a thing," Blundell said.

"More's the pity," grunted Major Gates. "Anyway, how many of them?"

"From the shooting, two men. Marksman got one skull before she blew. And, from the screaming when we arrived, there might be a female."

"Right. Get the area taped off and let's have a look."

"Sir!"

"Guardsman! Here!" Major Gates shouted. "Help ATO run out the tapes."

"Suh."

"And where's your officer?"

"Injured, suh."

"Badly?"

"No, suh. He was pretty well the one nearest the explosion. He's spewing his . . . he's feeling a little shaken, suh."

"Good. Send one of your lads to find him and tell him that SATO requests his presence here as soon as possible."

Less than a minute later, a young captain, whey-faced,

shakily approached the major who was now standing by the "pig," establishing his command.

"You wanted me, sir?" he asked, obviously still suffering from the after effects of the explosion.

"Son," said Major Gates quietly, so quietly that he couldn't be heard by other than the captain, "lay a cordon around this area, establish perimeter defenses against possible snipers, then report to the nearest M.O. Right?"

"As you say, sir."

"Good man. First class."

Soon, white tapes had been secured at waist height across each end of the street, effectively warning people from going near the scene of the explosion. Some troops guarded the street while others resumed searching homes in neighboring streets.

Corporal Jefferson, a bulbous swelling on his temple, approached the major, now conferring with an RUC inspector.

"Sir!" he said. "The television people want to know if they can film inside the tapes."

Major Gates swung around and saw one cameraman with his eye already to the camera's viewfinder, his left hand adjusting the focus on the special lens capable of filming with the minimum of available light.

"Just the thing," said Major Gates cheerfully. "Ask them in on the usual conditions and we'll use their hand-bashers. Save us rigging lights."

For the next hour, bomb disposal and forensic searched through the rubble with the aid of the camera crews' hand-held lights. The cameramen were allowed to film on the strict understanding that they never took identifiable close-up pictures of the EOD unit or their equipment.

The unit checked first that there were no more bombs or explosives in the rubble. Then they picked carefully through the shattered bricks, glass and wood of what was once three dwellings. They searched for the smallest piece of electrical wire or a fire-seared brick which might contain the impregnation of explosive, or the smallest slivers of human flesh. Each of the searchers wore rubber gloves and carried tweezers and each placed their finds in small plastic bags.

There was only one substantial find and that a street away. A forensic detective, gagging a little, identified it as a human thigh. A young soldier picked it up on a shovel and pushed it, quivering like jelly, into a large transparent bag. He later surprised himself by being sick only three times.

The search resumed at first light and by mid-morning the pathologist at the Royal Victoria Hospital was able to begin his postmortem examination of what few remains there were.

While he worked, Major Gates and Captain Briance watched from the next room, through a large rectangular window.

Normally, curtains were drawn across the glass but the major wanted the young captain to undergo a final experience of Northern Ireland's awful realities before he was assigned to his own bomb disposal unit.

Major Gates did the same with all his young officers. His intention was not to shock them but to try to save their lives and the lives of those around them. He reasoned that if they saw the effects of an explosion on the human body then they wouldn't take any chances whatsoever in their work.

The major knew from his long experience that to stay alive as he had an ATO had to be especially cautious, meticulously prepared and an absolute stickler in following the laid-down procedures for defusing bombs. He had little time, if any, for individuals, innovators or improvisers. To him, bomb disposal was a precise science in which the slightest mistake invariably meant death. His own survival had proved that.

"Caution and concentration," he always told his men. "Never take a chance unless it's irrevocably necessary. And then don't. Brothers, never hurry to your own funeral!"

His teaching had succeeded until now. Since he'd arrived in the Province late in 1969, not one of his charges had died, though some had had lucky escapes.

But, as he'd often said in the officer's mess, "You either have bad luck or you get what you deserve!"

Captain Briance, tight-lipped, tried to concentrate on the minutest, least significant details of the gruesome scene

before him, hoping in that way his mind wouldn't accept the
wilder thought that the pile of raw, bloody meat on the
white, slightly inclined slab in the next room had once been
a human being, maybe three.

"Stay with it, there's a good chap," Major Gates said
encouragingly, patting him lightly on the shoulder. "Stay
with it!"

He turned and winked conspiratorially at the RUC
sergeant sitting stolidly in the corner of the same room,
waiting to take a statement from the pathologist.

The sergeant, a veteran of such duties, smiled ruefully.
"The first's always the worst," he said in his unmistakable
Belfast accent.

Captain Briance drew a deep breath, his face grey. He
swayed slightly, steadying himself by leaning forward with
his palms against the glass.

The door to the observation room opened. A man of
about thirty strode in, white coat flapping. He paused when
he saw the three men in uniform.

"Not interrupting anything?" he asked.

"Not at all. Come on in," Major Gates said with a
welcoming smile. "Always room for another."

Edward S. Aicheson nodded and moved to the window,
standing beside Captain Briance. "Last night's explosion?"
he asked over his shoulder.

"Affirmative," replied Major Gates.

"Sweet Jesus, what a mess!" Aicheson muttered, shaking his head.

"Seen one before?"

"Once, back home, Major, but nothing like that."

"American, aren't you?"

"You got it."

They introduced each other, shaking hands. The major
used his Masonic grip but it wasn't reciprocated.

"What are you doing over here?" Major Gates asked
conversationally. "Last place I'd volunteer for."

"You gotta be where the trade is," Aicheson grinned,
mocking his accent for a moment. "No, seriously, there was
a visiting fellowship available, and since I'm specializing in

neurological surgery I reckoned this was where it's at.
There's some tremendous work being done here on new
techniques because of the troubles.''

"Out of bad comes good."

"That's right, Major. I can learn more here in a month
than in a year back home, though, mind you, we've gotten
our fair share of fellows shooting bullets into each other."

"Where's home exactly?"

"Boston, Massachusetts."

"Where the Irish come from."

"Go to, more like. Scratch most anyone in the old town
and you'll draw a drop of Irish blood."

"You?"

"Oh, yes. There's a fair amount in me, so the family
say."

"Where from originally?" the major asked more courteously than inquisitively. As he talked, he watched Captain
Briance, weighing him up for the future.

"Somewhere deep in the west, I'm told. Apparently on
the female side. Some place I'd doubt you'd ever heard of.
Listowel."

"In Kerry?"

"That's right."

"Funny, but I'm supposed to have some distant ancestor
from around that part of the woods."

"You? You, Major, with Irish ancestry?"

"Most of the British Army have, actually. Certainly most
of the field-marshals anyway. Right down to Wellington."

"Small world."

"Affirmative, and yet your Irish-Americans, maybe three
cousins removed from my lot, keep wittering on about us
moving out from here and allowing a blood bath."

"Some, Major. Just some. The Kennedys and so on
aren't exactly typical. They might like to think they are but
they aren't. Sweet Jesus, I wish we had your young soldiers
running things back in Boston. They make things work!"

"They're trained to. It's the best army of its size in the
world."

"No doubt there, sir."

"Thanks. Nice to know someone appreciates us, isn't it, Charley?" Major Gates said, warming to the American surgeon.

"Sir?" gulped Captain Briance, still staring through the window.

"Oh, come away, Charley," the major said. "Don't make a meal of it. I only wanted you to have a peek after all."

"May I be excused then, sir?" asked the captain, moving swiftly away from the observation window.

"From that, yes, Charley . . . hang on, though, I think he's finished."

The pathologist was removing his near-transparent rubber gloves. He tossed them into a waste-bin and left the mortuary.

"Interesting, gentlemen, to say the least," he remarked strolling into the next room, still wearing his blood-streaked gown. "How many did your people think, Gates? . . . Oh, hello, Aicheson."

"Good morning, sir."

The police sergeant fumbled in his breast pocket for his notebook.

"Two males and a female they reckoned, professor," said Major Gates.

"Well, certainly, two males . . . left their under-carriages."

The pathologist peeled off his gown, revealing immaculately tailored waistcoat and trousers, and tossed it casually into a corner of the room.

Captain Briance stood, transfixed.

"Undercarriages?" interrupted Aicheson.

"Their cocks, young man," said the pathologist. "Always count the genitalia. Can't go wrong like that. One of the softest parts but always seem to hang on to the last I find. We've a problem on the females, though. Certainly one. Definitely one. But I do think another one as well."

"How, sir?"

"Because I've got three tits in there, that's why. One pair and an odd 'un. And, unless we've a freak, that's two females, isn't it, Aicheson?"

"Even in Boston, Mass . . ." the major interrupted.

"Shut up, Gates," the pathologist said, not at all put out. "Or I'll order a perch in there for the vulture you really are."

"Jesus," murmured the police sergeant, used to most anything. "Three! That'll be problems!"

"I thought it might," said the pathologist even more smugly.

"It will," agreed the major.

"The bumf'll be something awful," said the police sergeant disconsolately. "They'll not be at all happy at headquarters. Any chance of identification, sir?"

"None at all," replied the pathologist. "I've taken the measurements of what bones and limbs I could. When I've worked them out, you might have some idea of height and build. Best I can do, I'm afraid, Sergeant."

"Long and short of it, eh? Looks as if we'll have to wait for the death notices in the *Irish News*."

"As you say, Major," the pathologist murmured. He walked through the door and then turned. "By the way, Aicheson, how's the child?"

"The one from the bomb? Holding his own, sir, but still unconscious. I've decided against operating, though. I reckon it's a deep concussion and he'll pull out given time."

"Good decision," the pathologist nodded. "I've had more clients on the slabs down here from surgeons who insisted on meddling than from those who let good old Mother Nature take her course."

"We must meet again," Major Gates said to the young surgeon as he too prepared to leave. "Perhaps a noggin some time? Discuss our Irish ancestors, eh?"

"Pleasure, Major. And take care now," Aicheson replied.

"You can bet your life on it," smiled Major Gates. "And mine for that matter."

Outside he found Captain Briance standing in the corridor, as pale as the cream-painted walls.

"Come on, Charley. What you need is a stiffener in the mess."

When they arrived back at Thiepval Barracks, the two officers went first to the major's office. There, on his desk, was a report detailing the finds made during the previous night's search of the Markets area.

"Look at this!" exclaimed the major, quite excited. "862 rounds of Kynoch 9-millimeter in all. Our stuff made in '56 and '58."

"Decent haul, sir."

"Yes, but see here. Look at where the bullets were found. Most in one house but they've spread the ammunition around seven places in just two streets next door to each other. I'd bet a year's pay there's a skull in every one of those houses. Classic sign of a terrorist cell, Charley. Remember that. Precisely what they used to do in Malaya and Cyprus. They all learn off each other. The brotherhood of international terrorism, that's what we've got here. Not a little local difficulty as some of these bloody politicians seem to think!"

"You'll mention it at the briefing?"

"For the Home Secretary? For my sins, I'm afraid so. Waste of an afternoon but there we are. Just thinking of it gives me a thirst. Come on, Charley!"

They walked out of the headquarters building, turned half-left and approached a high wire fence guarded at its only gate by two soldiers. This was the inner compound, containing the commanding general's house, tucked away within evergreen shrubbery, and the officer's mess.

The mess was reached down a narrow outside passage leading to the wooden front door of what was once a grand old house. Immediately inside, the large sombre hallway was all brown veneer panels. Half-a-dozen officers sat around, waiting to have lunch in the adjoining dining room, thumbing through copies of *Punch, Country Life*, and the *Illustrated London News*. The atmosphere was of disciplined order and comfortable calm, a haven from the nasty, untidy events of the world outside.

The actual bar was a smallish rectangular room off the hallway with a curved dispensing counter set in the corner nearest the door. It was fairly empty at this time of day.

"What's yours, Charley?" asked the major. "A drop of brandy to settle the stomach?"

"Why not, sir, seeing it was upset on duty."

"Quite right. A large brandy, steward, and a pint of Bass for me."

The elderly steward, a retired soldier, served the drinks while Major Gates wrote out and signed the chit of paper which would place their cost on his monthly mess bill.

"Nice one last night, Stephen," another major remarked, standing at the other end of the padded bar counter.

"The own goals? Even better than we thought. Four instead of three."

"Another one, eh?"

"That's what the old prof says. It's either that or there's a lopsided female skull in town."

"Like that, was it?"

"And some, brother! It'll be in ops. briefing notes."

"Look forward to reading them."

"You callous devil!"

"What about you then, old man?"

"Me? Can't you see my tear-stained cheeks?"

They laughed cynically.

Major Gates, still smiling, carried the two drinks over to a table by the large sash windows and sat down. He took a long pull at his beer, sighing appreciatively.

"Well, our Seamus certainly came through," Captain Briance remarked quietly, warming the brandy glass in his cupped hands.

"He did that, Charley. In spades. I wish he'd been there to see it rather than snug in his cell at the Crumlin, and preferably in the house when it blew!"

The captain raised his eyebrows. "Don't you feel anything at all about the skulls? About their families when they die? Anything?"

"Nope," Major Gates grunted, lighting his third Panatella of the morning. "It's their choice if they want to play games. They pick the game. They pick the rules. Not us."

"Odd though, isn't it?" Captain Briance said reflectively. "Our Seamus seemed a nice enough young fellow really, yet he throws up a perfectly decent job to come up here and take us on."

"Very odd. When I first arrived here, I couldn't understand it either. Not one iota of it. Oh, yes, I could see why the Catholics were upset all right. They'd had the muddy end of the stick in Northern Ireland for mumble-mumble years and not one blessed person had done anything about it. They could hardly get a job if they were up against a Protestant who wanted it as well. They couldn't vote in enough of their own councillors even if there were more of them in a town than Protestants. The plural voting system fixed that . . . dammit, a helluva lot of them weren't even entitled to vote. And, of course, if they couldn't get control of a council, they didn't have the houses allocated to them. Hardly a Protestant went begging for need of a council house. Thousands of Catholics did. I mean to say, it was bloody ridiculous. Take Derry for an example. Twice as many Catholics there as Protestants yet, thanks to the gerrymandering, the place kept returning a Unionist M.P. to Stormont. No wonder there was trouble. Those civil rights youngsters were on the ball about the carve-up going on. But that's all being put right now. As you'll guess, I'm no admirer of your darling Harold when he was Prime Minister but he was spot on in telling Stormont to pull its finger out and sort out this nonsense with the Catholics. Should have been done years ago! The Protestants brought a lot of this trouble on themselves, make no mistake, but now it's being sorted and everyone's equal under the law etcetera, etcetera, what do we have? Still more bombs and bullets. And what do they want? They want the Brits out, the very people who set it back on the tracks again. And who, might you ask, are precisely they? Not Dublin politicians, on your life. They know they couldn't afford to subsidize this place like the poor old British tax-payer does. The Catholic population in Northern Ireland then? No way! They know they'd be worse off if they were run by Dublin. Where would all the subsidies for jobs come from, the social security, the old age pension, the dole money? So, as I asked myself a long time ago when I stepped off the boat, just who are 'they' and what's it about?"

The major swallowed the last of his beer and edged the mug towards the junior officer.

"Christ, Charley, talking to you always gives me a dry throat," he smiled.

"My round, sir. Same again?"

"You'd better watch the old cognac. You're in ops this afternoon while I'm with our beloved Reggie."

"I'll just take a dry ginger."

"Good man!"

Captain Briance returned with the drinks and set them on the table. He glanced through the window at the well-kept lawns and shrubberies outside and thought it a rather incongruous scene in relation to what was happening many miles away. "You were saying, sir?" he asked tentatively.

Major Gates laid down his beer mug, brushing a knuckle against the side of his mouth to remove a speck of froth.

"Well, I was telling you about 'they,' wasn't I?"

The captain nodded.

"International communism, that's 'they,' simple as that. Marxist anarchists. Just like they've got in Germany and Italy. Same sort of mob. Sure, this lot call themselves the Provisional IRA but that's just window-dressing. Should be prosecuted under the Trades Descriptions Acts among other things."

Captain Briance looked doubtful.

"You mean someone like our Seamus? A communist?"

"Him?" The major smiled and shook his head sadly. "No, they just wind up boys like him: just wind up most of the poor punks with stories of the old IRA. It's a very convenient name to use. After all, it's worth some mileage. All the top boys, those who really matter in the Provo's Army Council, are about as near to the old IRA as Moscow is to Washington. They're always vanishing off overseas for their conferences and indoctrination lectures. If they can bring about a total breakdown in law and order, then they'll be in. They won't be satisfied till the whole of Ireland's a Democratic Republic like the ones behind the Iron Curtain. They'll make Ireland as threatening to Western Europe as Cuba is to the States. That, Charley, is what it's about."

Captain Briance was still doubtful.

"You mean there's no old IRA in this at all?"

"There's a bit. Of course there is. After all, it's a basic principle of the IRA to have a united Ireland one day. That's what pulls the suckers like our Seamus in. Another glorious campaign just like dad and grandad and great-grandad fought. What they don't realize is what's behind it all. And, let's face it, Charley, the only way they're going to have a united Ireland is to throw us out. It'd mean another civil war and I'd put my best shirt on the Protestants to win every time."

Major Gates stubbed out his cigar and finished his beer.

"I think a last half before lunch. What about you, Charley?"

Chapter 4
May, 1971

His eyes didn't flicker when he heard the keys chink and rattle, the locks turn, the murmurs and the footsteps further along the landing.

After four months, fifteen days and twelve hours of imprisonment, Seamus Aherne could time the warders' approach almost to perfection.

They were four cells away.

His gaze remained fixed on the light in the ceiling. By concentrating upon it, he could enter, for a moment at least, a world of aloneness.

He wished it could stay on throughout the night. If it did, he thought its trance-like effect might even shut out the sounds of his three cellmates as they evacuated their bladders or bowels into the tin bucket in the corner by the door, or panted and sighed and snorted as they exorcised their sexual fantasies by masturbating.

The warders were opening the door of the next cell but one.

If the light was with him through the night, thought Seamus, he might also avoid the nightmares, which persisted despite the tranquillizers prescribed by the medical officer.

Awful images of people torn limb from limb by bombs of his own making. They were always people he knew, his family or friends from the National School in Upper Church Street in Listowel.

They were next door now. The sounds of them echoed off the stone and metal of the Republican wing of the Crumlin Gaol in Belfast.

Sometimes, in his dreams, he ran towards the people trying to warn them. Always, a figure in khaki uniform, grinning, blocked his path. He would lie winded on the ground, watching the bomb victims disintegrate in the blast. Major Stephen Gates would be cackling with laughter.

The tiny spy hole, recessed into the cell door, clicked back. The key clunked in the heavy lock. The warder's voice was flat with boredom.

"Slop out, you Ras! Come on now, move it!"

Seamus swung his legs over the edge of the bunk, stars and blobs swimming liquidly before his eyes as they readjusted to normal light.

"Another day, another dollar," he muttered, his stockinged feet striking the harsh matting on the floor.

"Do you always have to fucking say that?" exclaimed the man in the bunk below, an IRA veteran from the early 1960s, Andy McCann.

"Why not?" Seamus answered. "And what else?"

He knew it was his turn, and he quickly dressed himself in the prison's blue denim uniform.

"It's all shit," he said lightly, picking up the tin bucket in the corner and walking out on to the landing.

Nobody argued about him pushing into the queue of prisoners waiting to "slop-out" the contents of the night-buckets. The essential thing for all was not to spill a drop, not to be ordered to spend the morning scrubbing down that landing and the landing below.

It was almost a social occasion: there was a camaraderie which lifted the participants above their menial, evil-smelling task.

"Good night, Vienna," Seamus murmured when he eventually reached the sluice basin and up-ended the contents of his cell's bucket down the waste pipe. Then he moved sideways to wash it out in the adjoining basin.

The prison officer standing by the door, fresh on duty, usually averted his eyes rather than watch what was happening in the sluice room. His early morning bacon sandwich was too valuable to risk.

Thus that part of the prisoners' daily routine became a favorite time for relaying messages and instructions.

Seamus had been approached while slopping out only
two days after receiving his five-year sentence for posses-
sing explosives from the court directly across the Crumlin
Road.

"Second landing. Cell thirty-four," the man slopping-out
beside him had muttered from the side of his mouth, his lips
hardly moving. "Ten o'clock."

Seamus had begun to protest, believing that the warders
wouldn't allow such movement from landing to landing.

"Don't worry about the screws, cunt," the man urged.
"Just be ready."

To his surprise, at a few minutes before ten o'clock, his
cell door opened, a prison officer motioned him out with a
flap of his wrist and he was escorted down the circular iron
staircase to the landing below and to Cell 34. Nothing was
said. Nothing remarked upon. It appeared simple routine.

"Thanks, Mr. Allen," a prisoner, standing casually
outside the cell, said to Seamus's escort. The prison officer
merely nodded and turned away.

"Through there," the prisoner ordered Seamus, opening
the unlocked door and pushing him inside.

Cell 34 resembled a bed-sitting room rather than the over-
crowded, squalid cell which Seamus had just left.

Along one wall, there was a single bunk covered with a
flowery blue bedspread, transforming it almost into a sofa.
Large colored photographs of idyllic scenes of the Irish
countryside covered two walls. A table, bearing a radio and
what were obviously family photographs, was set at an
angle under the high, barred window.

The middle-aged man behind the table waved Seamus
inside.

"Come in, son," he said in a flat, nasal Belfast accent.
"You'll excuse me for not standing, but the old legs are
playing up today."

"I'm sorry," Seamus replied automatically, surprised at
the cell's appearance. There was even a strip of carpet on
the floor.

"Sit down," the man invited, gesturing toward the bunk.
He pushed a pack of cigarettes and a box of matches across
the table. "Smoke?" he asked.

Seamus nodded and opened the pack. It was nearly filled with proper cigarettes, not the scraps of hand-rolled tobacco he'd become resigned to since beginning his sentence. He raised his eyebrows.

"Living in luxury, eh? That's what you're thinking?" the man at the table went on. "Just perks of the job, son, for the officer commanding the Republican wing."

"Then you're . . ."

"That's right, son, I'm Charley McCool."

"Of St. Matthew's?"

The man grinned. "You know the local history, then? Yes, I was with Billy defending the church against those fucking Prods. Unlike Billy, I got bullets in both legs. Still, they're all right now unless they pick up a wee bit of damp. I can always tell from the legs when the rain's coming!"

Seamus looked with undisguised admiration at the older man, legendary for his exploits in protecting Catholic areas from rampaging Protestants during the riots of 1969. He saw a man with steel-grey hair brushed straight back, deep lines on his forehead and around his mouth, and eyes which seemed both penetrating and kindly.

Seamus lit his cigarette.

"I thought, Mr. McCool, we weren't due any political privileges in here."

"We're not, officially, Seamus. But the governor and the Home Office accept realities if they're not flaunted in their fat civil service faces. They negotiate conditions and whatever with me and that way we can both get things done. It's a two-way deal." McCool shrugged. "It's the same in the Loyalist wing though, things being what they are, there are less of them."

Seamus leaned back against the wall, beginning to relax.

"I'm told you refused to recognize the court at your trial, Seamus."

"Sat with my back to the judge. It didn't really matter what I'd said. They'd me colder than Monday's snap. They put up the evidence and that was that."

"It's a worthwhile gesture anyway."

"Traditional, so my da said."

"You've seen him?"

"In the cells afterwards."

McCool nodded approvingly. "Keep the family links. They're important. We'll help with the cost of their travelling, if you like."

"They'd appreciate that. Money's pretty scarce back home."

"Isn't it everywhere? My wee wifie's still got three at home. Three away, but still three at home. Sounds like the football results, eh?" McCool stopped for a moment, perhaps thinking of his family. His hand slapped down on the desk. "Anyway, son," he resumed, "I've heard good things about your work with the Third Battalion."

"Uh-huh?" Seamus murmured doubtfully. He looked around the cell and particularly at the door and ceiling.

McCool smiled reassuringly. "We'll not be overheard," he said. "It's part of the arrangement that they don't bug our cells. We don't take any chances anyway. The fellow you saw outside can sniff a microphone from thirty yards, so he can."

"So it's safe to talk?"

"In here at least. But be careful anywhere else. Better safe than . . ."

"Right."

"Well then, your work with the Third Battalion?"

"Fairly routine, Mr. McCool. All the old stuff. Actually, I was working on a new 'un when they picked me up."

"At a bomb, wasn't it?"

"I liked to watch them. If I could see what they were doing, it gave me an idea sometimes of what might give them problems. Careless, I suppose."

"Pity. You were getting results. Lived in Andersonstown, didn't you?"

"A room in Slievegallion Drive. Three quid a week and walk the landlady's dog."

"Deliberate?"

"The area? Yes. As you know, it's the First Battalion's patch—that Ballymurphy and the Falls—so the Brits might get a wee bit confused finding me where I was rather in the north or east of the city where we're supposed to operate."

"Your da train you?"

Seamus shook his head. "He's not the man he was. He took ill during his last spell in the Curragh. He told me a wee bit, but it was Jack McKay who filled in the details."

"Where's he at?"

Suddenly, Seamus had the strong impression that McCool already knew the answers to the questions he was asking. It was more of an interrogation than a friendly chat. "Where he usually is. At home in Swords Road, Dublin. Works in his garage mostly."

McCool nodded, evidently satisfied. "Nice fellow?"

"A hard man and then some, to be sure."

"When did you join?"

"Late '68. After the first Derry."

"A lot did. Suppose they singled you out?"

"They knew of my family, Mr. McCool. Probably helped."

"It would. When did you come north?"

"When I was sent. September '69."

"No qualms?"

"Not really. I liked my job but . . ."

"Post Office, wasn't it?"

"You know a deal . . . yes, the Post Office . . . but once I became involved, once I joined, it didn't seem to matter that much."

"Willing volunteer then, Seamus?"

"You could say that."

"Inevitable, perhaps."

"Aye. Suppose so."

The chat-cum-interview between Seamus and Charley McCool continued for another half hour before it became clear that both had exhausted questions and answers.

Seamus came away surprised that the destruction of the bomb factory in the Markets had not been mentioned at all, remembering the coincidental date of his arrest. He also took away the feeling that, because of his particular skills, he was regarded as someone special among the IRA prisoners.

"The door of Cell 34 is always open to you, son,"

McCool had said at the end. "If you want anything, come here. If you feel the bonk coming on . . ."

"The bonk?"

"Depression. A special kind. Prison depression."

"Does everyone get it?"

"Most. If you do, drop in here before you see the medical officer. Like to know what's happening."

"Thanks, Mr. McCool."

After that interview, Seamus's life in the Crumlin Gaol was as pleasant as any prisoner's could be. Most of his fellow inmates deferred to him, though he insisted on taking his share of the menial jobs like slopping-out and peeling potatoes in the kitchens. He found it a time of thinking and, perhaps for the first time, a period of reassessment. His mind constantly returned to the question of the inevitability or otherwise of his chosen path. With his inherited background, he knew it would have been nigh-impossible to escape from adolescence without a leaning towards republicanism. He'd been well indoctrinated by Grandma Hannah and his father, Joe.

Strangely, he thought, he always connected his father with a bed, probably because of all these weeks and months he'd spent over the years by his bedside, listening to him. That's where he'd learned it all, wasn't it? At his father's bedside. Not that he didn't also remember his father as a lean, energetic man always ready with a laugh or a hug. But those days had been before Seamus really understood what Joe Aherne's life was about, before the four men from the Special Branch had called at the farm at Galey Bridge and taken him away into internment for the second time.

The first time had been in 1941 when Joe Aherne had joined 2,000 other IRA men at the Curragh Camp. He'd become active in the movement in the border campaign of the 1930s before acquitting himself well as the quartermaster during the IRA's bombing campaign in London during the early part of the Second World War.

Like many others, Seamus's father emerged from internment thinner and sadder. True, he had a better understanding of the Gaelic language and culture from the classes he'd attended in the detention camp as well as a more sophisticated knowledge of bomb-making gained in other instruction groups. But, he used to joke later, if it hadn't been for that spell behind barbed wire, Seamus might never have been. As soon as Joe was released, he proposed to his sweetheart of schooldays, Bernadette Burns, flushed with renewed longing for soft femininity. They'd married in the autumn of 1945 and Seamus had arrived in the summer of the next year. Joe concentrated on bringing the farm back to some sort of production after his time away, and on enjoying his new son, soon to be joined in successive years by two sisters, Shelagh and Mai.

He still attended IRA gatherings in North Kerry whenever work or domestic duties permitted and continued to take part in the Bodenstown march every June when Republicans gathered at the grave of Wolfe Tone, one of the leaders of the uprising in 1798 who committed suicide in prison after being sentenced to death.

This occasion in County Kildare, thirty or so miles from Dublin, was perhaps the most important in the IRA calendar, always ending as it did in speeches from the leadership which spelt out future policies.

Joe Aherne was among the IRA detachments at the Bodenstown Rally in 1949 to hear the IRA's new post-war policy put into public words for the first time by Cristoir O'Neill.

"The aim," he announced, "is simply to drive the invader from the soil of Ireland and to restore the sovereign independent Republic proclaimed in 1916. To that end, the policy is to prosecute a successful military campaign against the British forces of occupation in the Six Counties."

The new policy attracted recruits in plenty. The problem was to arm them. To do this, the IRA staged half-a-dozen daring raids on British Army barracks in England and Northern Ireland in the early 1950s. A campaign began late in 1956 which soured relations between London, Belfast and Dublin. And in its initial stages in 1957, it did help the return to power of de Valera.

Once more de Valera, IRA hero of 1916, turned the full

force of law and order against his old organization by reintroducing internment.

Joe Aherne, who'd designed a number of bombs exploded during the border campaign, was picked up along with 60 others, during the first Special Branch sweep on July 8th, 1958.

Most were to stay for ten months behind the five barbed wire fences at the Curragh but Joe was released before Christmas. Although conditions within the detention camp had improved considerably since the wartime days—some IRA men likened it to a holiday camp—Joe contracted a chest virus which needed medical treatment of a degree only provided in hospital.

The illness left him virtually a cripple for the rest of his life. The slightest damp and chill brought on bronchitis which kept him in bed for weeks on end. Worse, his weakness effectively barred him from all but the lightest work and the family farm, handed down by the Wilmots, gradually declined without a grown man to shoulder its grinding and necessary routine.

Seamus, in his own captivity, remembered that period of his life as one of its blackest. Barely in his teens, he couldn't escape the deep misery pervading the farmhouse.

He would lie awake listening to his father's angry, self-reproachful words during parental arguments about lack of money and, most usually, Joe's drinking bouts in Listowel at his relatives' tavern in Church Street.

The seeming injustice of it all drew him closer to his father. When he assumed, in his mid-teens, the position of virtual head of the family, the person who could do the heavy work around the farm, he became increasingly protective toward the semi-invalid.

After all, he reasoned, his father was not alone in suffering the after effects of the detention camps. One man had been so depressed following his release that he'd shot himself. Another was so psychologically diminished that he couldn't bear to cross the road any more.

Often, when Seamus was mucking out the cattle shed or feeding the pigs, he would glance around and find his father watching him, a dreamy, envious expression on his face.

Eventually, the teenager came to realize that his father was living out his dreams of a better life through him, that he saw in Seamus everything he couldn't and wouldn't be.

Sometimes he would sit up late with his father, talking, after the women of the household had gone to bed.

Joe Aherne would sneak a half-bottle of whiskey from his back pocket and pour his son a nip to be drunk with a deal of water.

"Just a drop to help you sleep, son," he'd wink, lifting the bottle to his lips and taking a swig himself.

"Slainte," they'd whisper to each other.

On such occasions, they'd discuss life in general and Seamus's future in particular. His mother and grandmother wanted him to become a farmer, to stay at Galey Bridge. His headmaster, Mr. Macmahon, thought he'd enough technical aptitude for another occupation. And Seamus himself was adolescently unsure about almost everything. Finally, it was his father who forced the decision.

"You get away from here, son," said Joe Aherne when they were talking one night. "We've had enough farmers in this family already and look where it's taken us. The country's full of small farmers, so it is. What Ireland needs is more people with brains and modern skills, so she does."

"But what about you?" Seamus protested. "You can't be working the farm on your own."

"And don't I know that? But we'll muddle along all right. Your sisters will be wed soon enough—pray to the Holy Mother!—and then they'll bring someone into the family to work the farm. Good catch they'll be. You just see, son. It'll be fine. Don't be paying any attention to the women. I'm not, althought they're always sticking their little poison darts in me. Just don't pay any attention to them. You listen to your teachers and do what they say. They're knowing better than any of us."

Reluctantly, after much argument and heartsearching, Seamus took his advice. When he was sixteen years old, in 1962, he sat an examination for the Post Office and was accepted as an apprentice technician. He had the choice of three training centers, Dublin, Cork or Sligo, and, without much hesitation, chose the Irish capital.

Rather to his own surprise, because of his rural background, he proved to be among the best of the apprentices at the technicians' training school sited within the walls of Dublin Castle.

For three years, he learned the intricacies of building and maintaining telephone switchboards, assembling delicate switching gear, indeed everything about a modern telephone and telecommunications system. When he wasn't in class or at the Post Office hostel, Seamus busied himself in discovering the delights of Dublin as well as those of the opposite sex.

His life, even after he became qualified and remained to work in Dublin, was almost totally self-centered, although he continued to be aware through newspapers and magazines of what was happening in the Republican movement.

The IRA, disappointed at the public's antipathy toward its six-year bombing campaign, moved even more to the left in the middle 1960s. Many who believed that violence was the only way to win back Northern Ireland left the movement, frustrated and disillusioned, to be replaced by those of subtler political thinking. The Army Council went so far as to appoint a well-known Marxist as education officer despite rumblings from the Irish-Americans in Clann-na-Gael who distrusted any form of socialism.

But the old traditions managed to survive and in 1966, the fiftieth anniversary of the Easter Rising, several bombings showed that there were still IRA Volunteers who believed in action rather than words. The most spectacular explosion toppled the statue of Admiral Lord Nelson off its plinth in O'Connell Street.

Behind the scenes that year, however, the IRA leader, Cathal Goulding, secretly committed the organization to support an embryo civil rights movement in Northern Ireland during an informal meeting at the home of a Derry solicitor.

And the next year, in his Bodenstown oration, Goulding revealed publicly the IRA's shift in policy when he admitted that the movement's narrow aim of ending partition by violence had been a mistake. In future, he announced, the

IRA would campaign to end social and economic ills, retaining at the same time the right to use force when necessary.

His policy succeeded beyond the IRA's wildest dreams. In little more than a year, the searchlight of world opinion swung on to Ireland following a march by civil rights supporters in Derry on October 5th, 1968, which was broken up by the Royal Ulster Constabulary with a series of baton charges.

The incident would normally have received scant attention outside Ireland but the dramatic television news film, satellited from country to country, roused indignation everywhere. The problems of Northern Ireland became the major topic of debate.

The IRA had stumbled at last upon a new cause. It didn't matter that few knew of its connection with the civil rights activists. Suddenly, Republicanism was almost respectable again cloaked, as it was, by the shining, radical zeal of university students like Bernadette Devlin, Kevin Boyle, Michael Farrell and the rest, all protesting about the undoubted discrimination of Protestants against Catholics in the fields of housing, employment and political representation.

Seamus Aherne, like many of his generation, was jolted from his complacency by those flickering television images of young people scattering this way and that from stick-wielding policemen, grotesque in their riot helmets. The marchers looked so innocent and defenseless; the police so menacing and cruel.

Like the IRA, Seamus had found a cause.

It appeared entirely natural to Seamus for him to want to join the IRA rather than the civil rights movement. What was good enough for his grandfather was surely good enough for him? After all, wasn't the IRA the shadowy influence behind the civil rights demonstrations?

He felt totally at home from the first. The words of his pledge of loyalty were almost second nature to him.

"I, Seamus Aherne, do solemnly declare that, to the best of my knowledge and ability, I will support and defend the

Irish Republic against all enemies, foreign and domestic, and that I will bear true faith and allegiance to the same. I do further declare that I do not and shall not yield a voluntary support to any pretended Government, Authority, or Power within Ireland, hostile or inimical to that Republic. I take this obligation freely without any mental reservation or purpose or evasion—so help me God!''

He attended a couple of desultory weekend training camps in the Wicklow Mountains, and, more importantly, began taking instructions from Jack McKay, a veteran bomb-maker from the 1940s.

All the while events in Northern Ireland were moving as inexorably as an Alpine avalanche.

In the May of 1969, with anarchy almost total, the IRA leaders in Belfast hurried down to their senior colleagues in Dublin. Their worry was how to protect the families in the Catholic ghettoes. They couldn't hope to match the undoubted firepower of the Protestants who managed to gain firearms certificates from magistrates on the flimsiest pretexts or, sometimes, acquire weapons temporarily from their fellow loyalists in the "B-Specials," the part-time constabulary.

The response in Dublin was disappointing. The IRA's Northern Command was told there were hardly any guns to be had, pretty well the whole armory having been sold to the Welsh Nationalists. The commanders from Belfast and Derry left Dublin empty-handed and unhappy.

The summer heat increased. The police, weary and hard-pressed, continued to dodge and skip stones and guttering pipes but now the sounds of shots were heard in the Belfast night. Protestant gunmen began hunting their Catholic rivals just as they'd done in decades past.

The IRA men, who could only muster a dozen revolvers and rifles in the entire city, defended desperately.

Finally, on August 12th, 1969, the point of no return was reached when the Northern Ireland government rashly authorized a march by the Apprentice Boys of Derry, a virulently Loyalist organization.

The rhythmic thudding and wailing of the Protestant

drums and fifes pierced through the thick walls and ramparts of old Derry, reaching, challenging the Catholics penned into their housing estates, the Bogside and the Creggan, outside those walls.

Trouble began with sharpened coins being flicked at the marchers in their solemn bowler hats and garish sashes. Then small stones beat down on to their heads followed by large pieces of brick and concrete. The police charged the mobs of Catholic youths, driving them with flailing batons out of the old city and back into their Bogside ghetto. For once, the Catholics stood their ground in the maze of narrow streets, ambushing the constables on street corners with hails of missiles. Policemen fell under the barrage and were dragged away by their colleagues, riot shields held above their heads.

"Fuck King Billy!" the Catholics jeered. "Fuck the Prods!"

"Up the IRA!" they shouted. "Up Free Derry!"

As the news of the action spread across the Province to Belfast, Protestant mobs stormed out of the bars in their own ghettoes off the Shankhill Road, inflamed with drink, infuriated at the Catholics' defiance in Derry. Petrol bombs set houses ablaze in the neighboring Catholic areas.

Catholic families fled for their lives or huddled under their beds and sofas while revolver and rifle shots smashed through windows and doors and whined down deserted streets.

Armored tenders of the RUC growled down the street, constables blasting away at the snipers with the 30-caliber Browning machine-guns mounted on the vehicles' turrets.

Rioting, murdering and burning continued into the next day and night with both factions hardly breaking for food or rest.

On August 14th British troops swept out of their bases in Derry and Belfast to take up positions between the factions. Catholics ran waving and cheering into the streets, clapping the soldiers as if they were a liberation force, their apparent saviors against the onslaught of the Protestant mobs.

Between them, politicians in London, Belfast and Dublin—by their vacillation, obstinacy and opportunism—had created a situation where the only winner could be the IRA.

Since the Dublin Government was unable to help the Catholics in Northern Ireland over whom it still claimed constitutional sovereignty, then the IRA would have to protect the minority.

The Dublin Government preferred not to notice as various individuals and organizations provided the IRA with thousands of pounds with which to purchase arms in Europe and the IRA in the South dispatched to Ulster what men it could. Among them was Seamus Aherne, who arrived in Belfast by train on September 22nd, 1969.

By this time, the Army had constructed what it called a "peace line" in the city from Cupar Street to Coates Street. This ugly strip of corrugated iron and barbed wire, searchlights and sentry posts, was supposed to be a barrier between the Catholic and Protestant ghettoes, between the Falls and the Shankhill. It satisfied no one except the Army and the world's media who took it as the final acknowledgment that Northern Ireland was a hopelessly divided community.

Seamus obtained lodgings with a family in Merrion Street, just off the Falls Road, not far from the Long Bar in Leeson Street which was used as an information center by the Republicans.

Each night, he helped mount the patrols guarding the Catholic enclave from any sneak attacks by Protestant gunmen.

By early October, the IRA had obtained two dozen more weapons and Seamus was issued with a .38 caliber Smith and Wesson to carry during the long nights.

It was a time for the IRA, like the British Army, to build up its strength and review its tactics. Many politicians on mainland Britain still refused to see the hand of the IRA behind the civil unrest and recommended, on October 10th, the disbandment of the Protestant part-time B-Special constabulary.

The Protestants were so infuriated that they poured on to the Shankhill, attacking police and troops, even trying to roll a lorry into them. Their gunmen flitted behind the mob, sniping at the security forces, eventually fatally wounding one policeman.

For the first time, on October 11th, the Army was given orders to return fire. It was a delightful irony for the IRA that the first two to be killed by the forces of the British Crown were Protestants whose entire *raison d'etre* was to remain subjects of that Crown.

The IRA had the chance to seize the initiative totally but, as so many times before, its leadership was split and in disarray.

Cathoal Goulding and his supporters on the Army Council and in its political counterpart, Sinn Fein, wanted the movement to recognize what it termed "the partition parliaments" in Dublin, Stormont and Westminster and to resume using political methods to bring about change in Ireland. They also suggested the possibility of amalgamation with the Southern Irish Communist Party.

This idea of a switch away from direct action was anathema to many IRA men who believed in the movement's traditional aims and methods. They banded together to form the "Provisional Army Council" which held fast to the old IRA philosophy that only physical force, not class politics, would bring about the re-unification of Ireland.

Sinn Fein and IRA groups, north and south of the Border, split. Most stayed with what was now called the "Official IRA." The others, usually more militant, pledged themselves to the new "Provisional IRA." Seamus Aherne, with his family's history, found it more natural to side with the Provisionals.

For a time there was vicious animosity between the two sides which manifested itself in a sharp, nasty shooting war in Belfast, centered mostly around Leeson Street, before a priest arranged a ceasefire.

After that, the Officials continued to man the barricades while the Provisionals adopted a more offensive policy.

Seamus was set to work designing crude nail grenades for throwing at Army foot patrols. These consisted of a dozen six-inch nails fixed through thick corrugated paper, a small amount of explosive and a detonator on a burning fuse taped to the contraption. They were simple but effective in confined spaces like narrow alleys. Later in 1970, he worked on bigger bombs which were laid at public utility targets—gas-holders, water pumping stations and electricity transformers.

His great problem was lack of sophisticated equipment. The supplies of stolen explosives were adequate enough but he had no access to modern timing devices. He fell back on methods used long ago in the Fenian bombing campaigns, tying wire around clock-winders or pushing tin-tacks through wooden clothes pegs.

It was simple but dangerous. Seamus knew that there could be no accuracy about the timing.

At least three of the bombs designed by Seamus went off prematurely, killing four IRA Volunteers, but that was a fact he didn't mention to his cellmates in the Crumlin Gaol whenever he discussed his work with the Third Belfast Battalion.

He did tell them briefly about the new device he'd designed which used a metal rod to arm it but they weren't particularly impressed.

To his chagrin, they regarded a bomb-designer as someone on the periphery of IRA active service. Their stories were all of gun battles with the security forces or the Protestants and, occasionally, of murdering informers.

"You southerners don't know what it's about," his cellmate Andy McCann would jeer.

His face had the pinched expression of a hungry rat. When he was excited, his high nostrils twitched and quivered like a rodent on the scent of food.

"You came up here, Seamus, believing it was about politics and civil rights, my son," he'd continue, unpleasantly patronizing. "Just like all the big brains down in Dublin. About civil rights and politics, that's what you thought."

Seamus would half-nod, perhaps agreeing slightly, certainly not wishing to give offense. Each of his cellmates carried the unmistakable stamp of men long accustomed to direct physical violence. Seamus knew that he was hardly capable of that himself except in the most extreme circumstances. It worried him and made him feel inferior in such a place as this prison where brutish violence simmered so near the surface.

"In Belfast, my son," McCann would continue his lecture, "it's always been about the survival of the hardest. Your own da helped bomb the customs posts on the Border for God knows how long and thought it was all about bringing workers' power to a united Ireland. Up here, down the Falls, it mattered as much as a limp prick waving in the west wind. Up here, we had to fight or die. It didn't matter or not whether you were IRA, though most of us were. Just being Catholic was enough, believe me, my son. In the Thirties, we tunnelled under the houses and garden walls just so the womenfolk could get from street to street, from house to shop without being plugged by a bullet. Why, the Prods would just as happily loose a few rounds down a Catholic loanin as they'd buy a packet of Woodbines at the corner shop. And all the while, you boys in the south were happy having your fist-fights with the Blueshirts or picketing some building site or other. Did you know, up here the Prods took out a whole family and shot the menfolk dead down to the wee-est boy? We went to a Proddie factory and hit all them. We even asked them to pick out the Mickies first so we knew who wasn't to be dealt with.

"Mind you, all that stuff ended back in the 30s when none of us had any work. Then the war came and we both got bombed, Proddie or not. But you still picked which bar you supped in 'cos we weren't that friendly. In those days, though, we both had to make the best of it so there wasn't too much energy left for fighting. And anyway, those bastard Bs were everywhere. They knew who was who and what was what and they carried the guns that mattered. Christ, in the old days, if they'd had a wee party at their barracks, they'd end up for an encore driving down the Falls and tossing a couple of grenades through a window just for the hell of it. No, Seamus, my son, up here it's always been a wee bit of a private war, whatever the hell you fellas in

Dublin might've been doing. We've admired your political principles but they've meant fuck all to a fool as far as the Belfast boys are concerned."

Always, it seemed to Seamus, his cellmates had forgotten the fear, the sheer terror, of their gunfights and bombings, only immortalizing the bravado involved. They had no regrets about what they'd done and, actually, were loath to place their legends within the framework of IRA history. It was somehow a private war.

To them, he realized, shooting and being shot at was regarded as almost an everyday part of life in the Belfast ghettoes. He wondered if their children would have a similar attitude when they grew up, would live out their fathers' legends once more.

He, at least, had experienced a fairly normal upbringing despite its deprivations and strong Republican overtones. He had not had to become involved. He'd had free choice, unlike many of the Belfast and Derry IRA, and the realization of that made him feel more able to withstand the ordeal of imprisonment. Seamus also knew that he could take a more detached view of what was going on outside the prison walls than men like Andy McCann, who cheered every shooting, riot or burning as a new victory.

Seamus wasn't so sure, couldn't share their enthusiasm for the news reaching the prisoners within Crumlin Gaol that late spring and early summer of 1971.

The first British soldier had been killed, and the tempo of violence had increased. Seamus's bomb laid by the BBC transmitter on Brougher Mountain had been partly instrumental in that. Instead of killing the Army patrol charged with guarding the transmitter, the bomb had devastated three BBC workmen.

That incident, along with others, had raised the political temperature. But Seamus's guess was that none of the mayhem and destruction had yet begun to affect those people in Westminster and Dublin with power to make decisions about the future of Northern Ireland.

He pondered the question during his first months in prison, walking round and round the exercise yard, watching the helicopters buzzing into Girdwood Barracks nearby, standing in this queue or that, or simply laying on his bunk gazing into the light or the darkness.

And when he'd plucked up the nerve, the confidence, to voice his ideas, he was surprised at how matter-of-factly they were received at first by Charley McCool in his Republican commander's cell on the landing below.

"So you think the tactics are wrong, do you, son?"

"Some, Mr. McCool," Seamus replied hesitantly.

"And why are you telling me now? Why now?"

"I've been thinking of it for some time."

"Strange, son. Strange now, when I was about to send for you myself."

"Me. Why?"

"Doesn't matter for the moment. You just be telling what's wrong for the present."

Seamus took a deep breath, wondering how to begin.

"Well, Mr. McCool, I think the emphasis on guns and rifles is wrong. We'll never beat the Brits in a shooting war. We'll never match them like that. They've the training and they outnumber us thousands to one."

"Who says there's emphasis on the gun?"

"That's all the boys along the landings talk about. When they laid such-and-such an ambush on an Army patrol, fired a few rounds and skedaddled, or when they knee-capped some poor sod or gave someone a head shot."

"Guns are necessary sometimes."

"We'll never hurt the Brits enough with them and that's for sure!"

"Guns are necessary for discipline, for raising money, even for finding recruits. There's nothing like the sight of a pistol of his own to give a youngster a powerful urge to fire it at someone," McCool said flatly, almost dismissively.

"I agree that. I agree all that," Seamus replied, searching desperately for the right arguments. "But the guns aren't hurting the right people where they should. Bombing can do so much more damage."

McCool nodded.

"If we blow up a factory, we hurt all the people with

money in that business. We cause unemployment and that costs the government a fortune here, let alone the social upset caused with people without jobs. If you ruin the industry, then you ruin the country. That's what we want, after all, isn't it?"

"Not totally," McCool smiled. "We want to hurt the Brits so much that they'll want to get out of this place. Not total ruin."

"Bombs are still the answer, not bullets. Don't you see? A few pounds of mixture, a detonator for 5p, a bit of wire and a battery, and we've a bomb for about £1 which'll cause hundreds of thousands of pounds worth of damage. And also, there's nothing like a bomb to put the shit up the civilians."

"So?" McCool shrugged. "We're using bombs, aren't we? Christ, son, you should know that if anyone."

Seamus shook his head. "You can hardly call them bombs! We've not the proper equipment to build real good 'uns and if we had I'm doubting if I'm well enough trained, or the others are, to make proper use of it. My Post Office training just about got me to a simple circuit and a makeshift arming rod."

"So what do you suggest then, son?"

"We find proper timers, maybe even remote control stuff, and we put bombs on top of the list of priorities. Not just fart about with them. And, last but not least, we also dig up a proper instructor from somewhere."

McCool looked at him for a moment, narrowing his eyes, then grinned broadly.

"You're right, of course, son. Dead right."

Seamus stared with amazement.

"Just testing the strength of your convictions, if I can use that word in here!"

McCool stood up and limped around to the bunk where Seamus was sitting. He leaned over him, speaking not much above a whisper: "Now listen . . . the Army Council agree with what you've been saying. They've been thinking the same. That's why I was wanting to see you . . . to tell you they've decided you're to get out of here."

"Escape?" Seamus whispered back.

"That's what I said. You'll be on a break-out in a fortnight or so."

"Jesus, that's good, Mr. McCool."

"Maybe so. Maybe not. It won't be so good for you if you're caught. Nothing's guaranteed, mind."

"I'll take the chance."

"You will, son. You will that."

He placed a hand on Seamus's shoulder in a paternal gesture.

"But one word of warning and I'll not be mentioning it again. There are still some not happy about the word on that bomb factory down the Markets a few months back. They're wondering awful hard where the Brits found the info on it and how they did when they did."

"That! Christ, I was inside here at the time, wasn't I? Why put me with that fuck-up."

"No idea, son. I'm just thinking. They're just guessing. Only you're knowing what happened if anything happened at all." He paused. "Let's have it like that, shall we? Any three ways, the big men are thinking you're more useful out than in so you'll be going."

"That's something, isn't it?"

Seamus hoped his voice sounded calm. Inwardly, he felt sick with shock at the mention of the bomb factory, at the clear warning.

McCool clapped him on the shoulder again.

"Don't worry, son," he said. "You'll be a big man one day. And that I'll guarantee or . . ."

He paused, his eyes harder, his mouth tighter, his grip harder, claw-like, on Seamus's shoulder.

". . . or you'll die in the trying, so help me!"

Chapter 5
June, 1971

The young housewife, slim and dark in sweater and jeans, stood at her kitchen sink listening to the birds singing and chattering in the small copse just outside the window. Tree branches, high up, swayed and dipped as a red squirrel foraged relentlessly. A patch of sunshine crept into the far corner of the courtyard surrounding the small, isolated cottage, once the stables behind the Victorian mansion fifty yards nearer the road.

Sharon Ayres thought there was little that could add to her contentment. It was a lovely day; baby Oliver, nearly three months old, was fast asleep in his pram out in the courtyard; and her husband would be home that evening.

Later on, she decided, she would walk Oliver down to the pine woods and sand dunes at the end of the road. They'd feed the squirrels, plentiful and nearly tame along the Lancashire coast, north of the Mersey.

Perhaps, by accident or design, she'd stroll past that particular dune where she and Roy had made love under a full moon on their way home from a late party. Her grey-blue eyes always softened at the memory of that and the shared bath afterwards when they'd tried to rid each other of intimately embedded grains of sand.

She took a deep breath and smelled the fragrance of the pine in the air. Then she grimaced to herself, smiling, as her nostrils also took in the earthier smell of dirty nappies soaking in their bucket by the sink. Anyway, Sharon decided, she wouldn't let that unpleasant chore spoil her mood. She bent down to lift the bucket and heard the voice at the same time as she saw the trouser legs and shoes.

238

"Don't cry out, lady! Don't scream! Don't do nothing!"

Something cold and hard jabbed into her back, into the gap of bare flesh between sweater and jeans.

"Slowly now!" the voice commanded, gruff and low yet strangely lyrical.

Her body went rigid with shock. She couldn't move. Her hands in their rubber gloves clenched tight beneath the scum of the soaking bucket.

"Up, lady! Up!"

But she couldn't. Her eyes, wide with fear, were fixed on the scuffed suede of the man's shoes.

"Come on," the voice urged.

A hand slid under her armpit, encompassed her full left breast and pulled upwards. She jerked straight and began turning her head. A snatch of breath rasped in her throat. Her heart fluttered out of rhythm. It had to be a nightmare.

There, close by her, in her kitchen, were two of Snow White's dwarfs.

"That's right, lady. Easy now," said a red-nosed Grumpy, so close that she could feel his body-heat.

"Don't be feared now," echoed a lop-eared Dopey over by the door.

And then Sharon realized that the men were wearing colored Disney masks.

"Who? Who?" Her voice was high-pitched and quavering. She saw the revolvers in their gloved hands pointing unwaveringly, black and shiny, at her midriff. She turned fully around, gasping again, and pressed back against the sink. Instinctively, she clasped the dripping wet gloves across her breasts as if to shield them from attack. "Wha . . . a . . . a?" She tried to ask something but her tongue had thickened and dried.

An image of Oliver, eyes tight shut, little fist near rosebud mouth, flashed into Sharon's mind. She lurched towards the door. "My baby!" she cried.

Dopey didn't move from the doorway. His gun was steady.

Sharon stepped back, clutching herself in anguish.

"The wee 'un's sleeping sound," said Grumpy, a

surprisingly reassuring tone in his thick Liverpool-Irish accent. "At least he was when we slipped in and found you day-dreaming out of the window. Just wait till you calm down, lady, and then you can bring him in."

The young woman knew she had to regain control of herself. She took a few deep breaths, eyes flicking from one dwarf mask to the other. She couldn't understand. Why hadn't she heard them? She must have been too lost in her happiness.

"Right," said Grumpy, seeing her compose herself. "Go and get the wee 'un and bring him in."

"But he'll cry if I wake him," Sharon protested automatically. "He always does."

Grumpy shook his head as if in amused despair. "Then, sure we'll be after helping you carry the pram in, lady. Anything to oblige."

He stood by the front door, just inside the glazed porch, while his companion lifted one end of the pram gently up the three steps, through the porch and into the large square hall which doubled as a dining room.

"Now sit yourself down, lady," said Grumpy when the pram had been maneuvered indoors and wheeled alongside the small, extendable dining table.

Sharon sat down warily, stiff-backed, by the table, one hand pressed into her lap, the other grasping the pram handle. She noticed the rubber gloves still on her hands and began irritably to peel them off.

"That's right, lady. Relax," murmured Dopey, sitting down opposite her, gun casually in hand.

"Now we can talk," said Grumpy. "In about an hour you'll be having a phone call from your man . . ."

"But he's away on a job," Sharon interrupted. "He won't ring till he's back at the airport this evening."

She heard her own voice as she spoke and realized that her natural Scouse accent, nasal and singsong, was reasserting itself over all her elocution lessons.

"Don't worry, lady. Don't be worrying at all," said Grumpy, leaning over the table. "Believe me, he'll be ringing all right."

"And when he does," Dopey continued, rubbing the barrel of his gun against his wobby rubber ear, "all you have to do is tell him that you've two nice gentlemen here for coffee who'll go away when he does what he's told."

"What's that supposed to be?" she demanded, beginning to feel anger rather than fear.

"Nothing to do with you, lady," said Grumpy.

"All you have to worry about is staying calm and looking after your wee 'un. We're not criminals. We're not after harming you."

"Then who are you then? What are you doing here?"

Sharon began to rise from her seat. Dopey motioned her down again with a wave of his gun. "Can't you tell from our accents?" he asked teasingly.

"Oh, my God!" Sharon exclaimed, suddenly understanding.

"That's right, lady. We're an Active Service Unit of the Provisional IRA. We're soldiers, not criminals, though I suppose you mightn't guess that from our masks. But we wanted to wear something which wouldn't frighten the babbie too much. Don't want him crying a storm."

"You see," said Grumpy, "all along we want to do what we have to do without hurting anyone. We're not enemies of yours."

Sharon nodded, her mind whirling with questions. "And if Roy doesn't do what . . . ?"

Grumpy shook his head. "He will, lady. Never fear. He will."

She sunk her head in her hands and started to sob.

"Put the kettle on," Grumpy muttered to Dopey. "Maybe a nice cuppa'll put her right."

He touched Sharon gently, almost paternally, on the shoulder. She reminded him of his own teenage daughter.

At that moment, Captain Roy Ayres was 2,000 feet above the Irish Sea in his charter firm's Bell 206 Jet Ranger helicopter, GTAX-4. Beside him was the client who'd hired him from Speke Airport in Liverpool to the Isle of Man for the night and then on to Belfast.

The customer, a florid, balding Irishman nearing middle age, called Black, had explained that he wanted the helicopter for his urgent business trip in preference to a small aircraft because he wanted to test the machine's performance, possibly to buy one himself for his own company.

Ayres had guessed that his client was probably connected with the gaming industry. Certainly he'd spent most of the previous evening at the tables in the small casino at the Palace Hotel in Douglas, the Manx capital. Not that it was any of the pilot's business how a client spent his money. He seemed a nice enough chap, though lacking the usual Irish loquacity, and had even given Ayres £10 pocket money to spend at the hotel.

The pilot noticed the grey, indistinct smudge on the horizon. He tapped his passenger on the forearm and pointed. "The coast, Mr. Black. Another ten minutes," he said into his microphone.

The Irishman nodded, smiling, and reached for the briefcase by his seat.

"Any further orders when we land?" asked Ayres.

Mr. Black fumbled for his mike button before replying. "I'll let you know when we're on the ground."

"Enjoying it?"

"Fine. Just fine, Captain."

Soon, the helicopter dropped lower on its approach to Belfast Lough. Its shadow danced across the small silvery waves and the decks of two coasters making their sedate way back to England.

The city could be seen clearly now, sprawling around the horseshoe-shaped lough, the huge shipyard crane of Harland and Wolff's raised above the docks like a yellow offering to the sky.

"Merseyair helicopter Golf Tango Alpha X-ray," Ayres called. "Request clearance to land at Sydenham."

"Roger, Alpha X-ray. Affirmative to land," crackled back the reply. "Nothing in the circuit. Wind northeast, twelve knots. Visibility good."

The helicopter whirred over the factories on the reclaimed land on the east side of the lough, across the perimeter fence of Belfast Harbor Airport and descended gently on to the grass about fifty yards from the main buildings. The rotor blades driven by their 317 hp Allison engine turned ever more slowly before drooping to a halt.

"Right, Mr. Black, what now?" the young pilot asked, removing his headset and turning cheerfully to his passenger. "Shall I . . . ?"

"I'm sorry about this."

"What? . . . Oh, Christ alive!"

The Irishman held a small revolver in his lap pointing directly at the pilot's chest. It was shielded from all but Ayres by the briefcase.

"Don't do anything silly, Captain. Please. For your own sake—and your family's."

Ayres struck a clenched fist against his thigh. "You're hijacking me?" His voice was flat and angry.

"Something like that. We want you to perform a wee service for us."

"I don't suppose I have to ask who you are?"

"Probably not."

"You realize you'll never get away with it."

Ayres sensed he was speaking like a character in a second-rate film. He looked into Mr. Black's eyes, calm and alert, and knew that, indeed, he could get away with it. He shrugged despondently.

"Well, what now?"

"A phone call, Captain. Just a phone call. We want to be sure you'll cooperate fully. There's to be no mistakes, no sudden errors of judgment."

"A phone call?"

"To your home, Captain."

"Sharon!"

"We want you to realize it's not only your future at stake if you decide to play hero."

"Bastards!" Ayres exclaimed venomously.

Mr. Black was unconcerned. His voice continued flat and hard, no longer jaunty and appealing.

"Possibly. But let's just get on with it, shall we? This gun'll be on you all the way so let's not be stupid."

To the men in the control tower, the sight was perfectly normal, simply a businessman and his pilot walking towards the main airport building.

When they neared the building, past three airport workers pushing a trolley, Ayres steadied himself to attack. It was an animal feeling. His deep anger allowed no fear for himself or anyone else. He stiffened his muscles, about to swing around suddenly. But it was as if the gunman could read his thoughts.

"Don't, for Sharon's sake," he murmured quietly. "And the babbie's."

Ayres' shoulders slumped fractionally, the threat registering. He shook his head slightly and pushed through the building's glass doors towards the grey public phonebox set on the wall a few yards inside.

Mr. Black stood so close to him while he dialled the nine-digit number that he could feel the gun pressing against his chest. At the other end of the line, the phone rang only three times before Sharon, his lovely Sharon, answered.

"Darling," he cried urgently before she could finish giving the phone number.

"Roy!"

"It's all right, darling! It's all right!"

"What's happening, Roy?" she almost shrieked.

He could sense that she was near to hysteria.

"I don't know, darling, but are you and Oliver all right?"

"There are two men . . ."

"I know. But are you all right?"

He'd wanted to be calm and reassuring but his frantic worry was clear in his voice.

"Yes. They haven't . . ."

"Are you sure?"

"It's horrible. They've guns and mas . . ."

Mr. Black leaned across and pressed down the phone rest, cutting off the call.

"That's enough, Captain," he said harshly. "We've work to do."

Ayres replaced the phone receiver slowly. He felt drained and weak. "If anything . . . if you hurt them . . . I'll . . . I'll . . ."

"Nothing will," the Irishman interrupted. "Now let's get on. The quicker we're done, the sooner you'll see them again. Once you've done what we want, they'll be left alone. You've my word on that."

"And what's that worth?" Ayres asked bitterly.

The gunman looked stonily at him for a moment, then jabbed him in the ribs with his briefcase and nodded towards the door. They walked quickly back to the helicopter and clambered into the cockpit.

"You know we can't take off without clearance and without filing a flight plan," Ayres remarked, settling back into his seat. "So it's no use going on."

"Uh-huh," Mr. Black replied, unconcerned, pulling three large colored photographs from the briefcase with his left hand. The other held the gun, pointing without the slightest quiver.

He handed the photos to Ayres who immediately realized they were aerial survey views of Belfast.

"See where we are?"

Ayres nodded. He could easily identify the airfield jutting out into the middle of the harbor.

"Right. See the big crane over there?"

"You can't miss it," said Ayres.

"Well, you fly directly over that, come down to 300 feet and head on the same bearing over the city until you see the first large piece of greenery. It's there on the photo. Girdwood Park. I'll tell you where to put down."

"Is that all?"

The sarcasm was ignored.

"It'll take no more than three minutes. Probably less."

"But I told you, we've no clearance."

Mr. Black's voice hardened.

"Fuck clearance! If they query, just stall. Got it?"

"Okay," the pilot sighed. "Shall I start up now?"

The gunman looked at his watch. It was ten minutes to eleven o'clock. He shook his head.

"Dead on five minutes to. That's when we go. Start the rotors a minute before."

The two sat in silence, occasionally glancing at their

watches. Roy Ayres thought of his wife and child and if he'd lose his job after doing what "they" wanted. He had no doubt who "they" were. Mr. Black waited impassively, hoping that the others would carry out their orders as well as he'd done. His main worry was the £55 he'd lost in the casino the night before. He would have to refund that if he wasn't to risk a bullet through the calf muscles of one leg, perhaps both.

Not three miles away, Seamus Aherne trudged around the exercise yard of Crumlin Gaol, hearing the monotonous tread of dozens of boots upon paving stone, the sound of men walking for the sake of walking with little enjoyment and no expectation of getting anywhere. It was a sound even more redolent of prison life than keys turning in locks.

He counted the prison officers on duty: six of them, with three more holding dogs in the far corner where workmen were repainting the main wall, not twenty yards from the nearest cell block.

Every time Seamus looked at that wall, he thought it had grown taller and thicker. He wondered idly if the remote-controlled television cameras ever relayed close-up pictures of the exercising prisoners and, if they did, how he would appear on the screen. He brushed a hand through his black, greasy hair.

Suddenly, from a cell above, he heard the distinct sound of metal striking metal once. It was the signal to begin counting.

"1 . . . 2 . . . 3 . . . 4 . . ." he muttered under his breath, glancing sideways at the two men walking with him, Frankie O'Riordan and Mickey Quinn, both veterans of gun-battles along the "peace line." They were counting too, just as they'd practiced together after Charley McCool had arranged for them to share a cell.

It took exactly a minute to circle the yard at the accepted pace, to be in the right position at the right time. And timing, as McCool said, was all.

". . . 49 . . . 50 . . . 51 . . ." they muttered to themselves.

Seamus noticed the prisoners on the opposite side of the yard starting to bunch together.

". . . 54 . . . 55 . . . 56 . . ."

They were nearly in position.

". . . 57 . . . 58 . . . 59 . . ."

"You Provo bastards!"

The cries rang out around the yard, swiftly followed by the thuds of fists upon flesh.

Seamus looked quickly across. At least half-a-dozen men had begun fighting with more joining in every second. Already two prison officers had been drawn into the brawl while others were hurrying towards the disturbance.

"Kerrump!! . . . Kerrump!!"

Two loud explosions echoed around the yard as "ship-yard spaghetti" grenades containing nuts and bolts, thrown from a passing car, detonated against the Army sentry-post at the Crumlin Road entrance.

These were followed by a fusillade of shots from a machine gun while the car accelerated away into the busy morning traffic. The bullets cracked and whined against the outer walls.

Inside the yard, all was panic and pain. The warders fought baton-to-fist with the prisoners, fearing a concerted, full-scale attack on the prison. The alarm siren wailing from high on the cell-block wall added to their desperation.

Seamus and his two companions waited a moment, backs pressed against the yard's inner wall, until the warders with dogs had charged past them toward the brawling scrum. Then they dashed towards the outer wall.

"Quick!" called O'Riordan, reaching the wall first.

Seamus already had the two half-sticks of explosive in his hand.

He thrust them into the gaps left between the bricks by the workmen, and immediately lit the short, dangling safety fuses.

The three flung themselves to the ground, covering their heads.

Automatically, Seamus counted away the seconds.

"1 . . . 2 . . . 3 . . . 4 . . . 5 . . ."

Kerrump!!

The explosions came together, lifting the three men off the ground, partially deafening them, momentarily winding them.

They forced themselves to their knees, coughing and spluttering in the cloud of dust and powdered cement. Around them they could hear broken bricks clattering on to the yard's paving stones.

Seamus pushed himself blindly into the cloud, arms outstretched. His knees crashed agonizingly into a pile of rubble but, through the clearing dust, he could see that the explosions had done their work. Before him, at thigh level, was a jagged hole about four feet high and three feet wide. He launched himself through it, rather like a diver entering a swimming pool, and tumbled on to the grass bank on the other side, the side abutting the open spaces of Girdwood Park.

For a moment, he lay there, gazing up at the cloudless blue sky. It had never looked so blue from inside the prison. He felt totally calm, almost disoriented, until first Quinn and then O'Riordan dived through the hole and landed on top of his legs.

The prison siren continued to wail and the sounds of the fighting could still be heard even from outside the wall. Then, overpowering every noise, came the battering cacophony of a helicopter flying low.

Seamus looked over towards the nearest clearing, now used as a sports pitch by the troops who'd taken over most of the park, and saw the red-and-white helicopter hovering with its landing skids about two feet off the grass.

"Come on, for Christ's sake, or we're all done for," panted Quinn.

They pushed themselves to their feet and began running. Seamus felt weary. Perhaps, he thought, it was the mental exhaustion of the previous twenty-four hours when he'd been unable to rest properly, always rehearsing the routine with the explosives, smuggled into the prison in plastic bags hidden in women's vaginas. He heard shouting behind him.

Before he could look back, O'Riordan shouted a warning: "They've loosed the fucking dogs!"

The thought of the German Shepherd dogs bounding over the grass, fangs bared, lent them speed. No one dared turn his head.

To his left, about a hundred yards away, Seamus saw a group of soldiers, apparently unarmed, break into a trot towards them. Ahead, closer with every stride, was the helicopter. The pilot was rigidly straight in his seat, concentrating on the controls. A man hung out of the door nearest to them, gun pointing, mouthing something that was lost in the roar of the machine's engine.

As they ran, the three prisoners ripped off their denim jackets, trusting in Charlie McCool's advice that the dogs would break their progress to sniff and harry the cloth.

Quinn reached the helicopter a yard ahead of the other two. He tumbled through the doorway and on to the wide bench-seat at the back. Seamus and O'Riordan collided in their haste to get through the narrow door. O'Riordan's greater bulk pushed Seamus aside. He slipped on the turf and fell full length. The helicopter began rising while Seamus scrabbled frantically to his knees. He gazed around wildly, thinking he was about to be abandoned.

The soldiers came nearer. One of them was obviously carrying a weapon. Seamus saw him drop to one knee and aim a rifle. The prison officers were still a good way off trying to disentangle their dogs, grouped and snarling and tearing around the discarded jackets.

He heard a shot ring out close to, clear above the helicopter's thumping, beating blades. He scrambled upright and felt a hand reach out for a grip on him, then another. Somehow, slipping and twisting, he hauled himself up. The helicopter banked sharply to the right and lifted. Somewhere on the fuselage, a bullet pinged off metal. Hands gripped Seamus under the shoulders and pulled him finally, safely, into the cabin. The door slid shut. He grinned up into the sweating and triumphant faces of Quinn and O'Riordan.

The middle-aged man beside the pilot was shouting above the noise. At first, Seamus couldn't hear him. He shook his head. The man leaned further towards him between the front and rear seats.

"For Jesus' sake," he roared. "Where were you? Did you think this was a fucking scheduled flight?"

Seamus shook his head again, too breathless to answer. The man broke into a wide grin. O'Riordan gripped Seamus around the waist and lifted him on to the seat. At last he was able to see out of the windows.

The helicopter was flying at about 200 feet straight along Crumlin Road towards the hills surrounding the city. It was so low that Seamus could clearly see the people's faces as they peered up at the machine. The houses and shops below resembled large models, complete in every detail even to the washing on lines in gardens and courtyards.

In the pilot's seat, Roy Ayres took a peek at the aerial survey photo as his hijacker traced the route with his finger. Within a minute, they were away from the city streets and flying over the heather and gorse of the hill slopes and the scattered homes on the outskirts near Ligoneil.

A message crackled indistinctly on the radio. Mr. Black leaned forward and flicked up a switch on the control panel, turning off the transmission.

The pilot banked away from the road below him, flicked across a spinning mill and descended even lower. Seamus thought at first that the helicopter was preparing to land in the open but then he saw, over a gentle rise, a large quarry deserted except for two cars.

Mr. Black jabbed his thumb downwards. The helicopter swung to the left and began its descent, sinking to the ground only ten yards from the waiting cars, its rotors swirling up a cloud of earth and small pieces of gravel.

No one waited for the blades to stop. They tumbled gleefully out, shaking hands in self-congratulation at the success of their escape so far.

Two men jumped out of the cars, shielding their faces from the stinging gravel, and waved the prisoners over.

"You, in here!" one ordered Seamus, pushing him into the rear seat of a large grey Volvo. "And keep down!"

Quinn and O'Riordan jumped into the other car, a red Austin Maxi.

Seamus looked back at the helicopter, blades now

stopped, Mr. Black was handcuffing the pilot to one of the struts of the skid undercarriage.

The middle-aged man patted Roy Ayres consolingly on the shoulder before trotting over to Seamus's car and jumping in the front seat. "Let's go," he called.

In convoy, the cars screeched away down a hard-rutted track.

"Listen, Aherne," Mr. Black called over his shoulder. "We're dropping you off in a minute. You'll hide up for the rest of the day and then be picked up again tonight. You'll find new clothes and the necessary instructions where we're leaving you. Okay?"

"Fine," Seamus replied. "I'll be on my own?"

"Uh-huh. The other two are decoys to lead the bloodhounds off the scent."

"Do they know that?"

Mr. Black shrugged. "They've a chance," he said blandly.

When they reached the end of the track, the vehicle carrying Quinn and O'Riordan turned to the left, tires screaming, while Seamus's car went to the right.

The Volvo sped along the narrow country road, green hedges blurred on either side, for little more than half-a-mile before it spun into a small car park behind a squarish, grey-stone building. Seamus lifted his head above the back window. The car skidded to a halt close to the building.

"In there!" shouted the driver, pointing to the nearest door. "Lock it behind you. Your stuff's in the next room through."

Seamus was out of the car and into the building in a second. "Thanks," he called, closing the door, reaching for the key, but the Volvo was already in motion. All he could see was Mr. Black with his hand half-raised as if saluting or waving farewell.

He locked the door carefully. He was standing in a narrow, dark passageway. He walked quietly along it to a room leading off to the right, a largish kitchen. By the sink, he saw a suitcase and a large envelope weighed down on the tiled floor by a bottle of milk and a quarter-bottle of Paddy whiskey. Seamus smiled, silently thanking someone's thoughtfulness. He picked up the whiskey and began unscrewing the top. Suddenly he stopped and listened. The silence was slightly disconcerting. It was the first time he'd heard silence since the Army had picked him up five months before.

"Slainte," he murmured, taking a swig of the whiskey. The spirit made him gag and splutter. "Jesus, it's been too long," he reflected.

On the wall, by a mirror, was a tiny notice. He took another mouthful, more carefully this time, while he read the instructions about how to switch off the lights in the building. He grinned when he saw the heading "Masonic Hall."

Seamus sat down on the floor, resting against a set of drawers, and tore open the envelope. Inside were two closely-typed sheets of paper and a leather wallet.

He checked the contents of the wallet first. Apart from a few receipts from restaurants in Belfast, there were currency notes totalling £64, rail and sea tickets, a driving license and a rectangular piece of plastic about two inches square.

"So that's why," he muttered, remembering how Charley McCool had somehow acquired a Polaroid camera, presumably from a friendly prison officer, to take two photographs of him. His hair had been smarmed with grease and parted down the middle; he'd worn thick-framed spectacles borrowed from another prisoner and he'd been told to puff out his cheeks. Peering into his shaving mirror, he'd been surprised at how much these touches of disguise had altered his appearance.

Now, seeing the finished product in the plastic identity card, he guessed that his old friends in Listowel, perhaps even his family, would have great difficulty in recognizing him from the photograph.

The typewritten instructions confirmed that he was to disguise himself once more, using the materials and clothes in the suitcase, and provided details of his new temporary identity.

He was a textile engineer called Alan Anderson, Courtaulds employee, on his way to its Lancashire mills for a conference. The plastic card was a Courtaulds identity pass for its factories in Northern Ireland. Clearly, Seamus decided, someone must have had friends within that organization who'd laminated his photograph into a genuine pass.

Next, he opened the suitcase and lifted out a smart, lightly checked grey suit on its hanger. He hooked this behind the door to allow any creases to drop out. There was a complete change of clothing, shoes, a wash bag with toilet gear, a wristwatch, properly set and wound, even a pack of cigarettes and a well-used lighter.

Finally, there was a packet of cheese sandwiches, the bread cut thick, and a documents file. He leafed through this and saw a number of letters, memoranda and instructions booklets, each bearing the distinctive Courtaulds' heading, many with his alias typed upon them.

Seamus settled down to eat the sandwiches and drink the milk, studying at the same time the instructions for the next stage of the escape.

The plan was as daring and simple as the actual break-out from Crumlin Gaol. On first read, he thought it almost too simple, perhaps suicidal, but the longer he read, the more he could perceive its chances of success.

Although he felt mentally and physically exhausted, Seamus didn't dare sleep during the next six hours or so spent in that kitchen. He was too afraid of missing the pick-up. Instead, he busied himself by washing the dust from the explosion out of his hair, shaving carefully, changing his hairstyle and checking the spectacles, memorizing his instructions and studying the Courtaulds documents.

The last thirty minutes dragged interminably. He kept examining the watch on his wrist but its hands seemed hardly to move.

He dressed in his new clothes and walked up and down, becoming used to the feel of them. Then he took the suit off again for fear of it being stained or creased. He packed the suitcase with his prison uniform and any rubbish, everything except the documents file and the near-emptied bottle of whiskey. He wanted a last drink before setting out.

But still there was time to spare, time to worry.

By now, he supposed, the news of his escape must have reached his family. Probably the Garda had already been around to check that the helicopter hadn't spirited him by some miracle to Galey Bridge.

Seamus wondered how they'd all taken the news. His father would have been excitedly proud, he was sure, and perhaps would have made it an excuse for a trip around the bars in Listowel. He could see his mother and Grandma Hannah being inwardly pleased as well, yet showing a stern face to any outsider. It was a strange feeling, wishing to know what others were saying but, at the same time, not wanting to know in case their opinions were hurtful.

Seamus read the instructions for the last time before burning them in the sink and flushing away the ashes. He wiped every surface clear of possible fingerprints, finished the whiskey, packed the suitcase and finally put on the suit once more.

He took a last look around the kitchen to make certain that there were no signs of his stay. Satisfied, he walked to the back door with the suitcase in his hand and the file tucked under his arm.

At exactly six o'clock, he turned the key in the lock and stepped outside just as a cream Belfast taxi pulled up. Seamus locked the door behind him before climbing into the back seat. The young man sitting beside the driver smiled nervously.

"Any bother?" he asked, a deferential tone in his voice.

"Quiet as a Croke Park crowd when Dublin loses," said Seamus lightly, handing him the key to the hall and the suitcase. Another suitcase lay on the seat beside him. He noticed it was monogrammed "A.A."

"Away we are then," said the driver, a grey-haired man with the inevitable paunch of a veteran cabbie.

The taxi moved out of the car park and turned left into the main road a hundred yards away. To Seamus's surprise, it braked only another hundred yards on outside the Glen Inn, a bar nestling just off the road. The young man in the front seat jumped out, waved once to Seamus and walked into the bar carrying the suitcase with its wealth of incriminating evidence. The taxi set off again.

Seamus wondered if the driver knew that his passenger was an escaped IRA man and whether he should talk with him. He decided silence was wiser. He rubbed the tiredness out of his face and turned casually to gaze out of the car window.

"Jesus!" he exclaimed, realizing for the first time that the taxi was heading directly down Crumlin Road toward the center of Belfast. "Hey!"

The driver glanced back at him through the rear-view mirror. "No worry at all, sir," he said over his shoulder. "I always take the quickest route."

"But . . ." Seamus began to protest when the all-too-familiar shape of Crumlin Goal loomed up on the left.

"Just settle back nicely and enjoy the ride," the driver interrupted, seemingly unconcerned.

Seamus risked only a quick peek as the taxi passed the prison. Workmen and soldiers were busy stringing more barbed wire across the entrance.

"Wee bit of trouble there this morning with this escape," the driver announced cheerfully. "And a fair palaver when two of them were captured at Coleraine."

"Was there?" Seamus replied as innocently as possible, grinning a sickly smile into the driver's mirror.

"So I hear, sir."

"Ah, well," Seamus sighed, re-opening the documents file on his lap, thinking for a moment of Quinn and O'Riordan back in the hands of the security forces.

In ten minutes, the taxi had threaded through the tail of Belfast's rush hour traffic and arrived outside the ferry terminal at Donegall Quay in the docks.

"Got your tickets, sir?" the driver asked.

Seamus pulled out the wallet from his inside jacket pocket.

"Aye, and the cabin reservations."

"Well, have a safe crossing and take it easy now."

"Thanks."

Seamus got out of the car clutching the suitcase and the

file stamped "Courtaulds" across its cover. A thought came to him. He leaned into the driver's window.

"How much do I owe?" he asked.

The driver laughed shortly. "It's on the company's account, sir, the old company. And sure, didn't you know that?"

"Of course. I thought it might have been."

Seamus slapped the taxi's hood lightly before walking into the terminal building. His nerves tightened when he saw an Army foot patrol by the ticket barrier and another patrol, with a group of policemen carrying sub-machine guns, by the queue of passengers waiting to have their baggage searched before boarding the ship.

He started to veer away from the queue toward the men's toilets, then sensed that even that might be suspicious behavior. Instead, he quietly joined the line of passengers, each shuffling forward with their suitcases and shopping bags, either lifting them or pushing them with their feet.

"Reserved cabin, is it, sir?" the man at the barrier asked automatically, already noting the answer in his hand.

Seamus nodded.

The man clipped together his ferry ticket and the cabin reservation. "There's a baggage check tonight, sir, if you don't mind. Just wait by the tables. It won't take too long, Mr. . . ." He peered at the tickets again. "Mr. Anderson."

Seamus nodded again. His instructions, now memorized, had emphasized that he should speak as little as possible in case anyone recognized his Kerry accent.

He touched his spectacles, pushing them further up the bridge of his nose, and joined the second queue beyond the barrier. His finger began to reach for the spectacles again. He pulled it away realizing the gesture might draw attention to himself.

"Is the suitcase locked, sir?" the constable asked at the examination table.

Seamus hesitated, unsure. He bent forward and pressed the catches. They sprang open.

The constable opened the lid.

Seamus tried to look anywhere except into the suitcase or at the young Army corporal standing behind the constable, rifle nestling in the crook of his arm.

He realized he was under the closest scrutiny. He adjusted the file under his arm, hoping someone noticed the lettering on the front.

"That's all right, sir," the constable remarked, closing the suitcase lid.

"Any identification with you, sir?" he added.

Seamus coughed chestily.

"Driving license, maybe, sir?"

Seamus fumbled for the wallet. In his nervousness, he spilled some of the contents on the floor.

The corporal moved forward. "Excuse me, sir." He picked up the driving license and the Courtaulds identity pass. He looked at them both, examined Seamus and then handed them back to the policeman who nodded.

"Mr. Anderson?"

"Uh-huh." Seamus nodded, coughed.

The policeman looked closely at the two documents. "From Ligoneil?"

"Wolfhill Gardens," Seamus answered without pausing, remembering his instructions, blessing his own good memory.

"Thank you, sir," said the policeman, apparently satisfied, snapping shut the suitcase. "Have a good journey. Mr. Anderson."

Seamus nodded, coughing again.

He lifted the suitcase off the table and began walking toward the gangway leading to the ferry. A sense of release was already flooding through him.

"Mr. Anderson . . . ?"

The voice came from behind him. He stopped. His knees bent, losing strength.

"Mr. Anderson!" the voice called again, closer.

He turned slowly, reluctantly. After all there was nowhere to run except up the gangplank.

"Yes?"

Behind him, beaming, the Army corporal held out the

Courtaulds pass and the driving license. "You forgot these, sir," he said pleasantly.

Seamus tucked them away in his breast pocket.

"Wouldn't do to lose those, sir," the corporal went on, the muzzle of his rifle swinging near Seamus's midriff. "Not your license and your identity."

"Right," Seamus murmured.

He walked up the gangway on to the ferry and handed his reservation tickets to the steward. Five minutes later he was safely into cabin 3A.

"Fucking hell," he swore, tossing the suitcase on the bunk. The locks snapped open on impact. There, lying on top of a pair of striped pajamas, were a tube of Alka-Seltzer tablets and a half-emptied bottle of Bushmills whiskey, aids common to many travelers across the Irish Sea.

Seamus sniffed, feeling rather humble. At the Masonic Hall at Ligoneil, he'd been grateful, but now, after the penultimate stage of his escape, he truly realized how much trouble and thought had been invested in the entire operation.

He stayed in his cabin, its door locked, sipping whiskey, until the thumping and vibration told him that the ferry had slipped its moorings and was heading toward the open sea. Then he left the cabin and walked along the narrow passageway to the open deck.

The last rays of the setting sun were orange and deep red on the slate roofs of the older houses near the docks and glinting piercingly off the glass windows of the larger office blocks rising behind.

From the rail of the ferry, Seamus thought Belfast looked benign and comfortable in its huddling, Victorian sprawl. Certainly, from this perspective, the city gave no hint of the embracing terror and hatred within its deepest core.

"See youse," he muttered thickly, knowing he was a bit drunk and very tired, turning away from the rail and making for his bunk and hoped-for sleep.

As the ferry sailed into the enveloping darkness of the Irish Sea, en route for Liverpool, Roy and Sharon Ayres shut the door of their small cottage on the last of the newspapermen who'd been waiting, clamoring, for the story of their experiences.

While they'd given their interviews and posed for photographs, eyes blinking into the electronic flashes, their sense of unreality about the day's happenings had heightened.

Roy remembered his feeling of foolishness when the firemen had come to saw through the handcuffs linking him to the helicopter. He'd thought himself so stupid, sprawled there in the gravel, surrounded by men in varying uniforms, all asking him questions.

Sharon had felt equally lacking when the police had come to release her and baby Oliver from the bathroom where they'd been locked in an hour previously by the men in the Disney masks. The police, of course, had been very kind and sympathetic but Sharon had sensed their mutual embarrassment that the forces of law and order had known nothing of her plight until the anonymous phone call, presumably from Grumpy and Dopey.

The young couple, shaking their heads in unison, walked into the kitchen to prepare their supper.

"I was just doing the nappies," Sharon began again, disbelief still clear in her voice.

"And I was just flying a client," her husband went on.

Suddenly, the horror returned to them, their hours of fear alone overwhelming them once more.

They clung together by the kitchen sink, holding each other tightly and rocking slightly.

"Dear God!" Roy breathed. "Oh, dear God, what a day!"

Chapter 6

Like New York or Boston, Seamus thought, Liverpool was a place familiar to any Irishman whether or not he'd ever seen it before. Its history was part of Irish history, its skyline marking the traditional gateway for emigrants seeking work, any work, in the richer industries of Britain.

He began whistling tunelessly to himself, swinging his suitcase, as he stepped onto the covered gangway with the other passengers after the ferry had docked under the splendor of the Royal Liver building with its two stone birds perched atop, sprigs in their thin beaks.

And then he saw the two uniformed policemen waiting at the bottom accompanied by three men in rumpled suits, clearly detectives.

He cursed himself for having become too casual: he'd forgotten his instructions to appear inconspicuous and remain on his guard at all times. But it was too late to do anything other than brazen it out, to continue playing someone who was literally on top of the morning.

He imagined eyes boring into him, following his every step. He cursed himself again for having packed the Courtaulds documents file in his suitcase. He puffed out his cheeks, still whistling, feeling naked and helpless inside.

The file of passengers stopped suddenly. There was a murmur of excited voices. Seamus lifted himself on to his toes and peered over the shoulder of the man in front. A small, old man wearing a light fawn raincoat was being held around the forearm by one of the policemen while a detective read from a piece of paper. Another detective joined the group and, together, they hurried the man off, one arm held high behind his back.

Passengers started moving slowly along the gangway again toward the remaining constable and detective.

Seamus elbowed himself alongside the man in front, hoping to give the impression that they were travelling companions. "What was all that about, for God's sake?" he asked loudly, flattening and sharpening his natural accent, ignoring the policemen.

"And how the divil would I be knowing?" the man alongside him replied. "Ask your friend in blue here," he added, nudging his suitcase in the direction of the constable.

"Nothing to concern you, gentlemen," the constable interrupted, his eyes blank with boredom and tiredness. "Just move along and don't hold the other passengers up."

The two men walked on to the deck, across a narrow bridge and into the bustle of Liverpool's commuters from the Wirral, all hurrying for buses after disembarking from the cross-river ferries.

"Going far?" Seamus remarked casually.

"The station. Lime Street."

"So am I. Share a taxi?"

The other man, older than Seamus by at least ten years, shrugged, swaying slightly. "Why not?" There was little enthusiasm in his voice.

When he reached the station, Seamus walked over to the bookstall next to the buffet, looking for something to read during the journey. The headlines on the newspapers leapt out at him, biting into his complacency. His eyes darted around, alarmed behind the plain-glass spectacles.

Was that policeman over there looking suspiciously at him? Were they playing cat-and-mouse with him, just waiting for the right moment to pounce?

"One of each," he mumbled to the girl by the papers, proffering a £1 note.

"Every one?" she queried, surprised.

Seamus nodded, stuffed the bundle of newspapers under his arm and moved off quickly toward the train without waiting for his change.

He picked a corner seat and huddled into it, not daring to gaze out of the window nearest the platform where the station porters were busy trying to appear busy.

It wasn't until the train pulled slowly out of the station and into the Edge Hill tunnel that he began to relax once more. He spread out the newspapers one by one.

"Security tightens after IRA escape," thundered *The Times*.

"Prison probe after IRA flight to freedom—MPs furious," announced the *Daily Telegraph*.

"Ordeal of IRA hijacked pilot," cried the *Daily Mail*.

"He slept through IRA hijack terror," screamed the *Daily Mirror*, featuring a large picture of a small baby in a pretty young woman's arms.

"My ordeal—by wife in IRA terror," declared the *Sun*, showing a similar picture.

Seamus shook his head in disgust. Only three of the papers concentrated upon the actual escape and the subsequent row in the House of Commons, the others being more interested in the human-interest story of Sharon Ayres and her baby.

If that was how the English press covered events in Northern Ireland it was no wonder the English had little understanding of the situation. In some ways it was a blessing. There was hardly a mention of his police description and the few photographs of him were smudgy and virtually unrecognizable. He was flattered, however, to be called "No. 1 IRA bomber," "top of the wanted list," and "IRA's leading bomb-maker." Not strictly accurate of course, but it was enjoyable to be a personality again rather than an anonymous number in Crumlin Gaol.

"Reading the free publicity of those bastards, are you?"

He glanced up, startled. The man he had met while disembarking leaned over the orange-colored table offering him a miniature bottle of Bell's whiskey. The man slid down into the seat opposite, pushing the newspapers aside.

"Bit early, isn't it?" Seamus said nervously, looking at his watch.

"And when the hell is it too early? If they're selling, I'm buying."

Seamus was far from happy at the intrusion. The man was a virtual alcoholic. He fumbled in his pocket for a cigarette.

"So what're the rags saying?"

"Not a lot. Usual things."

"All rubbish. All of it," the man went on aggressively, his voice already slurring.

Seamus unscrewed the small bottle, toasted the man and took the merest sip. "Why rubbish?" he asked curiously.

"Because the boys are just gangsters these days, and these press boys make them out like fucking Robin Hoods!"

"But you're from the south, aren't you?" said Seamus, thinking he detected a Dublin accent.

"That I am, but now I've the northern territory, sod it!"

The man finished the bottle in his hand, thrust it under his seat and simultaneously pulled another from his coat pocket.

"For what?"

"Shoes," the man sighed. "Used to be at head office in Dundalk before they moved me. Office politics, that's all. And, anyway, what's that to do with it?"

"What?"

"Whether I'm a southerner or not. Whether I'm from Howth or you're from Limerick. Does it matter? I've seen what's going on in the North and it's sheer bloody gangsterism, so it is."

"You're a wee bit strong, aren't you?" Seamus said apprehensively. He'd noticed that people in the seats across the aisle, probably businessmen, were beginning to cast curious looks at them, even craning to hear better.

"Look, sonny. I've seen 'em. I've seen what they're doing."

"I'm no stranger to Belfast. Everyone knows."

"Not the bombings, sonny. The way they're robbing the people, their own people, our people if you like."

Seamus began to rise from his seat. "The bog," he said by way of explanation, although the need wasn't particularly pressing.

The man shoved him in the chest, returning him back into

the seat, and swigged at his bottle. "You're not understanding anything, are you?" he whined. "How d'you think they came by the money to put down a deposit on that chopper they used yesterday? How did they pay off the prison officers?"

Seamus shuffled into the next seat, the one next to the aisle, ready to make his escape, thoroughly frightened at the way his "travelling companion" was drawing attention to them both. The drunken man gripped him by the right wrist, clasping his hand over his watch. Seamus tried gently to shake himself free but only succeeded in fluttering some of the newspapers to the floor. "I must . . ." he protested.

"No. No, listen. I've seen 'em. I've watched 'em. I've seen the gangsters with their collection boxes for this and that, their bingo tickets, their shoddy bits of wood carving or weaving. 'Buy this,' they say, 'and help the boys behind the wire!' And God, who's going to refuse 'em when everyone knows they'll be back with a bullet through the window—or worse—if you don't pay out? Look at their taxi service. You've got to use it since they've burned out most of the Ulster buses. It's the biggest protection racket since Al Capone. The poor bastards caught in between them and the Army haven't a prayer, though they're offering a wee few to be rid of each pack of vermin. I know. I've talked to the shopkeepers down the Falls when they can't settle their bills. I know where their money's going and every last penny begrudged, so it is! Many of them are just packing their traps and stealing away for the ferry rather than pay the extortion. What's the point of carrying on, they say, and, you know, they're bloody . . ."

"Excuse me," Seamus exclaimed, at last wrenching himself free and side-stepping into the aisle. He hurried through the automatic doors and into the nearest vacant toilet, to relief in more ways than one.

He remained locked in for more than half-an-hour. He thought about what the drunken man had said and dismissed it. He'd never met a Catholic in Belfast unwilling to subscribe to the Republican cause. In fact, he'd always found them only too happy to do so. After all, he'd never carried a gun while rattling the collection box at various functions.

When Seamus emerged from the toilet he peeked gingerly into his compartment. The shoe salesman had vanished, presumably to find more convivial company in the buffet car. Seamus took no chances though. He lifted his suitcase down from the rack and moved to another part of the train, settling down to read the newspapers for the rest of the journey.

After the train reached Euston Station in London, Seamus didn't follow the signs to the taxi rank in the basement but wandered nonchalantly into the busy road outside to hail a cab.

Only when the taxi was lost in traffic did he feel truly safe. He directed the first cab to Oxford Street, paid it off, then switched to another one which was cruising for business along the crowded street.

He paid this off at Paddington Station, and strolled into the Great Western Hotel.

As instructed, Seamus went to the reception desk, identified himself as Alan Anderson, and asked if any messages had been left for him.

The girl behind the desk flicked through the notes on a clipboard. "Mr. Anderson . . . Mr. Anderson . . ." she murmured. "Ah, yes, sir. Captain Black phoned for you earlier. He said he'd meet you at this address."

She handed him a slip of paper. Seamus checked that no carbon copy had been taken of it, and turned away.

"Aren't you booking in, sir?"

"Not yet. Later." Seamus lied, now knowing where he was to stay. It would have been too dangerous if he'd had the information before. He glanced down at the address. It was in Paddington itself, obviously not far away. He walked out of the hotel and into the pub across the road to ask directions. He had plenty of money for a few large whiskeys to celebrate the success of his escape.

Seamus's name, and the escape, figured prominently at that day's General Operations meeting at Thiepval Barracks.

The first item was a progress report on the construction

work at Long Kesh. Ostensibly, this was to provide more military accommodation. But senior officers knew that in reality the barracks blocks were being prepared to house prisoners in case the government reintroduced internment. Most of them guessed this was likely to happen some time that summer.

As the brief discussion ended, the commanding general warned once more of the need for extreme secrecy. "If anyone gets wind of this," he smiled without a trace of humor, "then all hell will be let loose—and not only in the streets. A number of promising careers, gentlemen, including mine, will take a very sudden and very prominent nosedive. And that I wouldn't like to happen. Right, next business. Yesterday's escape. How do you read it, Stephen?"

Major Gates squared up the file lying on the table in front of him, glancing up at the colored photograph of Her Majesty the Queen on the wall. "Fairly ominous, sir," he began. "I think we have to assume that the basic intention was to spring Aherne. The other two escapees were merely false leads to pull our attention away while Number One Johnny did his vanishing trick."

"You think he's away?"

"I'd bet my pension on it, sir. Wherever he is, he's not in Northern Ireland now. Probably south of the Border, but who knows?"

"If he is," interrupted the senior intelligence officer, "then we'll soon hear from the usual sources."

"I hope so," retorted Major Gates, rubbing cigar smoke from eyes ringed with tension and tiredness. "They're obviously pinning high hopes on the laddie and that means some nasty bombs sooner or later."

"Is he that good, Stephen?" queried the general anxiously.

The major nodded, opening the file. "He has the technical background, that's the worrying point. Given a good instructor and some decent material, he could be a real problem. My hunch is that's why they've sprung him. Their other bomb designers are pretty hopeless. All old-fashioned stuff."

"So what are we doing?"

"Well, I've warned the EOD teams to treat all devices with kid gloves. Otherwise, we'll just have to play it by ear until the new product is launched on the market."

Later that week Major Gates, his wife and daughter took Saturday lunch with the young American surgeon, Edward S. Aicheson, and his wife. It had been a long-standing appointment, twice cancelled at the last moment when the major had to rush off to examine a bomb.

The families ate in the half-filled dining room of the Conway Hotel in Dunmurry, one of Belfast's more select suburbs. They exchanged social pleasantries and shared experiences of life in the Province, each a trifle unsure of the other.

Elizabeth Gates, slim and capable, dark elfin charm hiding an independent mind, swapped shopping tips with Lindy Aicheson, blonde shininess and chattering veneer masking deep uncertainty.

Mary Gates kept silent, concentrating like a twelve-year-old should on finishing every last morsel of her roast chicken.

The two men attempted to keep their conversation from the grimmer realities of their respective jobs.

It wasn't until their wives took Mary for a paddle in the ornate swimming pool at the end of the hotel's garden that the major and the surgeon settled down to a real talk.

They sat drinking brandy on the terrace overlooking the gardens, both able to pretend that the hotel had reverted to its previous existence of a private—and decidedly stately— residence, all pillars and Georgian windows.

"It's strange sitting here, Ted," remarked Stephen Gates, using, as requested, the familiar version of his companion's Christian name. "We could be anywhere in Britain . . ."

"Or Massachusetts . . ."

"Or Massachusetts, yet not five miles away pretty well every crime in the book is being committed in the name of one cause or the other. They've come from all over the world—the soldiers, the media, people like you—and all because history has decreed that two factions should beat the living daylights out of each other and anyone who tries to stand between them. It's so bloody unreal in this day and age that sometimes I feel more like an actor than a soldier."

"You've gotten that feeling as well? Many a time I've looked at the mess of flesh on the table and had to pinch myself that I'm not in the middle of a bad dream."

The major grinned, smoothing the lapels of his hounds-tooth sports jacket. "I just pat my back pocket . . ."

He did so. The American heard the chink of something metallic.

Stephen Gates rose slightly out of his seat and lifted the flap of his jacket. The butt of his personal revolver, a specially tailored .38 Smith and Wesson, poked out.

"Always with you?"

"Always. You can bet the one time I'm not carrying it is when some skull will come after me."

The waiter poured more drinks from a bottle of four-star Hine.

Aicheson realized that behind the major's urbane manner, there was the calculating ruthlessness and arrogance of a man dedicated to the destruction of his country's enemies. He tried to change the subject.

"You know when we first met and you said you'd some Irish ancestors? Well, don't you ever think that you're fighting your own people?"

"No way. The skulls are no more representative of Ireland than my left tit. Sure, they've supporters, a hard core of maybe a thousand or two, but the majority who go along with them do so because they're scared witless."

"Do you think your Irish relatives support them?" Aicheson asked rather tentatively.

"That's a curious thought. Frankly, I don't know, Ted. I've never bothered to trace them back or even find out whether there are still any left over here. Way back, they're supposed to have been landowners in Kerry, apparently thrown out during the Land League troubles near the end of the last century. Always been a bit of a mystery, not really talked about in the family. They say great grandpa on my mum's side was a bit of a sod with the local girls on the quiet. He had to change his name from Sanders or something like that because he was afraid of getting the chop even when he'd moved over to Hampshire. Drank most of the money, they say. Certainly none came down to my dad. He lived and died a farm foreman."

"You've never wanted to find out more?"

"Not really," the major smiled, hoping he didn't sound patronizing. "What's passed is past. Leave that sort of thing to our American cousins."

Aicheson laughed. "Not me, brother. Or should that be cousin? My Lindy's the expert in our family. She's given up trying to prove she came over in the Mayflower so she's making me the direct descendant of the old kings of Ireland."

"Much luck?"

The surgeon shook his head in a mock-sad way.

"Not much. I reckon my folk were just like the rest of the Irish-Americans. Poor farmers who became poorer in the bad times. But Lindy's clipping all the papers like crazy. Our apartment down the road's looking more and more like a library. Funnily enough, I thought of you the other day, Stephen, when she surfaced with that guy who skipped gaol in that chopper. She swore he'd the right name and address to be a distant cousin. Aherne, wasn't that his name?"

"Affirmative."

"Well, I know for a fact my great-great-whatever grandpa married a girl back in Boston whose sister married someone called Aherne, who came from around where this guy comes from."

"Listowel?"

"Right in one, Stephen. Listowel. You know of him?"

The major nodded ruefully.

"Oh, yes, I know him all right. But, remember, there must be hundreds with the same name."

"That's what I tell Lindy, but you know women. She's all for spending part of our vacation down there searching parish records and digging around churchyards."

Seamus hadn't stirred in four days from his small bed-sitting room in the back streets of Paddington, about half-a-mile from the cavernous, glass-roofed railway station.

When he'd arrived there, the owner of the lodging house,

an elderly Wexford man, had asked no questions and clearly expected no answers. The lodging house provided no food but, each morning, the owner offered to buy groceries, drinks and books which had to be paid for in cash.

After four days of baked beans and sausages, cooked on a small gas-ring in the room, washed down with tea laced with whiskey, or cans of Guinness, Seamus began longing for a change of diet. He was also extremely bored with his own company and his only means of entertainment, a 9-inch black and white television set, which, like the room, had seen better days.

His instructions had been clear: stay out of sight for at least a week. Seamus decided, however, that a quiet evening out would do more good than harm.

He waited until early dusk, just after seven o'clock when the shadows were softening, checked his disguise once more and then went out. The streets were empty except for a few children playing ball on the pavements. Seamus wandered into the first pub he came to and ordered a large whiskey with a beer chaser, followed quickly by a second. The bar was virtually deserted.

"Where's everybody?" he asked the barman, ordering his third round, at last feeling some effect from the alcohol.

"Too early yet, Paddy," the barman answered cheerily. "We only get the locals here in the evening. If you want some action, try the places nearer the station."

Seamus took his advice and wandered out of the quiet side streets into Praed Street, the main road running alongside Paddington Station, and past St. Mary's Hospital, whose bulky ugliness disguised one of the finest medical facilities in the world. The opposite side of the road could hardly have been a greater contrast.

The cheap takeaway cafes jostled for space with sex-aid shops, pornographic bookshops and scruffy hotels. Red "Vacancy" signs leered into the gathering dusk, others simply winked out the two words "Sauna Massage."

The air was filled with the smells of spicy cooking, car fumes and the promise of forbidden sin.

Seamus found it irresistible. He'd never seen such a street

before. They didn't exist in Dublin, and if there were similar establishments in Belfast, they were well-hidden.

He bought two more large whiskeys in a pub opposite the hospital's main entrance, then risked a kebab in the adjoining cafe. It was surprisingly tasty and filling. By now, though, his stomach was fluttering with other than hunger for food and drink.

Seamus walked out of the cafe and into the next street, toward a beckoning "Massage" sign. He slunk past the converted shop window. The heavy brown curtains allowed no sight inside. He strolled over to the opposite corner and lit a cigarette, watching the doorway below the sign. He waited a good few minutes, wishing he'd taken another drink, before striding over to the enticing door and pushing it open.

An auburn-haired woman in her early thirties, smart and clean in a white overall, stood behind a counter in the narrow, curtained hallway. She smiled brightly at him. "Good evening, sir."

"Hello," he said hesitantly, not sure what to say next.

The woman was used to nervousness. "A sauna and massage, sir? The VIP service, sir?"

"Oh . . . yes, then. All right."

"That'll be £10."

Seamus gave her two £5 notes which disappeared beneath the counter. The woman handed him a numbered ticket as she called through the hatch beside her. "Rebecca will look after you, sir." She pointed to the inner door with a long, painted fingernail.

Seamus opened the door and stepped into a large room scattered with low chairs. In one corner, there was a tiny, curved bar with a half empty bottle of Yugoslav Riesling on the counter. A color TV flickered silently on a table.

A tall, suntanned girl, dressed in a tight-fitting blue gingham overall, stood at the head of a flight of carpeted stairs spiralling downwards. She was not much shorter than himself, with a swirl of black hair. A fluffy white towel hung over her bare forearm. She beckoned encouragingly to him.

As he walked down the stairs behind her, Seamus felt totally at a loss. "I'm in your hands," he murmured.

Inane pop music filled the basement area, little more than a square of threadbare carpet surrounded by numbered doors.

Seamus was shown to a small cubicle lit redly by a combined light and heater in the ceiling. One wall was covered entirely by a colored print of a Mediterranean landscape, the others with wallpaper simulating pine panels. The space was dominated by a waist-high couch covered with towelling and a wide strip of absorbent paper, leaving little room for a fawn bath, shinily clean.

Rebecca pointed to the only chair. "You can put your clothes there, sir." She placed the towel on the edge of the couch and took the numbered ticket from him. "The sauna and shower are just across the hall. I'll be back in ten minutes or so to see how you're getting on."

With another encouraging smile, she turned on her high heels and left the cubicle, closing the door gently behind her.

Seamus was as excited as he was uncertain while he undressed. He slipped his diminishing wad of £5 notes into one of his socks and stuffed that into his jacket pocket. He'd read court reports in the *News of the World* about what could happen in places like this.

He tucked the towel around his waist and left the cubicle. The sauna was empty and hot. Seamus reckoned it would seat four at the most. On the floor was a discolored saucepan, filled with water and a ladle. He picked it up and dashed the liquid on to the glowing heating unit. Steam hissed up into the wood-panelled room.

Seamus took off his towel and sat down on the wooden, slatted bench. "Jesus!" he exclaimed, immediately jumping up. The wood was burning hot to his bare flesh.

He folded the towel on the bench and sat down again. Within a few minutes, he was gasping for breath. He noticed globules of sweat forming among the fine hairs on his forearm. It really was becoming unbearably hot. He stood up, picked up the towel and crossed a narrow passage to the shower where he lathered himself with soap and stood under the fine spray of cold water. Refreshed, he went back to the sauna again. This time he felt the sweat forming under his hair.

"All right, sir?"

The door had opened suddenly. Rebecca smiled inquiringly at him. Seamus crossed his legs, trying to hide some of his nakedness. The young girl seemed totally unconcerned.

"Another five minutes, sir, and then we'll be ready for our massage, won't we?"

Seamus nodded without speaking. Rebecca shut the door once more.

"Gentleman in Number Four, Jane," Seamus heard her call to someone outside.

"How's yours?" another girl asked.

"Be done in ten minutes."

"There's one waiting upstairs."

"Okay. I'll start him off."

Seamus realized that if he stayed in the sauna any longer he might hold up the finely-tuned workings of the establishment.

He took a last shower and padded back to his allotted cubicle to begin drying himself, ready for he didn't know what.

The door opened quietly behind him and Rebecca entered as smilingly brisk as ever.

"Let me dry your back, sir."

She took the towel and gently wiped his skin, even patting his buttocks dry. Seamus looked down at himself. To his amazement, there were no sexual stirrings.

"Now, on to the couch, sir. On your front."

Seamus scrambled up and lay there naked.

He turned his head, watching Rebecca open a low cupboard beside the couch which contained a box of colored tissues and some clear plastic bottles.

She picked one up and sprinkled the contents along Seamus's back. The slight perfume of the oil filled the cubicle. It was cozy now, almost homely. Seamus felt the whiskey reach his brain again after its temporary retreat in the sauna steam. He began to relax as Rebecca started massaging him. Her hands were strong, kneading the muscles at the back of his neck.

"Hard day, sir?"

Seamus nodded, his head resting on a small paper-covered pillow. Rebecca had an Irish accent. Strangely he hadn't noticed it before.

"Soon have you relaxed, sir," Rebecca prattled on, massaging away. "Is this your first time here?"

"Uh-huh."

"Recommended, were we?"

Her hands were now rubbing and stroking his buttocks. She paused to pour more oil onto him. A hand slipped between his buttocks, a fingernail lightly scraping him before flicking between his legs and moving on to the back of his thighs. Seamus twitched.

"No, I was just passing when I saw the sign."

"You've a scar here."

"Yes," he replied, thinking for a moment of that bicycle accident when he was a small boy.

"Are you a mercenary? We get a lot of mercenaries here." Her hands dug into his calf muscles.

"No."

"You're not a copper, are you?"

Her questions sounded automatic with no particular curiosity behind them.

"God forbid!"

"What do you do then, sir?"

"This and that. Mostly that," Seamus joked.

She slapped his buttocks. "Turn over now, sir."

Rebecca begun running her clasped hands up and down his legs, each time moving them closer to his crotch.

"And what part of the old country are you from?" Seamus asked. He felt his penis beginning to thicken and lengthen. He didn't dare look down at it. He turned his head to the side, seemingly by accident.

"Galway, sir. The far west."

Her hands slid down once over his penis as she started to knead his stomach.

"I'm Irish too." Seamus's voice was strained. He'd

never felt so naked before, spreadeagled there on the couch.
It was delicious.

"I know."

"Kerry."

"Oh, yes."

Rebecca didn't sound that interested. She leaned over
him, to massage his chest briefly. Suddenly she stopped and
tapped his flat stomach with her long fingers. "Healthy,
aren't we, sir?"

"Try to be."

"I mean this, sir."

Her hand closed gently around his penis, now fully erect.
Seamus didn't answer. He looked directly into her dark
brown eyes. They smiled mischievously back at him.

"Any extra services, sir?"

"Extra?"

"Straight relief is £5; topless, £10, strip £15."

"Well, strip, I suppose."

"You've the money?"

"Of course."

Rebecca nodded. She unbelted her overall and deftly
removed her brief, light brown bra and matching panties.
Her slim, honey-colored body was firm, breasts slightly
pendulous, nipples pointed and hard. She sprinkled some
more oil and then began masturbating him, using both
hands, fingers linked to form a tunnel.

"Can I touch?"

"Yes, sir."

Seamus fingered her right nipple before sliding his hand
under her small, tight buttocks. She was open and wet
although she gave no visible response as he caressed her
wiry curls, even thrust a finger inside her velvetness.

"Too much to drink, sir?"

"A bit."

"Can't be all night, can we?"

Her hands moved more urgently.

"Why not climb aboard then, Rebecca?"

"Oh, no, sir," she said quite severely. "No sex here."

She worked over him for another minute, the only sounds
the slurping of her oily hands and his quickening breaths.

"You'll have to hurry up, sir," she said, exasperation growing in her voice. "My shift finishes in ten minutes. Please try, sir."

Seamus tried. Soon he felt his climax approaching.

"That's it," Rebecca said encouragingly. "I can always tell when your toes begin to curl."

And then it was on him. He groaned with pleasure. Rebecca covered him with tissues and wiped him dry, holding him until he began to soften.

"That's it. Always like to see my gentlemen come." There was a genuine note of achievement in her tone.

"A bath now?"

"Bath?"

"You're VIP service, aren't you sir?"

Seamus nodded weakly.

"That means an assisted bath but I won't be able to stay, sir. I'll run it for you though."

She turned on the water after squirting some foam into the bath, bending naked before him, unconcerned at totally displaying herself.

Seamus sat up, swung his legs over the couch and reached for the sock holding the money. He counted out £15 and then added another £5. He turned back to her, offering the blue notes. By some miracle, she was already dressed.

"Oh, thank you, sir."

"Can I see you again?" Seamus asked intently.

"Whenever you call, just ask for me," Rebecca said as she left the cubicle, bright, brisk smile back again.

"Goodnight, sir."

"Goodnight."

He bathed, dried and dressed quickly. He took a last look around the cubicle, grinning ruefully to himself, before tramping upstairs.

Rebecca was standing at the bar talking to the woman who'd been at the entrance.

Seamus walked swiftly to the door.

"Goodnight, sir," the women chorused.

"Goodnight," Seamus mumbled as he went into the street.

Chapter 7
July, 1971

"Will you write?"

Her voice was muffled in the pillow.

"And phone," he answered, his lips moving against the fine hairs at the nape of her neck, his tongue tasting salt.

"Every week?" Rebecca begged, turning over, pressing her smooth warmth against him.

"Twice a week at least," Seamus assured her, feeling his excitement growing again, sliding a hand down her back pulling her even closer, index finger slipping between tight valleys of flesh.

He raised himself slightly and kissed her. Her lips were still moist. He lifted his face a few inches and looked down on her beauty. Her eyes were shut, black hair spread on white pillow. His free hand followed his gaze slowly down her body, shaping, tweaking, caressing, stroking. And when she sighed deeply in her throat, ready, he moved gently over her and entered slowly, inch by inch until they were one body, thrusting and receiving in unison, quicker and quicker, deeper and deeper into the whirlpool of their pleasure from which there was no escape but inevitable flooding, overwhelming release.

They panted, foreheads damp, into each other's shoulders, still close, before he pulled away and lay next to her, one arm draped limply across her soft breasts. She shifted a fraction and nudged his arm lower, lifting his hand and placing it between her thighs, wanting him to feel their wetness there.

"Was it nice?" she murmured.

"For you?"

"Oh, yes."

"And me."

The tone of her voice changed.

"I wasn't easy, was I?"

"No."

"You didn't think I was just because I work there?"

"No."

"Sure?"

"You proved it, so you did."

"I did, didn't I, so I did?" she mimicked affectionately.

"You did."

"Sleepy?"

"A wee bit."

She kissed him on the cheek, then shifted decisively to her side of the bed.

Seamus turned on his side but shuffled back toward her so that their buttocks touched. He rubbed provocatively against her once. She linked her feet with his and was instantly asleep, satiated.

No, he thought, peering into the gloom of the bedroom, she certainly hadn't been too easy. Quite the contrary and she'd made that clear from the outset. He smiled to himself, seeing the trail of clothes leading from the door to the bed, laying where they fell or were tossed. No, she hadn't been easy.

It had taken two more visits to the massage parlor before Rebecca would even tell him that her surname was Fahey. And, during his next visit, she'd only agreed to meet him for a drink afterwards if he foreswore the "extra services." Even in the pub, she'd been very doubtful about spending her day off with him. He had had to promise never to go near the massage parlor again and to put their previous sexual intimacies firmly out of his mind.

"Outside the place," she said adamantly, "I'm just like any other girl. I'll not be having you think I'm easy because of what I do in there."

Actually, Seamus had been only too happy to accept her conditions. His visits to the massage parlor were already too expensive and his growing familiarity with the establishment had begun to breed self-disgust.

He slid a hand behind him and ran it over the curve of her hip, marvelling at the silkiness of her skin. The even rhythm of her breathing didn't alter. Suddenly, he felt extremely possessive towards her.

On their first date, they'd talked deliberately of inconsequential things. But each was aware of the other's probing, the gathering of titbits of family history here and there, the eliciting of scraps of information, the tossing of tastes and opinions back and forth, discovering those which matched, discarding those that didn't or filing them for future reference.

But it hadn't been until the early evening when they were eating curry at Veeraswamy's near Piccadilly Circus that Rebecca had found enough trust to speak of her past.

"It's so huge," Seamus had said. "I thought Dublin was big compared to Listowel—well anywhere's big compared to there—but London . . ." He spread his arms expressively, nearly knocking over his frosty glass of lager.

Rebecca smiled. "It took me months to find my way around. I kept losing myself on the tube and having to surface to take a taxi."

"Do you still?"

"Even after eighteen months, I'm unsure."

"You regret coming at all?"

"No, not really. I had to come and that's all there is to it."

"Had to?"

"I couldn't stand it there any more."

"Galway?"

"Not the place so much. It's beautiful and all but it's so damned small. That's the trouble. You see, I was courting a boy for two years and he apparently was going around the bars and bragging away, when he was in drink. Well, one Sunday, I was coming away from mass when I overheard these two biddy women talking about me, jawing away they were, saying what a shameless hussy and all I was and what a wonder it was that I wasn't showing yet and not banns fixed."

Seamus almost choked on his chicken biriani.

"Showing?" he spluttered.

"Showing . . . they thought I was carrying his babbie, that I was pregnant."

"And?"

"Of course, I wasn't," she said indignantly. "It was their dirty minds, that's all. Even Father O'Donovan, our priest, heard the talk and came to see me. He was just panting for all the details and whatever, God forgive him. Anyway, after that, how could I stay? I took what money there was and left. I'd heard they wanted nurses bad over here but my Leaving Certificate passes weren't good enough and I could only be a ward orderly polishing the bedpans and helping old men take a pee. I wasn't having that at all and then when I was near broke I met this girl in a Wimpy Bar, Geraldine, my flatmate, and she offered to fix me up at that place in Paddington. And there you are . . . The money's good, the work's all right when you're used to it." She paused, looking down on the table, crumbling a poppadom into her meal, a korma. "And I'll only say this once, though I'm not wanting to right now. I don't think I'm doing any wrong to anybody by doing what I do. I'm not selling myself like some of them are. I just shut my mind when they want me to . . . those things . . . you know . . . and when they want something else, something more, I simply tell them I won't."

"Have you ever tried for another job?"

"No, nor will I till I'm finding what I want."

"And what's that when it's at home?"

Rebecca shook her head, leaning across the table and brushing Seamus's lips with the index finger on her right hand. "Enough secrets for one day," she whispered. "Enough of mine anyway!"

"I've none," he lied. "Just a businessman trying to do business."

In the coziness of her bedroom, after their frantic love-making, the falsehood still preyed on his mind as part of the deception he'd played on Rebecca. He'd wanted to tell her his real name and his work even on that first date, but that would have been stupidly dangerous. As their relationship deepened, such a confession became too difficult. Simply, he'd been frightened of losing her, of scaring her away.

Twice a week, sharp at eight o'clock in the evening, he went to specially selected public telephone boxes around central London, waiting for the phone calls from Dublin, certain that he would be recalled shortly. After all, he'd believed, the situation in Northern Ireland was deteriorating quickly with the British Army arriving in ever increasing numbers to combat the IRA's campaign.

Despite the growing funds from bank and post office robberies, augmented by money from Clann-na-Gael in the United States, the movement had struggled to maintain its offensive with hit-and-run shootings and small-scale bombings, as well as continually promoting inter-community incidents to keep the temperature high on the streets.

Undoubtedly, however, the Provisionals' bandwagon of violence had been gaining an awesome momentum of its own, exposing the years of political mismanagement and neglect in Belfast and Whitehall, tearing away once more the thin veneer of civilization which cloaked the ugly hatreds and suspicions of centuries.

Everything indicated that something climactic was about to occur. Yet, in call after call, Seamus had been ordered to continue his aimless existence. He'd been puzzled and resentful at the Provisionals' attitude, his unhappiness deepened by Rebecca's desire to have him as a drinking and eating companion but nothing else.

Thus, on July 28th, when he was given his long-awaited orders to return to Ireland, he was eager to obey. They supplied a valid reason for saying goodbye to Rebecca without ever having to own up to his deception.

The next day, he sat with Rebecca at a corner table in the hotel bar, nibbling crisps and gherkins, his rail and ferry tickets already in his wallet. Outwardly, he'd been as attentive as ever. Inwardly, he'd been feeling rather empty, awaiting the chance to breach his news.

"Rebecca," he'd begun tentatively. "I've something to tell you and I'm not sure how . . ."

She had glanced at him, a secretive smile around her lips. "And I was going to tell you something," she had said.

"Women and children first, I suppose," Seamus had shrugged.

"Well, you know my flatmate, Geraldine?"

"Uh-huh."

"Well, she's going home to Manchester for a few days to visit her dad in hospital."

"So?"

"Well, I thought you might like to see me home tonight when I've finished work and maybe have a takeaway."

Seamus had straightened up in his chair, not sure if he'd heard correctly. "Tonight?"

Rebecca had nodded, eyes twinkling mischievously. "I couldn't let you there with Geraldine around," she'd explained. "She's had her boy-friends there in more ways than one but I couldn't. Not with someone listening in the next room. But tonight, there'll be no one."

Instinctively, he'd held out his hand to take hers.

"And what's your news?" she'd asked brightly.

He sighed and shook his head sadly. "I've to return to Ireland tomorrow. Definite orders from the boss man."

Her face had shown her disappointment. She'd pulled her hand away from his and gazed down at her lap.

"When did you hear?" she'd asked dully, not looking at him.

"Late last night," he'd replied, his heart sinking, anticipating she would change her mind now about their evening alone at the flat.

"You can't be putting it off?"

"No way."

She'd raised her face, eyes glistening with held-back tears. She smiled, wanly at first, then more happily. "Then your last night'll have to be one to remember, won't it?" she'd said determinedly, returning her hand to his and squeezing gently.

Twelve hours later, snuggled beside her, Seamus regretted not being frank with her. He'd half-suspected that he was in love with her. Now he was certain.

He slipped out of the bed and padded, naked, into the lounge next door to search for a pen and paper. Then he settled down to write a note to Rebecca, explaining everything and assuring her that he would phone soon from Ireland, begging her love and understanding.

Seamus placed the note prominently on the sideboard and went back to bed, eventually falling into a fitful, dreamless sleep.

He awoke to the caress of Rebecca's fingernails scraping lightly up and down, lengthening and hardening him. He luxuriated in the sensations from her practiced hand before turning hungrily, pulling her close.

"Last time?" she whispered.

"For a while, but there'll be many more, I promise you."

Their love-making was slower and surer, more a mutual celebration of their finding each other than a lustful snatch at momentary pleasure.

Afterwards they remained entwined in their oneness, loath to break apart.

"Don't you wish we could stay like this forever?" she breathed against his cheek, arms folded around his neck.

"Aye," he murmured. "And let the whole bloody world go by."

"Then why don't we?" she teased.

He slapped her buttocks slightly and rolled away from her. "Because I've a train to catch in an hour," Seamus replied. "That's why."

He jumped out of bed and hurried into his clothes while Rebecca lay on the bed, making purring noises like a contented cat and offering lewd suggestions about what they could do if only he'd return to her arms.

Finally dressed, Seamus leaned over the bed and kissed her once, deeply.

"I love you," he declared, looking into the depths of her eyes.

"This isn't all?" she asked mournfully. "Not just last night?"

"No, no. It's the beginning, you see."

When she heard the front door close, Rebecca turned her face to the pillows and began sobbing. "Oh, you bastard!" she cried. "You bastard, leaving me like this!"

It wasn't until early afternoon that she found Seamus's note and understood. For nearly an hour, she sat on the sofa reading it again and again, hardly believing its contents yet knowing they were true.

"You stupid, stupid, lovely, lovely Kerryman," she crooned, pressing the note to her lips, realizing that his "confession" was as great a commitment as giving her a wedding ring.

By that time, Seamus was aboard the British Rail ferry some thirty minutes out of Fishguard and headed across the seventy or so miles to Rosslare in County Wexford. He'd spent much of the train journey from Paddington in the buffet bar, attempting to stay awake with a mixture of black coffee and whiskey. On the boat, however, he felt comforted by the Irish accents all around him and nodded off to sleep, swaying to an unusually gentle swell across St. George's Channel.

When the ferry docked in early evening, he went directly to the tiny bar on the railway siding by the quay.

"If you've a long journey, sir," said the young barmaid, serving him with a pint of Smithwick's, "you'd better be buying what you want here. There's no refreshments on the train."

"No, thanks," Seamus replied, "I'm waiting for a lift." He nodded wearily at the middle-aged priest standing beside him, firmly clutching a plastic bag filled with bottles of spirits.

"All right, Father?" he said conversationally.

"And isn't all this travel the very divil?" complained the priest, downing a brandy.

"It can build a thirst, so it can," Seamus smiled, presuming that the priest had been on holiday in Britain and wasn't looking forward particularly to resuming his encompassed life in an Irish country parish.

"Mr. Anderson?" a voice asked at his side.

Seamus turned and nodded.

A young man, possibly still in his teens, cloth cap almost hanging off his right ear, held out his hand for the suitcase.

"I'm your driver."

"Right," Seamus said, swallowing the last of his beer.

"To Dublin?" he asked when they were out of earshot in the car park.

"No. You'll see."

After an hour's driving, Seamus had lost his bearings totally. He knew they'd headed north and inland, probably into County Carlow, but he didn't recognize the villages and townlands through which they sped.

Eventually, late in the evening, the car turned into a pair of high, wrought iron gates. By the lights of the headlamps, Seamus saw two men standing by them, both carrying what appeared to be submachine guns. A mile further on, the car scrunched to a halt on a wide patch of gravel in front of the pillars and terraces of a substantial, early Victorian mansion.

"Well, I see we've gone up in the world since I've been travelling away," Seamus joked.

"Only the best for Mr. M.," the young driver answered, mentioning the name of a prominent member of the Dail.

"This is his?"

"He's lending it, so he is, while he's away in the States on some lecture tour or other."

Seamus whistled through his teeth in amazement. He knew that the politician had Republican sympathies but he'd never dreamed of him actively supporting the Provisional IRA.

"You'll be going to your bed now," said the driver, leading the way into the house with a swaggering, natural authority beyond his years.

"No reception committee?" asked Seamus.

"Tomorrow. Be ready at nine."

The next morning, thoroughly refreshed by a deep sleep, Seamus stepped down the wide, winding staircase and followed the chatter of voices into a lounge overlooking acres of lawn and fields. He waited awkwardly in the doorway for a moment, recognizing none of the eight men sitting around the room.

Their animated conversation died away when they

noticed his presence. A stout man in early middle age heaved himself out of a deep chair and walked over, smiling broadly, greeting Seamus with a vigorous handshake.

"Seamus!" he exclaimed genially. "Your timing was never better."

"Timing?"

"Your arrival here. It couldn't have been better!"

"And why not?" he asked, puzzled, entering the lounge.

"The Brits went into Derry this morning. They smashed right through the no-go areas, so they did. Troops all over the place. Enough pandemonium to wake the dead."

"So there's no more Free Derry?"

"Was there ever? Did it matter, son? This means more volunteers than we can handle. It means an end to the milk-and-water Republicans like Fitt and Hume and Currie. From now on, they're either with us or agin us, and that's it. Oh, by the way . . . sorry . . . I'm the commandant here, Matt O'Neill."

They shook hands again. Seamus had heard of this man's reputation as a gunman during previous Border campaigns. He'd been credited with at least half-a-dozen killings, two of them especially callous. Matt O'Neill's avuncular, cheerful manner belied his true ruthlessness and dedication to the movement.

Seamus was introduced quickly, cursorily to the other men. Two had North American accents. Two were gutturally mid-European. And the remaining three bore familiar southern Irish accents.

He was waved to a seat and handed a steaming mug of coffee.

"Now let me explain again briefly for the benefit of our new friend," O'Neill began, standing close by Seamus, patting him encouragingly on the shoulder. "You're all here for training or, in some cases, just to sharpen up what you already know. You'll be finding out about each other in time but it'll be better if none of you say too much about yourselves or what your jobs'll be when you leave. That way no one'll be too embarrassed with too much information."

O'Neill patted Seamus again, then wandered over to one of the large sash windows and looked out at the countryside.

"We'll not be disturbed here," he continued. "The Garda won't be nosey if we don't go scaring the locals. That we've agreed."

He turned and beamed at the seven men in the lounge.

"Well, finally, before we all get down to work, just a word about the importance of your week or two here. According to our intelligence—and it's mighty high-grade, thanks to some friends in Dublin—Operation Motorman in Derry is only the start of a crackdown by the Brits. A lot of the boys have already skedaddled underground. When the balloon goes up, we want to be able to hit them hard where it hurts. They've started doing our work for us. Let's be sure we can finish it!"

After a further desultory conversation, the others drifted away, leaving Seamus alone with Matt O'Neill.

"You're seeming a wee bit worried, son," said O'Neill. "Didn't I make myself clear?"

"It's not that, Mr. . . ."

"Call me Matt, but don't be forgetting the rank."

"I won't . . . Matt . . . nor your reputation."

O'Neill nodded, smiling. "I thought someone with your background might have heard."

"I have that."

"Well?"

"What I'm wondering is why, if all hell's going to be let loose, I was left kicking my heels in London for so long."

O'Neill chuckled. "Didn't Charley McCool give you a few wee words of advice before you jumped the wire from Crumlin?"

"He did that, Matt. Oh."

"Yes. Oh, son. That's why. You were being watched in London. Sure, they wanted you out of the nick for your bomb skills but they also wanted to check whether you were an informer or not."

"And?"

"They must be satisfied or you wouldn't be here—or anywhere else, come to that. Mind, I hear that one or two of the Army Council didn't approve of your girlfriend. Bit puritanical. But I wouldn't let it worry you. Her family's known to us."

"Rebecca's?"

"That her name? Well, her da's helped in the past so she's in the family, like."

"Since you know, I might as well tell you I promised to phone her."

O'Neill smiled bleakly.

"Not from here, you won't, son. The local guards might not be unfriendly but the Special Branch will have the phones tapped as a matter of course. Write a letter and I'll see it's posted. But don't lick it down: I hate steaming them open. And why not one to your folks in Kerry? We're hearing you're awful famous down there."

There was enough sarcasm in Matt O'Neill's voice to tell Seamus that, despite his recall to the Provisionals, he was still on probation.

"Thanks, I will," Seamus answered, rather subdued.

"And, son, start growing your whiskers. You'll be needing all the disguise you can get when you head north again. Make that one of your jobs here. Okay?"

For the next three days Seamus was taught how to fire and maintain handguns and automatic weapons, using a miniature shooting range in the basement of the country house. He was also sent on an assault course built in a large copse next to the market garden.

"Toughen you up, son," O'Neill said pointedly. "After all your soft living."

Every evening after supper he listened to lectures about Irish history from O'Neill and talks on the tactics used by revolutionary organizations throughout the world. These included various offshoots of the PLO, the Basque organization, ETA, the Baader-Meinhof group in Germany, the Red Brigades in Italy, and even a cell of Croatians waging a campaign against Yugoslavia. Seamus hadn't realized that revolution was so interconnected.

His classroom work, as O'Neill termed it, began on the fourth day with the appearance of a man in his early 30s, introduced merely as Captain Jan. Although it took some time for Seamus to gather that his instructor was an East European army officer, attached to an embassy in Dublin, it was immediately clear that he was an expert on bombs.

Hour after hour till his eyes were red with tiredness, Seamus watched and copied "Captain Jan" as he built complicated circuits for activating explosives.

Seamus was taught how to construct trembler switches; how to set false wiring to confuse a bomb disposal officer; how to wire bombs into cars using pressure detonators which would trigger an explosion once the victim sat down in the driving seat; how to conceal circuits in a bomb; and, perhaps most deadly, how to set off bombs remotely with radio signals. These devices could be employed as "sleeper bombs," being placed in position long before their intended use and then detonated days or weeks later by someone miles away.

After ten days of intensive study, Seamus's notebooks were filled with diagrams and designs. He studied them with detachment, not relating them to the death and destruction they would cause. He deliberately fostered his detachment, glad that it was unlikely he'd ever have to meet his victims face to face.

He was content in his world of technical theory, even though it would soon end, particularly after internment, the detention of citizens without trial, was introduced into Northern Ireland.

Dozens of IRA supporters and activists, Provisionals and Officials, were arrested along with their counterparts in the Protestant para-military organizations like the UDA and UVF.

The British Government had found a use for the Nissen huts on the disused aerodrome at Long Kesh, ten miles west of Belfast.

Nightly, Seamus and the others watched the scenes in Belfast and Derry transmitted by Radio Telefis Erieann: rows of burning houses, young rioters attacking the Army, empty streets crackling with gunfire, barricades of gutted buses, refugees in church halls, ineffective appeals for calm

by politicians who'd helped light the fuse and wondered
why the powder keg had exploded.

Four days later, with the whole of divided Ireland in
torment, Seamus sat in the back of an estate car on its way
through County Donegal to the Border.

Beside him was one of the Americans, a deserter from
Vietnam, a native of Detroit called Teddy Block. In front
was a German with an unpronounceable surname known
simply as Hansi, and the driver who'd met Seamus at
Rosslare, Brendan Donaghy.

The mission, according to Matt O'Neill, had two objec-
tives. One was to drop Seamus back into Belfast, the other
to kill policemen or soldiers or both. But Seamus rightly
suspected that the mission had a third objective, to test his
own commitment to the Provos and, perhaps, to provide
them with another hold over him.

Two of them, the American and the German, were
mercenaries, pure and simple, each due £1,000 for every
murder of a soldier or policeman on the mission. It had been
quite clear at the country mansion that they were feared and
despised by the IRA: feared because they were so much
better murderers than IRA men; despised because they
killed for money rather than ideals. Young Brendan of the
smiling face and nineteen years was equally feared and
despised. A superb driver, he was also a psychopath who
delighted in taking life and causing pain.

Early in the morning of August 13th, the four entered
Northern Ireland along one of the hundreds of the un-
guarded country lanes which crossed and recrossed the
length of the border.

By ten o'clock they were parked in a side street about a
hundred yards from the police barracks in Strabane, a small
town just inside the border.

No one was near when the American leaned into the back
of the car, lifted a horse blanket and pulled out two Colt .45
automatic pistols which he handed to Brendan and Seamus
and then a Thompson sub-machine gun which he kept on his
own lap.

"Don't suppose you're joining in, Hansi?" he said to the
German in the front passenger seat.

"Is crude, Teddy. Too crude. I shall wait for the real shooting."

"Thought so."

"Too crude?" asked Seamus.

"Hansi doesn't like shooting anyone at under a quarter-of-a-mile range and then only one round in the breech," explained the American with a grim smile. "Reckons it's unsporting otherwise. Me? I take anything that moves."

Seamus felt a slight dampness on the gun in his hand. Was it oil or his own sweat? He didn't dare look.

"You get to the corner," the American ordered, "and give us the nod when the patrol's coming. Okay?"

"Sure, and then what?" Seamus tried to keep his voice steady.

"Just finish 'em off when we've done. That's all O'Neill wants. Simple. Okay?"

"Sure," Seamus repeated, climbing out of the car and walking the ten yards to the corner, pistol in the waistband of his trousers, hidden by his sports jacket.

He peeked around into the town's main street. It was quiet and unhurried as ever it was. There were no more than two dozen people in sight, mostly women with shopping bags.

Seamus looked back to the car and shook his head. He lit a cigarette, waiting, rubbing a hand over the beard stubble on his face.

Two or three minutes went by, long minutes during which he tried not to think of what was about to happen. He was alone and frightened. His life was shortly to be changed. There could be no going back. Until now it had been unreal, playing at history to please his father. Bombs hadn't been personal. Bullets were. And so were the men in the car. There were no false heroics about them.

Seamus glanced back at the vehicle, noticing all the windows had been wound down. He knew the three inside would have been ordered to dispose of him if he failed this test, if he tried to run away. He guessed that was why they'd hardly talked to him during the long journey to Strabane.

He began murmuring a well-remembered novena, "Oh,

Most Holy St. Jude Apostle and Martyr, great in virtue and rich in miracles, near kinsman of Jesus Christ, faithful intercessor for all who invoke you, special patron in times of need, to you I have recourse from the . . ."

And then he saw the flashes of blue uniform on the pavement, glimpsed between the shoppers, coming closer.

". . . from the depths of my heart, and humbly beg you, to whom God . . ."

Two RUC men, one a sergeant, the other a constable, were now in clear sight, perhaps thirty yards away.

Seamus suddenly felt stupid mouthing words which long ago had lost their power for him, ritualistic phrases meaning little in his heart.

He waved his left arm behind his back, signalling the car to be ready, gripping the pistol butt with his right hand before he risked another peek around the corner.

The policemen were only ten yards away. Seamus could see that the constable was young and nervous, staying close by the sergeant, fingers constantly playing near the holster on his shiny belt.

His left arm waved again, motioning the car forward. It eased quietly into second gear and drew level with him.

The barrel of the American's sub-machine gun glinted suddenly in a ray of sunlight, poking just above the rear window.

At that moment, the car accelerated, jumping on to the pavement at the corner. Seamus glanced around the brick wall once more, ready to draw back from the line of fire.

The policemen had stopped six feet away, their backs to him.

"Oh, Jesus!" he exclaimed aloud.

Between the blue uniforms, he saw a young woman standing in the doorway of the house just around the corner, a baby in her arms, presenting it to the policemen for their admiration and approval.

It was too late, much too late.

The machine gun began to thunder as the RUC men turned, alerted by the noise of the car.

The American had squeezed the trigger immediately the

uniforms had come into view, not knowing that they shielded the young mother from his position, crouched low in the back seat.

Seamus instinctively took a step forward although there was nothing he could do.

He was so close that he thought he heard the bullets thudding into flesh and the strangled cries of the policemen.

Holes exploded jaggedly across their uniforms, replaced an instant later by spurting blood, first at their waists, then up their sides and backs, eventually tearing open their cheeks and foreheads.

Bullets smashed into the windows and bricks behind, adding to the awful sound of carnage.

Seamus noticed an old woman further down the street, watching with mouth wide in horror.

"Aaaagh . . . !"

The young housewife, in apron and fluffy pink slippers, screamed a split second before the policeman started to fall away from her, pushed forward and sideways by the smashing impact of bullet upon bullet. The air around them was pink, darkening into red, with spraying blood and flesh and chips of bone.

"Aaaagh . . . !"

Her scream rose, piercing, and then gurgled away as the bullets stitched across her breasts and neck, wrenching the baby from her arms, tossing him high with the reflexes of her convulsive agony.

She was lifted bodily off her feet and thrown back into the shattered doorway of her home.

Her baby spun to the ground and rolled into the gutter, white shawl billowing, already spotted and stained with crimson life-blood.

As suddenly as it had begun not ten seconds before it was over.

The silence was harsh with the smell of cordite and the echoing screams of shoppers across the road.

Everything seemed to be moving in slow motion.

The young constable's feet drummed against the pavement with the last frantic order from a brain mostly smeared on the wall, dripping down.

Glass still tinkled from the windows.

The baby began to whimper in the gutter, kicking its legs and arms, miraculously unharmed but for bruising.

"Finish 'em!" the American shouted from the car. "Finish 'em!"

Seamus dragged his eyes from the twitching, ripped bodies and looked at him.

"They're done," he shouted back over the noise of the revving car engine. "All of them. They're done for! Oh God, didn't you see her?"

"Fucking finish 'em!" the American roared back, lips drawn tightly over his teeth, staring, eyes glazed, over the smoking barrel of the sub-machine gun.

Seamus's mind went blank. He dragged the heavy pistol from his waistband, took two steps forward and fired at point-blank range into the back of the constable's head, watching, almost microscopically, the hair part as the bullet struck and the shattered skull distended once more, quite perceptibly bouncing against the paving stone. He took another half-step and looked down into the sergeant's face, eyeballs white, rolled back, blood dribbling from both sides of his open mouth, displaying stumps of splintered teeth and gums. Seamus shut his eyes quickly and pulled the trigger again. A third eye appeared, blacky-blue, on the bridge of the sergeant's nose. The last suck of air ballooned the dead man's cheek and hiccupped in his throat.

He moved towards the woman as in a trance. She lay on the linoleum of her narrow hallway, skirt hitched around ample thighs, long dark hair obscuring her face.

"No, no!" called the American. "Leave her for fuck's sake. In the car!"

Seamus turned slowly, shaking his head, trying to clear the sounds, the sights. He ran back to the car and clambered in the opened door, falling across the seat.

Brendan shoved his right foot hard on the accelerator. The back wheels spun for a moment in the growing pool of blood in the gutter, then gripped. The car screeched away down the main street of Strabane, missing the baby's waving hands by less than six inches.

"Oh, Jesus!" cried Seamus. "Did you see her? Did you see her?"

"Tough shit," said Teddy Block, the American, barging his shoulder into him as the car lurched broadside around a corner, heading for the next rendezvous and, hopefully, a fresh vehicle.

Spent cartridges rolled back and forth on the floor, tinkling.

"Trust a Yank!" Hansi, the German, shouted over his shoulder.

"I didn't see her, goddammit you krauthead! I didn't see her till it was too late!"

"Anyway," Brendan chimed in, hugely enjoying the argument, relishing the drive and images of murder, "your man did well enough for a backroom bomber, didn't he?"

"Is one good thing from fuck-up," agreed the German.

"Two down already," Brendan chortled, spinning the steering wheel, "and not even lunchtime yet. That's really something! That really is!"

He'd already dismissed the young mother from his mind. After all, he'd thought, the Provisional IRA always issued a statement of regret after a mistake had been made, sometimes even paying the funeral expenses. Everyone, he knew, had heard the movement was generous in such matters.

"Christ!" exploded the American, feeling a sudden dampness, gazing down and seeing Seamus vomit bile all over his new trousers and shoes.

Chapter 8
August, 1971

"Sod that for a game of Indians!" exclaimed Major Stephen Gates. "Just come and look at this, Charley." He was in a foul mood, standing by the large map of Northern Ireland covering one wall of his tiny office at Army HQ in Lisburn.

"What is it, sir?" asked Captain Briance, skirting the clutter of chairs and filing cabinets to move beside his Senior Ammunition Technical Officer.

"Another abandoned car with those bloody French bullets in it. All .45 caliber and all with the SF headmark. Has to be the same gang of skulls."

"The ones who got Green?"

"Must be. And look at their route, curse 'em!"

Major Gates ran a finger along the line of colored pins stuck into the map, each indicating where a recent shooting had occurred and where stolen cars had been found abandoned, littered with spent cartridges of similar French manufacture.

From Strabane where the policemen and the young mother had died so horrifically, the pins traced a course through Coleraine, where the police barracks had been sprayed with bullets, Andersonstown in West Belfast, where a soldier had been killed with a single shot through the head, near the M1 motorway, where the major's personal driver, Corporal Arnold Green, alone in a Land Rover, had been hit by bullets from a passing car, and finally Strabane again, where a fifth stolen car had been found.

"They've gone in a circle, sir."

"Affirmative, Charley. The cheeky bastards used the

296

same border crossing to go out as they did to come in. We might as well cancel the alert for them. They've long gone."

The major knew it was simply bad luck that his corporal had been attacked. Incredibly, Arnold Green's bulk had saved him from death despite being struck by nine of the thirteen bullets which had riddled the Land Rover. But Major Gates viewed the incident as a personal insult. He vowed grimly that the score would be settled.

"Strange that," mused Captain Briance, interrupting the major's dark thoughts.

"What, Charley?"

"Why did they come right over to Belfast? The more travelling, the more chance of being picked up."

"Who knows?" said the major. "One of the skulls might have wanted to see his granny."

"Or deliver something or someone?"

"Could be, but we've missed 'em for sure, and I'm short one helluva driver."

Major Gates, like other officers, was under extreme pressure in these weeks following the introduction of internment under the Special Powers Act, approved by all political parties in the House of Commons at Westminster. Within a fortnight, thirty people had been killed, bringing the total deaths to more than a hundred since the beginning of the IRA campaign, and the bomb disposal units had been called to their 600th explosion since the start of the year.

And by early September, 1971, the major's problems had increased even further with the discovery of bombs clearly aimed solely at the disposal officers.

The earliest were cardboard shoe boxes with a burned out safety fuse laid on top to suggest that the bomb had failed to explode. In fact, they were still "live" and even contained anti-handling devices to cause detonation if they were moved at all.

Then came a spate of bombs made out of a sugar and weedkiller mixture packed in salt containers which again had switches on the bottom to set off the devices if they were picked up.

"Hell's teeth, Charley," the major complained to his

assistant on the fourth day of a new bombing offensive, "they really are having a go this time."

He sat wearily at his desk, sipping a mug of tea and puffing his usual small cigar, wondering how long his EOD teams could stand the pace. They'd virtually been on round-the-clock duty dealing with the wave of new bombs and Major Gates had hardly left his office, busy coordinating movements and offering advice.

"One good thing, sir, is that we know these brutes are fairly straightforward. At least we're pulling them over like nine-pins," said Captain Briance, smoothing back his dark hair and rubbing his black-rimmed eyes.

"So we can make 'em go bang and save some lives," the major shrugged. "But these are the best we've seen so far, Charley. One of their designers must have learned a new trick with anti-handling switches and they're churning 'em out like Model Ts. Let's hope they get fed up when they realize we're on top."

The red phone on his desk rang, the direct line from the operations room.

"Here we go again, Charley," the major sighed, lifting the receiver.

He listened for ten seconds and scribbled an address. "Right! Wilco!"

Major Gates looked up at his assistant, nodding towards the door. "On your bike, Charley," he muttered. "A package on the steps of the Orange Hall near Lambeg. There's no one left so you'd better buzz along."

The captain saluted and hurried out of the office, picking up his flak jacket from a chair.

Major Gates smiled wanly to himself. He could hardly remember ever being eager to reach a bomb incident. He supposed he must have been once, years ago.

Still, he admired Charley Briance's spirit. He could guess how near his men were to breaking point. He knew he was. He'd even sneaked a pre-breakfast whiskey that morning "to wake himself up."

The major leaned back in his chair and blew a smoke ring, gazing at the small board on the wall, showing the disposition of the EOD units. He shrugged. If there were another emergency he'd have to attend himself and that wouldn't please his wife. They'd arranged to have a rare evening out: dinner at a new restaurant at Holywood called the Pepper Mill. The King Prawns Andalusian were said in the mess to be a special treat.

The major ran a hand through his prematurely grey hair and settled down to study the incident reports piled in his in-tray. Each was a meticulous account of how particular bombs had been defused the previous day. They formed the basis of all the briefing notes carried by the ATOs.

He wasn't aware of time passing until his green phone jangled. It was a friend at 39 Brigade headquarters in Belfast.

"Have you heard?"

"Nothing."

"An explosion! First flash on our net says one of your boys has bought it, Stephen. Sorry."

The major stiffened in his chair, clenching his pen. His chest suddenly felt very tight. "Where?"

"No details yet. Somewhere between you and Belfast, I think. It's a bit confused. It's only just happened this instant."

"Right. Thanks, chum."

"And sorry again, Stephen."

"Right."

With his free hand he was already dialling the EOD unit in Belfast, at Girdwood Park. They'd just returned safely from an incident outside the Law Courts.

Stephen Gates slapped his palm against his head in anguish. It had to be Charley Briance, his newest ATO, the one with the young wife and baby back in North Yorkshire, the one . . .

The red phone rang. An impersonal map reference from the duty officer in the operations room.

It was Lambeg!

The major grabbed his hat and ran out of his office, down the slightly winding staircase, past startled military police-men, through the front hall and around to the car park.

His temporary driver, a young corporal, was slouched in the Land Rover's driving seat. The orders were swift,

shouted and direct. The driver simultaneously started the
vehicle, threw a cigarette out of the door, engaged first gear,
and switched on the siren and flashing light.

A torrent of thoughts went through Major Gates' mind as
they roared through the traffic towards Lambeg. What had
gone wrong? How near had Charley been to the explosion?
Was it possible he'd been simply badly injured? What had
he done wrong, if anything? Not Charley, surely? Not
young Charley who'd begged him for a chance to join bomb
disposal? Why not himself? Why hadn't he gone to the
bomb? Had his briefing been good enough? Was it his fault
after all?

Some of the answers were all too clear when the Land
Rover shuddered to a halt outside the Orange Hall near
Lambeg, less then fifteen minutes after the first alarm.

An infantry patrol stood around the building keeping
about thirty of the local people back from the scene. Four
marksmen were crouching by the dry stone walls along the
road, vigilant against any ambush. A military ambulance,
red crosses prominent, waited, engine running, rear doors
wide open. Two men in white coats were wrapping
something in deeply red blankets.

Major Gates took a deep breath, already knowing the
worst, as he jumped out of the Land Rover. He looked
towards the young infantry officer who'd started doubling
towards him. Then he saw the ladder perched against a
chestnut tree by the hall and a medical orderly clambering
up gingerly towards one of the higher branches.

"Up there?" muttered Major Gates, half gesturing with
his right arm.

"Fraid so, sir," said the infantry lieutenant.

"Thanks, chum."

He turned away, having seen the medical orderly lift
Charley Briance's head off the angle between branch and
tree trunk and place it gently in a black plastic bag.

His grief would come later, probably after he'd formally
identified the body. It was more important for him at that
moment to discover what had gone wrong. The lives of all
his other men depended on that. Emotions couldn't be
allowed to interfere.

"Any witnesses?" the major asked brusquely.

"Plenty, sir," answered the lieutenant. "Try the postman. He used to be in the ranks himself."

The postman had been the first to raise the alarm. He described the device as a box, standing on its end, about 12 inches high, 7 inches wide and 7 inches deep.

"Certain it was on its end?" queried the major.

"Definite, sir."

The major nodded, worried. He had never encountered a bomb in Northern Ireland placed in that particular way.

"Well, tell me in your own words what happened."

"Well, you see, your man arrived in his jeep like a bat out of hell. Bold as brass, he walked straight up to the thing on the steps of the hall. He crouched by it for a good minute, then he tied a line around it. He took the line out to the wall over there and pulled it. I could see the thing move a foot maybe but nothing happened. Then he walked up to it again, reeling in the line. He seemed a wee bit worried, like something was puzzling him, but not afraid in the least. Brave as a . . ."

"Just go on," the major urged testily.

"Well, then he took the line out in the opposite direction and gave the thing another pull. It moved again, I could see that from where I was. Then he told the lads to keep us all well back, took up his tool bag and went to the bomb again. I could see him fiddling around deciding what to use. I reckoned he picked a wee fretsaw. He knelt right over it and seemed to start cutting into the top or maybe a corner. That's when it went. A big crump. A sort of bluey-white flash and . . ."

Major Gates cut him short. He'd heard enough. "Thanks, Postie. I'd like you to give a full statement to the lieutenant here. All right?"

He took one last look at the scene; at the door of the hall, splintered and hanging off its hinges; the small hole in the concrete steps; the shocked people standing by; the pleasant rural setting.

Involuntarily, he glanced up into the green foliage of the chestnut tree, at the darker patch. He wanted to say something to himself, maybe a prayer, but there was nothing except hate. "Fuck it!" screamed in his head. "Fuck it and fuck them!" his mind repeated. His fingers scratched against his trousers like the claws of a new-landed crab.

The obscenities didn't help.

Back at headquarters, he managed to calm down. He didn't blame Charley Briance for disobeying orders, for tackling something outside his experience and training. He couldn't even feel bitter about the man who'd designed this latest bomb so cleverly. He'd lulled the RAOC into believing that he was only capable of building one trick into a bomb and then he'd put in two or three. Gates had to accept responsibility for the Corps' first fatality, for the waste of a promising young officer. All his anger was directed against himself.

He quickly flashed a warning to every disposal team to be on the watch for a new type of bomb, not very big, perhaps 15 pounds of explosive, but with an unknown number of anti-disturbance switches.

The orders were simple and to the point: lay sandbags around the bomb to muffle its effect, try to take an X-ray picture, a radiograph, of its innards, and then topple it complete to cause detonation. Until the bomb's secrets were discovered, Major Gates could only wait, pray and stall.

"What's gone wrong, Stephen?" asked the General Officer Commanding, expecting questions from the high politicians.

He was glad that night to shut the front door of his married quarters and infinitely grateful that Elizabeth was an experienced enough Army wife not to bombard him with questions and recriminations about one more cancelled night out.

After a makeshift spaghetti bolognese and a bottle of red wine, they talked quietly about Briance's death and what the RAOC wives could do for his young widow.

Young Mary sat listening, eyes wide, cuddled against her mother on the sofa. The Gates had never hidden the realities of a soldier's life from her. She knew it could have been her own father in the mortuary of Lisburn Hospital.

"If you've heard nothing about me," Stephen Gates would tell his wife, "that means it's all right. No news is good news. The bad news is going to come from a guy in uniform knocking on the front door."

For the next few days, the tension remained high in Army HQ, and in the married officers' estate just across the road, as the EOD units continued to joust with the new bombs.

By the twelfth explosion, Major Gates was convinced that the Provos had an unusually potent bomb-designer.

The Army had obtained radiographs of the devices, now christened "Lambegs," but they were useless because of the amount of decoy wiring inside the bombs.

But eventually a bomb disposal team pulled over one of the devices without it exploding. Within hours, Major Gates had had an exact replica made, minus the explosive, and that evening carried it home.

Elizabeth Gates took one look at it and smiled. She was well used to her husband's routine. "Coffee and sandwiches in the kitchen?"

"Affirmative, darling," he replied, kissing her on the cheek, wondering at her patience after so many years.

"Don't be too long. You've had an awful lot of late nights."

"As long as it needs. That's all. And I'll clean up the mess. Promise."

"Just see you do," she said, touching his arm affectionately.

He cleared off the table and settled down to work while Mary finished her homework and his wife watched television.

This was the challenge he relished, pitting his brains against another's cunning. He was confident of the outcome. He'd always been mechanically minded, forever tinkering with the farm machinery where he'd been brought up. He'd been going to study science at university, but that dream had been ended by compulsory conscription at the end of the Second World War. However, as he'd progressed in the Corps, he'd spent periods studying at the Royal Military College of Science but had never qualified for a degree. But then academic degrees couldn't save anyone who bungled a bomb!

To his dismay, though, the mocked-up "Lambeg" proved

too good for his delicate work with pincers and screwdrivers within intricate circuitry. Time after time, the little light bulb, substituting for the explosive, flashed on, telling him he'd failed, that, if it had been a real bomb, he would have been as dead as Charley Briance.

He got up and walked around the kitchen, gazing at the "Lambeg" from every angle, peering into its chipboard interior with its tangle of switches, taped over batteries and curling, striped wiring.

Major Gates poured himself a generous measure of his wife's cooking brandy in the pantry and sat down again. There had to be a way, he knew, but he couldn't see it. Whenever he broke one circuit, another would become live.

"Oh, bugger!" he murmured, tempted to give up the task.

He wondered about the man who'd designed the "Lambeg." Clearly, he thought, his object was to trick and confuse, to lure the bomb disposal officer into the maze of inter-connected circuits, to his doom, wanting to make him believe that there lay the solution. No, the major decided, lighting his fourth cigar of the evening, there was no way to dismantle the bomb quickly enough to avoid activating the detonator and thus the explosive.

And then a memory came to Gates from his days at grammar school, from a lesson by his science master, Mr. Ladd, nicknamed "Stiffy" because of his artificial leg. There might be one substance which could stop the bomb's relay of switches before they did their deadly work.

He rushed out of the kitchen and began a search of the house, calling excitedly to Elizabeth for help, waking Mary, before he found what he wanted in a small cupboard upstairs and returned to the "Lambeg."

Two hours later, he'd succeeded.

Not once but three times, he'd dripped the substance into the "bomb" and three times he'd managed to disrupt the wiring without the light bulb coming on.

"The brute's dead," he announced triumphantly to himself. "We've got to stun it first before killing it. That's the secret."

Chapter 9
September, 1971

The Republican Club in Andersonstown in West Belfast was smoky and noisy. A couple of hundred people sat around the tables in the converted warehouse, drinking and talking, flirting and arguing. Others stood three deep at the bar, elbowing, pushing, apologizing in their haste to reach the counter. A local showband beat its way towards exhaustion on a small stage. Men's faces grew redder, women's voices shriller, as the climax of the evening approached.

Unnoticed and unmourned, the music faded away. A roll on the drums drew eyes to the stage. The chatter and clatter died.

A rotund man in a cheap, creased suit heaved himself on to the makeshift stage and stood under the Irish tricolor draped across a romanticized portrait of Michael Collins. He raised his arms for total silence. Some of the drinkers felt for their wallets to check how much cash was left.

"Right, friends and fellow Republicans," the fat man boomed through the microphone. "You've had a good time tonight. I've had a good time tonight. But now's the time to remember those who're not having such a good time; those who can't be with us because of British imperialist suppression; those who're suffering in their agony while we've been enjoying ourselves."

He paused while a silence, heavy with guilt and drink, settled over the club, then his tone of voice rose, more vehement, almost evangelical. "Yes!" he shouted. "Yes! This is the time to remember all our boys behind the wire!"

Applause rippled out.

"Yes!" the voice echoed and reverberated. "This is the time we remember our debt to them and repay it by putting our hands in our pockets!"

The applause grew.

Four blushing girls in their early teens, wearing the berets of Na Fianna Eireann, the IRA's youth organization, trooped on to the stage with trays filled with an assortment of goods.

The MC signalled to the band, wet-shirted behind him. The drums rolled again.

"Now, friends," he began, lifting a piece of embroidery off the nearest tray, "this is from Johnny Hughes in Hut 6."

He held up the scrap of cloth so that the audience could see the words embroidered crudely upon it, green upon white—"Long Kesh 1971—The fight goes on."

Clapping hiccupped and was extinguished by disapproving glances.

"Now, isn't that great, friends?" the fat man continued, undaunted by the interruption. "What a message! What a memento to take pride of place in your front room!"

Stamping feet boosted clapping hands.

"Yes, a tremendous effort . . ."

The microphone began whistling. He tapped and slapped it back into audibility.

"Tremendous, but before I start the bidding, are there any of Johnny's folks here tonight?"

He shielded his eyes to look into the audience against the glare of the lights.

"Ah, yes!" the fat man announced triumphantly, gripping his fast-sagging trousers, pointing to a pinched-looking woman who'd stood up nervously by a table in the middle of the room.

"Mrs. Hughes, isn't it?" he called. "Johnny's mam, so it is!"

She nodded, haggard face lightening as even more clapping broke out around her.

"Well, that's the sort of brave lady we'll be helping out tonight, friends," the MC cried, sweat beginning to drop from wobbly dewlaps. "We'll be buying Johnny's mam a wee something as well as providing comforts for her gallant boy behind the wire!"

He held the cloth above his head, a hand still clutching his trousers.

"Now," he said, even more triumphantly, "what am I bid for this fine work done by Johnny Hughes in Hut 6 of Long Kesh concentration camp?"

"A pound," a voice called.

The fat man frowned menacingly at the bidder.

"And if that's who I think it is," he warned, "I'm not appreciating the jape . . . nor will Johnny's friends."

"Three pounds!" the same voice called again.

"Make it five!" another shouted.

"That's more like it," the MC encouraged.

"Seven!"

"Eight!"

"Nine!"

The bidding continued briskly until the rectangle of cloth sold for £15.

The fat man's perspiring beam embraced everyone. The standard for the evening had been set.

In quick succession, he auctioned more embroidery, metal ash trays, lumps of wood burned with Republican inscriptions, drawings and paintings, even miniature tricolors made of toilet tissue.

Seamus Aherne, standing close by the bar, drinking Guinness, estimated that the sale raised more than £500.

Certainly enough to provide some small luxuries for the relatives of the IRA internees and the internees themselves.

Other, more discreet collections from factories and shops who preferred not to be bombed out of business would help bring in his own pay and that of all on full-time IRA active service.

In addition, since internment, Seamus had heard, considerable funds had been raised by Irish-Americans, supposedly to help the Catholics in Northern Ireland who'd been burned and terrorized from their homes. He knew a goodly proportion of this money from the Northern Ireland Aid Committee, NORAID, had already been earmarked for the Provisionals' use. After all, the movement claimed, one of the Provos' main jobs was to protect such unfortunates, forgetting that their unfortunate circumstances might never have arisen but for the IRA's campaign.

"Another one?" the head barman asked, breaking into his thoughts, noticing his near-empty glass.

Seamus nodded. "Might just as well. I'm reckoning they'll be a few minutes yet."

"The big men?"

"Aye. Their meetings take longer and longer."

They smiled at each other, realizing they were among the few who knew that, while the audience enjoyed their evening's entertainment, the senior leaders in the Provisionals' Belfast Command were meeting in a room behind the stage.

The Republican Club was safe enough: in the unlikely event of a raid by the security forces, there were sufficient people around to provide a screen of protest and panic behind which the IRA leaders and activists could escape.

Seamus's nervousness that evening had nothing remotely to do with his personal safety. Since returning to Belfast, his beard had grown thick, his hair long, and he had put on at least two stone through a deliberate diet of Guinness and chip sandwiches.

His confidence in his new appearance had grown so much that he now moved freely in and out of the Catholic enclave with little fear of identification.

"Evening, Mr. Aherne."

Seamus acknowledged the greeting from an IRA Volunteer in his late teens who'd shoved his way to the bar for a round of drinks.

His self-confidence had increased as well, partly due to the deference shown to him by younger Provos, after his role in the Strabane shootings and the success of the "Lambeg" bombs.

Indeed, his increasing status in the movement had helped ease his mind over those bloody shootings. The policemen's faces returned to haunt him in occasional nightmares, but after all he'd only fired the gun when the two men were beyond all help.

"A drink, Mr. Aherne?" the young Volunteer beside him asked.

"Thanks but no thanks. I've business shortly."

He wanted all his wits for his chat in the backroom with the officer commanding the Belfast Provisionals.

He had a personal matter to raise and was unsure how his CO would react. He was hopeful of success, though, because he'd always got on well with the IRA leader, particularly since that bomb disposal officer had been killed.

Seamus had felt only elation when he'd heard of the RAOC's first fatality. Of course, he'd conceded a tinge of sorrow for the dead officer's family, wishing they could have known that it wasn't a personal attack by him on their loved one. He'd remember what his IRA lecturers had taught during his indoctrination, that the movement didn't attack British soldiers and policemen as people. It merely attacked what they represented.

Thus Seamus could divorce himself, as did his colleagues, from reality. If a member of the security forces died, it didn't matter because he or she was only a cipher of the authority standing between the IRA and its aims. If an innocent civilian died, it was simply bad luck. If a Provisional was killed, then he or she was a martyr to the struggle, a person to be singled out and transformed into myth.

The barman flicked Seamus's glass to gain his attention.

"They say they're ready for you," he whispered, leaning over the bar as if to polish it. "You know the way."

Seamus grinned. "Wish me luck," he winked and began threading his way past the crowded tables toward the small room behind the stage. Two young Volunteers stood on guard outside, hands tucked into their jackets. They nodded to Seamus and pushed the door open.

"Come in, son," invited the CO seated behind the trestle table, shuffling some papers into a briefcase. A haze of cigarette smoke hung over him.

"Evening, sir," said Seamus, standing to attention.

"At ease," the older man muttered, pointing at a chair. "Take a seat. I won't be a second."

Seamus watched as he finished putting away his papers. He wasn't a particularly impressive figure with his glasses and thinning, brushed-back hair. But his reputation com-

manded total respect. He was revered among the Belfast
Provos as a man of fairness and integrity who'd never send
his men on any mission he wasn't willing to undertake
himself. He also had an encyclopedic knowledge of Belfast
from his former occupation as a bookie's runner, taking bets
in factories and bars. He was also a person who wouldn't
hesitate to be totally ruthless.

"Now, son," the Provo leader said, putting the briefcase
by the side of his chair. "What d'you want?"

"It's a wee bit personal."

"So I gathered, but I must tell you we've been talking
about your bombs in the meetings."

"You saw the new designs?"

"They look good."

"Thanks," Seamus smiled.

"But the priming?"

"That's the trick!"

"You'll do it on the first one?"

The query sounded rather like a command.

"To make sure?" asked Seamus.

"Well, yes. It'll make the layers more confident when
they take the others."

Seamus thought of the spotty teenagers who had laid his
bombs up till then and had to agree. "I don't mind," he
said, an image flashing into his mind of the two killed
outside the headquarters of the BBC at the corner of
Bedford Street and Ormeau Avenue.

"Good," the officer nodded. "That'll be tomorrow."

"Yes, I heard from the bomb officer."

"Fine, that's settled. Now, what's all this personal stuff?"

Seamus hesitated a moment, unsure of how to begin. He
took a deep breath. "Well, sir, when I was away in London . . ."

"That girl?"

Seamus shook his head admiringly.

"Yes, the girl. How did you know?"

"It couldn't have been your landlady, could it? Mrs.
McGuinness, isn't it? Nice widow-woman so she is but as
plain as the nose on my face." He spoke brusquely,
obviously eager to be away to the bar or his bed.

"I spoke to the girl—to Rebecca—two days ago, and she says she's pregnant!"

His commander tilted his chair back, sighed and closed his eyes for a moment. "Son, son, son," he murmured. "Will you boys never . . . ?"

"I didn't mean . . ."

The leader of the Belfast Provisionals gestured despairingly. "If you were a married man, son, you'd know excuses don't count. If she is, she is. And if you're the one, it's down to you."

Seamus felt himself reddening around the cheekbones. "I didn't mean excuses!" he exclaimed. "I just meant I didn't mean it to happen."

"Do any of us?"

Seamus shrugged. "Well, it happened and she says . . ."

"You're not doubting her?" There was a warning note of disapproval in the CO's rasping voice.

"No, no!" Seamus said hastily. "Of course not. If she is, then it's mine."

"And so?"

"She wants to come over here."

"And?"

"Stay with me."

"And marriage?"

"Who knows?"

The man began to laugh. "I do, son. I know even if you don't."

"Can she? Will it be all right?"

The CO stood up, tucked the briefcase under his arm and moved around the table. He clapped Seamus between the shoulder blades.

"I appreciate your asking, son, but I don't want to interfere. You know the dangers as well as I do. Just you do what you think best."

He looked closely into Seamus's face.

"But remember your work and the oath you swore to the movement. We wouldn't be wanting anything to get in the way of that, would we?"

Seamus understood the implied threat.

"Nothing will, sir," he promised.

"Grand. Then, son, it's up to you." He took Seamus by the arm and led him into the club. The two guards followed, flanking them. "As long as you invite me to the wedding, eh? Now, what about a jar? All the yammering's given me an awful thirst."

"Just a quick'un," Seamus replied. "I've a phone call to make."

"Break the good news, eh?"

Seamus smiled. "Something like that." Ten minutes later, he was in the public call box around the corner from the club, speaking to an overjoyed Rebecca at the massage parlor in Paddington.

"You're sure it's all right?"

"It is. Don't worry. The big man okayed everything."

"And your landlady, darling?"

"No problem. She's already said you'll be company for her until we find another safe house on our own."

"You're sure you don't mind?"

"Me? Mind? Don't be silly."

"I'm not being silly. I just don't want you to feel trapped. You don't, do you?"

"No, of course not," he said, trying to fill his voice with reassurance.

He did feel slightly enmeshed however. His first reaction to the news of Rebecca's pregnancy had been one of shock. They had spent such a short time together and now, suddenly, there was a child on the way. It seemed an awfully swift way to be landed with such a huge responsibility. But later, after a few reflective drinks, he was rather pleased at the prospect of fatherhood. It would mean marriage, of course, but then the weeks of separation and longing, the letters and phone calls, had made him even more certain that he was in love with Rebecca.

"Are you sure?" she asked again.

"I'm sure I'm sure."

"When can I come then?"

"Soon as you like."

"I'll take the boat."

"Hang on!" Seamus called, hearing a noise outside the phone box.

"What?"

"Hang on!" he repeated, pushing the door open and listening. In the distance, there was the wail of approaching sirens.

"I'll have to go!" he shouted down the phone to Rebecca. "Write me when you're coming and I'll meet you."

"What's happening?"

"Nothing to worry about but I'll have to go."

"But . . ."

"Love you!" he called, slamming down the receiver and darting off down the road toward the club, hoping to raise the alarm.

But when Seamus turned the corner, he saw people already hurrying out the entrance, urged on by two policemen.

"What the hell's on?" he demanded of a man and a woman who almost cannoned into him.

"A bomb!"

"Bomb?" he said incredulously.

"Down the side alley."

"Oh, Jesus!"

"Must be the Prods."

"Well, it won't be one of ours, for fuck's sake. That's for sure!"

Within minutes, the club and all the neighboring shops and houses for a hundred yards around had been evacuated.

Seamus stood as close as he dared to the police cordon, watching the Army bomb disposal team begin its work.

At that distance, he could barely distinguish the figures of the Ammunition Technical Officer and his assistant moving cautiously in and out of the pools of light thrown down from the street lamps, going back and forth to the bomb with equipment. He thought he saw one of them carrying a long, cylindrical object, probably the radiograph machine for photographing the device's innards.

From the care and time they were taking, Seamus

reckoned that they must be dealing with a particularly well-made and dangerous bomb.

After almost an hour, a whistle shrilled its warning to the silent and deserted street. The ATO scurried back to the protection of a Saracen personnel carrier, unwinding wire as he ran. Police and a few onlookers like Seamus moved back even further, seeking what cover they could.

Crack!!! The sound echoed along the street and around the buildings. A cloud of dust puffed out from the alley where the bomb's mechanism had been shattered by the tiny explosive charge laid by the ATO.

The emergency was over.

Policemen muttered into their radios and then started to wave people back to their homes.

Five minutes later, traffic was moving along the street as if nothing had ever happened.

"I wonder who the fuck designed that one?" Seamus muttered to himself, scratching his beard and heading off toward his lodgings.

Until now, the Protestant bombs had been even less sophisticated than the IRA's. They must have discovered a new man with enough talent to worry the Army.

The bomb designer's identity was also worrying Staff-Sergeant Warren Palmer of the RAOC as he talked to Army HQ from his office in Girdwood Barracks. "Never seen one like it out here before, sir," he told Major Stephen Gates.

"Sure, Palmer?"

"Not out here, no. It was almost like the ones we handled in training."

"Really?"

"Whoever put it together knew what they were doing. A bit of a craftsman with a neat line in soldering. I'd swear he'd had professional training. And, if I didn't know better, I'd swear I'd seen his work somewhere before."

"But it was straightforward? You had no problems?"

"No, not really. I just took my time and followed the book of words."

"Well done! Well, have a quiet night."

"Sir."

In his office, Major Gates slumped back in his chair, smoking a cigar and sipping a large whiskey. It had been a gamble, an awful gamble, but it had seemed to work.

He rubbed his chin and smiled when he saw the black smear of boot polish on his fingers. He'd have to wash before going home to Elizabeth. He was glad he had arranged the roster so that young Palmer had been on duty to deal with the bomb. Anyone more experienced might have recognized his handiwork from the bombs he had made for training purposes back in England. And Major Gates had spent a great deal of time on the bomb for the Republican Club.

It had taken him more than two days to build it after that phone call from the secret Army intelligence unit, which wasn't supposed to exist, and didn't on paper.

He had been extremely careful to ensure that the device had been within Palmer's capabilities yet difficult enough to force him to work carefully and provide the time needed for the intelligence mission inside the Republican Club.

The major had even insisted on laying the bomb himself so that Palmer would face precisely what his senior officer had planned for him.

Earlier that evening, as dusk turned to darkness, Major Gates had been driven in an unmarked Army car along the M1 motorway leading into the heart of Belfast.

He'd hunched low in the back seat, feeling a trifle ridiculous with his blackened face, black beret covering grey hair, and black sweater, trousers, socks and sneakers.

The men from Intelligence had even provided a knife with a black lacquered blade. Major Gates had refused the offer of a gun. He reasoned that the entire mission was doomed anyway if he ran into a shooting match on his way to the club. The whole district would be alerted and on guard.

"Good luck," his driver muttered, allowing the major out of the vehicle just by the motorway intersection at Kennedy Way on the edge of the Andersonstown district.

"Just you be here, chum, when I get back," Major Gates had replied, starting over the rough ground beside the motorway, the bomb tucked safely in his rucksack, knife clenched between his teeth.

Once he'd started, he had no time to feel any nervous tremors. He tried to skirt as many houses as possible by ducking down alleys, but eventually, he was forced to make his way through back gardens, weaving in and out of their gates and clambering over wooden and wire fences.

His worse moment had been when he'd trodden on a pair of copulating cats. Their screeches of anguish had brought a woman to her window, bawling for quiet. As she'd pulled the curtain to see out, a square of light had jutted across her small garden, catching the major in midstride. He'd frozen still, quivering inwardly, praying that he wasn't silhouetted.

"Just like a ruddy oversized plastic gnome," he'd murmured grimly to himself when, after a seeming eternity, the cats had vanished into the bushes and the woman had closed her curtains again.

For the last hundred yards, the major had taken his directions from the lights and music flooding out of the club. To his surprise and relief, the entrance to the building had been deserted except for a courting couple who were too busy with each other to notice the figure slipping into the alley beside the club.

It had taken only a few seconds to prime the bomb and lift it from the rucksack before the major was on his way back towards the motorway.

The further he moved from the club, the more he abandoned his previous caution. Finally, he'd run at full pelt to the waiting car, tumbling gratefully and breathlessly into it.

"Move it, chum," he'd called to the driver.

The car sped away.

"Something scare you?" the driver'd asked casually.

"Just myself," Major Gates had panted.

The bomb had been discovered and the alarm raised before he'd reached his office. Then the worst part of the operation began for Major Gates, the waiting to hear that his EOD unit had been successful in defusing it. He'd had to resist the temptation to wash and change quickly in order to sit in the operations room and monitor radio transmissions from his men.

Anyway, that would have been a change from his normal routine and policy of leaving them well alone unless they requested advice and help. And the men from Intelligence had emphasized that everything should appear normal. Not only should those around the Republican Club believe it was a genuine, though routine, bomb disposal operation, the Army headquarters staff should also have no suspicions to the contrary. No one who didn't already know was to learn that it had, in fact, been a diversionary action to empty the club and allow the intelligence unit free access. Thus the call from Staff-Sergeant Palmer had eased the major's mind considerably.

He poured himself another drink from the bottle in the filing cabinet, smiling to himself, imagining the row if any hint of the secret operation should ever leak out. His career would be finished for certain and he didn't fancy life as a civilian just yet, life in the unordered, disorganized world outside where few knew their place and most were forever dissatisfied, not understanding their proper role in society.

That was one of the attractions of service life, he'd always thought, beginning to relax now. It was the certainty of it all. Sergeants saluted officers and officers saluted generals. The salutes went up, the orders went down. And if you did what you should do to the best of your ability, then there was a real chance of a contented mind.

The green phone on his desk rang.

"SATO," he replied unhurriedly.

"Thanks for the help, old boy," said the voice at the other end. It was from the unit that didn't exist.

"Everything go well?"

"Fine. And your chap at the sharp end?"

"He coped."

"Good."

"Enough time to do all you wanted?"

"Plenty. If any of the boyos so much as farts, we'll have him on tape. That particular watering hole is well and truly bugged."

Chapter 10
September, 1971

It was the middle of the afternoon and life in the hotel was as it usually was at this time of day.

In his eighth floor suite the general manager, Bryan Green, was dozing on his bed, gathering his strength for the evening's drinking, eating, greeting and placating, an ordeal which would last until the early hours.

Two floors below, in a bedroom, a middle-aged London businessman who'd drunk too much was desperately trying to achieve an erection while his thin blonde companion helped with growing despair, worried about collecting her children from school.

In the small alcove behind the cocktail bar, the barman counted his tips and considered a customer's complaint that he was putting too much ice into his drinks instead of spirits.

On the same floor, the chef was in his office, locked in a heated conversation over the phone. It concerned a substandard side of beef and the chef's commission from that particular supplier.

In the reception area on the ground floor, the hall porter announced that he was away for the afternoon newspapers, and set off for the betting shop up the road.

Behind the desk in the corner, the duty receptionist was telling the switchboard girl about her encounter with a journalist the previous night and her post-coital promise to provide him with an inflated bill for his expenses sheet.

It was an entirely unremarkable mid-afternoon in the hotel until the revolving glass doors began to swish around violently and noisily.

"Everyone stand with their hands in the air!" two voices bawled before the staff and half a dozen guests in the reception area could react.

Two men in athletes' tracksuits, balaclava helmets covering faces, stood there, sub-machine guns at their hips. One moved a pace at a time towards the reception desk. The other stayed by the doors, covering the lifts and the curved stairway leading to the first floor.

The switchboard girl, dark haired and pretty, began screaming hysterically as the gunman advanced. Slowly her eyes, wide and bulging, were fixed on his weapon. Her hands closed and opened convulsively over her breasts.

"Shut your gob!" the gunman shouted but her screaming grew louder, shrilling higher and higher, until her eyeballs suddenly rolled upwards and she slid untidily to the floor in a faint.

"Thank fuck for that!" the gunman by the revolving doors exclaimed, moving aside to allow two more hooded men through the entrance. Between them they carried a wooden box about two feet wide and eighteen inches high.

"Where?" muttered one to his fatter companion.

Seamus Aherne looked quickly around the lobby, sweating profusely. "Over there," he said, nodding towards the two glass phone booths at the end of the lobby furthest from the door to the coffee shop and bar. The bomb would be more difficult to deal with if laid in a confined space.

"Gently," he urged as they began lowering the box on to the brown and cream patterned carpet.

He slid his right hand underneath, feeling for the tiny, protruding metal rod. He pushed it in and then held a coin over it while the box was finally laid on the floor. The device was primed.

Seamus stood back to check that the bomb was pushed tightly into the corner of the phone booth. He looked at the wording, now revealed, on the wooden casing. He smiled under his mask, wondering if his instructor, "Captain Jan," would have approved of his attempt at psychological warfare.

On the one side, he'd daubed in red paint, "Ha-Ha-Ha";

down the front "Bomb"; and on the other visible side, "Tee-Hee-Hee."

Yes, he decided, it was definitely a message to worry any bomb disposal officer. The words would be a challenge to him, perhaps even unnerving him. At least, that was what "Captain Jan" had taught. The officer would certainly be uneasy from the very start and that was half the battle.

Buzz . . . zzz . . . zzz . . . zzz!

The insistent noise was growing louder as more incoming telephone calls stacked up on the unmanned switchboard.

"Come on!" Seamus shouted. "It's set. We're away."

The duty receptionist began crying hysterically, thinking the bomb would explode in a few seconds.

"You've plenty of time to get out," Seamus called, almost at the door, wanting to give the impression that the bomb contained a timing device.

But the screaming became even more piercing, swelled by shrieks of fear from a middle-aged American woman at the foot of the hotel staircase.

The noise unnerved the gunman by the reception desk. He turned to run out of the hotel and dashed straight into one of the floor-to-ceiling panes of glass by the entrance.

"Fuckin' hell!" he swore, bouncing back off the thick glass. He fell to his knees, half-stunned. His sub-machine gun clattered to the carpet.

A hotel guest, standing by a jewelry display counter, started to lower his hands and took a tentative step towards the weapon.

Seamus saw the movement from the corner of his eye. "Don't move!" he bellowed. "Don't anyone move!"

The second gunman swung the barrel of his weapon around to the guest who, in that split-second, thought better of his impulse.

The injured IRA man, nose bleeding, scrabbled for his gun, cursing loudly, then staggered to his feet.

Grabbing him by the shoulder, Seamus pushed him through the revolving doors and into the stolen car waiting outside, with its engine racing.

Two patrolling policemen, about a hundred yards up the

road, spotted the hooded men bundling into the car. They started to run, barging aside shoppers, unslinging their submachine guns.

But by the time they were anywhere near firing range, the vehicle was in the heavy traffic of central Belfast heading for the comparative safety of the nearest Catholic enclave, the Falls Road. There, another car would be waiting.

"Done it!" Seamus exclaimed triumphantly, pulling off the suffocatingly warm hood.

"Jesus, my ears are still ringing with all those caterwauling women," one of the IRA Volunteers complained.

"And that bloody switchboard! What a fucking racket!" said another.

"It'll be nothing to the noise when that bomb blows," Seamus added. His hands were trembling now the raid was over.

Behind them, the Provisional IRA's bomb gang had left scenes of total confusion and panic.

The two RUC officers were trying to push through the revolving doors into the hotel while frightened guests and staff jammed into the doors attempting to leave.

The switchboard continued to buzz away. The duty receptionist's screams had subsided to sobs but still she stood behind the desk, transfixed with fear, one hand over her mouth, the other pointing, wavering, at the large wooden box in the telephone booth nearest to her.

Once inside, the policemen saw the words on the box and moved swiftly. One ran behind the desk, slapped the receptionist back to her senses and pushed her towards the door, before lifting up the telephonist, now moaning, and carrying her out.

The other radioed his operations room, then picked up the Tannoy microphone lying on the switchboard.

"This is a police emergency," he broadcast, trying to sound calmer than he felt. "Please evacuate the building. This is an emergency. Please evacuate the hotel immediately."

Lights began flicking above both lifts bringing down chambermaids from the upper floors. Staff in white jackets ran down the staircase from the second floor.

The policeman saw the red button on the wall by the switchboard with a small hammer hanging below its glass case. With a swift jab, he smashed the case and pushed the button. Bells clanged their urgent, deafening warning throughout the hotel.

The general manager in his suite stirred and turned over restlessly, thinking for a moment he was in a dream. A second or so later, he jerked upright, fully awake. "Christ!" he exclaimed and reached for the phone at his bedside. The RUC men looked at the mass of lights, switches and plugs on the switchboard, shrugged helplessly and hurried out of the hotel to join an Army patrol which had just arrived.

In his room, the London businessman struggled into his clothes. He cursed the noise, his impotence, his wasted money and the threat of publicity if photographers were in the neighborhood. The woman from the escort agency slipped her dress over her head and stuffed her underclothes and tights into her handbag. It wasn't the first time she'd had to leave a hotel room at a moment's notice.

Major Gates heard the news of the bomb before the last of the staff had clattered down the outside fire escapes.

"Right—on my way!" he barked down the phone to the operations room, realizing that, for once, he'd have to abandon his policy of not interfering with his men. The tower of shining glass was so prestigious a target that the bomb demanded his presence.

His driver, Corporal Hosken, got him to the hotel just after five o'clock, travelling the last hundred yards down a deserted road, cordoned off and evacuated by the police. The bomb disposal team had already set up a temporary command position in a bar opposite the hotel.

"Well, what's the bad news?" the major asked the two RAOC captains, Alan Campbell and Derek Madeley.

"You can see it from here, sir," said Campbell, handing him a pair of high-powered binoculars.

They briefed him on how the bomb had been laid, mentioning the remark made by one of the bombers that there was time to evacuate the building.

"Time means timer, eh?" grunted Major Gates.

"Could be!"

"We'll see about that. Everyone out anyway?"

"Everyone."

Major Gates peered through the binoculars, focusing on the box in the phone booth. He smiled grimly when he saw the lettering.

"Cheeky sod!" he murmured. "How much do you think?"

"Pretty big, maybe 15 pounds, enough to blow the lobby and the windows," said Madeley.

"I'll buy that," the major nodded. "Thank the Lord, the place's built round the lift shaft. Chummy's put his package too far away from that to do any structural damage."

"Shall we just let it cook, sir?"

"Nope. We'll have the brute out without cracking a single pane, that's what we'll do. And then we'll kill it in full view. Chummy's thrown down the gauntlet. He's challenging us. So we'll show him what's what."

The major checked the lay-out once more. He pointed to the bar next to the reception area.

"Call up the sappers," he ordered. "We'll have sandbags between that bar and the bomb. Then we can work from there, from inside, and even move the guests back in there. At the worst, they'll have sand in their coffee if it blows. Okay?"

The three officers in their work clothes of camouflaged fatigues, sweaters and combat jackets walked out into the road, one of Belfast's main thoroughfares. The major looked at the surrounding buildings, noting that four television crews had set up their equipment in the second-floor windows of a bar along the street.

He strode over and called up to one of the cameramen.

"If you boys want to stay there, make sure none of my chaps' faces are on film, right?"

"Fine with us, sir," the cameraman replied.

"I'll let you know when anything's about to happen but settle down for a long wait."

"Understood. Thanks . . . and good luck!"

The major waved casually, rejoining his officers.

"We've all the equipment?"

"Everything."

"Right. Alan, you sort out the radiograph, and Derek, you brief the sappers. I'll have a sniff around the brute."

Major Gates pushed through the revolving doors and entered the deserted hotel. He felt suddenly cold and lonely. He always did when approaching a bomb. It was the moment of truth, the last few steps up to something unknown which contained the power to rend limb from limb, to totally obliterate in one second of awful heat and energy.

Someone had asked him once if, in those moments, he thought about the family or the insurance or whether the gas bill had been paid.

He had replied that he thought of nothing except the bomb in front of him. Every time it was the same, the sense of walking down a narrowing, darkening tunnel with only the bomb at the end. All else was outside his vision and hearing.

The major squatted outside the phone booth, his eyes searching for any hidden wires. There were none.

He dismissed the words painted on the box. He knew they were meant as a distraction. Instead, he noted the location of the screw holes, the flush fitting of the sides, the dimensions.

He listened, head pressed almost to the bomb, his absolute concentration filtering out the interminable buzzing from the switchboard and the clanging of the fire bells.

Was there a timing device in the bomb? It was a possibility. And that meant it would explode at any second whatever he did. That was one of the risks.

There were no sounds of whirring or ticking from the box. He doubted it contained a timing device. The IRA had already lost too many men through timers going wrong. He reasoned that this bomb was something a little special because of the target. It was probably laid by one of the Provisional's more experienced units who wouldn't have taken risks with their lives.

Major Gates sat back on his heels, teeth nibbling his lower lip, thinking. "Yup," he declared to himself and stood up. He began the long walk back out of the lobby, all ten yards of it, terribly conscious of the menace behind him.

But it wasn't until he was going through the revolving doors that he felt any fear. Then, it was so strong, so embracing, that his skin shivered under his uniform. Again, that was something that always happened.

"Sappers here?" he asked Captain Madeley rhetorically, seeing the Royal Engineers already unloading sandbags from their lorry and into the side door of the hotel.

"Just arrived, sir."

"Let's get on then."

He sketched the bomb on a pad, illustrating its main details.

"It's going to be hellish to get a picture because the brute's right against the metal of the phone box but we'll have to try."

"Who d'you want in first then?" asked Campbell.

"You and me, Alan, but not till the sandbags are up. Then Derek can watch us from there in case we make a cock-up."

"Do we need lights?"

"Better alert them but there seems plenty available in the lobby. Should be enough for the closest work."

Major Gates paused, scratching his forehead.

"And that reminds me; all those glass windows. We're not only sitting ducks for a sniper but we'll be giving free bomb disposal lessons for anyone who cares to watch."

"Screens then?"

"Yes, whistle up the manager and we'll borrow some of his sheets."

The hotel's general manager Bryan Green and Major Gates were old acquaintances. They had shared an interest in the hotel's security since its opening. They both had a taste for good champagne and cigars. And they were both Freemasons.

Captain Madeley, a rather gauche officer unversed in most things except his work, shepherded the hotel executive over from the far side of the road.

As always, Bryan Green looked dapper with his pomaded

hair and immaculate morning suit. Somehow, however, his
rasping Belfast accent clashed incongruously with his
appearance. The major, perhaps snobbishly, always expected this stoutish man to speak with an upper class
English voice. Yet, he liked him immensely, respecting his
courage and professionalism.

"Bryan, my dear chap," he greeted him, offering the
Masonic handshake, pressure on the second finger joint.
"What did I tell you?"

"What, Stephen?"

"When we talked before about security?"

"You said there wasn't much to do except the best we
can."

"Affirmative, old chum. And that's what we're going to
do with your help. The very best we can."

He outlined his plan and, with an encouraging pat, sent
Bryan Green scurrying into the hotel through the bar
entrance to gather some of the establishment's largest
bedlinen.

"Now," he told his two captains, rubbing his hands
eagerly, "when the glass is covered and the sandbags in
place, we can really get down to it."

After the large white sheets had been securely taped over
the outside of the windows, Gates and Captain Campbell
moved into the hotel with the radiograph machine.

"This is going to be the very devil, Alan," the major
remarked as they tried to maneuver the cylinder into the
small phone booth.

They tilted it this way and that, stood it upright, placed it
flat on the floor, taking exposures all the time, ignoring
safety precautions against radiation. Eventually, after half
an hour, with sweat dripping from their brows, they'd
covered the bomb from every possible angle.

By the time the two officers reached the fresh air again,
their heads were splitting with concentration and all the
buzzing and clanging inside the lobby.

The X-ray negatives were rushed to the radiology
department at the Royal Victoria Hospital for developing.

Major Gates looked at his watch. The time was nearly

seven o'clock. "Let's have a break, chaps," he said, longing for a cigar. They sat in the sandbagged bar, drinking coffee and smoking, until the developed plates arrived back from the hospital.

"Jesus H. Christ!" the major murmured as he began studying them. "Someone's been putting in overtime! Look at this!"

At first, all that the bomb disposal officers could see was a jumble of wires, switches and taped-over batteries with sticks of explosive fixed to the bottom of the box, lying on a metal plate. Then, perusing other X-ray plates, they began to trace the various circuits inside the box.

"At least six, possibly seven," the major concluded ruefully. "Some of them are dummies, of course, but which?"

"Can we cut into it, do you think, sir?" asked Alan Campbell.

"Possible. Look there and there. He's put clips on the joints at both sides with wires to the batteries. They'll either trip if we go in through the sides or else they're total decoys inviting us to go in through the top or the front where the real ambush is."

"I can't see any wires either to the top or the front."

"Neither can I. I think Chummy wants us to use the front door to get at the innards and when we do the circuit'll trip. So we'll go in at the top."

"Steam it, perhaps?" Captain Madeley said tentatively, suggesting the use of high-pressure steam to dissolve the explosive.

The major shook his head.

"Wouldn't be able to get at it. That's why he's used the metal plate under the stuff. He knows that trick well enough. No, the only good thing about this is that I can't see any sort of timer."

"Neither can I, sir."

"He's taped everything but they all look like simple batteries to me. No, he wants us to think it's on a timer so we'll get a move on and make a boo-hoo. This bomb's meant to bring the hotel and the whole area to a standstill. It'll only blow when you try to move it or kill it. So we'll assume there's no hurry then?"

"Affirmative, sir," his Ammunition Technical Officers chorused.

"You know," the major said reflectively, rubbing his tired eyes, "I reckon this brute's just a tarted-up 'Lambeg.' If we pull it over or move it, it'll go. Likewise, if we cut into the sides or front. I reckon Chummy's simply thrown in a couple more switches and a helluva lot of wire to confuse us. Otherwise, it's fairly plain sailing."

"Could be."

"We'll know soon enough anyway."

"Before we start, sir, can't we do something about the bloody noise? My head's throbbing like a tom-tom."

"You're right. So's mine . . . Bryan!" He called the manager over to the table. "Bryan," he said, gesturing at the empty coffee cups and the stubbed-out cigars. "Your hospitality is appreciated. So were the sheets for the windows. But, old chum, if you want us to go on, you'll have to stop that infernal din in the lobby. Can you fix it?"

"It's by the switchboard."

"You're not going through that lobby, friend. That's all we need. Mr. Green and his hotel going kerboom at one and the same time!"

"I can reach the switches through the back, through the luggage store."

"Then do so, Bryan, if you can. Derek, go with him."

The two set off into the labyrinthine corridors behind the hotel's shiny façade.

"Where's the equipment, Alan?" the major asked, squinting through the smoke of a second free cigar.

"In the bag, sir."

Suddenly instead of the cacophony of buzzes and clangs, sweet music from a violin orchestra flooded the building.

"That's better," laughed Major Gates. "Music to defuse by!"

Bryan Green hurried sheepishly back into the bar. "I pulled every switch I could, Stephen," he explained, "and the Muzak just seemed to come on. I couldn't switch it off."

"Don't worry," the major replied, standing up from the

table and waltzing a few steps on the carpet as if he'd a partner in his arms. "As long as it doesn't play the 'Dead March' or 'The Wearing of the Green'!"

His hawk-nosed face lost its forced smile. The lines around his mouth and chin set deep once more.

Captain Campbell recognized the signs and walked over to the sandbags laid three deep from the ceiling to floor, blocking the bar off from the reception lobby.

He picked up the bag of equipment and the neck-radios they would wear so Derek Madeley could hear every word and sound while they tackled the bomb. If anything went wrong, at least one of them would have an idea of what might have happened.

They walked out into the fresh air again, day turning to dusk, and back into the hotel through the revolving doors.

"Well, at least no one's pinched it yet," Alan Campbell joked as they approached the bomb again behind the cover of the white sheets.

The major's eyes flicked up at the clock above the reception desk. It was nearly ten minutes past eight. He knew the night's work had barely started.

They laid out their tools on the floor by the phone booth, checking everything was in place.

"This one, d'you think?" asked the major, picking up an extremely fine hand drill and bit.

"Will the liquid get through?"

"Should do, Alan. Let's try anyway."

Major Gates knelt before the box as if in prayer to the God of bomb disposal, hands clasped around the drill. He took one deep breath and lowered the tool to the surface.

The specially hardened bit cut easily into the chipboard of the box precisely at the point calculated by the major from the radiographic plates. He drilled slowly, hardly exerting any pressure, continually blowing away the shavings so that none might drop down inside. After two minutes' careful work, the drill met no resistance. The hole was made.

The major left the bit in the hole for a second. He took another deep breath. If the bomb contained a light-sensitive switch, then this next second would be when it triggered the bomb. He lifted the drill slowly and permitted himself a quiet smile. The bomb had been penetrated.

He looked back over his shoulder and winked at Captain Campbell.

Next, the major leaned even further over the bomb, shining a slim, powerful torch into its workings. He could just see two of the soldered connections amid the maze of green and white striped wire.

Like a surgeon in an operating theater, he held out his right hand and Alan Campbell placed a thin glass pipette in his palm, all the time talking quietly into his neck-radio, relaying each of the major's moves.

Major Gates slid the glass tube into the opening, released his thumb over the top and allowed six drops of liquid to fall into the box, hopefully on to some of the electrical connections.

He waited a few seconds before using the torch again, right eye pressed nearly to the bomb casing.

"That's two knocked out at least," he said quietly, straightening up, sighing, rubbing the aching muscles in the small of his back.

He shuffled around on his knees. Captain Campbell held a shadowy radiograph plate up to the light of the lobby's false chandeliers while they both checked the position of the other contacts and switches.

Three more times, the major drilled holes into the casing and dripped through the chemical whose bomb-disrupting powers he'd proved in his kitchen experiments.

He studied the radiograph plates constantly as he worked, always checking the work with Alan Campbell.

"Just there," the major murmured, another drop of liquid slithering into the bomb's innards. "That's right."

"Watch it, sir. That wire's a bit fine."

"Is that enough? Should be."

"I reckon that's okay, sir."

"Let's wait a mo. We're in no hurry."

"That should do it."

"Let's look at that plate again, Alan."

"This one?"

"Uh-huh. Now here's that other wire to the detonator. There's the connection."

A few more drips fell through the hole in the casing, effectively jamming the bomb's electrical circuits.

"Right. Got it."

"I think that's the lot, sir."

The major hadn't been conscious of the passing minutes and hours until he eased himself back out of the phone booth.

He brushed a hand wearily through his grey hair, feeling the strands sticky with sweat from his scalp.

The clock above the reception desk showed it was nearly fifteen minutes past ten o'clock.

"It's stunned, Alan," Major Gates muttered, smiling lopsidedly at his ATO. "Better tell Derek to organize the pulling line."

Captain Campbell spoke briefly into his radio.

"He's already got it prepared and made a plan."

"Good man. Let's have a smoke."

The major stood up and stretched, pulling the front of his trousers away from the sweat-stickiness of his crotch and thighs.

"And so ends the second act," he murmured, glancing down at the bomb.

There was an acute sense of expectancy when the two officers walked back into the bar next door. Bryan Green hovered near them, unsure, with two steaming cups of coffee.

The major waved him over.

"You can bring your guests back in here, chum," he said, taking a cup. "Got any grub for them?"

"Toasted sandwiches?"

"Why not, as long as you don't charge them? And make mine a ham and cheese, eh?"

"Can I pull it out, sir?" asked Captain Madeley anxiously. "I've hardly done anything all evening."

"All yours, Derek. Through the luggage door, down the ramp and into the car park. Have the sappers build a sangar there and we'll finally kill the brute once it's inside."

The captain turned away, enthusiastic.

"And, Derek," the major added, "better put some sand down outside to help it move. I don't want the bastard tipping over. It's safe when it's upright but I won't give a five-year guarantee in any other position. Let's not lose the game now, eh?" He beckoned to Bryan Green. "Fix me a line out on the receptionist's phone, will you?"

Back in the lobby, the pulling operation had begun. Inch by inch, the bomb, secured by a strong nylon cord, was moving across the carpet toward the luggage door which was wedged open by a single sandbag.

After every six inches or so, Captain Madeley, his normally puce features growing redder, crawled along the carpet to check the box's progress.

Once the bomb was outside on the ramp leading to the car park, Major Gates walked jauntily over to examine the phone booth. It was exactly as he'd thought. He picked up the coin on the carpet, the piece of metal holding in the anti-disturbance switch, and wrapped it carefully in his handkerchief in case it might yield some fingerprints.

Smiling to himself, he walked over to the reception desk, jumped up to sit on the counter, then dialled the operations room at Army headquarters.

"Where are you, Stephen?" asked the major on duty, surprised at the call. "I can hear music your end."

"I'm in the hotel. About twenty feet from the bomb. It's just leaving by the front door without paying its bill."

"God! Be careful!"

"Don't worry. Simply wanted to let you know we're winning. Anything else happening?"

"Quiet as the proverbial, old boy."

"Good. I'll see you later then, chum."

As he walked outside to watch the bomb's movement, the Muzak tape changed to the melody of "Moonlight Becomes You."

"Like hell it does!" he murmured.

The major tossed back his head and sucked in the night air, gazing momentarily at the stars and their shredding cloud cover.

He sensed a desperate weariness around him and within himself. His Explosive Ordnance Disposal teams were near the limit of their endurance.

By now, the bomb was sliding over grains of yellow sand, approaching the beehive of sandbags, the sangar, built in the car park by the Royal Engineers.

The major and Captain Campbell, munching sandwiches, drew up their final plans, checking again and again the radiographic plates.

"First charge here, Alan?" asked Major Gates pointing to a cross on the diagram he'd drawn on the back of a bar menu.

"Should open it at the very least, sir."

"And if it blows, well, it's in the sangar."

"Should save the windows."

"I bloody well hope so. I'm getting a little obsessional about them."

They grinned at each other, relishing a conspiratorial feeling about their expertise and shared danger this long evening.

"Half an ounce?"

"No more."

"Can I lay it, sir? I don't reckon I've earned my corn so far."

"Don't be silly!" the major protested, secretly pleased at the captain's modesty. "Of course you have and of course you can!"

Captain Campbell positioned his tiny, wedge-shaped lump of explosive against a particular joint in the bomb casing once the box slithered into the protective shield of sandbags.

He walked unhurriedly back to the new command position behind an armored personnel carrier, carefully laying down the wire connecting his detonator to the electrical circuits.

"When you're ready, sir," he said.

Major Gates shook his head. "Wait one, Alan."

He stepped into the road, cupped his hands and shouted up at the windows occupied by the television crews. The major wanted the triumph of the Royal Army Ordnance Corps to be properly recorded.

"Countdown starts at five," he called. "Five . . . four . . . three . . . two . . . one . . ."

Alan Campbell twisted the key which connected the circuits.

Kerr-rr-ack!

The explosion, red and angry, leapt out of the half-dark, silhouetted against the steady yellow lights of the hotel.

Dust blew up into the strengthening breeze, wafted away and settled.

"Come on!" the major said, gesturing his two captains forward.

In the light of the major's torch, they saw that the bomb casing was virtually shattered, its front and back hanging on by mere splinters of wood. Inside, switches and batteries swung gently, torn from their connections.

"Let's have another go," urged Major Gates, grinning broadly, almost totally satisfied. "We'll have a total victory!"

Captain Madeley, somewhat nervous, laid the second small charge inside the far corner of the casing. His walk back to the firing position betrayed quickening anxiety.

He looked, kneeling, at the major for permission to turn the key.

"Not yet," said the major.

In the darkness, he'd sensed people beginning to move across the road, presumably thinking that the bomb was safe after the first dismantling charge.

"Keep clear," he shouted. "Keep well clear. There's another charge. Five . . . four . . . three . . . two . . . one . . ."

The flash and crack of the explosion burst into the night.

Major Gates walked to the bomb alone this time, torchlight bobbing on the tarmac of the car park.

The breeze from the Black Mountain brooding invisibly above Belfast's sprawl grew into a sharp wind. Its gusts whirled down side streets, tinkling plastic cups and empty Chinese takeaway containers along the gutters.

Now, the loneliness was to be savored, a time for the inner communion between hunter and prey after a long stalk and successful kill.

The inside of the bomb was completely exposed, broken wires flapping harmlessly, batteries hanging off threads of black tape.

The major shone the torch on his watch. It was thirty minutes past midnight and the bomb was dead.

The major walked slowly back to his men, kicking at fragments. He saw their eyes shining in the hotel's light.

Suddenly, six feet from them, he smiled broadly and ran forward to shake their hands.

"We stunned the brute," he cried exultantly. "We carted it out and now we've shot it! We've won!"

They hugged each other without any self-consciousness and slapped shoulders and backs before the major called a halt. "Right, chaps," he said, perhaps a trifle curtly. "Pick up the pieces and I want your reports on the desk in the morning."

He left his men to gather up the remains of the bomb, ready for forensic examination, and drove down the road to Lisburn, blue light flashing on the roof of the Land Rover.

Just before one o'clock in the morning, he crept up the staircase and to his bedroom, determined not to wake Elizabeth.

But, as always, she seemed to sense his presence even in sleep.

"There's a message for you," she grunted, lifting her head off the pillow, pointing towards the phone by his side of the bed.

He picked up the piece of paper and read the Belfast telephone number scrawled upon it by the light of the night-bulb on the landing.

"I'll call from downstairs."

"It doesn't matter," Elizabeth replied, smiling blearily at him and scratching her head. "I'm awake now."

The major began dialling the number.

"How did it go, darling?" his wife asked.

"We won, hands down."

"I can see that."

"Ssshhh!"

The number rang and was answered within seconds. Major Gates recognized the voice immediately.

"You called?" he said shortly.

"Ah, SATO. Thanks for ringing back after such a busy night."

"It's late."

"Is it? Of course it is. Sorry," said the man from the intelligence unit which didn't exist, sounding indecently wide-awake. "Anyway, old man, I hear hearty congratulations are in order."

"Thanks, old man," the major replied with some irony. "But what do you want at this hour?"

"Sorry . . . but you did say to give you a bell if we heard anything."

"And?"

"Your fans were getting a blow-by-blow account while you and your boys were hard at it . . ."

"And?"

"They were more disappointed with the result."

"You heard?"

"Clear as a bell. They seemed to be blaming a chap called Seamus. Apparently, he as good as guaranteed that little package you unwrapped."

"Did he, by God?"

"Thought you'd be interested, old boy. To quote one of their happy band when the news of your win came through, 'We should have left that fucking Aherne in the Crumlin.'"

Chapter 11
September, 1971

"Zip me up, darling," asked Lindy Aicheson as she stood before the mirror in their room at the Listowel Arms Hotel.

"Uh-huh," Edward S. Aicheson murmured from the chair where he was reading that day's *Irish Press*.

"I said, zip me up, will you?" she repeated.

"Sure thing," he replied, still engrossed in his paper.

She sighed to herself and slapped the front of the newspaper. "I said, zip me up, will you?" she demanded once more and smiled warm and soft and fragrant from the bath she'd taken after their unexpected love-making.

Ted Aicheson jumped up, apologetic, and reached for the zip at the waist of her black cocktail dress. He slid it half-way up, then leaned forward to kiss the smooth skin just above her bra-strap.

"Hey!" she protested, wriggling. "Enough of that, Aicheson. Remember I'm a respectable married woman."

He slid his hands around her and squeezed her full breasts.

"Respectable women don't screw in the afternoon," he teased, breathing into her long, blonde hair.

She rested against him for a moment, rubbing her bottom against his groin, covered only by his thin dressing gown, before pulling away, pretending annoyance. "You're nothing but a horny, dirty-mouthed old man," she exclaimed, flattered by his renewed desire. If she hadn't moved away that very instant then, they would have ended up in bed again.

"I'm on holiday," he said lightly.

"And we've to meet your relatives in an hour."

"Suppose so," he sighed, making a last, playful grab at her. She twirled easily from his clutch.

"What was so interesting in the paper then?" she asked, deliberately changing the subject.

"Oh . . . that? There was a big bomb scene in Belfast last night. In that hotel where we ate last week."

"Oh, no! It's not blown up, is it?"

"No. The Army defused the bomb. The paper says it took them hours."

"Our intrepid major with the gun in his hip pocket?"

"Doesn't say but I guess he'd have been in the action somewhere."

"Seems so far away, doesn't it, Ted?"

"Another country, another century."

"Another planet?"

"That too."

"Glad we came?"

"Just now?" he smiled lecherously, slipping off his gown and posing before her like a body-builder. She threw his underpants and trousers at him, sparkling eyes savoring his nakedness.

"Now stop that! Just stop it!" she ordered laughing. "You know very well what I meant."

He shrugged resignedly, beginning to dress.

They'd arrived in Listowel three days before expecting to find another quiet and unhurried market town. The reality was different. Listowel had been packed with people attending the last day of the town's September race meeting.

The market square had been jammed with cars and only the help of a police sergeant had enabled them to double-park outside the Listowel Arms Hotel in the corner of the square.

"From the North?" he'd remarked, noticing the vehicle's number plates.

Ted had nodded.

"Well, don't you worry, sir," the sergeant had grinned. "You'll be finding a wee difference here."

And so it had proved.

The hotel had been a scene of controlled chaos when

they'd booked in. Their room had not been ready and the bar had been too crowded with racegoers for comfort.

"Come back in an hour," the receptionist had said, apologizing fulsomely. "By then, they'll all be at the track or drunk and we can sort you out."

Ted and Lindy had wandered out into the square, smiling to each other at the frenetic bonhomie pervading the town.

They had admired the two churches and the ruins of Listowel Castle, not quite knowing what they were, and then had decided to try their luck in Buckley's Bar, diagonally opposite to the hotel. This, too, had been packed with racing men, mostly dressed in checked sports jackets and brown trilby hats.

Ted had left Lindy standing by the grimy mirror covering one side of the room and pushed to the bar through the rising gabble.

"And didn't the man tell me so himself?"

"It's a three-legged donkey, so it is . . ."

"Four more Paddys, Pat!"

"I'd have had the forecast but for that one-armed jock . . ."

"Away with you! You wouldn't know Vincent O'Brien from Father Mulcahy!"

"Two gin and tonics, please," Ted had heard himself order.

"What's that, sir?" said the man behind the bar, expertly flicking Guinness froth from a glass with a plastic spatula.

"Two gin and tonics!" he almost shouted.

The exchange of misinformation around him died away as his nasal Boston accent registered.

Faces had turned towards him, friendly but curious.

"It's an American you are?" the tiny, gnomic man at his elbow had asked.

"Uh-huh. That's correct."

Ted had reached for his drinks on the counter.

"And here for the races?"

"Nope," he'd replied, handing a glass through the customers to Lindy. "Just a holiday."

"A holiday it is?" another man had chimed in, evincing total disbelief.

"That's right."

"In Listowel?" they'd chorused incredulously.

"Looking for ancestors," Lindy had volunteered, pushing to her husband's side amid a general touching of hatbrims.

Ted had shaken his head slightly, but it had been too late. The forthcoming races had been forgotten.

Questions had come from every corner of the bar. Their replies had brought more questions and even more answers until the Aichesons were overwhelmed with information about this family Aherne here and that family Aherne there.

Eventually, an old man sucking a sticky pipe had been ushered forward. All the information gathered by Lindy had had to be repeated in a loud voice because the old man's hearing aid battery was run down.

He'd ruminated through most of a pint of Guinness bought by Ted, who suddenly noticed that his hand was dipping into his wallet with increasing frequency.

"If it's you are after a Mary Aherne," the old man had finally pronounced, "who married in Boston and ran a bar, then you're after wanting . . ." He had counted on his fingers. ". . . her great-great-great-grandson, Michael, at Aherne's in Church Street."

"Ah, that's your man," everyone had agreed immediately with much nodding of heads. "You'll be wanting Michael Aherne."

"And where's he?" Lindy had asked, delighted at everyone's willingness to help.

"Well, he won't be there anyway!" the barman had declared, leaning his elbows into the spreading slops of beer on the counter.

"Where?"

"He'll be at the races with Johnny O'Hara from Ballybunnion," advised the little man still at Ted's side, now drinking the American's gin and tonic. "Always together," he'd added. "Inseparable they are except when Johnny's away on business and then they're not seeing each other."

"Hold on," Ted had said, lifting his hands. "Now just hold on."

There'd been a momentary silence.

"Now where will this Michael . . ."

"Aherne," the little man had interrupted needlessly, taking another sip of gin and tonic.

"This Michael Aherne be when he's not at the races with Johnny O'Hara?"

"At his place, of course," the barman had declared between two gulps of Guinness which emptied his glass. Somehow, in putting it down, he edged it invitingly towards Ted's side of the counter.

"O'Hara's?"

The little man drained the glass of gin and tonic, shaking his head. In doing so, he caught sight of the yellowing watch on his wrist.

"Dear Mother of Heaven!" he'd exclaimed. "It's twenty to, boys! Sorry, friends!"

Elbows had risen. Mouths had opened. Drinks had been swallowed.

Within a minute the racing men had left the bar. Some of them ran out, pushing each other through the door in their eagerness to reach the track in time to bet on the first race.

Ted and Lindy had leaned on the bar, carefully avoiding the damp patches, and looked at the barman expectantly.

"Now, what were they saying?" Ted had asked.

"Well," the barman had started. "There's this . . ."

The door had opened and the police sergeant who'd allowed the Aichesons to double-park walked in.

"Ah, so there you are at last. I saw you walking this way," he'd said, removing his peaked hat, rubbing his palms together.

Ted had winked at his wife and reached for his wallet again.

"Just a pint, sir," said the sergeant, not waiting to be asked. "It's terrible thirsty with all those cars."

"Must be," Lindy had agreed.

"Well, no rest for the wicked," the sergeant continued, before downing most of his Smithwick's bitter. "It's after . . ."

The door had swung open again, this time more violently.

Through it staggered a beefy man, more than six feet tall, cloth cap over one side of his head. The barman had started towards him, alarmed. The sergeant showed little interest.

The big man had swayed to the bar, face ruddy and sweating.

"And where the divil is this?" he'd slurred.

"Buckley's," the sergeant had answered, not even turning his head.

"Buckley's where?"

"Listowel."

"Grand!" the big man said, weaving his head, clearly sodden drunk. "Not far away then!"

"And where are you headed?"

"Tralee!"

"Well, you'll know the road then," the sergeant had said dismissively, supping his pint.

The man turned and, in turning, almost fell.

"He's drunk!" Lindy had whispered indignantly as the door slammed shut again.

"He's been in Dublin," the sergeant had explained.

"Dublin?"

"The All-Ireland Final."

"The Final! When?"

"Four days ago but your man's nearly safe home now."

"Can take more'n a week when Kerry win," the barman had added.

"And it's been known they end up in Liverpool," the sergeant added, visibly refreshed by his beer.

"Even Rome . . . in St. Peter's Square," the barman had breathed in some awe.

"Don't blather," protested the sergeant. "That's just old stories and can't you see our American friend here is wanting to buy another drink?"

In the next hour, the bemused Aichesons were treated to a rendering, for fifty pence, of "Danny Boy" by an old woman who'd wandered into the bar; an incomprehensible explanation from the sergeant about how he'd been transferred from his normal work in County Donegal and why he was drinking and not on duty; and finally, from the barman, a fairly lucid explanation about Michael Aherne and his bar in Church Street.

Slightly drunk, they wandered out into the square, now somnolent and quietly sedate in the warm afternoon sunshine. They drifted arm-in-arm past the banks and shops, drawn towards the occasional, distant sound of cheering.

"Isn't that the cutest!" Lindy had exclaimed, pointing to the narrow alley, Tay Lane, sloping mysteriously downwards from the rounded junction of William Street and Market Street.

They picked their way carefully along the cobbled surface, badly needing repair, turned a gentle corner and saw the river at the end of the lane.

Ted laughed aloud.

"Look! That's their racetrack!" he'd said, pointing across the narrow, meandering river to the wooden rails circling the large island on the opposite bank. In the distance, they'd seen a small grandstand and some white marquees.

Suddenly, as if from nowhere, they'd heard the pounding of hooves. A dozen horses, jockeys in multi-colored silks, had swept into view, staying as close as possible to the rails.

For a moment, it had seemed that they would gallop headlong into the river, that their momentum wouldn't allow them to maneuver around the bend.

Lindy had stepped back, frightened, hand to mouth, sensing the tremendous power in the horses only yards away.

"Sweet Jesus!" Ted had muttered, alarmed himself.

And then, in a flash of color and noise, the horses were out of sight, away down the far side of the track in the middle of the River Feale.

Ted had shaken his head in astonishment, laughing nervously. "Crazy!" he'd exclaimed. "They're absolutely crazy!"

The Aichesons' experiences in the next three days did little to change that opinion. They could hardly believe the contrast between the easy-going, exuberant, almost overwhelmingly friendly people and those they'd left behind in Northern Ireland.

That first night, they were greeted by Michael Aherne as life-long friends when they called at his bar. It was clear that the heavily built, crinkle-haired man in his late 50s was extremely busy with all the departing punters but business was dismissed from his mind immediately he heard of the American couple's relationship with his family.

He'd insisted over many drinks on arranging a family reunion party at his own expense and sent Ted and Lindy on their unsteady way back to the Arms Hotel well under the influence of the town's hospitality.

For the next two days, they had explored the country and coastline of North Kerry, relaxing more and more with each sight and sound: the old man plodding along the straight country road beside his donkey laden with bricks of peat; the four nuns paddling on the shining sands at Ballybunn-ion, habits clasped demurely at mid-calf; the farmer's wife who invited them into her cottage for fresh-made apple pie when they'd merely stopped to ask directions; the sudden hush in a crowded bar as Radio Telefis Eireann broadcast the Angelus; the gypsy children, tanned and cheeky, begging outside shops with their mother, babe in arms; the priest, on holiday himself, telling Bible stories to a rapt audience of small children on the terrace of the Greenmount Hotel, perched above the beaches at Ballybunnion; the sunsets, orange and dark purple above the hills; the quiet and sweep of empty, stone-walled fields, high clouds dancing shadows across them; the curious, gentle smiles of the elderly; the bold, inquisitive gazes of children.

Ted and Lindy Aicheson fell under Kerry's spell. No longer did they attempt to organize their time. Indeed, time was of no importance. They relaxed as they hadn't done since their student days, surrendering totally to each other and the people of North Kerry.

It was like their courtship in Boston when everything, visible or unseen, had been made fresh and exciting by their love. Then, the flower sellers along Newbury Street had seemed magically romantic and the pavement cafes so

intellectually chic. The Charles River, dit-dotted with
sailing craft and rowers, had looked as wide and important
as the River Shannon, particularly when the dying sun
reflected off the windows of the sky-reaching office blocks.
They talked of those times when they'd viewed the town
from Cambridge across the river, when it had appeared that
new Boston was growing perceptibly upwards from the old,
rough-bricked buildings, from the gold glittering dome of
the State House nestled comfortably among the dips and
rises of Beacon Hill, its narrow alleys and streets offering
continual glimpses of water. They held each other's hands
like they'd done those years before on the Common or in
Harvard Yard or when they'd strolled through Quincy
Market, sipping fruit cups and wondering how clever or
banal any trader could be to name his stall "Boston T.
Baggs." They ate snacks not formal meals, love-filled just
as they'd done when they'd motored out to Medford on a
Sunday for the "dim sum" savouries at that Chinese
restaurant.

And they'd talked again of smells and sights and colors,
just as they'd done during their honeymoon at Rocky Neck
on the jutting arm of Cape Ann, living in a friend's wooden
holiday home among all the other wooden houses painted
blue-green, white, red or grey.

They remembered their loving in a huge bed, how they
luxuriated in each other, despising the previous grabbing
and groping, the zipping and unfastening in the back seats
of cars or borrowed-for-an-hour apartments.

They stopped to look at flowers in hedgerows, recalling
the scarlet maples of September in New England and the
fresh picked buttercups and ox-eyed daisies in the vases on
the table at that little restaurant at West Wharf, the one
called The Kitchen, where they'd eaten late breakfasts
during their honeymoon, eggs and bacon and muffins, sex-
tired eyes adoring each other.

The guarded suspicion, fear even, generated by the ugly
brutalities of Northern Ireland slipped from their minds.
They no longer felt embarrassed about their presumption in
claiming kinship with these Kerry folk.

Now, the Aichesons found it natural to stroll rather than
stride purposefully, to nod to passers-by rather than avoid
their eyes as they did in Belfast.

"A fine evening!" Ted called to an elderly couple as he
and Lindy walked slowly along the west side of the market
square, deep in slanting shadow, towards the tavern and the
reunion party.

"It is that, thanks be," answered the strangers.

"Thanks be," Lindy echoed softly, clutching her husband's arm, feeling, like him, totally familiar with Listowel. Its peace of mind was deep within them.

When they reached the bar, simply signed "Aherne's,"
the chatter and juke-box music suggested that they were
among the last arrivals.

Slightly uncertain, they pushed the door open and
immediately saw the beaming face of Michael Aherne, his
paunch finding the gap between waistcoat and trousers.

"Hello there!" he cried, hurrying over. "So it's yourselves are here!"

He clasped Lindy in his arms and kissed her damply on
the left cheek before vigorously pumping Ted's right hand
up and down, pulling him into the bar.

The narrow room was crowded with more than thirty
people sitting or standing by a number of round tables
covered with white tablecloths. Two girls in their late teens,
faces shiny with exertion, bent and bobbled behind the bar
counter, serving drinks with practiced speed.

"Quiet now!" Michael Aherne called, clapping his hands
three times. "It's the guests of honor are here."

Faces, freshly young to wrinkled old, turned to the
Aichesons, smiling, assessing. For the next ten minutes,
Ted and Lindy were led around the bar, shaking hands or
kissing.

"This is Joe . . . he's my nephew . . . the son of
Bryan Aherne, my elder brother killed in The Troubles
. . . his wife Bernadette . . . their girls, Shelagh and
Mai, and their husbands, Sean and Patrick . . . and this is
Hannah, my sister-in-law . . . Bryan's wife . . . Grand-
ma Hannah . . . and my sister, Sinead, who'd be your

Mary Aherne's great-great-granddaughter just like you're
her great-great-grand nephew . . . and here's Kevin, my
second older brother . . . his wife, Maggie . . ."

The names and faces circled around them, too many to
remember at once, until Michael Aherne called a halt.

"Enough of that," he announced, pushing Ted and Lindy
to the counter. "They'll be having a wee drink before
meeting the rest of you."

With glasses in their hands, the Aichesons had time to
look around the bar again.

"I didn't realize there'd be so many," Ted remarked
ruefully.

"So many?" said his host. "And sure isn't this just the
half of them? The others are scattered over the world."

"I'll never remember them all."

"Don't worry, Ted. I've had them all written down."

He beckoned to a gentle-faced woman in her early
seventies, sitting quietly in the corner.

"Now this is Miss Quinlan . . . Mai Quinlan," he
said. "She's not a relative, a neighbor really, but she knows
who's who in Listowel."

"I wouldn't say that, Michael Aherne," the woman said
softly, brushing back a stray lock of grey hair, smiling
deprecatingly behind her spectacles, the epitome of an
educated spinster.

"Oh, come on now," urged the bar-owner, respect clear
in his manner although Miss Quinlan was obviously of the
same generation.

"Well," she admitted. "I have been talking to one or two
since you asked."

"Then you can tell them about it over supper. You'll be
sitting with us."

Miss Quinlan smiled and accepted a glass of sherry, duty
overcoming modesty.

There were more introductions before everyone was
called to a meal of porterhouse steak and salad with potatoes
boiled fluffily in their skins. The tables were so filled with
food that the bottles of wine and pints of Guinness were
relegated to the scuffed linoleum on the floor.

While the Aichesons and their host ate and drank heartily, Miss Quinlan pecked bird-like at her food, telling the story of the Ahernes of Listowel, the joys and tragedies of each generation, their achievements and failures.

As she talked, Michael Aherne pointed out the relevant branches of the family at the various tables.

And as the story went on, told with the disinterest of amateur scholarship, Ted and Lindy became increasingly aware of its Republican overtones. They looked uneasily at each other, wondering if questions would be welcome, particularly about that Aherne who'd escaped from Crumlin Gaol and who, according to the newspaper, came from near Listowel.

After his fourth glass of wine, Ted Aicheson, replete with food, decided to broach the subject indirectly.

"And are there Ahernes all over Ireland, Miss Quinlan?" he asked.

"All over the globe, Mr. Aicheson," she answered.

"As Michael here's probably told you, I'm working right now in Belfast, at the Royal Victoria, and I've heard of Ahernes up there. Would they . . ." From the corner of his eye, he noticed the glazed look of cheerfulness on his host's face suddenly change. ". . . be related as well?"

Miss Quinlan's smile tightened.

"They could be. Oh, yes, they could be," she conceded.

Michael Aherne hunched forward over the table, pushing aside the condiments.

"Is that what brought you here?" he asked bluntly, expression hardening.

"What?" Lindy said, all innocence.

Their host shook his head, then tapped the side of his nose knowingly. He laughed in the back of his throat, relaxing again.

"The Ahernes in Belfast? Or rather, should I say the Aherne in Belfast?"

"But we knew about the Ahernes in Listowel before we left Boston . . ." Ted began to say.

"Sure you did," the bar owner interrupted. "Sure you knew, but I'm reckoning it was newspaper stories about a certain Seamus Aherne which brought you down here finally."

He winked shrewdly.

Ted Aicheson spread his hands upwards on the table, shrugging, smiling a trifle sheepishly.

"Well, seeing as you're family now," Michael Aherne continued, "I don't suppose you shouldn't be knowing."

"About Seamus?"

"He's Joe's son. My great-nephew."

Michael Aherne pointed to a table further down the room. Ted looked quickly and saw a thin, sickly man in the act of swallowing a glass of, presumably, whiskey.

"And he is in the Provisionals?"

"Oh, yes. He's one of the boys all right. Joined them after Derry, not long since he finished his apprenticeship with the Post Office."

"Don't you mind?" Lindy asked, ingenuously.

"I mind," Michael Aherne replied, a trace of bitterness in his voice. "Oh, yes, I mind enough. We all do. But then, after all, he's his own man now."

"You worry then?" Lindy persisted.

"Worry? Worry? Of course, we bloody well worry, but he's doing what he thinks right by himself and the family and that's that. He's a good boy, Seamus. Always helped out around the farm when Joe had one of his turns. He was well liked. You see, down here we stopped fighting a long time ago. At least most of us did. Let's face it, there's precious little to be fighting about except income tax and not enough jobs and the pill. We've forgotten in one generation what it's like to have the troops marching up and down the street, right outside your own front windows, scaring the wee 'uns half to death. Miss Quinlan here . . . well, her da used to barricade the windows all day and all night so that Tan bullets wouldn't be coming through when they were out drinking and raping and looting. Why, some of them even pulled their funny business with Grandma Hannah before she was wed. In those days, the only good British was a dead 'un. Now the only bad Britisher is the one who doesn't come here on holiday spending money. Oh, yes, we've forgotten what it was like down here. And maybe we'll be forgetting even more in that Common Market. Then we'll be Europeans not Irish. Sometimes, it's seeming to me that you Irish-Americans remember more than we do. But then, you can be affording to. You're far away enough to be enjoying the luxury. We've forgotten and maybe we shouldn't have. But they've not been able to forget up in the North with all those Protestants sitting on their necks and maybe it's a good thing that some Southerners like Seamus and the rest of the boys haven't forgotten either and are giving them a hand to get rid of the Brits and . . .''

He stopped suddenly in mid-sentence, sensing that his words were coming too fast and with too much anger. He shook his head and sighed deeply.

"And don't you see how it sets me off at the mouth and this supposed to be a celebration?" He rubbed a large hand over his face, wiping away globules of sweat.

Ted lowered his voice, sympathy evident, glancing a warning at Lindy. "Have you heard how he is?"

"Seamus? All right as far as we're knowing. But there's not much we've heard since the prison break. One letter and a brief phone call, that's all. He's worried that if he gets in touch, then Joe and Bernadette will be in trouble. We already reckon the security boys have a tap on the phone but who knows what's happening? We're presuming he's back in the North but we just don't know. That's the worst of it, not knowing.''

"None of you've seen him then?"

"Not since he broke out."

"It must be very difficult," said Lindy Aicheson, realizing how embarrassed Michael Aherne was to talk about his young relative in the Provisional IRA.

He patted her hand, shaking his head again.

"Most things are difficult in Ireland, lass, particularly being able to forget. That's why this place makes a good living. That's why there're more bars in this town than food shops. We're not serving pleasure and company here, just oblivion.''

There was silence at the small table and an awareness that

the conversation had gone on too long and that those at the nearby tables had also been listening to the bitter words.

"Anyway," said Michael Aherne, regaining some joviality of manner, "how are you two finding Belfast, the city of ten thousand bigots?"

Ted coughed and cleared his throat. "It's different," he joked grimly. "Definitely different. You have to live every day as it comes. You can never get yourself away from the tension. Most times, some tiny part of you is afraid. Coming down here is like having a huge weight lifted from your brain. Lindy and I haven't gotten to understand yet how the people who live there all the time manage to cope without ending up on the funny farm. I know we hand out tranquillizers at the hospital like candy but that still doesn't explain it. You simply have to go on living, praying to the Almighty, or Dr. Paisley or the Pope that there's not a bullet or bomb around the corner with your name on it."

"D'you see a deal of it?" Michael Aherne asked, all previous aggression absent from his voice.

"I see the results of it pretty well every day in the operating theater."

"You must despair."

It was a statement, not a question. Miss Quinlan nodded agreement.

Ted took a long sip of wine, looking over the rim of the glass at his host. "To be truthful, sometimes I do," he sighed. "It's as if the whole world's gone mad up there. I can see both sides of the question, sure, even three sides, but I just can't figure that it's worth all the killing and maiming. No one's winning, everyone's losing."

"And isn't that the God's truth," Michael Aherne replied. "I'll only be saying that you've had to live through the last fifty or sixty years in Ireland to make the slightest sense of it all. It's gone on and it's still going on and you don't know whether you're proud or ashamed that you've a relative like Seamus involved. Most times, it's a bit of both."

He paused, then called to one of the girls behind the bar

for another bottle of wine, obviously wanting to end the conversation about Seamus Aherne.

Ted turned to Mai Quinlan, suddenly remembering an unasked question.

"Have you ever heard of a family round here called . . . oh, what was the name, Lindy?"

"Whose?"

"Stephen's old ancestor."

"The . . ."

"Yup," Ted interrupted quickly, not wanting his wife to mention Stephen Gates' military rank.

Lindy nodded and thought for a moment. "Sanders, wasn't it? He said it was Sanders."

"That's right. Miss Quinlan, have you ever heard of anyone with that name in Listowel? Apparently he owned land hereabouts at the turn of the century. A friend of ours thinks he's related."

The town's unofficial historian shook her head doubtfully, repeating the name softly to herself. "Sanders, no. I don't think so. Not Sanders. In Father Gaughan's book about Listowel there's mention of a land agent called Sandes but I don't remember Sanders."

"That Sandes was a real bad lot," Micahel Aherne interrupted. "I remember stories about him from my own grandfather. In the end, he had to leave town or else. A lot of people ran foul of the Sandes family. Awful drinkers and womanizers they were while they drove hundreds of poor devils into the ditch."

Ted smiled. "Doesn't sound like my friend's ancestors," he said. He wondered how Stephen Gates would take it when he heard that the only family bearing a name remotely like Sanders was one of the most notorious in the district.

The evening continued with toasts and singing until the floor of the bar was littered with empty bottles and glasses.

Ted tried to talk quietly with Joe Aherne, wanting to discover if any help was needed about Seamus, but found him too drunk to be coherent. His professional eye noticed the well-developed signs of someone who'd die in a year or so from cirrhosis of the liver. The realization sobered him slightly for the walk back to the hotel.

"Well, that was one hell of an evening," he remarked, putting his arm around Lindy's shoulders to steady her. She'd never had a head for strong drink.

"I guess we got what we deserved for prying. I thought Michael was really going to blow his stack."

"Uh-huh. At least we understand a bit more."

"Are you sorry?" Lindy asked, nestling her head to his chest.

"A bit. Stephen's going to have a real laugh when he hears we're related to the IRA."

Lindy giggled. "I'd have sorta liked," she said, "to have gone on thinking of your people over here as . . . well, like the stage Irish. You know . . . Barry Fitzgerald and Victor McLaglen in *The Quiet Man* . . . all begorrahs and bejabers and shillelaghs."

"They're happy to play it that way if they think you want them to be like that."

"Till you scratch them. Then they're different."

"Then you see why the Irish are some of the saddest people in the world. Really helpless melancholiacs."

"But they enjoy it, their sadness," Lindy suggested.

Ted smiled wanly, holding open the front door of the hotel. "They've had to learn to," he said.

Chapter 12
October, 1971

Everyone kept telling him not to worry, not to be nervous, and to act naturally. As Edward S. Aicheson sipped a weak whiskey and water, young men and women with clipboards and large stopwatches kept dashing in and out of the hospitality room on the top floor of Broadcasting House in Belfast.

Their remarks to the man sitting with him ranged from the profane to the incomprehensible.

"The Derry film's gone down in the sodding soup!"

"The two-way from London's okay after Manchester has the first five!"

"Billy can't VT his piece so he'll have to go live at the top after your intro. Okay?"

They all smiled at him in passing but it was mere courtesy, not real friendliness. When he'd first arrived at the fortress-like building the television people had gone out of their way to make him feel special, thanking him profusely for coming. But now that he was securely in their clutches, safely within their peculiar world, he had become just another titbit to be fed into the medium's voracious maw.

"You're down for four minutes," someone had told Aicheson and that was precisely how he felt at that moment, merely a time-unit, a face and a voice capable of filling a slot in "Scene Around Six," the nightly television program broadcast by the BBC to the people of Northern Ireland.

The knowledge of his own temporary unimportance made him even more upset at having allowed himself to be persuaded into this by Major Stephen Gates.

"A fine pal he turned out to be," Aicheson murmured to himself.

"Pardon?"

His companion, the presenter of the program, thought the half-heard remark was directed at him.

"Sorry," Aicheson smiled, reddening slightly. "Just talking to myself."

"Don't we all over here?" grinned the presenter, a chubby, cheerful young man. "And isn't it the only way of not offending anyone?"

He returned to the yellow pages of his script, underlining words here and there, leaving Aicheson to his dark thoughts.

It had started out innocently enough over lunchtime drinks at their flat on the Sunday after he and Lindy had returned from their holiday. They'd regaled Stephen and Elizabeth Gates with their impressions of country life in County Kerry and then teased him about the possibility of his being related to the despised land agent Sandes.

"Wouldn't surprise me in the least," the major had joked. "Always was attractive to women. Always was a bit of a rake, eh, Elizabeth?"

"Not that you'd notice," his wife replied, trying to look severe but only breaking into giggles.

Ted Aicheson was so absorbed in describing all his distant relatives in Listowel that he failed to notice a certain thoughtfulness come over the major when he mentioned his relationship to Seamus Aherne.

"I feel sorry for his father," said Aicheson, pouring another round of drinks. "I guess he's headed for an early grave with a bottle in each hand. And having a boy in the Provos can't help much."

"Can't," agreed Major Gates, tugging the lobe of his right ear. "All the worry and whatever must have some effect."

"Sure does," said Lindy. "And they all reckon he was a fine son before he got mixed up with the IRA."

"Probably was," the major agreed again. "He threw up a good job to go in with them and now he's about as popular as a barman with no arms."

"What's happened?" Aicheson asked. "What've you heard?"

The major smiled mysteriously, shrugging. "We hear things, you know. Apparently, your Seamus isn't too popular with his friends right now. He promised more than he could deliver and lost the Provos a fair number of brownie points. They don't like being left with egg splattered all over their faces."

"You won't tell me what it's about?"

"Not won't, Ted. Can't. Official Secrets Act. But I can say your precious relative isn't too high on the totem pole at present. In fact he could be in deep trouble."

"D'you know where he is?"

"Somewhere in town, that's all. If we did, we'd lift him and stick him back inside. Probably the safest place for him."

"Oh, I do wish we could help the boy," Lindy remarked, looking appealingly toward her husband.

"He's not much younger than you," said the major. "He's no boy. He's an extremely dangerous terrorist."

"But his folks are real nice," protested Lindy. "Real nice."

"So was Hitler's mum by all accounts," the major replied, sharpening his voice, an idea forming in his mind. He cupped his jaw in his hand, little finger flicking at his lower lip. The Aichesons waited expectantly.

"It might be worth trying," the major mused, deliberately allowing the sudden tension to increase. "Yes, it might . . ."

"What?" Lindy pleaded.

"Well," he said after another pause, "it'd have to strictly be unofficial, of course, but how about if we plant a story in the newspapers about how ill Seamus's dad is, quoting Ted, asking chummy to think about giving himself up? After all, you say his family have hardly heard from him. At least, I reckon there's a chance he'd contact you, Ted. You know, long-lost American cousin and all that guff. It might give you the chance of talking him around."

Aicheson looked doubtful.

"He'll probably think it's a trap."

"Almost certainly," agreed Major Gates. "You'll just have to persuade him otherwise."

"And what'll you be doing while all this is going on, Stephen?"

Major Gates looked hurt and innocent. "It'd be nothing to do with me," he said. "Nothing whatsoever. Any advice from me is strictly on the old-pals basis. After all, you might have the police sniffing round, asking questions, and I can't be involved with that."

"Police?"

"They'll probably want to know what you're up to, if you can give information on chummy's location. That sort of thing. You have to remember he's an escaped convict."

"That'd be difficult."

"Shouldn't be, Ted. Not necessarily. Just plead the big-hearted, open-handed Yank who wants to help and you'll get away with it."

Aicheson sniffed, still doubtful. He took a long pull at his glass. He suspected that the army major had an ulterior motive behind his suggestion but more important to him was the thought of trying to help Seamus and, thus, his new-found friends in Kerry.

Like many in a closed profession where years of intensive study were obligatory, Aicheson wasn't particularly world-ly-wise. He guessed that one of his faults, if it be a fault, was to take people too much at their face value but had not yet acquired enough natural wariness to protect himself from his weakness.

He looked across at his wife, raising his eyebrows quiz-zically.

"Oh, can we please try, darling?" Lindy pleaded in response.

"It's up to you, of course, old chum," the major intervened. "But it might be the only way of saving the poor sod. Even if it doesn't work and you never hear from him, well, at least you can say you tried."

He leaned back in the easy chair, smoking his cigar, apparently disinterested and unconcerned. In fact, his mind was seething with plans and theories and thoughts. Mentally, he crossed his fingers.

"How would I get in touch with the press boys?" asked Aicheson, still undecided.

"Don't worry about that, Ted," the major replied, smiling encouragingly. "The chaps in our information room can pass the word. It'll be quite painless, you see."

"Uh-huh," Aicheson muttered, clutching hands to head, thinking. Finally, after a minute's silence so intense that the major thought he could hear his watch ticking, the American looked up and grinned. "Okay then, Stephen. We'll have a go. Will you fix it?"

Lindy clapped her hands with delight.

"Leave it to me, old chum," said Major Gates, trying not to appear too pleased nor too smug.

He was as good as his word. Two days later, at the start of the second week in October, 1971, Ted Aicheson was interviewed by a journalist from the *Belfast Telegraph*. The story appeared the following afternoon, headlined "SURGEON'S PLEA TO 'IRA RELATIVE':

"An American surgeon working in Belfast made the dramatic disclosure today that he has a relative in the Provisional IRA.

"And the surgeon, Mr. Edward S. Aicheson, 31, appealed to the man: 'For your family's sake, quit the terrorists.'

"Mr. Aicheson, who's working at the Royal Victoria Hospital on a two year fellowship, made the appeal in an exclusive *Telegraph* interview.

"He declined to name his relative but said that the man came from County Kerry and that his parents' given names were Joe and Bernadette.

" 'If he gets in touch with me at the hospital,' said Mr. Aicheson, 'I'll give him enough proof that we are, in fact, related.

" 'I'll also provide as much help as possible if he wants to start a new life away from all this senseless and terrible killing.'

"Mr. Aicheson, from Boston, Mass., made the discovery about his relative during a recent holiday in the South.

"He said: 'My wife and I traced a family in a small town in Kerry who are related distantly to us on the female side.

" 'It was great meeting them but then, at a reunion party, I learned that one of the younger men in the family was a Provisional, supposedly in Belfast.

" 'I was very upset at the thought that while I'm trying to save lives, he's trying to take them. It seems quite ridiculous.

" 'I'm sure if he realized just how ill his father was and how worried the rest of the family were, then he would reconsider his actions.'

"The surgeon, specializing in neuro-surgery, said that he wouldn't name his relative for fear of the Provisionals blocking any contact between them.

" 'I don't want to cause any trouble for him,' added Mr. Aicheson. 'I simply want to help and maybe save someone's life. After all, that's what my whole existence is about.' "

The tone of the newspaper article hardly pleased him. He realized that to many in Northern Ireland he would appear to be a naïve meddler. Indeed, this was one of the first comments made to him by the two detectives from the Royal Ulster Constabulary who called on him that evening at the flat at Dunmurry.

They told Aicheson that they'd already identified Seamus Aherne in their files from the scant details in the newspaper and then proceeded to threaten and wheedle and bluster, making it very clear that they expected to be told if Seamus should make contact.

The next morning a telephone call came from the BBC, inviting him to appear on its local television news program. He changed his mind about further publicity, deciding that if he gave his appeal the fullest exposure then no one would be able to accuse him of acting secretly. He would adopt Stephen Gates' advice and pose as the disingenuous American that he appeared to be. He had had time to regret his decision during the seemingly interminable wait in the small BBC hospitality room.

Eventually, though, he was led into the television studio along narrow corridors, past a canteen, and up and down flights of steps. The journalist who was to interview Aicheson was all smiles and reassurance under the hurtfully bright lights of the studio.

"Just take your time, sir," he advised while a girl dabbed powder on Aicheson's nose and forehead, even combing his hair. "Don't think of all the people out there, watching. Imagine you're simply talking to a nice old lady alone in her front room."

The interview began gently with Aicheson being allowed to explain how he'd discovered his relationship with a member of the Provisional IRA. Then, to his discomfiture, came some sharp, almost impertinent questions.

"You're absolutely sure this man is a terrorist?"

"His family tells me so and I have read about him in the papers."

"Then why do you want to help him, Mr. Aicheson?"

"I simply want to meet him, to try to talk him round, to have him stop what he's doing."

"You say you don't want to cause any trouble for him?"

"That's right."

Aicheson felt sweat forming high on his brow. He hoped the camera, red light glowing, couldn't detect it.

"Why not?" the question snapped back.

"Why not what?"

"Cause trouble for him. After all, you say he's a terrorist."

"I think he needs help."

"What sort of help?"

"I don't know precisely," Aicheson replied, realizing how weak his answer must have sounded.

The interviewer lifted one eyebrow, hoping the cameras would catch the expression. He'd been practicing it.

"Don't you think some people, like the relatives of IRA victims, will be upset that you want to help an IRA man, even though he's your relative?"

Aicheson shrugged, trying to think, conscious of the lights and the curious stares from the others in the studio.

"They probably will be," he conceded. "But, you see, my whole object is to have this man stop . . ."

"Isn't that rather the job of the security forces?" the interviewer said coldly.

"They haven't gotten far," Aicheson snapped back, anger growing.

"You're not saying that you can succeed, Mr. Aicheson, where the forces of law and order have failed?" the interviewer asked curiously, more quietly, a somewhat smug expression on his face.

"No, I guess not," Aicheson floundered. "No way."

"You're not in sympathy with this relative of yours?"

"Again, no way. I abhor violence."

"Then why bother with him? Aren't your motives as misguided as those of your fellow-countrymen who raise cash for the IRA?"

"No, they're not. I think they're wrong too. Just like I think the IRA is wrong. All I want to do is simply help the guy. Is that . . ."

"Mr. Aicheson, thank you."

The interviewer cut him off smoothly, ending the interview before Aicheson could finish his statement, protest clear in his voice. Off camera, he gestured with his palms and smiled at the American as if disclaiming responsibility for the public humiliation.

Aicheson, emotionally drained, was ushered quietly out of the studio as the program's next item was introduced.

"Fancy a drink before you go, sir?" his guide asked, leading him back down the corridors, one of them decorated with originals of cartoons about Ulster politicians.

"Uh-huh. I surely do."

This time, he took the generous glass of whiskey without any water, wanting the jolt of neat alcohol.

"You did very well," the BBC man said conversationally, helping himself to a drink as well. "Our Don can be a wee bit hard at times."

"Don't I know it? He really chewed me up and spat me out."

"Oh, I wouldn't say that, sir. I thought you came over very sincerely."

Aicheson shook his head.

"I came over as a fool," he said. Adding quietly, "But maybe I guess that's no bad thing."

"Oh, I don't . . ."

"Can I use your phone?"

"Of course," said the BBC man, indicating the instrument on a corner table. "Just pick it up and ask for an outside line."

He told Lindy that he was about to start home before asking rather tentatively what she'd thought of his appearance on television. Her hesitation provided a more truthful answer than her guarded reply.

Aicheson drove down Lisburn Road towards Dunmurry blaming Stephen Gates for the entire idea, angry at having been made to look so mixed-up during the interview, too angry to understand that the aggressive, one-sided interview was exactly what he should have hoped for.

Major Gates, to the contrary, was feeling rather pleased with himself as he drank his second pint of Bass in the officer's mess at Army Headquarters. He reckoned that Ted Aicheson had portrayed perfectly a well-meaning American blundering into a situation which was none of his business. No one could have mistaken the young surgeon for anything else. Certainly, someone would have to be extremely cynical and far-sighted to think that the American was the key figure in a plan that'd been hastily put together by the major and his acquaintance in the clandestine intelligence unit.

Indeed, the major's professional judgment was absolutely accurate as far as Seamus Aherne was concerned.

His first reaction had been one of shock when he'd seen the story in the *Belfast Telegraph* the previous evening. He guessed immediately that it referred to himself and thought instantly of telephoning Michael Aherne at the bar in Listowel to find out what was going on. But he'd quickly rejected that as too risky in case the Irish security branch had already tapped the line.

He'd spent that night and the next day in an agony of indecision, worried that his superiors in the Provisional IRA might have recognized him from the article although he knew they dismissed anything in the *Belfast Telegraph* as anti-Republican propaganda. However, the last thing he wanted after the abject failure of his new bomb at the hotel was another question mark against him. He'd already noticed the doubtful looks and taciturn remarks from some of the other members of the Active Service Units who occasionally frequented the Republican Club of Andersonstown.

Seamus's only comfort was that since Rebecca Fahey's arrival in Belfast he was able to discuss his dilemma with someone trustworthy. Her advice was to the point.

"Give the fella a call. What harm can it do?" she said, smiling up at him as she sat on a cushion on the floor of the front room of the house off Lenadoon Avenue, lazily comfortable in the heat of the hissing gas fire.

"None really," Seamus agreed, stroking her long hair. "On television he looked a right clown. When I first read that thing in the paper I was thinking that it smelt like a pretty obvious trick. I don't give a toss if he's related to me or not. All I want to know is what he's saying about our dad."

"You're sure you can't get in touch with them at home?"

Seamus sighed deeply. "If our dad is ill, or rather, iller than he usually is, then having the special branch boys sniffing around the farm won't help. He really does hate those bastards."

"Then ring this fella," Rebecca urged, scraping a long fingernail against the palm of his hand.

"I'll sleep on it," he replied.

"We'll sleep on it," she whispered, now moving her fingers to caress the inside of his thighs. He looked down at her, feeling a stir of excitement in his loins. Their appetite for each other's bodies had been nigh insatiable ever since he'd collected her from the ferry terminal in a borrowed car.

Thankfully, the Provisional commanders knew of her arrival and hadn't bothered him since. Seamus suspected that they were quite relieved to have an excuse for leaving him alone while they considered his future as a bomb designer. He'd already submitted a new design based on the hotel bomb, the improved "Lambeg," but this time containing a delayed timing device. He thought that his drawings were being shown to other, more experienced and trusted designers for their opinions, perhaps even his first instructor, Jack McKay in Dublin. Seamus didn't mind. He was thoroughly confident of his new work.

Meanwhile, he welcomed the chance to be alone with Rebecca, alone that is except for his landlady, Mrs. McGuinness, who'd shown surprising tact in leaving them alone, always off to bingo or a bar or shopping. Not that they would have noticed her presence, so rapt were they in a rediscovery of mutual passion and affection. Even the thought of the tiny being developing inside Rebecca had not affected the uninhibitedness of their loving.

For the first time in his life, Seamus experienced living with a woman, watching one in the intimacies of toilet and dressing and make-up, discovering grips and tiny brushes on the dressing table, noticing her clothes pushing his own to the most distant cavities of the drawers and wardrobe, smiling ruefully at her bland illogicalities and her refusal to acknowledge them, and, most of all, accepting her downright untidiness.

Far from upsetting him, Seamus was totally fascinated by these glimpses of the female world, wondering all the time if his mother had been the same.

That night, after repeated love-making, they did, in fact, sleep on Seamus's dilemma, awakening in the morning to the same conclusion that nothing could be lost and, perhaps, peace of mind gained, if Seamus should contact the naïve American who claimed to be his relative.

In mid-morning, he walked to a phone box six streets away and dialled 40503, the number of the Royal Victoria Hospital. He listened intently when the hospital switchboard answered, alert for any clicks or changes of tone which might have signified that the telephone line might be tapped. He could hear none.

"Dr. Aicheson, please," he asked.

"Mr. Aicheson, you mean," the man on the switchboard corrected, using the correct prefix for someone who was not only a doctor but a consultant surgeon. "Connecting you."

There was a pause for a few seconds before Aicheson—his New England accent unmistakable—came on the line from his office.

"Mr. Aicheson?" Seamus queried.

"This is he. Who's calling?"

"Maybe a relation," Seamus said guardedly.

There was an audible intake of breath at the other end of the line.

"It's you then?" asked Aicheson.

"I saw you on the telly last night. You said our dad was ill."

"He is if it's your father."

"Tell me about him then."

"He lives on a farm near a stream at a place called . . ."

"Don't say it," Seamus warned urgently. "Where did you meet this man who might be our dad?"

"At a party at a bar in the town run by your great-uncle Michael."

Seamus knew then that the American had met his family. He wasn't particularly concerned that this man was almost certainly a relation. What really interested Seamus was that this American might have news of his father.

"How is he?" he asked.

"Sick."

"Badly sick?"

"Sick as anyone can be, I reckon."

"Tell me."

"Not over the phone. Let's meet," Aicheson suggested, anxious to gain an opportunity to persuade Seamus to leave the Provisionals.

"Why the hell should we?" Seamus answered impatiently. "You could be setting me up."

"I'm not setting anyone up," Aicheson protested vehemently. "I simply want to help. Remember we are related."

Seamus lit a cigarette with his right hand, pushing the match box against the side of the shelf in the phone box. He thought furiously.

"You say you only want to help?"

"That's right. I only want to help."

"How?"

"Maybe get you out of the fix you're in. Maybe stop your family worrying, particularly your father."

"He's really bad?"

"Really."

"I'll not come to you," Seamus said, finally making up his mind. "That'd be as good as cutting my throat in public."

"Then I'll come to you. Anytime. Anywhere. You name it."

"Maybe," Seamus conceded, desperate to hear about his father, worried by the American's opinion of his condition. "I'll be ringing you back," he added. "I'll have to work something out."

"When?"

"Tomorrow. Same time," Seamus said, putting down the phone and hurrying out of the booth and away down the road. His wristwatch told him that the conversation had lasted barely ninety seconds but he knew from his work with the Irish Post Office that that was long enough for a tracing operation to be well under way. To prolong the call any longer would have been inviting trouble.

"Blast it!" cursed the officer from the secret intelligence unit when he heard the news. "Just Andersonstown, that's all we know?"

"Just Andersonstown. He rang off too quickly," confirmed one of the unit's sergeants who'd been at a telephone headquarters watching the attempts to trace the call.

"But he's calling back?"

"He said he was."

"Well, we'll just have to wait, won't we?"

"Suh," answered the sergeant, who was bored with the job. He would have preferred to have been out in the unit's new undercover van, touring the Catholic enclaves, the IRA's heartlands, masquerading as a street laundry.

The next call from Seamus to Ted Aicheson was even briefer, allowing no chance of his location being traced. He didn't even phone at the appointed time. In fact, Aicheson and the unseen phone tappers had almost given up hope that he would make the contact. The surgeon was about to leave the hospital for home when the call came just before six o'clock.

"Be at the Elbow Room in the Ormeau Road in fifteen minutes," Seamus ordered briefly, not even introducing himself.

"Will I need my car?" Aicheson asked.

"Maybe. Just be there."

Seamus put down the phone.

The intelligence officer cursed again when he heard his sergeant's report a couple of minutes later. He knew there'd be no time to tap the phone at the bar and hardly any time to mount a proper surveillance operation. He rapped out some orders, rather pessimistic about their successful outcome. He knew he should have taken more account of Seamus Aherne's knowledge of telephones. He should have realized just how wary his quarry would have been about talking on open lines.

Despite Belfast's chaotic rush-hour traffic Ted Aicheson reached the bar, diagonally opposite the BBC studios, with two minutes to spare. He felt empty to the depths of his stomach as he pushed through the grimy, though finely etched, glass doors, wondering if Seamus would be waiting for him inside.

Immediately, it was clear that that couldn't have been the plan. The bar was deserted except for three elderly, down-at-heel men whose clothes were as dirty and as ravaged as their faces.

Aicheson walked to the horseshoe-shaped wooden counter, instantly sensing an aura of despair about the establishment. It was a gaunt, bare room, offering no concessions to comfort or attractiveness. Like so many

similar bars in Belfast, this was no place where young
people or courting couples might gather. This bar was
dedicated to those who wished to drink seriously without
any frills. Its atmosphere was pervaded with the loneliness
of its habitues for whom alcohol was the only escape route
from the disappointment and emptiness of their own lives.

The barman, as spare and unwelcoming as the bar,
wandered over to Aicheson, noting his well-cut suit and
mistaking him for a broadcaster from over the road
dropping in to see how the other half lived.

"A drink?" Aicheson asked, his mind on Seamus.

"Yes, we do sell 'em," the barman sneered.

Aicheson flushed. "Sorry. A Jamieson Crested Ten, I
guess."

He picked up his whiskey, poured into a cheap, thin
glass, and sipped. Somewhere in the cavernous recesses of
the bar, a phone shrilled.

"It's for someone called Aicheson," a gin-thickened
woman's voice called to the barman.

He looked disapprovingly around his four customers.
"Anyone called Aicheson?"

The American nodded. "That's me."

"The phone. Take it upstairs," said the barman, jabbing
his thumb towards a door at the side of the bar. "And tell
your friend not to make a habit of phoning here."

Aicheson nodded, embarrassed by the barman's animosity, and walked over to the door. He pushed it open and saw
it led to a carpeted stairway going upwards.

As he went through, the main door of the bar opened
behind him and a young man in a long, light brown raincoat
entered quietly.

"So you're there?" Seamus said straightaway when
Aicheson picked up the dangling phone.

"Hardly a cocktail bar you chose."

"It is that but you won't be having a second drink."

"Good."

"Go out through the side entrance, the one at the bottom
of the stairs from where you're talking. Turn right and walk

twenty yards. You'll see a battered old blue Anglia, registration EKU 316D. Get in. The keys are under the front seat in an envelope along with your instructions. Got all that."

"A blue Anglia?"

"Right. A banger. I'll talk to you in a wee while and then, for Holy Mary's sake, check you're not being followed."

"Check."

The line went dead.

Aicheson leapt downstairs, loath to leave a fine whiskey unfinished, gulped it down and hurried into Bruce Street through the side entrance of the Elbow Room.

He turned right, as instructed, and could just make out the blue Ford Anglia car in the gathering gloom.

A young man with rather piercing blue eyes, wearing a long, light brown raincoat, brushed past him on the pavement, apologizing in a thick, rasping Belfast accent.

Aicheson walked quickly to the car, noting that the narrow street was now deserted, opened the nearside door and pushed up the driving seat. There was the envelope.

Inside were some car keys and his written instructions. He had to drive to the Post Office in Andersonstown, wait ten minutes, then ring a phone number from the call box outside the building.

Aicheson shrugged to himself, noticing that the handwriting was scrawled and uneven: the writing, he thought, of someone under fairly severe mental pressure.

The drive took about twenty minutes in the decrepit car, minutes in which Ted Aicheson couldn't help but wonder if he was doing the correct thing, whether he should simply return the vehicle to its original parking place and then go quietly home to Lindy.

Aicheson remembered suddenly Seamus's instructions to check that he wasn't being followed. He looked guiltily in the rear-view mirror, driving along the Falls Road, and could see no headlights behind. He steered the car to the side of the road in front of the dark and wire-shuttered Post

Office, just opposite what seemed to be some sort of park with tennis courts.

"Sweet Jesus," he sighed, nervous tiredness beginning to grip him. The Post Office looked more like a Second World War fortification than a place of business. Just a sign of the times, he knew, with the IRA often choosing such establishments for fund-raising robberies.

When the allotted ten minutes had passed, Aicheson walked over to the public phone box and dialled the number on his sheet of instructions, ready to push in a 2p coin when the connection was made. As the digits tumbled, he heard a helicopter above but dismissed the noise as merely a routine sound of the troubled city.

"Anyone follow you?" Seamus asked immediately, breathing hard, not bothering with any greeting.

"Not that I saw."

"And not that I saw either."

The remark surprised Aicheson.

"You're near then?" he said. "Were you watching?"

"You arrive? Yes, from the sports club across the road. That's why I wanted you to wait before calling. So I could get where I am now."

"You're surely careful," Aicheson said.

"I'm alive and free, so I have to be."

"A poet too, I guess," Aicheson grinned into the mouthpiece, encrusted with grime and flecks of tobacco.

Seamus grunted unappreciatively.

"Now drive the car straight down the road, past the church on your right, keep to your right at the junction and keep counting roads leading off to your right. You want the eighth on your right. Turn up there and pull in when you see a light flash twice. Got it?"

"Real James Bond, eh?" the American said dryly, now beginning to savor the danger. His tiredness fell away. He was very awake, very alive.

"It's my life," Seamus growled. "For fuck's sake, watch for anything and everything and if you don't see my signal just drive off and forget tonight."

"Bit late now," Aicheson drawled but the phone was already dead.

The helicopter was still above when he pushed through the door of the phone box. He glanced up, picking out its navigation lights among the darkening clouds.

He waited a moment, watching the few passing cars. None slowed, quickened, turned, or did anything to suggest their occupants were at all interested in him.

The ill-used Anglia coughed and spluttered on its way again along the almost deserted road. It passed under the eyes and rifle barrels of an Army Observation post, wired and netted and camouflaged, before reaching the eighth turning on the right, a road leading into a fairly new housing estate.

Aicheson peered carefully into the rear-view mirror; no other vehicle had turned behind him. Nobody, he was sure, could be following. He looked back through the windscreen. A light winked twice about thirty feet ahead on his nearside. He changed down and rolled to a stop by the curb.

No one approached. His eyes tried to penetrate the darkness, flicking left and right. He could see nothing but the glow of lights behind curtained windows further up the road. He switched off the car's lights and continued to wait, nerves taut.

The rap at the window on the passenger side came so suddenly, unexpectedly, that his body actually lifted an inch or so from the driving seat. His head switched to the left. All he could see was a hand beckoning urgently to him before vanishing into the darkness. Aicheson scrambled out of the car, not thinking even to remove the ignition keys.

"Come on, for fuck's sake," a voice whispered hoarsely from a patch of stygian shadow. "Up this alley and quick about it!"

The American broke into a trot, following a bulky, dark-clad figure he assumed to be Seamus Aherne.

They turned two corners, crossed a well-lit road, loped across what seemed to be a playing field and ran through two more alleys in another housing estate before stopping outside the back door of a house identical to all those they'd already passed. Seamus knocked softly three times. A key clicked in the lock and the door swung open. He pushed Aicheson into an unlit room, took one last look around and then followed him.

The light flashed dazzlingly on and Aicheson saw that he was standing in a rather small and untidy kitchen.

By the inner door, a slim, attractive young woman, her long hair in a ponytail, stood with a hand still on the light switch. He turned his head, eyes adjusting to the light, and saw a tall, youngish man, bearded and thick around the waist, leaning, panting, against the back door.

Aicheson wiped a layer of sweat from his forehead, smiling, unsure, thinking that his immaculate grey suit was hardly the ideal clothing for a jog around the back streets of Andersonstown. "Phew!" he exclaimed, wiping his face again, not quite knowing what to say.

"So you're my American relative who wants to help?" Seamus said a trifle sarcastically, looking intently at Aicheson, still breathing hard.

"That's right. So you must be Seamus?"

Aicheson pulled out his right hand. Seamus looked at it for a moment, then slowly extended his. The two men shook hands.

"And this is Rebecca," Seamus said. "She's my fiancée."

"Congratulations," Aicheson smiled, shaking her hand, feeling the fine bones and long fingers.

Rebecca blushed and looked down at the floor.

Aicheson turned back to Seamus who was still leaning, winded, against the back door. "I guess you've taken a helluva risk in seeing me," he said. "Thanks."

Seamus shrugged non-committedly. "We haven't much time," he said shortly. "No time for jawing about nothing in particular. You said that our dad's a very sick man. What's the trouble with him?"

Aicheson gazed around for a chair. He couldn't see any.

Seamus nodded and pulled out a stool from beneath the kitchen table.

"Well, Seamus," Aicheson began, sitting down, "you have to realize that I didn't make a formal examination of your father but I did have a pretty close look at him at that hooley your great-uncle Michael threw for Lindy and me . . ."

"What's the matter with him?" Seamus interrupted impatiently.

"I don't suppose it's any news to you that he's got a drinking problem."

"He's always liked a drop. Maybe it helps him forget."

"A drop?"

"Well, sometimes more than a drop if he had the cash."

Aicheson nodded, noting the dark rings under Seamus's eyes and the almost imperceptible tremor in his fingers. This was a man, he could see, living on his nerves.

"Well, to be frank," he sighed, "I'd say the booze is near killing him. Right now, I'd guess he should be hospitalized and treated for cirrhosis. And, right now, I'd wonder if it's even too late for that."

"Too late?"

"His liver's shot to hell. Soon it'll pack up altogether and then his body will simply poison itself. I tell you, it's not exactly the method I'd choose to shuffle off the mortal coil."

"You're certain?"

"Well, as I said, I didn't . . ." Aicheson paused, shaking his head. "Yes, I'm certain."

Seamus rubbed the back of his hand nervously across his mouth. "What can I do?" he asked.

"Go and see him," Aicheson urged. "Talk to him. Persuade him to be hospitalized. Get out of this thing you're in and stop him worrying. Your family said he listens to you."

"We always got on well," Seamus conceded. "That's true. Maybe, if I asked, the big men might let me off for a wee while. But then, if I go home, the Garda would probably snap me up. It's a bad choice."

"Maybe for you. Not for your father."

Aicheson fumbled in his jacket pocket for a handkerchief to mop his forehead, feeling a drop of slithering sweat on his skin.

Seamus gazed down at the floor, then looked appealingly across at Rebecca.

"If they did arrest you, they wouldn't extradite you from the South," Aicheson continued, pressing his argument as he sensed Seamus's resolve weakening.

"They might. After all, I did break gaol. It's mighty uncertain if that's a political offense."

"Well, it's your choice but anyway that's what I wanted to talk to you about, your family and you leaving the Provos," Aicheson said, finding his handkerchief at last and pulling it from his pocket.

Seamus laughed humorlessly. "Leaving the Provos? You must be . . ."

Aicheson shook his handkerchief. A round, shiny disc, not much bigger than a coin, entangled in the handkerchief's folds, fell on to the cracked linoleum covering the floor. It tinkled metallically as it rolled a few feet before settling just by the stained gas cooker. Aicheson gazed at it with amazement.

"Fucking hell!" Seamus snorted, starting toward it, eyes blinking with fear.

Aicheson's groping fingers reached it first. He held the disc up, turning it, gleaming under the light. Seamus tore it from him. He threw it to the floor and ground it under his heel, crunching it into a tangle of metal, plastic and wires.

"What . . . what?" Aicheson stammered.

"A fucking bug!" Seamus screamed. "You were fucking bugged!"

"But . . . but how?"

"How the fuck should I know?" Seamus cursed, his eyes wild. "They must have . . ."

A boot crunched into the lock of the back door. It

splintered open, hitting Seamus on the right shoulder, spinning him around, pushing him forward. Another crash came from the front of the house, through the small hallway.

A crouching figure in combat fatigues, face smeared with black, burst through the back door, stubby machine gun covering all three in the kitchen.

Another soldier slid around him, thrusting Aicheson roughly aside. He threw the inside kitchen door open as Rebecca cowered in the corner. The American could see more troops running through the front door, some beginning to take the stairs two at a time. He began to protest, shouting incoherently.

"Shut it, cocker," called the first soldier, through the door, ramming his weapon not too heavily into Aicheson's buttocks, forcing him against the gas cooker.

Seamus's face was white and shocked, his mouth moving soundlessly, as he was spreadeagled against the wall, hands and legs thrust apart in a position only too familiar to him.

Rebecca started to sob, both hands covering her face, dropping to her knees as if in prayer.

"Well, this is a nice place for a family reunion," murmured Stephen Gates, stepping into the kitchen, dressed incongruously in a tweed sports jacket and flannel trousers. "Hello, Ted," he nodded towards Aicheson, who was speechless with surprise. The major flicked a suede shoe against the remains of the electronic device which had been slipped into the American's pocket outside the Elbow Room, enabling the Army intelligence unit to monitor his movements from the helicopter.

"Tut-tut," he sighed. "Damaging government property . . . still, there's always the one in that old heap of metal you drove up here, Ted."

"Bastard!" exclaimed Aicheson. "You limey bastard!"

The major looked evenly at him, shaking his head. "All's fair in love and war, old friend," he said, disregarding the insults. He turned to Seamus who was squinting viciously at him over his shoulder. "Nice to see you again, laddie," the major said heartily but without a trace of a smile. "Been a long time, eh? You were bloody careless for a phone man. You should have remembered that phones in most bars have extensions."

Seamus spat before the soldier behind was able to crash the stock of his weapon between the prisoner's shoulders. The gob of saliva spattered harmlessly on to the linoleum.

Chapter 13
October, 1971

Major Gates reckoned he had a thicker skin than most, but his memory of the searing row with Aicheson after the raid on the house off Lenadoon Avenue was to remain with him for months afterwards.

When Seamus Aherne and Rebecca Fahey had been taken away in handcuffs—she to be released in the morning without being charged—the major offered to give the American a lift back to his car, still parked outside the bar. Aicheson had looked coldly at him before holding out both arms in front of him, wrists close together.

"You'd better put the cuffs on, Major," he said bitingly.

Stephen Gates understood how deeply upset his former friend must be. "Maybe even the leg irons too, Ted," he said wryly. "That's what the tough boyos sometimes need though we're not supposed to use them."

"I'm not bloody joking," Aicheson continued, a chill in his voice. "You've treated me like a criminal so why stop now, you bastard?"

The major stepped toward him, in the small kitchen, wanting to put a friendly hand on his shoulder, wanting to calm him.

Aicheson twisted away. "You really took me for an idiot, didn't you?" he murmured bitterly. "You talked me into this all the way. You saw what I was doing and let me go on. You used me to capture Seamus. You betrayed me, for me to betray him!"

"It was necessary, Ted," the major said quietly, hooking out a stool and sitting down at the kitchen table, willing to listen.

"Necessary?" Aicheson snarled, unsure whether he was angrier with himself or Stephen Gates. "Necessary to stamp all over someone who thought you were a friend, who trusted you? Necessary to follow me, to sneak in the shadows, to plant your bugs on me? Necessary to set me up as a Judas goat?"

"It was necessary," the major repeated patiently. "If we . . . if I could have done it any other way . . . it was a chance, an opportunity, I had to take and it came off."

"And sod everything and everybody?"

The major nodded reluctantly. "Yes . . . if needs be."

"Even a friend?"

"Yes."

Aicheson swung around, pointing an accusatory finger. It actually quivered with indignation and rage.

"Just who the hell do you think you are? Almighty God? How can you play with lives like this?"

Major Gates hunched over the table, pressing his thick fingers together. Under the stool, his ankles were clenched tightly together. His head seemed bowed to the scorn and insults. He said nothing.

"Let me remind you, Major," Aicheson went on, "that I'm an American citizen carrying a United States passport. Not one of the poor Catholics you seem to enjoy kicking from pillar to post!"

The major rubbed a hand wearily across his eyes.

"You had no right . . ."

"Shut up," the major murmured.

". . . to do what you did. Legally you had no right to plant those devices on me, no right to break into the house, no right to stick a gun up my nose, no right . . ."

"Shut up," the major repeated, more loudly this time.

". . . to tap phones without a warrant, which you must have done, no right . . ."

Major Gates' unusually large hands banged down on the flimsy table, the vibration lifting it off the floor. "Now, just shut up and listen, Ted," he roared, his voice startling a soldier still posted in the hallway, midway between front and back door. "Don't you tell me what I can or cannot do in this town. Don't you dare tell me what I can or cannot do about some hairy skull who's already murdered innocent people with his bloody bombs!"

Aicheson opened his mouth to interrupt. He saw the fury in the major's hooded eyes and decided otherwise. At that moment, the Army Officer resembled more than ever a hawk in the wilderness about to swoop on its prey.

"Do you think I wanted to do it, Ted?" the major exclaimed vehemently. "Do you think I even wanted to be here, losing my friends and my sanity and my sleep? No way, soldier. No way. None of us want to be here. The British Army have learned the hard way about running colonies and provinces and whatever and trying to back gracefully out of them without getting our throats cut. You bloody Americans think you know the lot. Well if you don't learn a lesson from that cock-up in Vietnam, you'll learn it in some place, believe me . . ."

"What the hell has . . . ?" Aicheson tried to interrupt. The major waved him to be silent.

"Listen and I'll tell you something. Listen and you'll learn, my New England friend," Stephen Gates continued angrily. "The bloody natives haven't spears any more. They've bombs and rifles and bazookas and know-how and a world-wide supply organization run from Moscow or Peking or just down the road as far as I'm concerned. It's not so easy, chum. To even hold them to a draw, we've got to play their game. The name of the game is survival and that's what we're going to do. There's no way Her Majesty's imperial bloody troops can solve this one. We bloody well know we can never win and, anyway, who wants us to? All we can do is hold on until the bigwigs in London and Dublin get it into their thick heads that the only solution is for people to get used to living and working together, north and south of the border. But that'll only happen when they want to. Some maniacs say that everything will be sweetness and light if the British Army pulls out. Well, shall I tell you what'll happen then? A very bloody, nasty civil war, that's what. The Prods'll bash the Catholics and they'll call in the Provos to defend them. It'll be the greatest thing since sliced bread for the IRA. And don't you bloody Americans realize what they want? It's not simply a united Ireland. We all want that one day. It's the only thing that makes sense. No, what they want is a communist republic of Ireland, and that's what you freedom-loving Yanks are supporting them for. You're not only mad, you're pathetic!"

Aicheson looked incredulously at the major, hardly believing what he'd just heard. "I always second-guessed you for a hard bastard," he said, sitting down opposite Stephen Gates. "But I never realized how twisted you were."

"Twisted?"

"Yes, twisted and downright wrong. You're like all professional soldiers: you don't give a tinker's cuss about the people you're dealing with. You don't really think about what you're doing over here, the harm you're doing, the enemies you're making for generations to come. God, why do you think those young kids are out on the streets most nights throwing stones and bottles at soldiers and police-men . . . ?"

"Because their uncles in the Provos tell 'em to," snapped the major.

"You're wrong. So wrong. It's because they think that if they don't attack first, then they'll be attacked themselves. You raid their houses, smash their belongings, search the family car, take their dad away for questioning and beating, all in the name of security. Haven't you ever thought of winning their hearts and minds? Not you especially—that'd be asking an elephant to dance a minuet—but your government, your politicians sitting on their arses and pontificating about this Irish solution and that through their well-oiled rectums."

"Save it for the social workers!"

"That's why you're winning a battle and losing the war."

"Just like your people are doing in Vietnam," the major jeered.

"Maybe. But at least we're learning from our mistakes. You British never learn anything. You're behaving like this is the Irish revolt of '98 that these people, these Catholics, have no more rights than the peasants had then . . ."

"Nor should they if they support the skulls."

"Let's face it, you don't give a shit about the Irish!"

"You're probably right, old friend."

"Don't call me that! Don't you patronize me! Our friendship ended in this house tonight!"

"As you like. But as I said, you're probably right. Why should we give a shit for the Irish anyway? They've meant nothing but trouble for us for hundreds of years. You see, Ted, it's true that we recognize the Irish have charm and wit. Oh, yes, they can be extremely charming and witty, but their attraction is seedy. Over the years, I'm afraid we British, maybe even we English, we Anglo-Saxons, have treated them like a slightly crazed maiden aunt. Of course we were bloody grateful when they fought for us and of course we've given them enough to keep them in genteel poverty. But when they have a mad spell and turn against us, well, we shake our heads sadly at their ingratitude and wait till they come to their senses again. Sometimes a course of electric shock treatment is necessary and we administer it, naturally telling them that it hurts us more than it hurts them."

Aicheson shook his head, fascinated. "Unbelievable," he murmured to himself. "Absolutely unbelievable."

"Really, historically," the major continued sarcastically, "it would have been kinder if we'd treated the Irish like you Americans treated your Red Indians, simply wiped them out and put the survivors in the prison camps you euphemistically call reservations. Then we could have sent around coachloads of tourists to buy their souvenirs and admire their out-of-date culture. The simple fact you have to grasp is that the Irish, just like your Red Indians, are a total anachronism. Their great times were the times when Christianity carried a flaming sword, when it was a blessed thing to slaughter some poor sod who happened not to agree with the prevalent idea of God. Sad, maybe, but those times have passed. No, it's all about compromise, live and let live, abstentions at the United Nations. And that's the rub. It's all or nothing here. You Americans deal with the Irish believing that they will and do compromise. We British know they're incapable of even understanding the word."

Aicheson raised his arms in disgust, then clasped his hands behind his shaking head. "You're talking balls. Wild generalizations, bloody wild ones."

The major sniffed and grinned, taking a small cigar from a crumpled packet. "Of course I am. I know that. But what I'm telling you is what most British people on the mainland believe. Okay, so most of the Northern Irish want to remain in Britain. I'd wager my hard-earned pension that the majority of the British don't want the Northern Irish. They might not want to do the dirty on them by breaking all the politicians' promises, but the truth is that they don't particularly care. The Northern Irish are costing the mainland, ordinary Briton an awful lot of money and lives. The time may come when they say to the smart politicians in Dublin who're always ready to play the problem for a few votes come election time, 'Right, chums, we've had enough. You claim the six counties of Ulster. Well, brothers, here's your chance. You sort 'em out.' And then you'll see the fur fly, my angry young American. It'll be the biggest bloodbath since I don't know when, say since Genghis Khan first lifted a horse's tail. And then all your politicians after the Irish vote in the good old US of A can really start wringing their hands and shedding the crocodile tears."

Aicheson recognized truths in the major's vicious statement. But he was still outraged by what had happened that night. High on his cheekbones two red spots glowed. "You think that excuses your conduct tonight," he glared. "Weaseling your way into my confidence purely to use me as a decoy. It's bloody unforgivable."

"Christ alive!" the major exploded. "I've been trying to make you understand. It's a love-hate relationship, deeper than any we have with you Americans. Sometimes we love the Irish, sometimes they hate us and vice-versa. We're like Siamese twins except we're bound together by history and geography and economics. The Irish are the flea in our hair. We're the dog nipping at their ankles. Christ, don't you understand we could have played it hard tonight, done a street-to-street, house-to-house search for your precious Seamus, turned Andersonstown into the Warsaw ghetto till we found him. If we took the gloves off, we could end this little emergency in a matter of weeks. You Americans have to remember that if we didn't have the Irish as neighbors, we'd have to invent someone like them!"

"And invent friends like me?"

The major smiled, conceding the point. "Yes, and friends like you. But remember, you didn't get hurt tonight."

"There's other kinds of hurt than an accidental broken jaw, you bastard!"

"The only thing hurt tonight, here tonight, Mr. Edward S. Aicheson," he grated, "were your delicate Boston bloody feelings."

"I'll never forgive you," Aicheson cried. "I'll never bloody forgive you."

"So break my heart," said Major Gates, standing up and tangling his feet in the stool. He kicked it aside and moved toward the back door.

"You'll be in deep trouble because of this!"

The major stopped by the door, leaning tiredly against the frame for a moment. His voice was angry no longer. "Don't threaten me, Ted. Just don't," he said quietly. "You could still spend the night, or perhaps two, under interrogation. You could even be charged. You know that."

"And then I'd tell 'em what happened," Aicheson said defiantly. "By Christ, I would."

"Spitting out your teeth and holding your broken ribs, you would," the major growled. He felt tired, so tired, and depressed, very depressed, when he knew he should be feeling exactly the opposite after the night's capture. "So d'you want a lift or are you going to walk?" he added, turning back to Aicheson, attempting a weak, conciliatory smile.

"Is there a choice, goddamnit?"

"No."

Ted Aicheson shrugged and followed the major through the back door. The RAOC driver took the surgeon back to his car in Ormeau Road before driving Stephen Gates on to Lisburn. During the journey, the British officer and the American said not a word. Nor would they ever again.

"That bastard Gates really stitched you up, Seamus," commiserated Mickey Quinn, one of Hut 8's occupants in the gaol at Long Kesh.

"Does it matter, Mickey?" answered Seamus. "I'd had a good run. They were bound to get me in the end and put me back behind the wire."

"Bad timing, though," Quinn smiled. "Just when you'd moved your girl-friend in."

Seamus shrugged. "In more ways than one with a wee 'un coming along."

"Aye, it is that. Maybe they'll allow you to wed her. You know, special parole for the ceremony."

"Maybe, but I doubt it. Not straightaway at least, not with the escape."

"Maybe not, Seamus, but if I were you I'd give it a few weeks and then have a word with Charley McCool. He can fix it if anyone can."

Seamus nodded agreement. That had been his second surprise after arriving at Long Kesh, discovering that McCool was an inmate too.

In fact, it was rumored that McCool had been asked if he would transfer from Crumlin Gaol to Long Kesh since he was respected as someone who could bring the younger, unrulier IRA internees under control and make the prison routine more manageable for both the guards and the guarded.

Charley McCool was not a collaborator, but he was astute enough to recognize that there had to be a tacit deal with the prison administration if the IRA was to maintain control of its members in the internment camp. McCool had set up a command structure in the Republican compound which was the envy of the Loyalist internees in an adjoining compound. In return, the prison hierarchy left him virtually in charge as far as discipline among his men was concerned.

The camp presented a bleak landscape of Nissen huts and barbed wire, fences and watchtowers, reminiscent of Second World War prisoner-of-war camps. McCool furthered the military comparison by ordering parades and drills and physical jerks, setting strict timetables within the Republican compound. His lieutenants organized lectures about the history of Ireland, classes to teach the Irish language, and various courses aptly termed "vocational." These were, in fact, instructional classes about the tactics of guerilla warfare, about weapons, using replicas modelled in wood, and, with Seamus's arrival, about bombs.

"Might as well make yourself useful, son," McCool had told Seamus at their first interview, about a fortnight after he'd come to Long Kesh.

"I don't mind at all, Mr. McCool," Seamus replied, smiling enthusiastically. "But how can we get away with it without the screws finding out?"

"Like we get away with everything else in here. By keeping our mouths tighter than Paisley's mind. Okay?"

"Suits me."

"And, son," McCool added, sitting at the desk in the small anteroom to Hut 9 which served as the IRA commandant's office and private bedroom, "no more disappointments, eh? A lot of people invested time and money in you, your training and your escape, and, frankly, they don't feel they've had too much return on that investment."

"I tried my best, for Christ's sake, Mr. McCool," Seamus protested, alarmed at the sudden menace in the older man's rasping voice.

"Sure you did but some of the big men are wondering real hard if you've the stomach for the job, whether you may be just a wee bit of a paper tiger. Indeed, I tell you straight, son, there's some who reckon you need a proper whacking for what's been going on."

"They're still upset about that hotel bomb?"

"Not so much upset. Mighty resentful, I'd say, at us being made to look fools. The big 'un and what happens? The Brits make heroes of themselves and we get our noses rubbed in it. And then you get yourself picked up like that. Personally I'd never have allowed you to bring that lady over here. Distractions, that's what's led you astray. Maybe this is all just a wee bit of fun for you, a way of keeping up the family traditions."

Seamus flushed, stung by the criticisms. "I'm as committed as ever I was, Mr. McCool!" he exclaimed. "True, things haven't been going my way lately but you're forgetting the 'Lambeg.' That had the Brits over a barrel."

"Aye, for a while. But what since then? Very little, I'd say."

Seamus bowed his head, licking his lips, realizing the truth of the statement. "You know," he said, "I gave up a lot to volunteer, Mr. McCool."

The Provisional's commandant in Long Kesh sighed. "Oh, dear, son. You gave up a job. No more. I'm wondering if you'd ever be prepared to give up your life or whether the Republican blood in your family has run a bit thin."

"I'm prepared . . ."

"No, listen, son. I don't want your assurances and promises on the spur of the moment. I want you to go away and think and work. I want you to consider that maybe, in the not too distant future, we might be asking some of you boys behind the wire to take up a hunger strike, to starve yourselves to death like Terence MacSwiney did during the Tan Wars, God rest him. I'm not asking you now. I only want you to think about it, son. Okay?"

Seamus nodded, hardly daring to speak. The concept of actually starving to death was too horrific. He thought about it for the next days, particularly at night, just before sleep. He couldn't see himself being able to go through with such a thing. He realized, not for the first time, that he might be a physical coward. He hated himself for it.

The phase of self-doubt passed gradually, however, as late autumn became winter at Long Kesh, and everyone's main purpose in life became keeping warm and occupied. Seamus's classes in bombs and bomb-making were well established. He enjoyed passing on his expertise. It gave him a sense of confidence. The pupils were only too willing to learn and Seamus discovered that he had a fair knack for teaching.

He looked forward to his weekly visits from Rebecca. At first, they were emotionally trying but soon—he wasn't certain why—the pangs of longing dulled. He went through the motions of reassuring her that he would try to arrange a marriage before their child was born but somehow, after she had left to return to Belfast, the minute-to-minute effort of simply existing in the camp was of greater importance. After a few weeks, it was hardly mentioned, neither of them wanting to plan ahead when there appeared so little chance of an immediate future together.

"It must be the bromide in the tea," Mickey Quinn joked one night. "You're forgetting what your old plonker's for!"

Seamus laughed but continued to wonder why he was feeling so apathetic towards Rebecca. The only thing they had in common, it seemed, was the unborn child.

His greatest joy came from the infrequent visits from his mother and father. His father looked comparatively better than he'd been led to expect after Ted Aicheson's dire statements. His mother explained that he was being more careful in his drinking habits, now that his worry about

Seamus had partially lifted. At least, his mother said, they knew now where he was and that he was safe from any immediate danger.

Yes, Seamus often reflected that life in Long Kesh suited his purpose quite well. He knew precisely how to behave within the strict rules laid down by Charley McCool. He was still a Provo, demonstrably so with all the parading and ritual. He could preen like a peacock in front of the warders and watching Loyalists, sometimes even noticing a gleam of slightly fearful respect in their eyes.

For the first two months, he felt comfortably remote from the dreadful conflict continuing outside the closed world of the camp. Then, on New Year's Day, 1972, he was called to Charley McCool's room in Hut 9 to be given the news about Jack McKay, his first bomb instructor and probably the Provisionals' most important bomb-supplier.

"He died like the hard man he was," said McCool somberly. "By God, he was a hard man!"

"Do they know what happened?"

"Oh, yes. Jack McKay wouldn't allow himself to die without giving that information and him with his eyes and balls blown clean away by the explosion."

"And?"

"Well, it seems he was mixing the stuff in his garage."

"On the Swords Road?"

"Yes, at his home, and the shovel hit the floor, scraped it like, and put a spark into the explosive. Whoosh! That was that!"

"Terrible, terrible," Seamus muttered, picturing the scene of bloody carnage. "He was an awful decent man."

"Well, he's gone to his reward now," McCool shrugged. "And that means you've proper work to do, son, until someone else outside can be trained up."

Seamus looked surprised.

"What on earth can I do behind the wire?"

"You can start drawing some proper designs again and we'll smuggle them out. Keep on with your lessons but make the designs your first priority."

Seamus did as he was ordered and within a few weeks his designs were being put into production.

And those early weeks and months of 1972 were to bring the movement to the edge of success, not only through its own efforts but through another gigantic misjudgment from the authorities, handing the Irish Republican cause yet another day to be commemorated in its bloodstained history.

On the afternoon of Sunday, January 30th, thirteen people in Derry were shot to death when British soldiers opened fire on the remnants of an illegal, though comparatively inoffensive procession under the civil rights banner.

The dramatic TV films caused horror and recriminations and questions throughout the world; the bodies lying in pools of blood; the soldiers with rifles aimed and firing at seemingly unarmed and fleeing civilians; a Catholic priest, later to be a bishop, frantically waving his white handkerchief as he escorted a group carrying a fatally-wounded youngster through the horrible, deadly confusion.

Another "Bloody Sunday" had been added to that one of 52 years before when twelve civilians had been shot at Croke Park, Dublin.

The reaction was swift. The British Embassy in Dublin was stoned and burned by a mob and the bombing campaign moved to the British mainland. A car bomb exploded outside the Old Bailey in London. One-hundred and eighty people were injured, many horribly.

Within a fortnight, the British Prime Minister, Edward Heath, dissolved the Northern Ireland Parliament at Stormont. He was angered by the mistaken advice from the Northern Ireland Premier, Brian Faulkner, who'd demanded internment, promising it would curtail the violence. From now on, Northern Ireland would be ruled directly from London.

The backlash came from the furious Protestants with riots and shootings and bombings.

It was a nightmare time for Major Stephen Gates and the RAOC bomb disposal teams. They worked with hardly any respite as the bombs grew bigger and better. The previous year, nearly 11,000 lbs. of explosives had been detonated in terrorist bombs and 3,000 lbs. successfully defused. The scale of the warfare increased so much that, in 1972, 50,000 lbs. exploded and nearly 20,000 lbs. were defused.

The major was under constant pressure from the weekly General Operations meetings to stem the tide of destruction but he was too busy actually dealing with the devices and deploying his men to analyze the backlog of bomb reports. When he did, late on a relatively quiet Sunday afternoon, the pattern immediately became clear.

The Provisional bombers were using new timing devices. That was to be expected. It was the method of wiring that interested him. Stephen Gates shuffled through the reports from his Explosive Ordnance Disposal units, placing them into three piles.

The first was for those about which he had a growing suspicion; the second for bombs clearly of Protestant origin; the third for those of indeterminate manufacture.

After scrutinizing the bomb reports once more, the major had twelve sheets of paper in the first pile. He picked them up from his desk and read them through again. "If it's not him, it bloody well ought to be," he muttered to himself. He leaned his elbows on his desk in the small office and lit a cigar.

He sat thinking for nearly five minutes before re-examining the bomb reports for the third time. In his own mind, he was certain. Most of the bombs being laid by the Provisional IRA were wired in an unmistakable way. They were, he knew, to the particular method of wiring equipment and connection used by telephone engineers in Britain and Ireland. They had to be the work, somewhere along the line, of Seamus Aherne.

The major rang his acquaintance in the secret intelligence unit. He had heard whispers that the Provos were running bomb-designing courses in Long Kesh.

"Thanks, chum," said the major, replacing the receiver.

He looked up at the wall bearing all the maps and charts. "The silly sod!" he remarked. "What a silly sod!"

He prepared his plan before the next G. Ops meeting. The commanding general was, as usual, in full cry about curtailing bomb warfare. But, for once, Major Gates had a suggestion.

"I'm pretty certain I've identified one of the Provos' designers, sir," he said, gazing around the conference room at the weary and grey faces of the other senior HQ staff.

The general perked up visibly. "Well done, Stephen. Is he accessible?"

"Extremely, sir."

The general lit his third menthol cigarette of the meeting and took a deep puff. At all times, he was an extremely careful and evenhanded man. That was why he held his position. "You mean," he said, slowly inclining his head, "you know where he is?"

"Affirmative, sir."

The general leaned back in his chair and gazed at the ceiling. "Do you have a plan, Stephen?" he asked quietly.

"Yes."

"Will it involve us?"

"Not necessarily, sir."

"Publicity?"

"Shouldn't be too damaging. Not as damaging as chummy's bombs or those made to his pattern."

"Take him out, Stephen. The whole bloody place is falling apart so we've got to get down on the carpet with them. Take him out, Stephen, if necessary with maximum prejudice. We just can't afford to keep that sort of type around."

Major Gates looked evenly at the general. The general shook his head slightly, his eyes despairing.

"As you say, sir," the major replied.

The major didn't even use the special intelligence unit to implement the operation. Two nights later, Corporal Hosken drove him along the M1 motorway toward Belfast. When the unmarked vehicle approached the Kennedy Way intersection at Andersonstown, the corporal slowed it on to the hard shoulder.

Major Gates pushed open the back door and tossed a load of files and papers on to the bank at the side of the motorway. The car sped away into the night.

"And that's your lot, your murdering bastard," the major murmured, settling back in his seat and lighting another small cigar.

At first light, the local Provisionals were gleefully examining a pile of Army documents which had apparently fallen from a lorry while in transit.

Some of the papers were deliberate forgeries. Most were out of date and useless. Only one was in any way genuine and confidential. It was the official record of Seamus Aherne's interrogation at Holywood Barracks.

Two days later, during a glorious, early April midafternoon, Seamus was summoned to Charley McCool's office in Hut 9. He strode across the compound, whistling cheerfully, hoping he was about to receive a reply to his request about marrying Rebecca.

In the last few weeks, as her advancing pregnancy became more obvious with each visit, he'd decided that marriage was the right and proper thing. McCool had seemed fairly sympathetic, privately thinking that such a ceremony might attract favorable publicity for the Provisionals, and had promised to press the application with the prison authorities.

When he first stepped into the IRA commandant's office, Seamus was certain that everything had been arranged, noticing straight away the file and papers on the desk. "Afternoon, Mr. McCool," he said, rubbing his hands together theatrically. "It's come through then . . ."

The door slammed shut behind him. Suddenly two men were at either shoulder. One of them was a grim-faced Mickey Quinn.

"What the . . . ?"

"Shut up!" rasped McCool, his eyes boring into Seamus. He held out a flimsy sheet of paper. "Read that!"

At first Seamus couldn't take it in. An official notice convening a court-martial, with his name on it. "I . . . I . . ." he stammered, fingers quivering.

"Read it again!" snapped McCool.

And on the second reading, Seamus understood. His eyes flicked to the official-looking file on the desk, its cover turned towards him. He could read the wording on the front. He shivered, feeling very cold.

"You're confined to this room under close arrest until the court meets this evening," McCool announced, limping towards the door, avoiding even a glance at Seamus. "You've the right to study the evidence."

For the next four hours, Seamus stayed in the office-cum-bedroom with Quinn and another Volunteer called Billy Fogarty. They didn't speak to him and, after a couple of vain attempts at conversation, Seamus kept his own silence as well.

He felt numb and physically sick reading and re-reading the meticulous record made by Captain Charles Briance of his interrogation all those months ago. Seamus smiled wryly at the thought that the dead Ammunition Technical Officer, killed by his "Lambeg" bomb, might actually revenge himself from beyond the grave.

Just after eight o'clock, Seamus was led into the next room and pushed into a chair in front of a trestle table covered with an Irish tricolor fashioned inside the camp.

Charley McCool was hunched forward over the table, flanked by his two closest lieutenants, Raymond McCartney and Terence Walsh. He looked expressionlessly at Seamus, then swept his eyes along those grouped behind the semi-circle of chairs before the table, themselves forming an arena for the participants in this much-respected IRA ritual.

"Now before this court-martial comes into session," McCool said solemnly, "let me emphasize that it will be conducted in a proper way and according to the rules laid down by the Army Council. The legal officer here . . ." He gestured towards another of his lieutenants, a gunman named Donal O'Hare. ". . . will be advising the court if there is any question of the interpretation of the rules. The accused has declined by his silence the opportunity to be represented by a defending officer and will therefore conduct his own defense with the guidance of the officers of this court-martial. He has been given a copy of the charge sheet, a copy of the order convening this court and unrestricted sight of the main exhibit to be used by the prosecuting officer."

Seamus gazed at the bulb swinging gently above McCool's head, reflecting off his grey hair, emphasizing the deep lines on his face. The meager, yellow glow reached just far enough to illuminate the principals grouped in the middle of the hut. He was unable to see the spectators, his comrades in the deep shadows, though he thought he could detect eyes gleaming with expectation, lips moistened with anticipation.

Strangely, Seamus's fear had vanished now that the court-martial had begun. He felt numb still but hoped that he possessed enough strength of will to endure the ordeal with at least an outward semblance of courage. He knew the verdict would inevitably go against him. All he could hope for was leniency. But, however foregone the conclusion, Charley McCool insisted that the proceedings be run with the trappings and particular nuances of a legal court of law. His brooding presence invested the room, tatty and shabby, with a semblance of dignity and pomp.

"The legal officer will now read the charge," McCool announced.

Donal O'Hare stood up and cleared his throat before reading from a light-blue writing pad. "Seamus Aherne, a sworn Volunteer of the Irish Republican Army, is accused of giving vital information to the enemy on January 24th, 1971, contrary to the terms of his sworn oath."

"How do you plead?" McCool asked quietly.

Seamus opened his mouth to reply.

"Stand up," the legal officer ordered harshly.

Seamus pushed the chair back and stood slowly. His legs almost refused to obey. They felt like rubber. Mickey Quinn, by his side, held his elbow, seeing his unsteadiness.

"Guilty," he said hoarsely, his left eyelid starting to twitch.

There was a gasp around the hut.

"Guilty?" queried McCool, raising his eyebrows.

"Yes," Seamus muttered, "but I'd like a chance . . ."

"You can talk after," McCool rasped. "Sit down!" He addressed the entire hut, his voice carrying and echoing off the wood. "Since the prisoner has pleaded guilty there's no need for the prosecuting officer. The facts are simple."

McCool went on to explain the circumstances of the raid on the bomb factory off Cromac Street in Belfast and how four Volunteers, two men and two women, had died in the subsequent explosion.

"Until only a few days ago," he continued, his voice rising and sharpening, "it was not known how the enemy obtained their information. There were suspicions, of course, but it was assumed to have come from their own intelligence sources, through their own cunning and observation and not through the word of a self-confessed traitor."

He picked up the file recording Seamus's interrogation by Major Stephen Gates and Captain Briance.

"And then this . . ." McCool slapped the file on to the table. ". . . came into our hands, discarded by chance or choice, but discarded nonetheless. It is here in black and white, the enemy's own document, showing that the accused, Aherne, told the Brits where the bomb factory was and was therefore directly responsible for the deaths of four of his comrades."

"I don't . . ." Seamus began to protest, rising.

McCool waved him down sternly.

"Do you want to ask any questions about this document?"

"No."

"You've read it?"

"Yes."

"What it says is true?"

"Mostly. I just want to say I never intended . . ."

"Quiet!" McCool said menacingly. "That makes no difference to the charge."

Somewhere behind Seamus a spectator sniggered.

McCool peered into the gloom. The snigger became a coughing fit.

"The accused admits his guilt and admits the truth of the document which conclusively proves that guilt . . ." McCool paused, waiting for the coughing to stop. ". . . but before the court's decision is made and announced, the accused has the right to address this court. Do you want to, Aherne?"

Seamus stood up again. For a moment, he swayed. Quinn steadied him again. "I just want to say I never wanted anyone to die. I wanted to lead them off the track . . ."

His voice was hard and desperate. ". . . For God's sake," he said more boldly, "I'd been beaten and kept without sleep for days. I hardly knew what I was saying at the end when these officers began hollerin' and hammerin' . . ."

"Did the officers hit you?" McCool interrupted, his tone concerned, his face grave.

"Not exactly," Seamus hesitated. "But the sergeant would have done and I could hardly stand up from the beatings and no sleep and not being able to think stra . . ."

"Did they or didn't they hit you during this interrogation?" McCool persisted.

Seamus swayed again, his eyes suddenly mesmerized by the colors of the tricolor, knowing how much danger he was in, unable to help himself. "Well, no," he mumbled, shaking his head. "No they didn't have to. I'd already taken all I could. I had to tell them something. They threatened . . ."

His voice died away as he slumped back in his chair.

McCool picked at his fingernails, gazing down at the notes he'd been making. Terence Walsh, to his right, began exploring the cavities in his teeth. Raymond McCartney puffed out his cheeks, leaned back and inspected the hut's cross-beams and rounded ceiling.

The silence in Hut 9 was tangible. It lasted more than a minute while everyone looked at Seamus and he looked sullenly at the floor.

"The officers of the court will retire," said McCool eventually. "We're doing this properly but we can't be here till the crack of doom."

They walked solemnly and in step to the anteroom. The discussion was brief once the door was closed.

"Agreed?" said McCool.

"Have to," the other two chorused.

"But how?" asked Walsh.

"Hanging?" McCartney whispered.

McCool shook his head.

"It's been arranged. Let's face it, Aherne's been set up by the Brits. We all know that but the fact is he has to be hit. It has to be for morale and discipline. Dammit, he's as guilty as sin, wherever the information came from."

The other two nodded.

"Well," McCool continued, "it'll be done in such a way that we'll be able to claim that the Brits did it. They'll argue but they'll not try too hard to disprove it. After all, I'm guessing they'll get what they want. Your man dead."

"But won't that make him a martyr?" McCartney asked, surprise in his voice.

"I don't give a fuck what it makes him," McCool said viciously. "As far as I'm concerned when he's dead he can be anything he likes. His family can think he's the greatest hero since his grandfather. That'll be no bad thing. But the main point is that the boys'll really know what happened. Maybe the truth'll filter out, maybe, but in the meantime it'll keep them strictly in line. Agreed?"

"You know best, Charley," said Walsh.

"Aye," agreed McCartney.

The whisper of conversation died away as soon as the three men trooped back into the main hut. They stood behind the table. Quinn urged Seamus to his feet.

Charley McCool took a deep breath. "Seamus Aherne," he began huskily, then coughed to clear his throat. "By your admission to this properly constituted court-martial, you are guilty of the offense as charged. By powers from the Army Council, this court sentences you to death. There is no appeal." He swept out his right hand in front of him. "Take him out," he ordered curtly.

Seamus's eyes widened. He wanted to speak but no words came. Quinn and Fogarty grabbed him by the wrists and hustled him into the anteroom, pushing him down into a chair with its back to the door.

"Wha . . . wha . . . what?" Seamus stammered, his mind blank.

Fogarty shrugged and pulled out a hip flask. He unscrewed it and handed it to Seamus. He took a pull, nearly choking on the raw spirit, a sample of the secretly brewed camp poteen. "Jesus," he muttered, feeling the raw alcohol explode inside him. He took another pull, gasping again.

Fogarty held out his hand and took the flask back.

With tears in his eyes from the emotion and the poteen, Seamus peered up at the two men on either side of him. They gazed back impassively. He wondered if this was how a beast in an abattoir felt. He didn't know what was happening, what was about to happen, when it would happen. "Oh, Mother of Mercy, keep me through this night . . ." he muttered.

His mind was full of images now.

They flickered back and forth: scenes of childhood; playing on the sands at Ballybunnion; the market at Listowel; Grandma Hannah leaning over his sick bed; a glass shining and filled with whiskey; Rebecca's face in ecstasy beneath him . . .

So much, he thought. So much and so little. But it was true. Your life did . . .

He didn't hear the third man, Donal O'Hare, enter the room behind him, didn't hear anything, felt nothing until the thick blanket was pulled down over his head and shoulders. And then it was darkness and struggling panic.

All images vanished from his brain.

"Aagh!" he cried agonizingly, the sound muffled to a groan, as the first blow struck the side of his face and glanced down, breaking his right collarbone.

And again.

He whimpered and groaned twice more as two lead-filled pipes and a chair leg spiked with nails crashed down in close succession on his skull. Then he felt nothing. His body's reactions were independent of his stunned, bruised, lacerated, dying brain.

Seamus slumped slowly sideways off his seat and on to the floor. The light in the room was strong enough to reflect the shadows of the men bending over him, raising their arms, unnaturally extended by their weapons, and striking down in rhythm, each in turn. Their arms rose and fell. At first there was a sharp, cracking noise as their blows connected. Within a minute or so, however, it was a sound akin to a housewife mashing potatoes. When the blanket was becoming sodden with blood and other pinker and greyer substances, the blows ceased.

The three executioners carried Seamus's body to the window, opened the shutters and the frames, waiting to observe the searchlights bathing the compound outside in a pale, creamy light. Then, with a sudden heave, they rolled the body through the window, hanging onto the blanket so that it stayed inside. Carefully, they closed the window and shutters before checking the floor for bloodstains. There were none to be seen. The floor would be thoroughly mopped over before the guards discovered the body outside and the wrangle would begin about how Seamus Aherne had died. Charley McCool would claim he was beaten to death by the guards; the prison authorities would say it was by his own colleagues. And nothing would ever be officially admitted or decided.

The three men walked back into the main room of Hut 9. McCool was still sitting at the table, his hands outstretched across the tricolor. "Well?" he asked.

"It's done," Quinn nodded, wiping a hand across his face.

Charley McCool looked around the hut at the men standing silently, at their expressions of awe and fear. "He never stood a fucking chance, boys. Never!"

McCool closed his eyes. His lips moved in a silent prayer for Seamus Aherne and, perhaps, himself.

Chapter 14
April, 1972

It was an impressive funeral. The furor in the newspapers had ensured that, the accusations and counter-accusations, the charges and denials about an internee beaten to death in Long Kesh. Everyone, north or south of the Border, Protestant or Catholic, member of the security forces or rank-and-file IRA, believed what their heritage, upbringing and duty demanded they should. Truth was swamped by rumor and, therefore, what was believed came to be the truth.

By their numbers alone, the people of Listowel demonstrated their certainty that Seamus Aherne had died at the brutal hands of the authorities and, thus, was worthy of elevation to the pantheon of Kerry's Republican martyrs. They stood in their hundreds, silently lining the streets of the small town as the cortege moved circuitously from St. Mary's Church, across the market square, down William Street, into Courthouse Road and then into Upper Church Street to the cemetery.

Police snapped to attention and saluted when the gleaming black hearse inched by, coffin draped in the green, white and orange Irish flag, a black beret and a pair of black gloves on top to denote the dead man's service in the Provisional IRA.

Seamus's family walked behind. His mother, Bernadette, snivelled quietly into a shoulder pad of Joe Aherne's Sunday-best suit. He looked straight ahead, staring blindly at the coffin. The sisters, Shelagh and Mai, clung on to their husbands' arms, weeping copiously behind borrowed veils.

Only Grandma Hannah walked alone, scorning all support but her stick, silver hair peeping beneath black shawl, stern and unyielding in her seventies, clutching a sprig of hawthorn.

Ted and Lindy Aicheson paced hand-in-hand behind Seamus's aunts and uncles, cousins, cousins by marriage, second cousins and schoolfriends. They looked totally out of place. It wasn't their expensive clothes. It wasn't their haircuts. They simply appeared different from the other mourners because they knew themselves to be different. They knew they had no feeling for this particular ritual of death. They had been brought up to believe that a funeral was an occasion for remembrance of a person's life, an expression of regret at the death, and the declaration of trust in the everlasting life.

But this funeral was a celebration of death. Beneath the Ahernes' natural grief, there was a feeling of grim pride in the way of Seamus's death, as if his dying was more important than his living.

Suddenly, as they'd left the church and begun walking in the procession they'd felt their prized links of kinship with these people snap. The Aichesons realized that tenuous family history was not enough. They were no more a part of these people and their beliefs and culture and town than any other outsider. They were American, perhaps even Irish-American. But these people were Irish.

Their sense of awkwardness was heightened by guilt about Rebecca Fahey. Immediately Seamus's death had been announced amid fulsome tributes in the *Irish News*, Ted Aicheson had hurried to the house off Lenadoon Avenue, hoping to give comfort.

Rebecca had only allowed him into the dingy hallway. Through the slightly opened door to the lounge, Aicheson had glimpsed three men sitting down, obviously drinking from a bottle of whiskey placed in the middle of the rug in front of the gas fire.

"How are you?" he'd asked, sniffing alcohol on her breath, noting her eyes reddened from tears, smudged through lack of sleep.

"How d'you expect?" she'd shrugged.

"Have you had anything?"

"From the doctor?"

"Yes."

"Some tablets but they're not much of a help."

"Do you need anything then . . . anything else?"

She'd glanced around toward the door to the lounge.

"No. They're looking after me all right. A woman's staying and they've given me money."

"The funeral? His . . . are you going?"

"Yes, if I can."

His professional gaze had assessed her shape beneath the grubby maternity dress. "Look, Rebecca," he'd said, almost pleading. "We'll be travelling down to Listowel, my wife and I, can't we give you a lift?"

She'd shaken her head emphatically, lifeless hair swinging at her neck. "I'll be taken, I'm told, and brought back. Maybe taken to my folks in Galway, if they'll have me, though that's an awful long shot."

"What about Seamus's family?"

"I'll not be imposing on them if I go. I'll stay away in the crowd."

"Imposing?"

"They've enough grief, so they have. They're not knowing about the . . . the . . ." She tapped her stomach lightly. "Well, they're not knowing and I'll not be telling and I don't want you telling either!"

"You sure?"

"Yes. I'll not be wanting their sympathy or whatever. I'll cope. I've had to so far."

Aicheson's hand had stretched for the lock on the front door. He'd heard no noise from the lounge. Clearly, the men there were listening to the conversation. He was frightened of them without knowing precisely why.

"Maybe when we start off, we can call around for you, check if you need a lift?" he'd suggested.

"If you like," she said without much enthusiasm. "But really, they're looking after me. They say they'll take me."

Aicheson had known better than to inquire who "they" might be.

"So we'll call," he'd added lamely.

"As you like."

"You know . . . you do know . . . I'm really sorry."

"About leading them here that evening?"

He'd felt regretful that she'd brought it into the open. "Yes."

"Don't be," she'd smiled tiredly. "If it hadn't been you, it'd been someone else."

"I'll see you then," he'd said, stepping on to the path.

"You can."

"And yourself?" he'd asked finally, inclining his head downwards.

"The lump? He's fine. Any day now."

"I can guess."

"You can? Of course, you can. You're a . . ."

"Yes . . . when I'm not interfering."

"Goodbye then," she'd said with some finality, shutting the door.

The next day, Seamus's body was released by authority of the Home Office after two post-mortem examinations and driven to Galey Bridge. There, it lay in an open coffin for viewing in the front room of the farmhouse, heavily bandaged head just visible, the rest of the body shrouded and covered with Mass cards.

That same day Edward S. Aicheson resigned his fellowship at the Royal Victoria Hospital, pleading immediate personal problems, settled the difference on the lease of his flat in Dunmurry, booked two Aer Lingus tickets to Boston, and said what few farewells he deemed necessary.

He and Lindy barely discussed his decision, both realizing it was inevitable and irrevocable after Seamus's death. They did talk about what could be done for Rebecca and her child when it was born, even mentioning the possibility of adoption, but somehow the conversation petered away to nothing. The responsibility was too much for them and they recognized it. Soon, they hoped, they would start their own family and that would be more than enough.

After Seamus's burial, they spent the briefest time possible at the wake at Michael Aherne's tavern in Church Street, muttering appropriate words, issuing half-hearted invitations to Boston, making empty promises to return to Listowel one day.

They hurried back to the hotel, collected their suitcases and set off towards Shannon Airport. The town was almost deserted in the mid-afternoon, bathed in a warm April glow, as the Aichesons drove out of the market square, between the shops and bars in Church Street and past the neat houses in Upper Church Street. Lindy slid a comforting hand on to her husband's thigh, pressing lightly. She recognized of old the haunted look in his eyes. She'd seen it first when one of his early patients had died.

He smiled at her with as much warmth and reassurance as he could summon and slowed the car to a halt by the metal swing gates of the cemetery.

Seamus Aherne's grave was only a few yards into the burying ground beside the last resting place of a young gypsy girl who'd died a year earlier. Her grave was covered with flowers sealed into boxes of clear plastic. The fresh flowers heaped over Seamus's grave seemed alive and blooming in comparison. Among them they noticed Grandma Hannah's sprig of hawthorn and wondered.

The masons had already done their work. The cross of the headstone was simply inscribed—"Seamus Aherne: 1946–1972."

Underneath were three words—"Killed Serving Ireland." The unequivocal statement brooked no argument.

"Was he?" wondered Aicheson.

"What?" Lindy queried.

"Killed serving Ireland."

"They think so and that's all that counts surely, darling?"

"I guess so."

They crunched back along the gravel path towards the car.

Aicheson stopped suddenly.

"Whose Ireland anyway?"

"Darling?"

"That he was serving. Whose Ireland?"

"Who knows? Does it matter now?"

"It sure as hell might one day," he said, thinking of Seamus Aherne's unborn child.

THE SNOWBLIND MOON
JOHN BYRNE COOKE

"An epic canvas created with sure, masterful strokes. Bravo!"
—John Jakes

"*The Snowblind Moon* is an intensely readable story."
—*The Washington Post*

"An epic tale . . . lyrically beautiful."
—*Los Angeles Times Book Review*

BESTSELLING BOOKS FROM TOR

☐ 58725-1 *Gardens of Stone* by Nicholas Proffitt $3.95
   58726-X   Canada $4.50

☐ 51650-8 *Incarnate* by Ramsey Campbell $3.95
   51651-6   Canada $4.50

☐ 51050-X *Kahawa* by Donald E. Westlake $3.95
   51051-8   Canada $4.50

☐ 52750-X *A Manhattan Ghost Story* by T.M. Wright
                                              $3.95
   52751-8   Canada $4.50

☐ 52191-9 *Ikon* by Graham Masterton $3.95
   52192-7   Canada $4.50

☐ 54550-8 *Prince Ombra* by Roderick MacLeish $3.50
   54551-6   Canada $3.95

☐ 50284-1 *The Vietnam Legacy* by Brian Freemantle
                                              $3.50
   50285-X   Canada $3.95

☐ 50487-9 *Siskiyou* by Richard Hoyt $3.50
   50488-7   Canada $3.95

Buy them at your local bookstore or use this handy coupon:
Clip and mail this page with your order —————————————

TOR BOOKS—Reader Service Dept.
49 W. 24 Street, 9th Floor, New York, NY 10010

Please send me the book(s) I have checked above. I am enclosing
$_____ (please add $1.00 to cover postage and handling).
Send check or money order only—no cash or C.O.D.'s.

Mr./Mrs./Miss _____

Address _____.

City _____ State/Zip _____

Please allow six weeks for delivery. Prices subject to change without
notice.